MY SONG'S GIFT

POPPY MINNIX

CITY OWL
PRESS

MY SONG'S GIFT
Duet of the Gods, Book 2

CITY OWL PRESS
www.cityowlpress.com

Cover Design by MiblArt. All stock photos licensed appropriately.

Edited by Tee Tate.

For information on subsidiary rights, please contact the publisher at info@cityowlpress.com.

Print Edition ISBN: 978-1-64898-307-8

Digital Edition ISBN: 978-1-64898-308-5

Printed in the United States of America

Praise for Poppy Minnix

"*Holiday Hotel* is a fun holiday story I'll be reaching for every Christmas going forward. I started smiling on page one, and I swear the smile stayed stuck on my face the entire time I read it. My cheeks hurt. It's that good." – *Imogen Keeper, Author*

"Poppy Minnix's vibrant descriptions in *Caribbean Competitors* rush through you, sucking you into the push and pull of Xia and Apollo's relationship until you realize it's three a.m. and you gotta be up in two hours! I loved every minute of this delicious romance and can't wait for more!" – *Codi Gary, author of Things Good Girls Don't Do*

"*Holiday Hotel* should be named Happiness Hotel! I loved this story of Cozi who finds herself and a second chance at love on an impromptu vacation. I highly recommend this story for people who love Happily Ever Afters and Christmas cursing." – *JL Bowman, Author*

"Poppy Minnix brings a fresh breath of air to Greek mythology in *My Song's Curse*. The characters jumped off the page and stole my heart." – *Cassandra Kay, Host of Punchkeys Podcast*

"Putting a new twist on an old story, Poppy Minnix kept me on the edge of my seat." – *Raisa Greywood, Bestselling Author of Demon Lust*

"From the steamy flirting to the classic lore, this story's magical from start to finish! Lula's fun voice will captivate you like it does all of humanity." – *Jackie Norling, Author*

"Just like the myth, *My Song's Curse* will lure you in and captivate you. You won't want to stop turning the pages as you root for Alex and Lula's love to endure the odds in this steamy, fun, and flirty romance." – *Lumen Ros, Paranormal and Dark Fantasy Author*

To those who exit their comfort zone.

Chapter One

LULA

THE MORE I STARE AT THE DECORATED MAP ON THE WALL, THE MORE my chest goes tight and cold. My palms sweat, my stomach balls, and my forehead aches until I have to rub between my brows. I need to focus. I need to find my sisters.

Slipping the knotted thread around the pushpin in eastern Minnesota, I run the red line from the convenience store where Venora was last seen, to the place a private plane took off without airspace permission seventeen miles from her house. Are they connected? Who the hell knows anymore? Every lead we've followed to where Venora and Hazel could be has turned out to be of zero help.

Tapping each black pin, I walk the length of the world map that I've hung in the kitchen of the house in Belize. Alex crinkles his nose every time he sees it. He's right—I've built a murder board like the ones in crime shows, and though that makes my sore soul ache, that's what we're dealing with, and it's helping me organize the information. Or lack of information. The yarn and sticky notes piece nothing together yet. I thumb the first one and the tension in my lungs intensifies. *Gerty.* I felt the break in my soul when Moros murdered her a month ago. At least we assume it was the God of Doom, since he was using her to harm the humans, thereby gaining the attention of the gods. My remaining sisters and I felt her passing. A week later, Alex saw him with Venora, but couldn't get to her fast enough for a rescue attempt. I tap the fourth sticky note in the chain of events. *65_?* Among a crowd of enthralled humans and pursuing gods, Venora yelled to, "find Hazel at six hundred fifty—" something. Definitely an address. Moros slapped her unconscious, stopping her from telling Alex the rest, and got away. It has to be where she's locked away. Ven wouldn't have given up Hazel's location if she were merely hiding. No, they've been captured by the God of Doom. That's the only fact I have to work with.

But how to find them? My vision blurs as I look for any hint, connection, or missed clue. But there's nothing.

"Where is he holding you?" I whisper. "Give me something." Moros has gone as silent as my sisters, so the moment Alex feels the tug on his attributes, or the news pops up with something that reeks of inhuman malice, we strike. I'm so tired of waiting for something to happen.

The heat of a familiar body warms my back. "How do you feel?" Alex splays his fingers against my stomach.

He's grown quieter, tiptoeing around me—all the guys have because of my potential pregnancy after my accidental heat with Alex. Which is likely one reason he secretly sends Rath traveling through the shadows to check for evidence of my sisters without telling me. I want to go too, so I can do something useful, but then Rath returns each time with a frown and empty hands. My irritation subsides, and Alex wraps me up in his arms and tells me we'll find them. Rinse and repeat.

Resting my hand over his, I run the tips of my fingers over the ridges of bone, bumping over veins until I encircle his thick wrist. He's so big and warm and golden. His thumb caresses an inch above my shorts as he waits for today's news.

I lean back against him. "No change." The probability of pregnancy at this point is slim if I'm being generous. I shouldn't think about the possibilities, and not only because it's more unlikely by the hour. An Olympian war threatens to engulf us. Bringing a child—a hybrid—into a world where a crazed, divine king forbids it is not a smart action—not that I cared in the throes of my heat. However, the thought of not being alone again, of having a tiny voice waking me instead of seabirds, and having that little one be part Alex...the hope is there, even if it's illogical.

I blow out a breath and reach to touch the pin for the mystery private plane. "This may be something. And..." I glance back at him. "I'm going too."

He wraps his body tight around me as if I may slip away from him. "Lu." His raspy morning timbre against my ear sends a wave of chills across my neck.

I turn in his arms and give him a determined stare-down. "I'm not pregnant. It's been too long. I'd be showing signs within a week and we're past two."

The battle I was gearing up for fizzles when I see the disappointment in his eyes, the slump of his big shoulders. Though he looks like the one needing comfort, he asks, "Are you okay?"

I have to clear the emotion from my throat to speak. "That's a loaded question and you know it."

He sweeps my curls aside and rests his forehead against mine. "I know." The sweet gesture settles my stress.

"I'm good enough. Okayish." Terrified. Irritated. Lost beyond these arms holding me tight.

His grip loosens, and he glances over my shoulder to study the map. "Comus will be up soon. He'll know if there's any news we can follow. Then we send Rath"—he taps my lips before I protest—"because he's the only being who can travel through shadow and doesn't yet have a bounty on him decreed by the king of Olympus. Lula, I can't lose you, and we don't have enough information yet."

I nip his finger. "I am useless."

"You are not." His fingers glide into my hair, wrapping the back of my head, and I can't help but melt against him. "But it's not your time yet." His lips brush mine sweetly, then firm. He pulls back a moment, but I follow, chasing his warmth, sinking my fingers into his soft, golden hair and inhaling him—citrus and sugar that smells like life and hope. His arm wraps around my waist, acting as a bumper as we crash into the wall. I nearly protest when a sticky note flutters to the ground, but then he kisses me like we haven't spent every available moment exploring each other, and this becomes the most pressing thing. Apparently, we both could use a distraction.

I clutch the hard muscle of his shoulder. "We should go upstairs."

He guides my head and I sink into him, going boneless. It's incredible, the way he affects me. How every cell of my body tilts to him, tugs and aches to get closer. I don't get it, nor do I care. I only know that this deity is mine and I am his, and this minute in time is ours. He pauses his perfect kisses to stare down at me with golden eyes that have been too worried lately. How I lucked out meeting him—the grandson of Zeus and Hera—I'll never know, but I'm thankful for it.

A throat clearing makes me jump. Rath sits on the kitchen island, white-blond hair covering one light blue eye as the other watches us with mischief, as if he's been there all along. Hell, he may have been.

I peek over Alex's shoulder and raise an eyebrow. "Yes, creeper?"

Rath grins wide, sharpening his already cutting cheekbones, but I know him well enough to see that it's fake. "Good morning."

"Morning." I tilt my head and give him a careful smile. "Are you okay?" He looks like he needs to talk. I hope he and Artemis aren't fighting in addition to all the other stuff we're dealing with.

"Just dandy." He slides from the counter. "Alex, I have a question for you."

"What's going on?" I ask. "It's not my sisters, is it?"

Rath shakes his head, but pulls a side glance at Alex.

Alex kisses my forehead and steps away from me. "I'll be right back."

My shoulders rise with tension. They've let me into their divine group, shared their plans to overhaul Olympus, but still talk among themselves. Alex has been pacing the beach and Rath has been away more than he's been here, doing whatever mysteries he does. Comus usually goes with him, sometimes returning, sometimes not. After the day the four of us sat down on the dock, and I agreed to help in their fight against Zeus and the old ways of the gods, I didn't expect silence and inaction. Maybe it annoys me because I went nearly two centuries never having a back-and-forth conversation with anyone other than my sisters—and now I want in on everything. I want all the words. Maybe I can help something—anything—move forward. What are they discussing today and why can't I be there? Maybe there's news I should hear.

I stand, determined to follow, when my phone rings. Alex pauses in the open door as I pull my phone from my pocket. "It's Grace," I tell them. "I have to take this." I give Alex a look I hope tells him I'm coming to find out what they're so keen on keeping from me.

Chapter Two

ALEX

WALKING AWAY FROM LULA HURTS, AND I'M TEMPTED TO BACKTRACK, say "hello" to Grace before hanging up on her, palming Lula's lush hips, and carrying her upstairs for yet another round. No matter how close I get or how tightly her body clamps to mine, whether it be from sex or kissing or simply staring at each other, I crave more. She satisfies like nothing I've experienced in my three thousand years, yet five seconds after parting from her body, I want to be back against her. If I fill her enough, maybe the connection will hold her to me, even with how upset she'll be when I explain how I met her.

If she'd grown up in Olympus like the sirens should have, she'd see why I needed to follow her, study her, make a plan around her without her knowledge. Then again, if raised by Olympians, Lula would be something else entirely. She's perfect as is. Whoever created the sirens made them with peace in mind, but with all the secrets behind their creation and history, it's clear they were submitted to vengeance and jealousy before being cast out of Olympus. Lula's life among humans hasn't been easy, but somehow, she's remained kind. Better than me. Better than all of us.

She's everything I desire, and I've been teetering between confessing and weathering her reaction or remaining silent in my guilt-ridden suffering. The cliff I stand on gets higher and sharper each day, neither direction a path I want to travel. A thousand times I've opened my mouth to tell her and failed to speak the words.

I watched you from afar long before you saw me.

I used you until I loved you.

My gods, do I love you.

Freezing at the door, I watch her walk the hall, talking with Grace about siren pregnancy and how annoyed they are that their eldest sister didn't tell them that when a siren goes into heat, any other present siren will as well. That had been a shock, a problem, and the best day of my long existence. The reminder of that day in the secret getaway I call Shangri-La makes me want to take Lula upstairs, play with her pretty auburn curls, and take her again and again until she wears out and does that adorable little telltale nose scrunch right before she drifts off. A million moments of just us is my goal.

Rath's hand against my shoulder makes me jerk. Unfortunately, I can't ignore the rocky path that lies ahead if I want to wake up with Lula beside me for the rest of eternity.

I clench my jaw and step outside. Salty air mixes with the scent of plumeria and washes away a bit of tension—for half a second.

"Morning," Comus grumbles, one hand in the pocket of his shorts, the other holding a mug decorated with a cartoon T.rex in a top hat. His wiry, dark hair and beard are always in seven directions before the day begins, but he's even more disheveled than usual. "Have you felt anything?"

"No. Not a tug or vision leading me to him." I've waited for my attributes to fire off, buzzing my brain to alert me to the God of Doom stirring up war on the Earth realm or Zeus if he were truly preparing his army, but besides my constant state of stress, my mind is quiet.

"He was doing a good job feeling Lu against her murder board." Rath dodges my half-assed elbow jab. He's poking because the pressure is too much; he's worried about her, and how our secrets and the growing tension in Olympus are going to pan out. We've waited for a century to get Zeus off his throne and are aiming for a peaceful exit, but with a bounty on the sirens, a mad god on the loose, and an illegal tryst between Lula and I, change is imminent, and we're not sure we're going to pull off a rational chat about it. There are more plans that need to be put in place. We need to test Lula's ability to control darklings, and for her to be on board with that plan. We need to keep the sirens safe, and Zeus has to give up on me being betrothed to Ichnaea. We must find Lula's sisters. The only thing I have control over is coming clean to my siren, and I'm not even prepared enough to do that.

Rath returns my elbow jab. "How is she?"

"Not pregnant and wanting to go with you to find her sisters."

His lips tighten and he squeezes my shoulder. He knows I'm a mess about keeping everything from her; how part of me wished she were pregnant, and Zeus would recognize that as enough proof that Lu and I belong together. But dreams are a wicked thing to lay plans on. We have reality to deal with before I can hope for the future I want.

When Comus purses his lips and blows out a long breath, I know that reality is of the worst kind.

I start my daily round of pacing. "Just say it."

"Da called."

And Comus's father, Dionysus, only calls for one reason. I pace, trying to ease the anxiety that has me at my breaking point. The laps of intrusive waves slipping over shells and sand help mute the resonant prattle in my mind, though it can't wash away the dangerous future we're up against. We've done a good job through the years of manipulating the Olympian council to warm up to the idea of change and peace, but my grandfather's patience runs thin—with Moros and with me. "Zeus wants us there, doesn't he?"

"Yes." Comus stares out at the water. "*Post haste.* And my father only mentioned that Moros is one of the agenda items before he hung up on me."

"Do you think they know about you and Lu?" Rath crosses his arms and glances back toward the house.

"They may by now." I pace, trying to sink the tension raging through me into the yielding sand. "If he hasn't already, Grandfather will have the oracles scrying for information on me if I don't go to him." I snort. "Post haste."

Comus swings his legs around, dropping his feet over the edge of the dock. "No one has gotten a glimpse of the oracles since Moros showed back up on Earth. I'm not even sure if any are in Olympus. We could search if time allows."

I halt in the sand, facing the water. "Zeus nearly bolted me to death last time he felt I slighted him, and if Rath shadows in and they find him poking around, they'll banish if not charcoal him." I glance at Rath, shoving my hands in my pockets. "I've seen Zeus use that green death bolt of his once in three thousand years. Let's not have you be the one to break his peaceful streak. Avoid Olympus as much as possible. I may be the most unlawful Olympian walking, but he thinks he needs me, so let me be the shield for now." I may be safe from my grandfather's wrath, but I'm not safe to be around. "What if Lula and I have to separate until this is resolved?"

I don't even need to see them to know they both wince. I did this to her—dragged the woman I love into danger because I couldn't stay away. Zeus will attack. Even if Olympians beyond us don't walk Earth anymore, if Zeus pinpoints her location, he'll send Hermes or ride his lightning right to us. When he realizes how much I care for Lula and don't plan to marry Naea, the punishment will make the liver-eating eagle he cursed Prometheus with seem tame.

Rath steps beside me. "Then you separate, and we keep working toward unseating Zeus. Then you get back together. This isn't a hard concept."

I give him a wry glare. "Sure, but the execution? Utter torture."

"We do what we must. But we have a big enough army to always have someone with her," Rath says, taking his choice of words to a place I fear we're headed. *Army.* "Hell, we could hide her in Olympus if need be. Zeus would never think to check one of our allies' homes."

I raise my eyebrows at Rath. "All our allies know I watched her before we met. Bringing Lu into that when she's the only one in the dark? It's not right. Not that it ever has been. And—" I start my furious pace again. "And if she sees the serial killer from the night we met and realizes he's my deity friend, it's over between us." I tug at the hair brushing over my eyes. The time for dragging my feet is up. "I have to tell her."

"Alex." Rath's tone is gentle. "She's not ready. She's still pissed at Amah for keeping things from her."

Lula's oldest sister won't explain why she has such a problem with me. Though with the siren heat, bounty, and lack of control over me, Amah has reason to be skittish of the gods.

I turn toward the house. "I've put it off for too long."

"You cannot be considering this right now." Comus curses under his breath. "Brother, we have a direct, immediate summons to meet with the Council. We have to go."

"I don't want someone else explaining this to her. What if Zeus knows exactly where we are and is only luring you and I to Olympus so they can attack Rath and Lula? In nearly all outcomes, she finds out I haven't been honest with her. If I lose her, it will be because I told her the truth, not because she found out I'm a dishonorable liar. And if I lay it all out, she'll still help because she's Lula."

"Alex," Comus warns.

I turn on him. "You want to move forward? This is how we do it." I smack my chest. "I can't do anything else with this lie hanging in the air. It's suffocating me."

Rath straightens and Comus closes his eyes and blows out a breath one second before Lula's voice asks, "What lie?"

I turn to face the love of my eternity and hope this isn't the last moment she looks at me with those sweet, stunning green eyes.

Chapter Three

LULA

ALEX LOOKS LIKE HE MAY CRY OR THROW UP. RATH'S EYES STICK TO the sand and Comus rubs his forehead as if this all just went way south. My stomach lurches. "What lie?" I ask again.

"I need to talk to you," Alex says.

"Are my sisters okay?" The tremble in my voice obvious even to me.

The firm line of his lips molds to a frown. "Not about them."

He has to go to Olympus, doesn't he. I bite my bottom lip. Does Zeus know already? His personal oracle, Pythia, is the greatest seer the universe has ever known, according to the guys, but Alex and I are so fresh into our relationship. I need another day—all the days. "Is he coming for us?"

"Alex," Comus says with warning, but Alex ignores him, takes my hand, and tugs me toward the house and into the mudroom.

Comus and Rath follow behind us, but they pause in the doorway. Rath's hands are in his pockets, and even hidden away, I can tell he fists his fingers.

I turn to Alex. "What happened? Tell me."

"I—" He stares past me. "I'd never hurt you on purpose."

Fear grips my chest and sends swirls of adrenaline racing through me. "I know. What happened?"

"Don't, Alex." Comus steps closer. "It's too soon—"

Alex slams the door, leaving us alone. He steps into me, resting his forehead against mine, fingers gripping my hips.

"What's too soon?" I wrap my arms around his neck and let his sweet citrus scent mixed with Belize sunshine waft over me. "Alex?"

He drags me closer and inhales against my neck. We stand as if nothing else exists in this screwed-up universe but us until he shifts out of my arms, running his hand through his waves. "Zeus summoned me back to Olympus."

My panic shifts into an angry lead ball in my stomach. "Does he know what happened between us? You can't go."

"He wants to discuss Moros. That's not...I'm not—Lula, I haven't been...fuck, this is so hard." He presses his thumbs to his eyes and blows out a lengthy breath. "I love you."

Swallowing down the knot in my throat, I nod. "I love you too."

He drops his hands to his sides. "I saw you before you saw me. When we first met."

"When the men attacked me downtown?" Maybe he's feeling guilty for not stopping them before they punched me in the stomach. I couldn't talk for a few minutes, but it worked out, and I discovered my thrall doesn't work on deities. Then he kissed me. The only thing keeping me from grinning over that memory is the utter dread lining Alex's features.

"Before." The way he speaks one word makes me straighten, moving farther from him. The house is silent and drops in temperature, especially on the back of my neck.

"When?" I ask.

"I—" He works his lips in thought. I've never seen him so unsure of words. "Followed you. I understood what you were before I met you."

"But we were strangers." We met during one of the oddest nights of my life. "I don't understand."

"We were, but I found you—we found you before, and thought you could help us. And then we wanted to see how you handled certain types of beings and—" He reaches for me.

I push away his hand. "Help you? Types?" What could deities need with a siren? We're good for controlling humans and otherworldlings. I rub my temples. The night Alex and I met had been surreal. What were the odds of meeting a serial killer and a vicious gang in one night? *Types.*

Alex's face scrunches as though he's with me on this treacherous mental path. "I…" He bites his bottom lip.

"You sent them to me?" I ask. "The psycho who—who told me he wanted to cut me open. Um…Jordan. Then the gang? You staged everything?" Comus didn't want him to tell me this. Rath—my eyes burn. Rath wouldn't look at me. They planned that night and I fell into Alex's arms. Why would they do that?

"No." He winces. "Well, not entirely."

Do not trust those we cannot control. Amah's words are a loud mantra in my mind, challenging the racing heartbeat in my ears. *Be careful around deities. You don't know what they want.* My oldest sister was right, and I've been refusing to speak with her. Did she see this coming? Did she know all along? No. This can't be.

"How long?" My voice comes out in a harsh whisper. "Why?"

"We need you, Lula. You belong with us."

His detour from the question speaks volumes. I take another step back, trying to ignore the pained grimace on his face that urges me to reach for him. This cannot be real. I'm often trailed by humans and otherworldlings who see me or hear me speak. But Alex? The night I met him, he popped out of the shadows with a ferocity that drew me to him like a homing device. Was it concern for me on his face all those months ago, or did I read him wrong? Was it possession instead? I place both hands over my chest, willing my lungs to work.

"Lu," Alex says, a rusty scratch.

I shift away from his reach. He acted as though he needed me, that my kisses and conversation were a gift, but was it my deadly voice he was after all along? Did he think he owned my power because he's a deity? That's what Moros is doing with my sisters. But Alex? No.

"Talk to me." He ducks his head, eyes pleading, reminding me of the first time he touched me. He'd taken my hand, pressed it to his chest, and told me not to fear him and that he wouldn't hurt me. I am hurt.

I slash at one hot tear trailing my cheek. "How long?" The

command is firm. Were he human, he'd speak within a second, answering to the hour.

He takes half a minute, biting his lips together and rubbing the back of his neck. "About a year."

A whimpering gasp comes from the incredulity stuck in my throat. I let him in when I shouldn't have. It was too quick. He was the first man that had free will around me, and I fell for him so hard. Amah was right. Will she be happy I figured out what she understood all along? I wrap my arms around my waist, caving in on myself. "Oh my god, I'm so stupid."

"No, you're not." Alex takes a step closer, offering a palm. His open hand may as well be a viper with the way I recoil and smack it away. He locks his fingers behind his neck. "I wanted to tell you sooner, but it was never an easy time. I couldn't find a way."

Quiet moments, while few, were there. He had slept in my bed, woken next to me. There had been spans of silence in my kitchen, staring at each other over the island while prepping dinner or eating by candlelight. I'd wanted to give him all of me, tell him everything. At first, I didn't because of Amah's warnings. She told me not to share our secrets with the gods. Then our sister died, and he was there for comfort when no one else could be. He was comfort and love.

I shared nearly everything, and he didn't.

"Why?" There should be more to that simple question, but my teeth lock tight and if I pry them open, only pain will come out. *Why didn't you tell me when you understood how I felt? Why me?*

I only harm. My voice is control and death. The power of it is darkness and pain. What was his nefarious goal for me when he said he loved me?

"We thought you would fit our plan. And you do. You're perfect. I didn't expect—"

Turning, I stalk toward the stairs. It's true, then. He met me so he could use me. He understood what I was, and he came out of nowhere like a…well, like a golden god. A tempting male I could have a conversation with. One I could fall in love with and enjoy sex with and—

A hand grabs my shoulder and turns me. I slap Alex so hard, pain stings my palm.

He barely flinches. "I'm sorry, Lu."

"You stalked me." My voice is tight and tear-laden. "You—Alex, I don't—what in—" I throw my hands up in the air, my voice unable to continue, and make my way up the stairs. "Leave. Just go." I need space to figure this out.

"Please," Alex says from the foyer.

"Leave me alone," I yell and slam the bedroom door, locking it as if that would do anything against the gods. This explains his nervousness. Why he's been pacing the beach while talking to the guys. Not because his attributes were calling or because Zeus might punish us for having sex. I gasp and cover my mouth, placing my hand over my stomach. What if being with me during my heat was part of his plan? Was the disappointment in his eyes because I'm not carrying a new generation for him? A hybrid he told me would be more powerful than Zeus; one that would be hunted down with far more ferocity than the king of Olympus had used to find my sisters and I?

I jerk at the light knock on the door. "Go away, Alex."

"I'm sorry," he says as if that can solve the rip in my heart.

I throw a pillow at the door. It bounces off the wood with a not-angry-enough whomp.

"I have to go to Olympus, but want to talk more when I return. Waiting so long to explain this to you wasn't right, and while it's not an excuse, I feared your reaction. I didn't expect to fall in love with you, but I did. I'd never hurt you, Lula. You are always safe with me. You and your sisters."

That's what he's after—what he's always been after. He needs the sirens for the plan, though I'm still not entirely sure what that plan is. I told the guys I was on board, and they've told me they're trying to get the Council to step down peacefully. They would say that. It's not in a siren's nature to kill, but Moros is using us to murder crowds of humans. Is Alex working with him or trying to fight fire with more fire?

I sit on the bed, hand over my heart as I try to calm down so I can think. I need space from them, but I'm never alone because they're trying to keep me safe.

But are they?

No. I can't believe Alex or the guys are that good at faking the care they have for me and my sisters. Alex and I have barely been apart for months and Rath and I bonded. He told me about his relationship with Artemis. He wouldn't have lied about that, right?

They could have though. Before the gods walked into my life and I could carry on a two-sided conversation with them, I watched humans from a distance or, in recent decades, on television. But actors make easy-to-catch dramatic expressions, and once humans see me, they zone into a complacent shell even before I utter a word and enthrall them. Deities and their ability to lie is new to me.

The bedroom, with its white linens and dark wood floor, doesn't seem big and luxurious anymore. It's a tower, and I'm a naive princess who saw it as a paradise because I didn't know better. Except I did, because Amah warned me so many times. In our last conversation, she told me to get away from the gods and she would tell me the secrets I'm itching to understand.

With a flick of my finger, I had ended the call and chosen Alex over the siren who raised me because I trusted him. I lower my hand from my trembling, chewed lips and eye the wardrobe, the window, then the door.

I need to talk to my sisters.

Chapter Four

ALEX

I REST MY PALMS AND FOREHEAD AGAINST THE DOOR AS IF THAT WILL somehow bring me closer to Lu. I waited far too long and handled things poorly. It's not like I thought she'd shrug, say she understood, and cuddle with me, but there had been hope.

What I didn't expect was the terror on her face when my words sunk in. I predicted anger. The slap could have been a punch or kick to the balls and I'd have taken it with understanding because it's Lu. She's had two mortal lifetimes of holding her tongue around others, and while conversation is flowing between us, when expressing herself gets difficult, she goes silent and sometimes physical. Not scared though, and that was fear in her green eyes.

"Alex," Comus says from downstairs. His voice is careful because he understands that with Lula, I'm not my rational self.

She has my mind twisted in an intricate knot when I should focus on righting the realm. The men and I spoke of this; how fessing up could mean delaying our plans and altering the role she doesn't yet understand. But she distracted me long ago, slowing my progress when she became a priority I didn't expect. My motives have shifted —gravitated to keeping her and her sisters safe. Which we are failing. One dead. Two in the hands of divine monsters, two more under our protection, and three others scattered to the winds of the Earth realm.

I don't trust that Moros and the gods that escaped Olympus to join him can't find the other sirens before we do. I can't let Lula lose another sister. Even if she doesn't speak to me ever again—that thought seizes my chest—she'll be safe. Maybe if I explain everything to Grace: Comus, the plans, the absolute truth of it all, together they will understand that we've always had the best intentions and would let us house the other sisters as well. Or they will hate us for the remainder of eternity. On the edge of my vision, Rath drops out of the shadows and leans against the wall a few feet away, probably unsure if I'll lash out at him in my frustration. Not today. He can help her navigate this.

He stayed with her last time Comus and I went to pin down Moros. That night, he fell in love with her too. Not like I am, or as he is with Artemis, but they have a bond that's rare in his life. His ability to get her riled up enough to yell about her family is an art form, and she brings a playful side out of him that's innate, but rarely used for fun.

"Let her calm down," he whispers. "Go argue for her sisters, and if things go well, bring Grace to her."

How I wish we could. She needs her sisters with her, but the danger doubles if they're together. When we got Grace to our safe house in the Alps, it was the first time Lula had seen one of them in the flesh in decades.

Pushing off the door with my palms, I nod. "I'll be back in a few hours. I love you, Lula." I don't expect a response, but I wait a long minute just in case. Only silence replies.

Signaling Rath to follow, I head downstairs and into the kitchen.

"She didn't yell." Rath hops up to sit on the counter.

"Not much." Comus leans against the stove. "Did she slap you?"

"Yeah." I rub my cheek. That may be the last time she ever touches me. I ball my fists. No. I'll make it right, or at least…hope she forgives me. "She was scared."

"Of you?" Comus asks, tilting his head.

"I don't know. It was like the first day we met, and she'd thought I was an incubus." I look to Rath. "Ideas?"

"She said Moros, Zeus, Olympians—discounting us—and being

pregnant scared her. None of those have to do with your stalkerish behavior though."

"Careful," Comus warns, glaring at Rath.

Usually, Rath's poking at a time like this would end in punches, but...

"He's right." I shrug. "She's upset at Amah too, but that's about trust, which I just blew to smithereens between us as well. She doesn't think she's pregnant, because sirens should know within a few days if they go on a food binge. That hasn't happened."

Rath taps a beat on the marble. "If she will talk to me, would you mind? I don't want to think she's lumped us in with Zeus and Moros, but it's possible. At least until she calms down and thinks everything over."

That would be terrible. I open my mouth to stretch the cramped muscles from clenching my jaw. "You may be the only one of us she will talk to for a bit." My phone rings—the one that connects me to the Council. I close my eyes and attempt to find my calm. We should have left a while ago, but I couldn't walk away from Lula one more time with this lie standing between us, then come home to her sweet, trusting kisses while she wasn't aware that we met under false pretenses.

"That will be your dad, as mine isn't talking to me at the moment," Comus says.

Last time we visited the Council, we unveiled that we knew they were spying on us with human technology—that we handed them for that purpose. It was a risky reveal, but we're still standing, possibly because Deimos stabbed Ares and ran away with Moros. There's nothing better than a Council member attacking their father and escaping with Olympus's nemesis to make our deceptions more palatable. I answer and Dionysus growls, "Where are you?"

"Hang on." I hand the phone to Comus, who rolls his eyes.

"Hello, Da." He goes through a volley of pauses and mm-hmms. "We'll be right there." He presses a button and hands my phone over. "The Council is waiting. Da sounds nervous."

I glance toward the stairwell, listening for any movement. "I'm nervous too. We'll return as soon as possible."

"I'll keep you posted," Rath says. "She'll calm down."

Calming down isn't the half of it. Forgiving me so she can trust me again is my worry. Keeping her away from Zeus, Moros, or any other deity who would harm her is on the top of the list of items to carry out so I don't go insane.

I nod and step back, calling my attributes forward with the memory of a lavender field in France. Portal travel is convenient but blind. I won't take the chance that Olympians could see or smell Belize and question me about the location if we arrive among a crowd.

Bringing my hand down to split the energy between locations sends a burst of relief and power to my fingertips. Creating a portal from one Earth spot to another is easy, and I'm glad I get to use my attributes, unlike the other deities in Olympus. The Council allows Comus, Rath, and I to walk among the mortals and otherworldlings so we can report the non-divine's progress and evolution—a quick and terrifying event to the old gods, not that they would ever admit it.

The chill hits us as we step into a field speckled with dead flowers, withered into frosty clumps in the setting light. Comus follows, and I take a deep breath. Lula will be okay.

Rath will keep her safe. He's the only being in the universe with his own private realm, though no one can stay there without touching him. It's not a long-term option, but they could play one hell of a game of hide-and-seek with their enemies.

I close the portal and open another to Olympus, right outside the massive marble building where I spent most of my childhood years. Mount Olympus appears as a foggy mountain to the humans. They can't see the homes spread in a circular pattern on an enchanted hill halfway up. The last tendrils of light glint off white structures and columns, making the golden walkways glow. Two chatting maids freeze at our sudden appearance. Their himations are diaphanous, one blue, one pale yellow, and they both wear their hair in tight braids encircling their heads. The demigoddess on the left grins at Comus and raises a dark, arched eyebrow. They both curtsy low. "Greetings to thee," they say together.

"And to thee," Comus says.

I bow my head to them and move inside to wait for Comus. Flirting for information isn't in the cards for me at the moment. My mind is on my sad, angry siren and what my grandfather has in store for us. Besides, they'd probably give me the cold shoulder anyway. I'm not the only one who's noticed the special treatment Zeus gives me, and he had me betrothed, blacklisting me from Olympian beds other than Ichnaea's. Comus laughs as the demigoddess in pale yellow—Uralia, I believe—tickles fingers through his beard and speaks close to his ear. All the whispers in this place, and most of them are silly games of flesh and fancy. We know that Olympians have thoughts that things could be better, but the only power most have is sticking their heads in the sand, and we haven't yet pushed for more. The moment Comus turns from the demigoddesses, the twinkling mischief and grin on his face drops into a curtain of irritation.

"Anything?" I ask, pushing off a column to match his quick stride.

"No."

I chew at my lip and turn a sharp corner. Zeus's house is a blend of home and politics. Mostly politics. The wing of bedchambers runs along the back of the nearly square structure, separate from the Council rooms, but it's still odd to have them in the same building. Why does he need everything so entwined? It's too close. He needs to escape ruling to at least dream in peace. Maybe that's why Hera has disappeared. Or why a guard follows him, standing near as if the Titans the king conquered long ago may spring from the nearest latrine at any moment. Though, here we are. Revolutionaries with a century-old plan to peacefully overthrow Zeus, walking in unchecked, welcomed for now—or treated that way to give us a false sense of safety. I can't remember when I last relaxed in Olympus. If the maids had followed us in, guards would have shooed or possibly punished them for trespassing without a summons from the king. Lula would have a spear to her throat, unless we'd have arrived at the outer ring of lesser demigod homes or the broken houses of departed satyrs. The nymphs are allowed to stay in their huts in the forests as long as they serve the needs of the gods, but Zeus ordered the dryads to leave for their fae realm before the break. Zeus doesn't pay attention to those locations anymore, making them good for private conversations with those we can't pull from Olympus without being noticed.

Beyond Mount Olympus is now a heavy impassable fog instead of the world below. When was the last time Zeus traveled to his earthly temple? Would he even recognize its crumbling marble walls? It's been two thousand years since the king broke the connection between Olympus and the mortal realm. Now we sit over Greece like a shadow, so close, but too far from where we should be. Unlike the structures on earth, Olympian houses, temples, alters, and statues stand in flawless carved marble. The weather is temperate with no rainy days, and plain, draped himations are still in fashion. In turn, Zeus reduced our inspiration cycle to a trickle between Earth and this perfect, stagnant cesspool.

Two guards with golden chest plates and matching helmets stand by the main doors of the Council room, spears locked together to block the path. An embossed eagle graces the top left of the plate and a mohawk of purple-dyed horsehair spikes from the reflective domes atop their heads. Deimos's betrayal must have freaked out Zeus for him to have his royal guard acting as doormen.

With a sharp click, they jerk the spears open so we can pass.

Here we go.

Chapter Five

ALEX

Comus and I stagger to a halt at the room's new layout. The purple fabric held by a golden cornice still drapes on the back wall, but the throne that sat under the royal curtains now bellies up to a massive round table; the kind we've used for maps and topography studies in times of warfare. Zeus smiles, though he looks tired and bag-eyed, with an obstinate wrinkle on his forehead that shouldn't stick to his youthful appearance. His dark beard is longer and more scraggly for him. He waves his hands apart, showing off the eight other thrones that circle the table. Two are empty, and this cannot mean what my hopeful mind concocts. I glance at Comus for confirmation that this could be a fresh beginning for Olympus, but his furrowed focus sticks elsewhere. I follow it past the feast of fruit and meat and the intricate goblets of ambrosia that fill the room with a sugary cinnamon fig scent. Dionysus stares back. His brown skin has gone ashen, and the muscle in his jaw ticks in time with the finger he taps on the table. I nearly retreat, but he gives the slightest shake of his head. Beside him, Athena settles in her throne, arms crossed and scowling. Apollo does the same. Hermes isn't present. *Shit.* Those rational four are the peace in the Council's circle of madness. Artemis refuses to meet my gaze—nothing new there, but Ares glares, his crimson eyes filled with the smug warning of impending war. We fit like oil and water. Nothing good will come of this meeting if he's pleased to see me.

These are the elite leaders. The remaining original majors. The closest, beloved children who go along with Zeus's entitlement issues and treat him with the delicate care he demands. With the unease around the table, something is horribly wrong. I itch to pull out my phone and text Rath; to warn him to be ready. To keep her safe.

"You are in the Council room," Zeus says in a stabbing reproach.

Comus and I bow, giving each other the side-eye as we dip. I'm treated exceptionally well for an Olympian, one step under the Council, though we haven't a clue why. Comus is not, even if he is Dionysus's son. Rath can't be seen without threat of disembowelment. Whatever is happening here isn't what I expected.

When we straighten, I plaster on a grin and approach. "Please forgive our rudeness. The alterations of the room shocked us a bit."

"And why is that, Alexiares?" Zeus asks.

I've held a thousand conversations in my head with multiple versions of my grandfather challenging my every word. It's possible for him to be kind and understanding. Or be a murderous monster. A simple phrase that he'd consider a threat can not only alter my fate, but endanger others. He's tipped into defense mode lately, but we've begun the next phase of the plan: explore the truth. I lift my chin. "Because Olympus doesn't change."

"And how does that make you feel?"

That throws me. Feelings are the last thing on our leader's mind. Has putting human technology in his hands given him a bug, and now he's studying modern psychology? I glance at Comus for guidance, but he squints in confusion.

Looking back to Zeus, I shrug. "Change is good." It's a dangerous statement in this crowd, but we've been living on the edge for a while and it's time to press forward.

"Sit." Zeus's scowl deepens. "Do you think Moros being on Earth and torturing the non-divine is a *good* change?"

"Of course not."

Comus and I slip into the unadorned marble thrones. They're not carved like Athena's owl-head backrest or Dionysus's seat of woven grapevines. The unease of this weird setup settles in, sending a chill traveling up my spine. Even Zeus's throne with the massive eagle-shaped armrests is only a few inches taller instead his usual place steps higher than anyone else.

I tent my fingers to hide their tremors, rest my forearms on the cool surface of the table, and lean forward. "But Moros is doing what he always does. There's no change in his behavior, so the question is moot." I add a touch of snark but continue, ignoring Zeus's frown. "That's beside the point. The God of Doom needs to go back to the hell realm."

Zeus's raised shoulders settle a couple of inches. "He does. The location of his last attack was Germany. Has your attribute called to you since then?"

"No." Lula and our situation may keep me distracted, but I would have noticed that particular tingle in my mind. "Not Moros. Just skirmishes and unsettled events. Nothing on a worldwide scale."

"Anicetus said the same."

I've spoken to my twin, but why isn't he here if he was in on this discussion? "He'd be good to have here. As the unconquerable one, he has the best chance of coming out unscathed from Moros."

Athena shifts in her seat, and Dionysus stops his rhythmic tapping and looks to the king. Comus's father is the closest thing to a friend Zeus could wish for. Dionysus is certainly his right-hand man. For the God of Wine to be staring down his king in clear disapproval, Zeus is doing something underhanded.

Zeus bares his teeth as if trying to smile but failing. "As of late, Anicetus has not proven that he is thinking correctly."

Comus gives the slightest huff, and I couldn't agree more. *Then where does that put us?*

Over the last few meetings, Comus and I have become more vocal about a lot of things the Council won't discuss. I called out the king of Olympus for having secret plans involving me, and also breaking the universe. For some crazy reason, he didn't strike me down on the spot. I've become the one deity he won't discipline like he wants to. He better not be harming my twin. I tap the table and Comus gives a slight nod. We'll find Anice right after this. Comus squares his shoulder. "Moros is on Earth and is using an innocent species to harm humans, and now has Deimos and another demigod at his side. Have you questioned the guard who attempted to attack Alex?"

"No," Ares says. "Because he's dead."

I furrow my brows. "Dead? How?" There hasn't been an Olympian death since our first battle with Moros two centuries ago.

Ares crosses his arms and leans back, eyeing Zeus who gives him a glare. Why is Ares not following Zeus's every move like the guard dog he is?

Zeus leans forward. "He was not willing to speak, therefore—"

Ares interjects. "I could have made him—"

"Silence!" Zeus bellows, his voice rumbling through the room like thunder.

Excellent. So my grandfather got impatient and offed the one being who could tell us why a Council member rode off into the sunset with the God of Doom, which annoyed Ares because he didn't get to torture someone for the first time in centuries. Business as usual in Olympus. Since Comus and I are hearing about this now instead of through the maid's gossip, I assume this hasn't left the Council room and there will not be an Olympian mourning period for the guard.

"Have you questioned any other guards?" I ask.

"All of them," Dionysus says.

"Anything come of that?" Comus asks.

"No one will talk."

We haven't talked either until recently because we understand how Zeus deals with information he doesn't like. If his own army has Moros followers, that means we may have to focus more broadly on dangers in Olympus.

Zeus leans forward, mimicking my stance. "Are you one of them?"

"Are you fucking serious?" I sputter. "I want to keep the humans safe. I would never—"

"Have you spoken with Hera?"

"No," I say. "I haven't seen my grandmother in centuries. Have you?"

Even under a dark beard his jaw muscles bunch. "Now is not the time to be contrary. Has she met with you?"

"Again, no."

Zeus glances at the Council members in turn, gauging their faces for something I'm unaware of. He gives a slight nod when his gaze lands back on me. "Yet you have spoken to the sirens."

Yet? What does my grandmother have to do with the sirens? "A siren." He only knows about Lula, and fortunately, doesn't know details.

When I shift in the uncomfortable chair, an I-caught-you grin from Zeus invites my fist to meet his smug face, but that wouldn't help accomplish the peaceful overhaul we've planned. "You were following one, correct?" he asks. "In America. Where did she go?"

"I haven't the slightest idea," I lie.

Zeus scoffs. "You expect me to believe that you met a siren, and she did not tempt you?"

Rath was the only one untempted by the sirens we studied, though he didn't need to speak to weave into Nysa's world, not that his devotion to Artemis would have faltered. I'm not sure which of the three of us are worse. Rath watching Nysa from the shadows, Comus pretending he was a human lover of Grace, or me falling for Lula when I should have been upfront with her, bringing her in as a partner, not a test subject. "Of course, I was tempted. There are many tempting bodies on Earth and in Olympus."

"Which one?" Zeus growls. "The daughter of Aglaope?"

Dionysus shoves himself back in his chair, seeming to silently ask the coffered ceiling for patience.

An icy chill invades my chest, and my jaw aches with tightness. "No clue. She didn't announce her lineage."

Zeus looks over my head, as he does when he's said too much or wants to say more but is filtering himself. We both have our tells. "What is her name? Where is she located?"

"Siren. East America. I wasn't paying as close attention as you do, so please, share the story. Give us what you know about them so that we can help you. Why did Moros bring up Aglaope? He said you were supposed to give her to him?"

Dionysus winces, which is a good warning for the explosion Zeus is barely holding back. What is my grandfather's deal with the sirens?

He stands, fingertips spread on the table. "So you know nothing we can use to find Moros or the other sirens?"

I tap my temple. "Only my attributes when I'm called. You have it out for them, don't you?"

"Alexiares," he says through gritted teeth.

We need more. Something that will help us keep them safe. "You brought them up. If we work together against Moros, we will succeed, but hunting an innocent species isn't a good use of time unless there's a reason for it."

Athena clears her throat and looks away as Zeus gives her a warning glare.

Comus leans forward. "Someone cursed them to walk among humans, yet we must interact with them and the otherworldlings blindly. If you would open the ancient libraries so we could understand the history of these species—"

"Not up for discussion, son." Dionysus takes a sip of ambrosia.

"Have you enforced your bounty and searched for them?" I ask, picking up where Comus left off. A scrap of information would push us forward. "Are you walking the Earth now, or did you send Hermes?"

"Enough." Zeus slaps the marble and strides to the doors, tossing them open. The guards uncross their spears, snapping them upright. I step around the throne, expecting that Zeus wants to take a walk as he sometimes does to see if he can get more information one-on-one. "Arrest him." The command is so nonchalant, I nearly miss that the guards are heading toward me.

Comus yells, "What?" over my, "Excuse me?"

Zeus makes his way back to his throne while the shorter guard puts himself between me and Athena, jerking my arms in front of me so the other can lay a golden chain over my wrists and connect it with one sharp move. "Alexiares, he who wards off wars, son of Hercules and Hebe, it is our duty to escort you to the barracks."

I glare at my grandfather as he settles back on his throne, then eye the thin metal encircling my hands. How odd to use something so dainty. Does he think I won't fight this? I need to get outside and away from these idiots.

"What reason could possibly lead to this?" Comus asks, facing off with Zeus.

"Protecting an enemy of the divine, consorting with a non-deity, and failure to obey his king." Zeus's frown tells me I am in the deepest of deep shit. "If you care to join him, son of Dionysus, continue speaking."

"That will not be necessary," Dionysus stands. "Comus is loyal to his friends but more so to Olympus." He stares at Comus, imploring him to behave.

"I am." Comus takes a step back from me, balling his fists at his sides.

This is the best day Ares has had in a long while, according to his smug grin and straight spine. Artemis is pale, probably afraid if questioning happens, I'll unveil her fucked-up relationship with Rath. The last thing I want to do is bring attention to him. Rath will keep Lula safe until we find Anice, or I get out of this chain. Athena and Apollo, both on their feet, appear to be watching a train wreck occur when they didn't even know they were near a railroad. Whatever the Council expected, it wasn't this. Except for Dionysus.

"You are making a massive mistake," I growl.

Zeus remains still as a statue. "You will wed Ichnaea in two weeks. I am only affording you that much time so that you may get your mind in order."

"I've been betrothed for centuries and now, in the middle of chaos, you want me to marry?" I raise the chain, surprised at the odd weight of it. "By force."

"If you will not bend your damned stubbornness in this case, Alexiares, I will make you bend."

Comus slams his palms on the table. "You cannot mean—"

One bright streak of lightning strikes between us, sending singed food flying and cracking the circle of marble. The Council members, Comus, and the guards scatter back. I've felt his bolt too much to flinch. There's no escaping it, though the pain doesn't come this time.

Zeus chuckles in a steady, loony rhythm. "Take Alexiares away. I will question him shortly."

A crunch sounds before the table buckles, caving inward with a grinding rumble until a pile of useless stone, charred food, and melted gold chalices lay in the middle of a circle of thrones, all empty except for one smirking king.

Chapter Six

LULA

I'm tempted to go find Rath when the inevitable knock sounds against the door. I had unlocked it, waiting for him to check on me, and for a half hour I haven't moved from the bed, sitting crossed-legged and staring at the walnut armoire where I stashed my bag. My world was stable. Not close to perfect, but close to better. I had a mission, plans, and a team. Now I sit; same mission, new plans, and no team.

"Lu?" Rath asks through the door.

The bed squeaks when I turn toward the window, making me flinch. Common house sounds will not give my plans away. "Come in." My voice is as creaky as the mattress, floorboards, and hinges on the wardrobe, though I'd never noticed the sounds until today.

Rath steps inside. It was nice of him to knock, instead of popping in as his attributes allow. The concern softens his sharp-featured broodiness. Maybe he's playing it cool while worrying about his plan falling apart. The sunny day outside burns into my memory; puffed clouds, swaying trees, and gentle waves. I will miss this view.

"How angry are you?" he asks.

The new light he brought down on himself casts unease all over me. Even after many hours of heart-to-hearts, I'm talking to a stranger. A powerful, underhanded stranger. Still, I want to share with him. It's become a habit now, this reliance on conversation—what I thought was honesty.

I force a sarcastic smirk. "Can Alexiares's attributes detect a war he created?"

Rath snorts and steps closer. "Alexiares, huh? Are you level-red-angry, Lu? Spouting formal names and starting wars." The boyish way he tilts his head is so human. "I'm sorry." His voice is warm, his tone gentle, and I can't help that it calms me.

"Why would he—you—do this to me?" Part of me doesn't want to know, and would Rath even tell me the truth?

Scrunching his nose, he sits on the bed next to me. "Olympus has needed to change for longer than either of us have existed. It affects us, doesn't it?"

"It didn't have to affect me." Alex and the guys didn't need to bring me into this as if lying and plans to overthrow the king of Olympus required a siren.

He shrugs. "Sure. You could have gone on living the way you did, scattered from the people you love, running to a new place every couple of years, walking among humans you can't even speak to." He raises his brow because he knows I'd have to lie to deny it. "Instead, you get us. We found you and knew you were the right partner. The universe is a mess we can't clean up without friends." He nudges my arm.

I bite my lip to keep from telling him that friends don't stalk or tempt others to love them. They don't possibly knock them up, then tell them about said stalking. Alex was more than that. Rath and Comus were my friends.

At least I thought they were.

"What did you need me for?" I ask. It better not be controlling humans.

Rath twists his lips. "Originally? We were hoping you could enthrall the darklings."

My stomach takes a long swoop though I've stayed still. "Darklings? Why?"

"If we can get the portals open, they will attack, and you could prevent that. Or you could command them so the Council can realize there are creatures who need them and ones who don't. Maybe it would tempt older Olympians to engage or leave and start a new universe."

"An exodus?"

"Alex told you about that, huh?" Rath asks.

"He mentioned it a couple of times." The event would allow a god to leave and start over in a new universe with fresh attributes and influence.

"Many say they've felt an exodus for a long while, but no change has occurred."

I huff. "And you think that parading darklings around will convince the Council to walk away?"

"When you do the same thing for thousands of years, a new evil creature to influence may look like paradise."

"You were the new one in Olympus, right? After how many years?"

His brows furrow tight, and I wait for his answer. "Seven hundred," he says.

"And how peaceful have the Olympians been with you?" I already know the answer. They debated killing him, the first baby born in nearly two millennia. After deliberation, they kept him alive, only to shun him, treating him as they would a bug, or...a human. "After seeing you, shiny and fresh, did they decide they needed a new beginning?"

"It's different, Lula. My father is reviled. I'm a deity, not a creature."

I cluck my tongue. "If they can't show kindness to another divine being, what makes you think that a darkling-wielding siren with Zeus's bullseye on her back will do anything to convince them to leave in peace?"

"Because it's you." He puffs his cheeks before blowing out a long breath. "It's not something you have to worry about now. Those were the plans before. Too much has changed, and we have to alter them again. You need to talk to Alex to work all of this out."

"No, thanks." I ball my fists.

"I understand that you're mad, Lu, but he was trying to do the right thing."

"By lying to me?" I shouldn't be talking about this further. How do I know he's telling me any truth at all?

"He withheld because he was afraid of hurting you."

"He was doing things he knew were wrong before today. My heat. How we met." I swallow hard. No more stalling and no more secrets. If Alex and Comus return before I get back, I'll never get away. I let my lip tremble and I sniffle.

"Oh, Lu," Rath sighs. "Can I get you anything?"

Absolutely. At least his reactions to my sadness are the same. "I want ice cream. Like sundae supplies with chocolate and every topping. An ice cream feast. You owe me."

He gives a slight smile and stands. "I can handle that. Will you be okay for twenty minutes?"

I need more time. He travels so fast through the shadows that if I don't get far enough away to switch cars, he'll find me. I hop off the bed, heading toward the stairs. "Yes. I'm going to take a bath. With wine. I'll emerge when I'm ready."

He nods and follows me to the kitchen. I pour a glass of Chianti while he checks the fridge for inventory.

"Do you need anything else while I'm out?" he asks. I've been the one wanting to cook since I came here. Sharing that part of me is another joyful memory now clouded by a thick fog of rage.

What would take a while to collect? Croissants from Paris? That may be suspicious. "Lasagna supplies and ice cream. Do you remember what to get?" I walk toward the stairs. *Get out already.*

"I do. Call my cell if you need me." He slips into the shadows.

I tighten my jaw and try to keep calm as I walk upstairs. No one in this realm can see him when he's in shadow form, but he can spy on everyone else. He won't stick around for long. He's a gentleman...I think.

The radio in the bathroom has a decent selection of stations that are loud and distracting. Leaving the glass of wine on the counter, I wait another minute, then shut the door and dart back into the bedroom. My bag is heavy, packed with enough stuff for a week. By then I should have a better handle on how to move forward.

Downstairs, I take granola bars and apples, stuffing them in the bag, then take a picture of my map on the wall. If Rath is watching me, he'll dart out of the shadows and snatch me any minute. The jeep's keys are on the hook next to the garage door. It starts up with a rumble. Chills travel my spine as I swing onto the road, and hope Rath doesn't notice the tread marks in the sand.

I cannot believe this. None of it. I woke in love and happy. Alex took every marvelous thing I thought made our relationship real and threw them out the window. Now it's time to rely on the only beings I can trust. I dial Grace.

"Hello again, sister." There's a smile in her voice that I'm sad to crush.

"Prax isn't there, is he?" I ask.

"Rath took him to Olympus this morning for a meeting. He should be back later, though I'm on the fence if that's good or not. Nothing like a siren heat spent with a stranger to make things awkward."

I place my hand over my heart. Thank goodness. "You have to get away from the house. Is there a vehicle or something?"

"Whoa, what? Um, no. What happened?"

I blurt out what Alex told me in a long run-on sentence, then have to pull to the side of the road because I can't see through my blurry, wet vision. Were Alex and I ever anything?

"Lu." There are tears in Grace's voice. "Maybe it's not what you think. I saw you two together, I heard him. I don't believe he was lying when he said how much he loved you. My heat could have gone so far sideways, but he stayed strong."

"What if they knew, Grace? He watched me for a year. He studied us. I can't trust that he didn't know exactly how our bodies would work. Anything that happened over the last few months is now up for scrutiny. What if Zeus and Moros aren't even real?" That sits wrong with me, making my face scrunch. Alex lied and stalked, but I've looked into violent eyes before, and his are tender. No one can hide psychotic for long. I settle my head in my hand. I don't know gods though. They've had eons to learn how to bend others to their will.

"No, Lu. Prax did nothing but talk about what kind of leader Alex was—how he's ruled by strong morals."

"He wants to use me."

She's quiet except for shuffling through the line. Hopefully, she's packing. "Any word on Venora or Hazel?"

"No. But hang on. I'll send you my research map." I pull the phone from my ear and do just that, then glance all around me to make sure I'm not being watched or followed.

"Okay. Got it. Uh, I have no idea where to go right now."

"Start walking toward the nearest town?"

Grace laughs. "It snowed last night. A lot. There's a shed though. I'll see if there's a snowmobile, not that I'd know how to drive one of those."

In my panic, I forgot how Grace doesn't like open vehicles. She's more of a carriage traveler. "Well, get going as quickly as you can. You probably have at least forty-five minutes. Once Rath discovers I'm missing, he'll come to find you."

We say our goodbyes and hang up. I wipe away the wetness from my cheeks and start driving again. It would be foolish of me to stay crying on the side of the road until Rath finds me.

Ten minutes later, the tropical forest and glimpses of ocean turn to small buildings, road signs, and sidewalks. Rath hasn't popped into the passenger's seat or appeared in front of the jeep, so I may get away with this. I pull over at a tiny store where two women are talking next to an old pickup. I hop out, grabbing my bag. "Do you speak English?" It's not the words that matter with my power, it's the intention.

The woman with black spirals surrounding a lovely round face shakes her head while the younger one nods. "Yes."

I make eye contact with the woman who doesn't speak English and point to the jeep. "Drive that vehicle two towns over and leave it there." She hustles into the driver's seat and pulls away, kicking up a tiny cloud of dust in her wake.

The remaining human looks to be in her early twenties and has bright red braids that hang to her hips. She stares at me, waiting for my instruction. Guilt swirls into the mess of emotions I'm carrying. I step toward the idling truck she stands next to. "Drive me to the nearest airport."

Chapter Seven

ALEX

We wait in the shadows of Zeus's corridors while the royal guards make a sweep, clearing out Olympians so we don't create a scene when they walk me to the barracks. The immense building's silhouette looms in the dark four blocks away. It would dwarf all of Mount Olympus without Zeus's house balancing out the structure. As well as rarely used cells for prisoners, it's the army's training grounds, and holds the arsenal of archaic weapons I learned to wield as a seven-year-old. I haven't touched a mace in a thousand years, and the thought that I may have to pick one up again makes my stomach ball even tighter. *Two weeks.*

While I'm ready to fight, refuse, and beg, I'm aware of the truth. My objection will fall on willfully ignorant ears. As soon as I'm settled into my cage, Zeus will tell me it's time to perform my divine duty, force a ceremony on me, and lock me in a communion room with Naea until she walks out pregnant. Over the years, he's offered her up like an exquisite dinner with maids and nymphs as appetizers. Past snippets of my conversations with Zeus echo in my head, grating the last of my nerves. "Alexiares, you have so many to bed. Why not wed Ichnaea, give her your seed, and enjoy all the lovers and pets you wish?"

Because I should have a choice and my choice is no. I've gained the insight that lesser goddesses and enslaved non-deities have always had, and it's time Olympus altered its path so we don't continue to have a history riddled with sickening violence. Zeus and the Council shock me with continued deplorable behavior, shading over any good Olympians have done. Dinginess now shrouds our visits here, even as we walk on trashless streets under bright blue skies. My love for Olympus has become love for an Earth full of potential.

Comus faces a wall as if he's studying a tapestry and taps at his phone. He's no doubt informing our small group of every detail and trying to find my brother. I'm no longer sure that this revolution we've worked toward will end in peace, but the way we're living must end. The rules of one jaded king can't rule Olympus, but something has to break besides the marble table. What if violence is the only path? I test the strength of the bindings again and shift with impatience. I'm not sticking around to accept this version of my fate. Lula could be in danger. Comus turns, raising a mischievous eyebrow at me and glances at the guard on my left— Trantus. I found that out while trying to be cordial. Comus thinks we should taunt the guards? I tilt my head and he raises his chin. Maybe he's right. Even if I can't escape, it's possible we could get information out of them if we use Rath's method of poking until they rage the truth at us. If anything, it may give me the distraction I need.

"How long does it take to clear out the civilians, so they don't protest the wrongness of what's happening?" I ask. If Zeus approved this idiotic plan, we have far more hope to gain control using strategy than I thought.

Trantus turns his head to stare at me as if utterly shocked I would object. Zeus probably even speaks a word to him occasionally.

I lift a shoulder. "Don't give me that look. This is a pathetic display of power, and you know it." I'm so used to keeping diplomacy in each of my well-considered words that saying what's on my mind makes my brain tingle. Not in the same way attributes fire off, but in a tumbling release of excitement-laced fear and needed risk.

The other guard, Olineus, prods me toward the door.

"Oh good. We are finally getting this parade started."

"Go," he barks, pressing the spear's shaft against my back.

I shrug him off. "I'm thirty-two-hundred-years-old. I'm aware of the barrack's location." Doesn't mean I will get there.

Comus pulls his phone out to text again, no doubt warning our allies that we're on the move. We walk into the dark of Olympus, the path highlighted by a few lit sconces and a nearly full moon in a cloudless sky. Escaping would be best before we catch up to the other guards.

"I said I know the way." When I elbow out of the grip of the guard, Comus slides between us. I raise my hands to open a portal to an alleyway in Los Angeles. If they follow us through, the humans there will think we're part of a movie. Nothing happens. I try again. There's no tingling in my fingertips, no tug at my brain, or pull on the veil's curtain. My attributes are gone.

Olineus chuckles and darts around Comus to shove me forward.

"This is enchanted, isn't it?" I ask, staring at the chain.

"Of course," the guard says, as if I'm asinine for not considering that Zeus would involve witches again. Maybe I should have, but last time, he broke apart the realms. I didn't think he'd come back for more after that. "Now go." Olineus gives me another shove.

Comus grumbles from behind Trantus and meets my eyes.

"Find my brother," I say.

Olineus gives a whistle, and two guards pop out next to a small blessings altar, then follow Comus. They squeak or clank with each step. Nothing to do in thousands of years and they haven't thought to work on their stealth game.

"Hey Comus," I call out into the night, ignoring the shushes. "You're being followed."

Comus turns to walk backward. "Oh, I heard them. Hello, gentlemen. Enjoying a romantic evening of...worship?" He lifts his voice on that last word, making it a teasing song. Both guards stumble to a stop as they glance at each other, then keep after Comus, who pivots and heads in the direction of Anice's house. "If you tell me where Anicetus is, we can all get some *relaxation* time. This may be a delightful date for you two, but I prefer privacy. Except on—" They turn a corner, slipping behind a columned archway that spins words into unheard mumbles. Anice isn't answering his phone if Comus is goading the guards. I ball my fists. We're not ready for this revolution.

We need extra time to solidify another plan so we're all working the same way toward the goal we share. Comus has done a superb job figuring out who wants change in Olympus, but we haven't asked for allegiances yet. We have a group of fifteen against a couple hundred. I set the pace to a sludgy stroll as we travel in silence, passing gardens and columns. A confrontation ahead catches my eye as meandering Olympians try to skirt around a line of glinting gold.

"What's going on for you to block us?" Prax looms over the guard in front of him. I'm both happy to see him and irritated that he's having to put himself on the line as a troublemaker. Three wide-eyed maids follow him, carrying armloads of fabric. *Perfect.* Prax's eyes narrow as soon as he sees me. "Alexiares? Why are you in chains?"

"Zeus ordered my arrest because I won't marry Ichnaea and pop out a new generation of divine soldiers for him," I say loud enough to carry, and get a hard nudge. "Sure, I'd love to have children, but since the king outlawed reproduction two millennia ago—"

Olineus elbows me in the side. "Quiet."

Never again. I raise my voice to finish my sentence. "I can't imagine the other Olympians will approve."

"Alexiares." He and Trantus grip my arms and drag me forward.

"You didn't see this coming?" I ask them as they push me to move faster. "When was the last time you cleared the streets? Using a crier to announce something big was happening would have been almost as effective."

The maids whisper to each other. The watered-down demigod and demigoddess servants are powerful—our gossip nuclear weapons, inhabiting divine bedchambers as much as public spaces. They speak more freely than full-blooded deities who must adhere to the behavior expected of majors. That's a massive mistake on Zeus's part, but that won't help us with peace until he sees them as more.

The hard grip of both guards comes loose with a well-timed jerk. "And I can't believe the Council executed a guard."

"Enough!" Olineus swings around, holding me back with his spear. The long blade at the end is too close to my jaw.

I lean closer until the metal pinches my throat. "You damage the goods, and it will be your demise everyone keeps secret."

He steps to the side, face pale. "Come on. Quickly."

A few other Olympians join the others, murmuring as more guards cross to ask them to disperse. Faces pop up on the unguarded side and four young Olympians wander into the street.

"Were you there?" I ask the guards. "Did you witness my grandfather's version of questioning? Did the accused stutter a word before the king got impatient?" Memories of Zeus's bolt sting my eyes. So many have perished under it. Fewer have lived through the tortures he's inflicted. I did. Even if they sided with Moros, no one deserves the physical punishment Zeus and his lackeys can dish out. "Did Zeus even know that guard's name?"

"We do not speak of it," he pitches over his shoulder, then halts to wait for the others to move the growing crowd. He falls back to stand next to me. Trantus throws him a nervous glance. He's my height but lanky. Nearly all deities appear as humans in their twenties to early thirties, except for those kept younger, cursed older, or those who want to age—though I haven't seen an age change occur in anyone but Rath since the break. When a deity is stressed, it shows. Ages them. Darkness soaks around the guard's bloodshot eyes, his lips are tight, and he holds his spear in a white-knuckled grip. This demigod is struggling. He should.

The bravest of the maids skitters between two guards and approaches on fast sandals. "Were you there, Oli? What happened?"

"Leave, Jemiasis," he grumbles, dragging me forward again. "This is none of your business."

I recognize her name but can't place her attribute. I've been working in the Earth realm for so long, I've forgotten, or never learned, all of my brethren. My close ties with Zeus put me out of touch with the others, but with the way determination narrows her eyes, I should have done a better job keeping up. She grumbles something under her breath, straightens up, and strides to the other demigoddesses. Get ready, Olympus. We've set a gossip bomb to launch.

"You screwed up," I say. "Now, you'll have to work hard to get any servant in your bed."

He jerks me forward with enough force that the attention we've drawn turns from curiosity to concern. Questions start ringing out asking what I've done and if there's an attack. As we pass, others follow. I relax at seeing a familiar face standing on a garden path. The Goddess of Dawn is one of our taxiarchs, though until today I wouldn't have used the military term to describe what we hope will complete a new, better Council.

Eos defines airy. She's an early morning sunbeam cast into a softly curved goddess with dark amber hair that flutters on an invisible wind. We spent a century comforting each other when Zeus broke the connection between Earth and Olympus. Zeus killed off her mortal lovers and my mind had been reeling from helping him disable the portals. In her grief, she wanted a child. I refused because of Zeus's newest law. That was the one time I was glad I followed his rule. When he decided I needed to marry Ichnaea and I stalled, he would have severed any link between another goddess and me. I'm not sure I could have weathered that heartbreak.

Eos gives the slightest flare of shock at the chain. I glance back where Comus went, elbowing Olineus to hide my movement. She tilts her chin up, as if my getting arrested is normal. She's the child of Titans, only slightly younger than Zeus, so she's seen many terrible things. Her bored reaction is perfect. As if we're not on the brink of disaster, she wanders that direction at a careful stroll, reminding me why she's with us. Our calm, intelligent daybreak.

Deities step out of white marble homes as we pass. Several stare, whispering as they fall behind and follow. The four young gods have picked up a fifth member. Plutus. Ichnaea's lover stares on in silence as the guards maneuver me to the darkened edge of the path. Does he know yet? Does Ichnaea?

"What's this about?" the tallest god of the bunch asks. They've encircled Plutus, hiding him efficiently.

The guards tighten their hold on my arms, but they can't keep me quiet without making a scene. "My grandfather's arresting me," I say, loud enough to carry. "Claims I'm protecting an enemy of the divine —the meek siren species. You wouldn't know about them because libraries are only accessible to the Council."

"Alexiares," Trantus growls, jabbing me in the side. "Don't make us silence you."

I shrug. "What? They're curious." I'm far from done but we're steps from the barracks. The crowd slows, standing on the dark green grass in front of a small marble temple decorated with columns and a carved scene of a chariot race. Trantus drops his hand from my arm to greet the guard at the barrack doors, and I spin to face the crowd. "He's also forcing Ichnaea and me to marry against our wishes in two weeks. I'm sure your invitations are forthcoming." Expecting the attack, I hold firm to my spot when Olineus shoves me. "I'll be in attribute-dampening chains. Much like this." I lift my hands to show the wide-eyed crowd.

I get the slightest glimpse of Plutus's horrified face blanch before Olineus lays me out with a hell of a punch. There are as many shouts as there are gasps. I sit up from the ground and shake off the headache. "That was dumb," I murmur, voice thick with the heat blooming on my jaw. The grumbles get louder, and I realize this could go sideways faster than I imagined. I hoist myself up as two gods from Plutus's group come forward. The others and Plutus slip around the corner, hopefully not aiming to do something stupid. I throw my hands up to halt approaching deities, some curious, some seeming to want to help. *Not yet.*

"It's okay," I tell them. "Do not allow them to tempt you into violence." I wipe my lip against my shoulder, leaving a red streak on my shirt, and glare at Olineus. *Idiot.* At least he didn't use his spear. He signals to the barracks without touching me.

"Disperse," yells Trantus. "You shall return to your homes, or we will involve the Council."

The eyes of the crowd widen, and they chatter. Two health deities approach—a god and demigoddess who work with Anice's wife. Concern paints every feature on their faces. They've seen war before, and battles start with a need and bloodshed. Now, we have both.

I give them a slight smile, ignoring Trantus's wide arms as he tries to herd me inside. "What's happening isn't right," I tell them over his pauldron. "But we will not fall prey to the brutality of olden days. I refuse to fill your hospital with broken deities. There can be a peaceful solution to these dark times." I hope.

They both nod, shoulders sinking. They do not appear surprised at anything unfolding. Possibly because they are close enough to Iaso to realize her arranged marriage isn't a happy one. She's become a dear friend to her husband, but my brother is in love with another god. It seems the more we return to Olympus, the more deities we find forced into a life they wish was different. The only happy Olympians are the young ones born on the cusp. They didn't experience the full connection with humans. They haven't walked in rain, fiddled with inventions, spoken to humans, or used their attributes as intended. The rest of us ache for what they're missing. We will have it back. Two thousand years is too long to be on lockdown, not doing what we were made to do.

Deities split and wander off, some lingering as I'm guided into the doorway of the barracks. Olympus will know my grandfather's actions by midday tomorrow.

Chapter Eight

ALEX

THE BARRACK'S SCONCE-LIT ENTRANCE ROOM IS TWO STORIES TALL, but only wide enough for the three of us to walk. Scenes of war and dark legends of injustice shift along the ceiling from the flickers of fire below. Darkling hordes of berserkers, incubi, and goblins overrun tiny humans who wear expressions of terror. If the Council saw the weaponry mortals have created, they'd rethink this ancient art.

Through the set of double doors, we take a left and pass through the breezeway next to the building's center garden. Stoic, uniform hedges stand at attention around a circular fountain. We cross into a private detainment room. Golden bars connect the white marble floor to the ten-foot ceiling, separating the visitor from the prisoner. A low cot sits under a narrow slit in the wall where moonlight pours in. Tucked in the back corner is a latrine and a mounted basin with a faucet. At least they didn't put me in the dungeon.

My heart hammers in my chest, and tingles roll across my fingertips. I flex and jerk, but there's no give to the chain. I struggle, but together, the guards guide me in and shut the gate. A clink of metal ricochets off marble as the lock catches. *Fuck.*

Olineus and Trantus take their places beside the door.

I take in every etched carving and vein of marble, looking for weakness. I've never been in this room. Not on this side of the bars, at least. "Did you know Moros has imprisoned two sirens and is forcing them to harm humans? The fault is not of their own, yet the king has placed a bounty on the entire species." I pace four steps and pivot. The guards ignore me. "Are you carrying out the murders or is Zeus doing it himself?"

Under his purple, feather-plumed helmet, Olineus's brows furrow.

I sneer in disgust. "He didn't share that in questioning, did he? Yeah, that's right. Instead of fighting the one responsible, the king will attack innocent women—Olympus's own creations—and have a royal wedding for his demigod grandson." I roll my eyes. "Priorities."

"They're not to be harmed," Olineus says, making me pause my steps.

I grip the bars. "No? Just captured and brought to the king?"

"Shh," Trantus says, but it doesn't stop Olineus from nodding.

My knees go wobbly, but I try to hide the utter relief rushing through me and straighten, refusing to release the breath I'm holding though it wants to leave in one great whoosh. Even if they found the sirens, we'd have a chance to get them out.

In the distance, a door slams and my brother's enraged voice bellows, echoing along the hall. "You want to stop me? Fine, arrest me and place me with Alex. This is atrocious. Going through with his asinine orders only speaks of the Council's insanity."

The guards exchange a glance and take their role as statues.

Anice is royally diplomatic...until you push him far enough. Then he's a pissed-off bull ready to charge at the tiniest sliver of red. Every Council member may as well be painted crimson.

"Change is not feasible at this time, Anicetus." Dionysus's calm timbre floats through the corridor. "He broke the laws and must be held responsible, no matter how much it pains the king."

Comus's voice joins the argument as they come closer. "Zeus is no more pained by this than he is shooing a fly away from the bullshit that falls from his lips. He lives for power, and this is his game."

"Yet again, son," Dionysus grumbles. "Hold your tongue." They burst through the door, Comus in the lead. Red highlights his cheeks, and a sheen of sweat coats his brow. Anice isn't the only one ready to gore someone.

"They bound your hands?" Anice shouts. "What the fuck?"

"Anicetus," Dionysus growls. "Lower your voice." He turns to the guards. "Please go fetch ambrosia and a meal." When only Olineus moves, Dionysus starts shutting the door. "And an additional blanket. It is much appreciated."

"This is utter bullshit, and you know it," my twin growls, running his hand through his golden hair. He keeps his shorter than mine, and I toss my head to get strands out of my vision. Anice grips the bars and gives them a jerk.

I place my hands over his. "Anice."

"So…" Comus flicks a bar.

"The bars are enforced with a core of adamantine," Dionysus says. "As is the chain. Zeus will not stand for anyone to attempt a rescue. Let things settle."

I'm in a cage I can't get out of. Rath probably couldn't get in either and Zeus doesn't let things settle, he punishes. I've felt the burn of his bolts, the tiny breaks in bone from his thunder when the Olympian way forced me into an impossible dilemma.

What will Zeus do now that I'm protecting an otherworldling?

If he thinks violence will make me give Lula up, he's wrong. I'll die to keep her out of his hands. I only hope her last memory of me isn't how I kept a terrible secret from her. Comus blinks at me and I glance at the pocket where he keeps his phone. He shakes his head. Nothing from Rath yet. Lula must still be holed up in our room. Now Rath is definitely going to be the one to talk to her.

Anice steps closer to him and spits out, "What Zeus has done is an abuse of power. We won't stand for this new low. I will *not* leave."

Every muscle is strained and ready. If anyone touches him, he'll come out swinging.

"Anice." I get as close to him as the bars will allow. "Brother, I need you on the outside in case questions or *errands* arise."

My twin exhales long, turning frightened, fiery eyes to me. His attributes work in a similar way to mine with calls of war. Moros will strike again soon, and without me, Anice is our shot to find him. He grasps my hands and leans his forehead against the bars. I do the same. We've spent a long time apart, oddly going through the same issues—we both helped close the otherworld portals that linked to the Earth realm, stranding otherworldlings because Zeus feared other gods would invade Olympus. We stood by as the king used his witches to part Olympus from Earth. We're both in love with those we're not allowed to be in love with. I have his loyalty, and he has mine.

"Keep yours safe, brother," I say. "We will fight this, but with intelligence, not fists." I lift my head to look at Dionysus. "What do we do to postpone this sham ceremony?"

Dionysus sighs. "Time's up, Alexiares. He believes that you harbor a siren and I cannot share more, not that I understand much." He raises a hand when I open my mouth. "And do not treat me as if I am one of you. I am not. We need to work together, but that will not happen until after the wedding. It is best that we all consider each word we choose to release to the winds." He keeps his voice low and leans closer. "And we assume you have human technology upon you, though it has not yet been sought." He glances at my pocket and I wince. I'm glad they haven't taken my phone yet.

An abrupt knock sounds before the door flings open and the guards take their stations. Dionysus heads out. "Make sure everyone is secure for the night. We have much to discuss in the morning." He does the best and worst job of staying out of things. We need him, but so does Zeus. I do not envy Dionysus's stuck place.

A maid with bedding in a basket slips in, followed by Ceraon who's holding a tray of dishes. My brother doesn't relax at the sight of the god he secretly loves, only stands stiffly as the guards carefully unlock the gate so I can receive my incarceration gifts while Comus picks my pockets. Even I didn't know Anice and Ceraon's relationship was deeper than close friends until Zeus set up a communion event between Ichnaea and me, then asked Anice to bed her when I got the hell out of there. Zeus lost his mind on so many levels that night, and I reunited with my twin.

As usual, Ceraon's smile is warm, even in the dim light. "I heard there was a need for food and ambrosia. I happen to have brought both." He bows his head at me, setting the tray on the cot. "It's an honor as always, Demigod of Warding off Wars."

The scent of cooked, herbed fish replaces sterile air. "Same, Demigod of the Meal. My brother could also use sustenance. Perhaps you can share your gifts with him as well?"

"With pleasure," he says as he's guided out of the cell by Trantus.

"It's what I do." The bars clink shut and Ceraon waits by the door, still appearing jovial, though there's the slightest squint to his eyes and a tightness to his grin. "After you, Anicetus. I'll take you to the reserved kitchens where all the good treats hide."

Anice reaches through to attempt a hug, but his arm won't fit through the bars past his elbow. I return his affection as well as possible before he pulls away and storms out. I give Ceraon a grateful bow. Comus and I need to talk about so many things in real words instead of eyebrows and nods, but it's not possible with company.

Comus purses his lips. "I'll be back soon, brother. You'll want to hear about that date."

He'll inform and organize our group, carefully direct the gossip that will burn through Olympus, and keep tabs on the sirens. He's got his work cut out for him.

And I'll sit in a gilded cage, hoping we get out of this unscathed.

Chapter Nine

LULA

At a gas station with a fruit stand attached, I tell my silent chauffeur to call someone she can trust to pick her up and take her home. I don't want to break her brain with too many commands, so I keep to short words to create a believable story for her family and friends: she was taken at gunpoint, but the attackers only needed a ride. Nothing bad happened. Once she fulfills my command, she'll wake from the siren mind fog, and with her grogginess, everyone will think she's experiencing shock. I hope. Today will confuse both women I enthralled, but I can't help that now.

Humans aren't all that resilient, but they have an amazing ability to let things go, even when they experience a chunk of time that's partially remembered, out of their control, and completely unexplainable.

An older man in a loose, white shirt stares from behind a hill of pineapple as I walk as far away from earshot as possible and dial Amah.

"Lula?" she asks with a tremble in her voice. It's not her typical cheery greeting, but our last conversation didn't end well.

I take a breath, but it only tightens my throat further. "He lied."

"Oh." She sighs as if she expected this. I suppose she did with all the warnings she gave me. "Are you safe?"

"For now."

"And Grace?"

"She's out of the house. I'm making my way—"

"Shh," she interrupts. "Not your location, okay? The phone may be recorded."

They wouldn't. My face aches and crumples.

Amah has acted as my mother since I was three and I lost my own. When she sent me into the world and crossed over the seas, I thought I'd die of loneliness. I had begged her to stay, offered her anything if I could come with her, and told her I'd fail at this make-believe human life. She wiped my tears, complimented my strength, and taught me a thousand ways to disappear if I got into trouble before she could get to me. I've forgotten most of those lessons. Or maybe the changes of each new era chased them from my mind. Running through streams and hiding in barns isn't the easy escape route anymore, and once I was on my own, I quickly learned that there wasn't much I couldn't handle with a word. Not until a century and a half later, when a demigod dragged me to him and kissed me. Why she taught me those survival skills when we hadn't met gods before is beyond me, but when I chose Alex's words over hers, it must have been a real slap in the face.

"Amah, I don't know what to say. I'm just…I'm sorry," I whimper and cover my eyes from the painfully bright sun.

"It's okay, dear one. I'm sorry too. We can only rely on ourselves in this world."

That hurts. She's always used that phrase, but I didn't understand why. Alex proved her point. I'm back to being alone, and now foolish too. Fixing what I've done may take time we don't have.

I let my hand drop and steady my resolve. "In our last conversation, you told me you needed to tell me some things about myself and that you would see me if I left Alex. I've left, Ma. Can we meet?" I need her. The line is silent. Maybe she only offered such enticing information because she thought it would make me leave Alex. "Ma? Did something change?"

Amah clears her throat. "I'll meet with you, but we have to be careful. He will keep searching for you."

"I know." Alex will not be happy I left. Nor the others. A

desperate part of me wants them to fight for me as if they care. I'm colder out of Alex's warmth, and would love to bounce ideas off Comus. The ties severed between Rath and me ache. I thought he understood me. We connected like old friends who hadn't seen each other for a hundred and eighty-three years.

"No, you don't understand." She gives a rare, frustrated huff. "Damn phones and their ability to record. Lula, I need to tell you so many things, but you have to know that he—that they—will stop at nothing to find you. Do not say anything that may lead them to you. Be so careful." Each word comes in slow warning.

"You really think they're listening." It's not a question. There have been a hundred times that Alex, Rath, or Comus had time to put a tracker or bug on my phone. Comus took it from me when Gerty died, and he handled my messages. I was busy in Alex's arms, absorbed with the pain in my chest from my broken soul, unable to pay attention to what the God of Revelry was doing. Who would think a deity with such attributes would track someone? "They could have all our numbers." They could call any of my sisters and plead for their help to find me, and the sirens would come running. I'd do the same for them.

"Lula, we can do this. Do you remember where we met that April? The rain had soaked you to the bone when I embraced you."

My nose tingles, and I attempt to calm the hyperventilation with a hand on my chest, eyes to the glowing clouds. The place in Canada? It was a hundred years ago. "Is it still there?" We live in a quickly changing world. Technology creeps in, people leave, roads change.

"Yes. It's the same. Do you remember the way?"

"I think so? At least, the general area." I had taken a train, then a carriage.

"Get to the closest airport to that location. I'll send someone for you that will ask you a question that only you and I know. They'll bring you to me. Do you understand?"

"Yes." My chest tightens further. She's in this with me, but only because I dragged her into it. Her and Grace. "I'm sorry. I didn't mean to drag my sisters into this."

"This isn't your fault. I never thought—" She blows out a long breath. "I blame myself for not preparing you better."

"How could you have prepared me for this, Ma?" The outside seems to pause and slowly linger as my thoughts spin in reeling circles. Palm leaves halt their rustling dance against each other, cars pass but slowly, with soundless engines. "You knew this could happen?"

Amah gives one short sniffle. "We can't talk about this now. I'm already close to the area and you will be there by tomorrow, do you understand me? Destroy your phone and leave now."

"I'll be out of contact." My voice is a tiny chirp compared to before. Did she meet Alex before? She said she'd never spoken to a god.

"The modern age has spoiled us. Get a new phone if you need to, but after I call everyone, I'm tossing this device. I'll give you numbers when we're safe."

My thoughts barely grasp her words. "Did Alex kill my mother?"

She's quiet for too long. "No." Her voice is sharp as talons. "But she was taken by a god. Now, Lula. Now."

"Love you." I choke out and smash my thumb against the phone to hang up. Relationships lost and relationships regained. My heart hurts.

I MOVE AS QUICKLY AS I CAN THROUGH THE SMALL AIRPORT, HEAD ducked, hiding under the huge hat I took from a woman in the parking lot. The big sunglasses make everything inside unnaturally dark. It's been five hours since I left. Alex must know by now. He's discovered the full glass of wine and empty tub. My missing clothes.

Did he roar and throw a fit; stomping around the house to check each room and the hidey holes within? Did they find the abandoned jeep?

Keeping my voice low in lines, I tell humans to give me space, then move on with their day when they're supposed to. I command agents and security guards with whispers of determined intent as they run my credit card through. The cameras are watching, and I already pull enough attention. If Rath searches here, I can't have suspicious officers and staff following me. Besides, paper trails only go so far and missing money stands out. I don't want any type of tracking tying me to a specific area.

I have a thousand questions for my sisters, but they've discarded their phones, cutting our ties. All but me. Except Amah took it upon herself to cancel my service, because she knows me, dammit. It's for the better because I dialed Alex and listened to the empty, broken space between us for longer than was necessary. Does he regret telling me?

I'm on my own to sort out the truth from a pile of lies and misunderstandings—at least until tomorrow. In three flights and seventeen hours, I will see my sister, hug her, apologize a thousand times, and hope I'm ready for her secrets. Whatever happens, I'll get Venora and Hazel back and keep the others safe. Even if that means accepting what Amah's been so afraid to tell me. It must be a nightmare made real for her to act the way she has.

A small crowd waits to board the plane to Miami. Their movements shift to a sludgy crawl as I make my way forward. Some reach out for me as I pass them. I bite my lips together to keep my words at bay. Fingers trail over my arms and my hips, making me jerk and dodge. This is why sirens don't do crowds. "Go sit down until the flight is called," I whisper. "Except for you four. Wait here." The family of three and a woman in a business suit stare at me, unblinking as the surrounding group sits on the chairs or floor. It's weird, but with the few around me, hopefully not weird enough to be flagged as an issue. I wince and walk to the gate staff, handing over my ticket. Get me on that plane.

THE BACKMOST COACH SEAT THAT THE AGENT BOOKED FOR ME KICKED someone from their flight. Hopefully their trip wasn't as dire as mine. I hold the brim of my hat with trembling fingers to hide. I'm going to make it. Unless Rath is here, but I don't think he is. I can sense him in a room, like an energy spike in the atmosphere even when he's in the shadows. All I'm sensing now is the ball of nerves writhing in my stomach and the ache of loss hollowing out my chest. I'm irritated that not only did Alex lie and scare me, but I still want to curl up against him. As mad and confused as I am, I'm half tempted to turn around and go back. Are they worried about me or concerned that they lost their siren?

They don't matter right now. My sisters do.

I hope Grace made it safely to town. She's had a century more experience than I do at disappearing. Even if she had to find a cave with a bear, I bet she would come out unscathed and toting along a new furry friend. I'm sure when we speak again, she'll have a hundred stories we will talk about for the next century, and those are the thoughts I must cling to: a future to heal from this. We'll go back to virtual movie nights, post-break-up dance-offs, and long conversations about the activities of humans. It's not a perfect life, but it's good enough and I appreciate those moments with my sisters. Even at a distance.

A young woman sits next to me, waiting for my words. She appears to be of college age with big brown eyes that still shine with naive hope and immature dreams. Did I ever have that look? *Yes.* When I met Alex.

"Do you have a book?" I whisper.

"Yes."

"Read and enjoy it." I wiggle further down in the seat, hiding from the stares of others. It's going to be a long trip.

Chapter Ten

ALEX

Sandal slaps against marble echo from the corridor as the sunlight pokes through twilight, beaming a rectangle across the room, past the bars and over the heads of Trantus and Olineus. They returned moments before sunrise, trading off with the two others who refused to speak no matter how much I poked at them all night. Zeus's himation whips in the wind of his strides as he halts a foot from the bars and clasps his hands behind his back in his typical patriarchal stance. "We have much to discuss, grandson."

What a loaded word. *Grandson.* I wasn't the first, nor the last, but unlike the others, Zeus imparted that role upon Anice and me. Our grandfather doted on us. Brought us into his home for meals and trained us in Olympian expectation as if we would inherit the castle one day. Except he'll never leave. He guards his property with a golden army and an electric fence brought straight from the skies.

The leeway he's always allotted me made his punishments crueler. He'd placed me on a pedestal, then used me as an example to Olympus. In his mindset, the archaic, abusive ways are a tradition to keep, and I wanted things to change. The worst infraction I'd managed through the years was when I protected Comus's sister from a Council member the only way I could. Dalia's communion event was torture for us both, but Deimos didn't have his chance to break her as a vendetta against Comus. The God of Terror may be another grandson, but his and Zeus's relationship was never familial. That made the punishment all the more damaging. Strike after strike ripped through me while Olympus watched on. For a moment, I had wished for Zeus's bolt of death instead of the lashes of a thousand high-voltage whips. The love I had for my grandfather burned away with my skin. The edge of each happy childhood memory singed as black as my fingers had been. My allegiance melted along with my corneas. I was in an unconscious stasis for weeks. When I woke, it took months for my vision and hearing to return, and longer for my hair to grow back and for my charcoaled fingers to show pink again, but my loyalty has yet to appear.

I found my staunch allies the night I'd wished for death. Comus put himself on the line to walk forward to pick my charred body off the ground to take me to the healers. He still hasn't left my side. Eos, Helios, Praxis, and Zephyrus watched over me for months. Anice was warned to stay away, though he's told me that was the worst thing Zeus ever commanded of him.

"Speak, Alexiares," Zeus commands, interrupting my thoughtful silence.

My throat dries as I pull from the painful memories. What punishment will he divvy out now? How could it be worse? Yet, I cannot bend. Not when we're this close.

I don't even get off the bench to greet him. No more bowing or even standing in his presence. Maybe it's the lack of sleep, or the successful lockdown he organized. I haven't seen Rath; therefore, he can't get through. I need my brothers and Lula.

"Why am I here?" I ask, rubbing my wrists, sore from too many attempts to break the chain.

"I no longer trust your judgment." Zeus strokes his beard. "Not that it was impressive before, but you have become irrational."

I lift my hands, showing him the chain. "And this is a sane move." His eyes flash in anger, but I'm too exhausted with this game to remember my diplomacy. "You decide that after a two-hundred-year engagement, two weeks is perfect timing for a forced wedding, and had your guards parade me down the main streets."

Trantus's spear tips to the side and he looks to the floor, tight jaw peeking out from under his helmet.

"Tell me about the siren," Zeus says.

Never. "Tell me why I'm here."

"Where does she hide? I must speak with her."

He hasn't found her yet. I fight to hold the tension in my shoulders and the scowl on my face so I give nothing away. "I have no idea what you're talking about. I met her months ago and we parted ways." Empty words that will keep Lula safe flow with ease past my lips. "Haven't seen her since." I will lie and lie again for her.

But not *to* her. I'll never make that mistake again.

"She has beguiled you. You are not yourself."

The only way I hold my tongue is by biting it. My feelings for Lula are as real as the blood running through my veins. The urge to explain every nuance of the emotions I've discovered rolls through me, but it's moot. Zeus cannot grasp love and devotion—only primal necessity and political posturing through arranged marriage. If he would drop the scorned-king act for a second, and walk with the humans, maybe he'd pick up on a dose of humanity. Or perhaps it's time to stop hoping he will come around. The days of longing to show him the beauty of the new era has ended. "I am as I've always been."

"Alexiares," Zeus growls. "Guards, leave us."

My neck tingles with Zeus's golden eyes piercing into me. The guards clank themselves out, and I hold my breath, expecting another bolt—though he likes witnesses, the more the better. But they still fear him and have yet to find something that means more than pain. Deities hold too much patience in that sense than humans though, because death is not something we're required to face. Mortals are braver than we are because of their inevitable end. I've learned from that.

"We are searching and will find her," Zeus says. "I will dispose of your toy, and you will have no one but Ichnaea to fall back on."

With an eye roll, I glance back at him, needing to see his expression. "Who's searching?" He has so few with traveling attributes and I'd put them on my team before his. Except for Pythia and Hades.

Zeus's oracle could pinpoint Lula with the right information. Me being with her could give Pythia what she needs, and I love Lula; she owns my heart. Zeus has punished lovers by using oracles to discover who the women truly loved, then disposed of the competition. He can ride his lightning, though he doesn't do it much. Hades can travel in fire to anywhere he wants in the universe. How close are the brothers now?

"How could you have waited this long for Ichnaea?" Zeus asks with a snort. Looks like we're going to have a conversation of questions and no answers. "She is beautiful. Why have you resisted her charms all this time?"

"I don't want Ichnaea like that. Never have." I miss her friendship and the wry humor she's had to hide since Zeus threw us into this situation.

"Will you ever learn that what you want is insignificant? Only the good of the divine matters."

A laugh bursts from my chest, the tight filter I keep now lost to stress and sleepiness. I sit up and rub my face with both hands as they're still tied. "How many atrocious actions have you performed under that guise? You've lost sight of what's good for *all* the divine."

"I maintain the Olympian way," he growls.

"That's the problem." I prowl from the cot. Golden bars play referee to keep me from strangling him. "We're not meant to live unchanged. What about Earth and our people? Olympians are miserable under your rule, and a third of them haven't even tasted what they're missing." I give a teasing half-grin to his scowl. "If they only knew."

His eyes narrow further. "Tread lightly, grandson. My care for you has limits."

"You care as a gardener cares for his crop. I'm valued as long as I produce what you want and don't infringe on your prized plants. If I don't obey, you will snip me down and grow another in the hole I used to occupy."

"I will do what I must, as will you."

"And what you feel you must do is an opinion you should reconsider, as I have." I turn again and sit on the thin cot. "I do not want this."

"You have no choice in this matter."

I open my eyes and level a glare at him. He needs me for something. Where is the line I can't cross? It's become fuzzy and gray over the years. "There's always a choice."

He smirks. "Not for you. In two weeks, you will marry, commune, and produce an heir worthy of my bloodline."

There's excitement in his eyes that sends a chill down my spine. It's like I'm a rare gem he's quested to find and he only needs to reach a little further. I tilt my head. "Why me? Why do I have the green light to bring children to Olympus, where no one else does?"

He snorts as if I'm the crazy one. "I have been patient. I have watched humans—"

"No," I interrupt. "I've watched humans."

He glares. "I understand their ways and their inventions through the eyes of others. Their progress is out of control. This…technology"—he waves his hand through the air and crinkles his nose—"is dangerous."

"But what does that have to do with me in this damned cage?"

He gives a smile, and while it's not friendly, it doesn't mock as expected. The concern that slides into his gaze is more concerning than this cage plus his thousand wrong ideas of how the world works. What is he so afraid of and how can I get the information out of him? "There is no more time, Alexiares." His exhausted tone betrays the morning light and his fresh himation. "I will not tolerate their destructive nature. They threaten everything I have created." He turns to leave but this conversation is far from being done.

"You created?" I growl. "You command the skies and either fuck or fight everything you meet." I continue as he scoffs. "Demeter helped the humans flourish, Hermes shielded them as they traveled and shared stories, your wife bound them by marriage and protected women. You and your Council don't even acknowledge newer deities whose influence trickles to the humans in the new age."

He scoffs. "My Council is detrimental to—"

"War, wild animals, and terror? You've pushed away those who give calm grace to the realm, and replaced them with those whose traits add edge to your mindset alone. Why was Hermes not at the meeting? Did he tell you to leave the humans be? Who else's opinions do you disregard at your Council meetings? Pythia's? Or is she why you're doing this?" The shock of his gaze makes a gasp escape my throat. "Is that it? What do you know? We can tackle this toge——"

"That is enough, Alexiares." He grips the handle of the door. "The only thing you need to understand is your place."

All is lost if I do not get something out of him. He needs to break.

"The humans won't go backward." I shrug. "They're not like Olympians, patiently waiting at a halt. They've evolved beyond you, old man. It's a beautiful thing to see something we've influenced flourish beyond what we thought they could do, but you don't see it that way, do you? I won't bring a child into this world as long as we're under your rule."

The glare Zeus gives me makes my muscles seize. "You will fall in line."

"Not your line." I should stop goading him, but not thinking through every answer is addictive. Rath must feel this way. It's potent to say what you think, knowing there's a danger to it, but also progress in the response. Where is the line where he'll strike?

He stays still, hand at the ready, but not dragging open the door. His brows furrow, creasing stress lines to his set jaw. He wants to tell me. He knows something, needs something, and he wants me to coax it from him. I tilt my head. And he won't harm me until that happens. I may be the most powerful Olympian right now—a card holding straight shooter who can tell him everything his yes-men are afraid or not allowed to say. I bite my lip to hold tight to my thoughts while they mill. There is a strategy here. Zeus fears the turn of the flock, and I'm not sure he realizes that not everyone agrees with him. There is something else that involves the sirens, but I don't think I'll get to that until he accepts me as a partner in this mayhem.

I clear my throat and steady my voice. "The humans are a monumental part of the realm. Even the more gifted otherworldlings follow their lead, and yet you dismiss them. You should have walked the Earth realm you claim as your own, yet you disconnected us from them. You were wrong and you don't know how to fix it."

Zeus abruptly steps away from the door and takes two steps toward me. "Otherworldlings. Non-deities." He shakes his head. "Abominations."

"No. Creations from other realms. Realms you made me cut from the Earth because you feared their gods."

"I fear nothing," he says with spit. "I was *not* wrong."

"You fear Moros, and I think you fear sirens, though I'm not sure why. You target them, acting as though it's a personal vendetta. Is it? You remember them, as does Moros. Tell me what happened and I can help take them from him." *And hide them from you.*

He turns away from me as if he's going to walk out the door again, but stays perfectly still. The hollowness of silence is hard to bear. He's supposed to be grabbing the bars, sputtering about divine bullshit, but he doesn't. His shoulders slump, fingers dangling loosely at his sides as if all his determination leaked out and he's left a lost child, awaiting direction. "The only way you can help is by following my orders. Do not test me, Alexiares. Too much rides on..." His strained voice holds emotion I've never heard from him. "You will stay here until your mind is clear. When you realize your place, I will allow you to show your son the ways of the realm."

Oh yeah? He may have two thousand years of age on me, but I wasn't born yesterday. "You will kill me at my child's first cry."

"That would pain me greatly."

But it's true. Stepping forward, I come nose-to-nose with the bars and embrace the truth in my voice. "I will never commune with Ichnaea. I'll leave or die before I follow one more order from you without a solid reason."

"That is why you are here, my boy. You will not leave, and if I need to involve the witches to make you ready for your wife, I will."

"You are overtaken by madness."

"I make choices for the betterment of the world." He whips the door open so quickly, I flinch for the marble to shatter or crackle with lighting. "Watch him. Allow the God of Revelry to see him for five minutes and no more. Kill the God of Shadows on sight."

The damn chain around my wrists has to go. The guards fall back into position on either side of the doors. I glare at them too. "You're all insane."

They both frown, but stay stock-still as the stomping grows quieter.

Wrapping my fingers around a bar, I yank. It doesn't bend an inch. I pace again. There's no hope for rational thought from Zeus, and his Council stands stoically behind him as he continues dragging us to a breaking point. Is this what happened when the Titans ruled? Was Zeus the hero of the Olympians during the Titanomachy—the one urging for a better world, or was he seen as the lesser of two evils, possibly even positioning himself as the one to fear over the Titans?

Quick steps pull my attention and Comus breezes through the door, eyes wide and nostrils flared. He practically slams into the bars as Olineus says, "Five minutes."

Comus's breaths come in rapid flutters as he leans close. "Lula ran."

Chapter Eleven

ALEX

GRUNT. THUD. SWAY.

The building will fall.

Pain holds my focus and keeps me on task, though numbness is setting in—tingling my bloodied left hand. It's crushed and still bound to my right, but with every hit, there's a sway. The indented circle of crimson against pristine white is my target, the splattered, cracked ring around it, the double zone. I've made myself a gruesome dartboard.

To save the unbroken bones in my hands, I front kick the cracking wall. *Grunt. Thud. Sway.* Chunks of marble hit the floor with a refreshing clack.

Good. Fuck this building and fuck my grandfather. I hope he's in here when the entire thing comes crashing to the ground, because this godsdamn building will fall. I will drag myself out of here by my teeth, then find Lula. It's the strongest plan I've had in decades. *Grunt. Thud. Sway. Clack.*

"What is the meaning of this?" My grandfather's voice booms from the doorway.

I'm done. To hell with strategy, rule-following, or politeness. The love of my eternity is missing because of me. She's in danger, vulnerable, and unprotected because I have to think things through—

have to analyze every situation for each outcome when I should have done the right thing. But stalking and using her was never the right thing.

I lift my still bound and now bloody hands toward my wide-eyed grandfather. His face contorts between fury and nausea. My crooked fingers twitch. "I'm flicking you off, but you can't tell because my hand is completely fucked."

Back to business. *Grunt. Thud. Sway.*

"Halt!" His bellow rattles a sizable chunk of marble to the floor, making me chuckle.

Next to the crater, I let the wall hold my weight while I catch my racing breath. Comus said Rath was a worried disaster. At least he found Grace seven miles from the house. She won't speak to him or Prax. I'd send Comus to her, but if they're running from us, sending the man she thought was a human—the man she took to bed for the only type of relationship sirens are used to—will confirm how untrustworthy we are to them. Lula won't answer her phone, and Grace doesn't seem to have hers any more. The sirens have shut us out, and I can do nothing except break this wall.

Grunt. Thud. Sway. Clack. Clink.

"Alexiares, answer me." Zeus's words have a delicious edge of desperation.

It adds kerosene to the fire in my blood and the broken bones in my hands. "I'm in here, detained because you're an asshole."

My rationality left with Comus, when they dragged him from me and closed him out, leaving me with a pile of splintered plans. But I've made a new one. Burn everything to the ground and maybe...maybe we'll find something worthwhile in the ashes. I can't stay still for long. The chill on my body isn't only from sweat, and the flames of pure rage may as well be flicking from my hands with the searing pain shooting from them up my arms. If I stop, I'll slip into shock. Zeus steps closer, studying the beast I've become.

I snarl at him over my shoulder. "The only reason you haven't electrocuted me is that you need something. You want to wring semen from my unwilling body so you can force a child upon a realm that would be far better off without you."

There is a tie to fate that he won't say. Pythia has been missing for years, rumors ranging from her traveling with Hera to Zeus locking her away. I'd wager on the latter. I'll disappear, hiding on the Earth forever if she's scried that a child not yet produced will be a weapon. Zeus said I'd produce an heir worthy of his bloodline. His version of worth is how high he can stand over everyone else, even if he has to use a pile of bodies to touch the stars.

"This is my realm," he yells. "The humans would be nothing without me and you need to learn your place—"

I bellow with the pent-up rage of a berserker and spin to face him. The room continues on, making me waver. "*You* need to learn *your* place, you pretentious piece of shit."

The guards shift on either side of the door, side-eyeing each other. Zeus hasn't kicked them out yet. Welcome to the family, boys. Enjoy the behind-the-scenes shit-show of Olympian life in the upper echelon.

Zeus's face reddens as he scowls. "Cease this madness before I am forced to reprimand you."

My laugh is loud and deranged because with everything that's going on, madness is precisely where my mind should be. "Reprimand? Ha!" I wave my swollen, bloodied arms around my gilded cage. "So this is a reward? Making me marry and impregnate someone against my will is an incentive under your rule? To hell with you and your fucked-up sense of management, old man. Now, leave me alone so I can get back to busting my way out of here and finding the only person who matters." I turn and kick the wall again and again and again.

Grunt. Thud. Sway.

Pain radiates through my ankle and shoots up my knee and thigh like an iron spike through my heel. Have I broken something in there as well?

"Who matters?" Zeus asks.

Dammit. The pain is getting to me. Deteriorating what's left of my filter. I flick him off again. Well…raise a fist.

"It's the siren, is it not?"

"It's not." *Lie.*

"Answer me, Alexiares!"

"Humans matter." I attempt to switch legs, but my kicking leg won't bear weight. I can still do damage with it though. "Otherworldlings matter."

Grunt. Thud. Sway.

Clunk. Clatter. Nice.

"The ones who want to unite the universe instead of ruling it matter." I inhale long and line up for another kick. "You do not—"

Thunder rumbles and I'm struck with enough electricity to send *me* clattering to the floor. The burn replaces the aches from my injuries. It sizzles under my skin, but I can't move to scratch it. The air I suck in crackles when my lungs restart. *Fuck. Ow.*

"Sire?" A fuzzy voice speaks from behind a wall of cotton, but two sets of sandals are at eye level on the other side of the bars. "Sire, a situation has arisen." The clarity increases with each word as my senses reset.

I pipe in with a raspy laugh that tastes of ash. "This entire kingdom is a fucking situation."

Inhaling a lengthy breath, I drag my ass off the floor and hobble back to the cracked wall, noting the crunch in my right ankle. Definitely broken.

My grandfather growls. "Explain."

The royal messenger's purple plume bobs in front of his face. How would one fight with that thing looming in their vision? At least he can attempt to hide his fearful expression by wobbling his head.

Back to it.

Grunt. Thud. Sway. Clatter.

Unfortunately, the pain that had gone numb reset as well, and my vision swims with a gut-punch of agony that radiates in all limbs, though my left hand took the force. Maybe a shoulder?

"There appears to be an uprising," the messenger says slow and cautious. "They are demanding to speak to Alexiares."

That stops my next assault on the marble, but I should keep going. A tiny light highlights the massive dip of jagged stone painted with my blood and skin. A break? It can't be much further to the outside.

"Who is demanding to speak to me?" I ask.

The nervous demigod looks to my grandfather, who rolls his hand through the air. The guard stands straighter, clanking his gold pauldron against his breastplate. He swallows hard. "A...sizeable group with a blend of Olympians. Anicetus and Comus appear to be the representatives."

We have assembled. "Send them in."

Zeus shoots me a glare. "*I* will speak to them."

As they stomp away, I call after them. "Tell Comus I could use some aspirin. He'll know what I'm talking about."

At the bars, I listen for any sign of conversation. Zeus opens the entrance doors, and the low roar of a crowd rumbles through the halls.

"Do not continue like this, Alexiares." Olineus is solemn, like a concerned friend. What a joke.

I hold his gaze, though it's tough with the spinning room. "You stand for your ideals, and I'll stand for mine. Now shush. I'm listening." No exact words come through the open doors. No chanting "Free Alex" or something humans would do, but a sea of murmurs.

"Get out of my way." My brother's voice comes through livid, breaking through the garbled discontent. "I will speak to my brother."

"Anicetus, this behavior is uncharacteristic of you," Zeus says. "Do not follow in Alexiares's footsteps."

"I will follow in his, but never yours. Never again."

Careful, brother. He hasn't settled down at all.

Anice barrels through the door and gasps, freezing at the sight of me. Dionysus does the same. Comus skirts in and rushes to the bars. "Who did this to you?"

Blood covers my bound arms and drips crimson onto the white floor, joining splatters throughout the room. Two bones protrude from the back of my left hand, but the real pain lies in my shoulders and elbows, radiating heat into my fast-moving lungs and heart. My hands only tingle with numbness.

"I did." I signal with my chin to the broken wall behind me and smirk. "Bringing down the house."

"Did you blast him?" Anice looks at my grandfather with fire in his gaze, then back to me, eyeing the red patterns of lightning on my arms that haven't healed yet. "You did. This is inexcusable."

Zeus bares his teeth and opens his mouth to respond, but Comus cuts him off. "We request an armistice, a healer, and a meeting with the Council. *All* of the Council."

I raise my eyebrows. *Damn, Comus.* This is happening.

"An armistice?" Zeus's eyes are wide. "This is not a war."

Comus points to me. "You're holding a peace-seeking Olympian prisoner in the barracks. One you threaten with marital enslavement and rape, then torture with lightning. While he diligently worked under your command, you used human telecommunications to record his conversations."

"You understood and provided the invention," Zeus says.

"We understand technology because we interact with the Earth realm, unlike you and the Council. But you took advantage, arrested, then attacked him when he was of no threat to you. Look at what you've done to *one* deity. One you claim to respect above others. Shall I go on?" Comus stands taller and faces Zeus. "You, the self-pronounced king of Olympus, have declared war upon your people. Your own *family*."

Dionysus steps closer and puts a hand on Zeus's shoulder but doesn't even attempt a reprimanding scowl at Comus. I must look like shit. Zeus blinks and his mouth gapes. After everything he's done, did he not expect it to come to this? Comus's hands tremble as he reaches for the bars. We wanted full peace—the first exodus that didn't go down in history as a divine blood bath. If this path doesn't divert, we will spin the world into chaos, and because humans now record everything, if our battle falls to Earth, it will be remembered. That is not how we want our reunion with the Earth realm to go.

My grandfather finds his words. "I will send Apollo to gather healers, then you and I shall meet."

"No." Anice reaches through the bars to cup my cheek. His palm is hot against my skin. "You will send Apollo directly. And Iaso."

"Yes," Comus agrees. "And once Alex is functional, *all* Council members shall meet with *all* of our group's taxiarchs, and only after you give your word for a peaceful armistice."

Zeus frowns. "You truly believe we are at war?"

I huff a wheezy laugh. "Look at me and repeat your question. Go back to your Council room of empty thrones and a broken wartime table and tell us that peace is what you've had in mind. Ask yourself what good has come from your sole decision to break apart our realm and lock down Olympus." I raise an eyebrow. "Do you agree to the armistice?"

For a moment, I think he may use the teeny, rational fragment of his brain, but then thunder rolls outside. With a sneer, Zeus turns on his heel and storms out with Dionysus following, leaving me alone with Comus, Anice, and two silent guards. "Well, that happened." Comus sighs as though he's been holding his breath. His shoulders sink.

"Holy Hera." Anice winces, then points. "Your hands. I think you broke every bone."

"So close." I nod back at the pinpoint of light sifting through the wall, but the motion makes my stomach swirl and I waver on my feet. "Have you found her?" I whisper.

"No," Comus says. "There's no sign of her anywhere, including Olympus."

Anice reaches through to hold me up.

I lean my forehead against the bars. Now that fury isn't fueling my actions, the damage I've done to my body creeps over me. "It's okay. I'll live." The skin is already stretching to cover the gaps. I need the bones set. I try to snap my forefinger into place, but there's not enough strength with the angle of my tied wrists. Oh. My *broken*, tied wrists. My stomach swoops. "Okay. Think I'm going to sleep now."

Comus helps Anice steady me. "Can you call Iaso to make sure they're en route?"

Anice exits, then returns moments later. "On their way."

Though he sways in my vision, the nervous concern in his eyes borders on fear.

"What is it?" I ask. "Why do you look like you've seen a ghost?"

Anice purses his lips. Is he afraid to tell me or confused? "Our mother is on her way to see you." His brows are furrowed as he stares out the door. I've been avoiding my mother. I don't enjoy lying to her, and she will want to know about my journey on Earth. My last few months have been Lula, and that won't work for conversation. He sucks his teeth. "Along with our grandmother."

"What?" Comus blurts. Even both guards turn to peer out the door, then snap to attention. I haven't seen Hera for a solid century. She disappeared right after the break of the realms two thousand years ago and randomly pops in and strolls around as if she's been in Olympus all along. When she's here, the queen is more formidable than her husband, except she doesn't yell or throw lightning tantrums. She simply listens, watches, judges, and corrects the issue with no fuss. That could mean cursing someone's entrails to vacate their body, or shutting them up with a blue-eyed stare. No one stares down my grandmother. Not even Zeus.

I can avoid my mother, but if Hera wants to talk, we will, and I'm not in the state of mind for this. The only one who understands her attributes is her, however, she always seems to know everything. Did she come to stop this revolution, and how?

I'm even more trapped than I was before. I want to stand up and pound the wall again, but my body is done. Jerking my shoulders into action only makes Comus shush me.

"We have to get out," I whisper.

He grimaces. *Too late*. Two fuzzy figures appear in the doorway in shimmering himations. One gasps and rushes forward.

"Alexiares?" My mother reaches for me but draws back as she stares at my hands. She covers her mouth in a look of horror that would make me shift behind Comus if I could move. "Hera, we cannot allow this." I don't like the tear rolling over her cheek and wish I could wipe it away. Hebe is the Goddess of Youth and surrounds herself with children—or she did when they were among us. The young avoid pain, not understanding that sometimes the cost is worthwhile. But she shouldn't have to witness this.

"Mother," I coo. "I'll be okay. It's just…little stuff."

"He harmed you." She kisses Anice's cheek and bumps him out of the way. Her fingers in my hair send specks of ash drifting from the tips. At least it's not gone this time. She scowls and jerks her attention to my grandmother. "He used his bolts on my son."

Hera glows with power and regal intent, reminding the universe that while Zeus conquered the Titans and proclaimed himself the king, deities termed Hera queen long before that. She's the only one who can influence my grandfather, but she doesn't. At least, not anymore. Tightly bound brunette curls complement her equally rigid lips. The most cheer I've been able to pull from her in a while is a raise of her mouth and a grin in her eyes. The blue is a galaxy that holds the pattern of eternity. When she wants to—like now—she punctures into my mind and spills out my closely kept secrets, seeing everything I am, was, and will be. At least, that's how it feels. I drop my gaze. We are so fucked.

She steps forward. "Leave us."

Her voice is as harsh and deep as I remember it, and I smile, nostalgia replacing nerves. "Hello, Grandmother."

Comus squeezes my side, and his hands fall away.

My mother strokes my cheek through the bars as Comus and Anice clear the room, taking along the guards who shut the door without a fuss. The pain in my arms lessens, and energy seems to leech into my body from the surrounding air. I stand straighter and inhale deeply, smelling ambrosia and warmth.

"Greetings, grandson." Hera steps forward, chin lifted. "Does your state pertain to the rumors I was told?"

I try hard to tame my face from any guilt. We've been working for a long time against the Council, and while Hera hasn't been active, she once was and still could be a major influence. "Which ones?"

"That my husband wishes you to marry Ichnaea and imprisoned you because you refuse and are protecting a siren?"

My mother gasps. "Alexiares?"

Well, that's a better interpretation than *I'm trying to unseat the crown because Zeus is a disease upon the Olympians and then I got caught up in a siren heat phase.* I nod and close my eyes. "That about sums it up."

"Does she have control over you?" Grandmother asks, assessing me.

"No. She doesn't."

My mother taps my face, and I open my eyes. "He needs help right now."

Hera nods. "Go seek the healers."

After a gentle kiss on my forehead, Hebe rushes from the room.

Warm energy hits me again when Grandmother steps forward. I hope it's not my body shutting down to cope with the damage. "Why do you reject marriage to Ichnaea?" she asks. "It surprises me that you never took a wife, but it is admirable that you have not littered Olympus with illegitimate children."

That is something I've tried hard to avoid, though the law Zeus put in place helped in my decision. "I don't love Ichnaea. She was my friend before Zeus demanded we marry and breed while no others are allowed. Now, we are not allowed to speak without being expected to procreate on the spot. He wanted me to commune with her in her fertile period a month ago. Set up a dinner and communion night."

Her lips tighten further. "Did he?"

"Yeah—yes." Hera is the queen and Goddess of Marriage, Childbirth, Family, Skies, and Life. Zeus goes against everything she stands for. He's her festering wound in male form, and she's attached to him, whether it be by her vow or actual love. That's another secret she holds tightly.

She takes a step closer and lifts my face with a delicate finger on my chin, forcing me to meet her eyes. "But you *are* in love." There's no question in her voice. "Does the siren hold your heart?"

I'm not sure who banned deities from being with non-deities, though I always assumed it was Zeus out of fear that hybrid children would take over, but it's possible my grandmother could have been the initiator. She has that pull.

"I wish to know, Alexiares. You will tell me." There's a sadness in her gaze along with determination.

I've never been able to lie to her, and the fight bleeds out of me on the shirttails of a raspy exhale. "Yes. I love her like no other in my eternity. She's kind and cares for the realm and its inhabitants. She holds unbelievable power, yet wields it to improve humans."

"Which line is she?" she asks, dropping her hand from my face.

"What do you mean?" I only want to keep Lula safe and I'm not sure where this questioning is going.

"What original siren holds her bloodline? Thelxiope, Aglaope, or Peisinoe?"

"I don't know." Lula never outright said it, but I believe she's from Aglaope.

"You do. Do not lie to me again." Hera crosses her arms. "What's her eye color? Is her hair golden, bronzed, or obsidian?"

"Her eyes are green, and her curls are red."

"There is no such siren." She watches me with a tight squint.

"She's proven herself by voice and demeanor."

Hera shakes her head. "There is no siren with red hair. Green eyes and bronzed locks mark the line of Aglaope, blue and gold brands Thelxiope's daughters, and brown and obsidian belong to the descendants of Peisinoe."

Maybe sirens evolved alongside humans. I shrug. "I only know what I know." Which is that I love her; green eyes, red hair, curves, and warmth. Her cleverness, stubborn sass, and trust—the way she trusted me to comfort her and keep her safe. I wasn't worthy of her.

Hera taps my chin, bringing my attention back to her. "And my husband will not allow you to bring her as a pet?" She narrows her eyes.

I do the same. "That is a wrong practice." The statement comes out with more spit than I should direct at the queen, but the thought of witches making Lula barren and enslaved to Olympus burns hotter than my broken fists. "I would not make an enemy a pet, though some do. No. Zeus put a bounty on her species because Moros has returned to the realm and is using sirens to kill humans."

She nods. "That is indeed a problem." Uncrossing her arms, she pats my cheek. It's a rare sign of affection that equals hugs and making cookies in the human realm.

I lean into her palm. "Will you help me fight this?"

She turns toward the door and the chill rushes over me again. "I have work to do, Grandson."

Chapter Twelve

LULA

An hour into my third flight—a small jet headed out of North Carolina—the Fasten Seat belt sign brightens the dim cabin and we drop right. Gasps and squeals sound through the cabin, and I suck my lips to keep my sounds to myself. I don't want to be in a plane crash. If I were a demon, I'd bounce from the flaming wreckage and go brag over beer, but I'm not. I heal a smidgen faster than humans, and I'm immortal, but not if I get smashed into a mountain. Minutes into what feels like a U-turn, the airplane tilts back into place, balancing on the orange sliver of horizon peeking over bumpy clouds. Every minute ticking by creates another knot of confusion in my mind until my leg bounces so much, I think I'm shifting the entire aircraft. As I go to stand, the whir of the engine lowers and we sink nose first, leaving my stomach squished against my lungs. If I move a step I may throw up, so I sit and put on my seat belt. When we drop out of the clouds, the evening sky is a fading violet. The region is hilly, with a bubbly sea silhouette of shadowy green trees.

I gulp down nausea and shakily stand, making my way to the front. The flight attendant sits behind a curtain beside the cockpit. She stares at the phone in her lap, long, red nails on thin, dark fingers clutched tight around the device.

"What's wrong with the plane?" I ask, taking the jump seat next to her and clicking the seatbelt.

"We're making an emergency landing," she says in a drawl she didn't have when we departed. She had told jokes and added a colorful array of adjectives to the safety speech. "Keep your seat belts fastened. Thanks." She's enthralled.

"Did they give you a name or message for Lula?" I ask.

"No," she keeps her eyes on her dark screen.

"Turn on your phone."

She does and I take it from her. She deleted her call log. Who'd reroute the plane? Amah? That has to be it. She needs me in another place. What changed? Nerves bounce around my stomach. Did someone find her or is she spooked that I'm being followed?

I bite my lip. What if the guys told Grace what happened and convinced her to help them? I'd love for all of this to be a misunderstanding, but I'm not sure I could view what Alex did as anything other than wrong. Plus, controlling an aircraft is dangerous. Amah and Grace would fabricate a valid story, but the pilot and attendant could lose their jobs if there's no actual danger. I wish I was near a window so I could see how close we are to landing, or get an idea of where we are arriving, but we drop in sharp swoops and I'm not moving.

The landing is fast and the worst I've experienced; a tumble to the Earth, then wheel-skipping lurches and a sideways skid where I crush my eyes shut and wait for the roll. It doesn't come and we bobble to a stop. Humans mumble and shift, peeking out the windows and looking up front. Releasing my death grip on the chair, I stretch my fingers and fumble with unlocking the seat belt. I rush to the door. Out the window is a dimly lit field and row of trees. No lights, no airport, buildings, or cars. A touch on my arm makes me jolt. "Everyone sit in your seat," I say at full volume. The man leaning toward me retreats, and passengers bumble through the aisle, knocking into each other and shuffling until seated again. I grab my bag from under the seat in the back row and stride up front while the final mechanical whir of the engines taper off. "Stand," I command the flight attendant. Only when she's up does she look at me, dark eyes half-lidded. "Open the door."

She gets to work moving levers while I search for a weapon which is nonexistent on an airplane. Drawers have pamphlets and packs of chips. There are some light medical supplies, but nothing sharp. I pull out a packet and toss it in my bag. If Alex is here and making my sister command airplanes, he will get a face full of vomit sawdust. The cockpit is locked. The outer door hisses and pops inward before the flight attendant gives it a shove, and it swings out, crashing against the side of the plane. "Stairs?" I whisper, poking my head out into the dim night. Headlights beam, bobbing over the field as a car comes closer. I should run and dive into the patch of trees, but it's a decent drop, and it's already too late—they would see me.

"At the airport," she says. *Fabulous.*

"Can you speak to the pilot?" I ask.

"Yes."

"Please tell her to come out here."

She wanders to an intercom and pushes a button, but there's no click. She jams her finger on it over and over. My sister thought of everything to cut off communication. I grind my chattering teeth. I'm used to Belize weather. This is late fall somewhere on the east coast and the chilly air seeps through my shirt. Is this where Amah is? It reminds me of the woods near my house.

A black, pricy sedan with darkened windows pulls up. An unfamiliar man steps out of the driver's side and into the light spilling from the plane. His brown hair is shaved close, and he has a beaky nose with the most structured nostrils I've ever seen. He takes a creepy trolling gaze over me. Besides the car, there's nothing but bushes and a marred field where we landed. The back door opens and I hold my breath, waiting for one of my sisters to appear. Another man steps out and smiles up to his eyes.

I tilt my head and duck to see if there's anyone else inside the vehicle, but it's empty. "Do you have a question for me?" Amah said she would send someone.

The smiling man's grin fades away, but he doesn't answer, and moves closer. He's tall and on the thinner side, with hair that lays in long red waves over his shoulders. "I have many."

My world does a spin. There's a fuzzy wiggle of a memory just out of reach. "Tell me who you are."

"We'll get to that. Hello, Lula."

Every muscle tightens to run. A deity. Without taking my eyes off them, I backtrack my steps. I'll close them out and command the pilot. Leave this place and—

"Wait," he says. "Give me a moment."

I pivot to him. "Who are you?"

"Come here." His tone is coaxing. "I'll help you down."

He's a deity. Which one doesn't matter because all of them are bad for sirens.

"Not a chance." I dive to close the door, but it's flat against the side of the plane, the handle inches from the tips of my fingers. Even Alex wouldn't be able to get into a closed metal tube. Rath would, but he's not here. I stretch, gripping the opening's edge, but only graze the raised metal. I stop struggling to reach, and glance at the man regarding me with tilted-head curiosity. "Who are you?" Grace isn't involved, so there's only one of two possibilities remaining.

"Lula, we're due for a long conversation." He beckons me. "But not here. Come now, there isn't much time."

"Why?"

"There was an emergency landing and police will arrive soon. We need to leave unless you care to make more of a scene?" He signals to the aircraft.

"I didn't make a scene. One of my sisters did." I glance at the humans, innocent faces staring back, waiting for a command. The flight attendant still rhythmically pushes the lifeless button. Sweat dots her skin even with the chill, and a trickle of blood drips from her nose. Guilt gives me a solid gut punch. I've been yelling and it's affecting the mortals. I lower my voice. "Who rerouted the plane?"

The red-haired deity puts his hands in his pockets and nods at the other who pulls his phone out and starts dialing. He passes it over.

"I did." The leader holds up the glowing screen. "So I could find you. Would you like to talk to your sister?" His words are gentle, as if he knows how much they mean to me and he's trying to calm me. That can't be though, and chills rise on my skin. Maybe Alex wasn't the only one watching from a distance. The stranger deity waggles the phone in an offering I so badly want to be real. He has to be lying or…

"Which sister?" I ask.

If Amah has a damned house of deities she didn't tell me about, the talk we will have is going to go far differently than I expected. Although, nothing has gone according to plan since Alex.

He tucks both lips between his teeth for a moment, reminding me of Alex's pauses, but he brings the phone to his ear. "You may speak to her." He pushes a button.

"Lula?" Hazel's sweet voice rings out. "Lula, are you there?"

My knees give, and covering my mouth, I let myself sink to the metal floor. "Hazel. Are you okay?"

"I am," she calls out, and I envision her smiling face in my mind. She doesn't sound hurt. She sounds like she does when we have a movie night and too much wine. Cheery with loose-lipped excitement.

"Tell her what she needs to do, Hazel." The deity's smile returns.

"Lula, do you hear me?"

I nod my head. "Yes."

"Aw, hey, don't be sad. I covered our bases with the pilot and the tower at the nearest airport. Hop in the car so I can see you."

"It may be a few days." The deity's dark eyes stay glued on me.

Why? I want my sister.

"Oh," Hazel says, sounding as downtrodden as I feel. "Well, soon then. Just come on. I miss you and want to catch up."

She sounds normal. Like she wasn't stolen by a monster months ago. Like she hasn't been missing, didn't call or write, and she hasn't been mourning Gerty's death.

"Is Ven okay?" I ask.

"Yes." He turns his head to the side, and a police siren whoops in the distance. "Thank you, Hazel. Tell Deimos to take you out to celebrate tonight." Deimos. Alex told me about him. He's the god who threatened Comus's sister and brutalized a goddess so badly, she threw herself off a mountain. Was that the truth? But he's taking Hazel on *a date*.

"Really?" she says, happiness returned. "Okay, I—"

He presses a button and passes the phone back before leaping forward to extend a hand to me. "You must come with me now. I will explain everything."

"I see lights." The other deity opens the driver-side door.

"Hazel is safe and happy," the deity below me says. "As you will be. Now come." The last command is harsh and he jerks his hand in the air.

I stand and turn to the humans. "Forget me." Snatching my bag, I sit on the edge of the floor. He catches me by the waist when I drop and steadies my feet on the ground. The need to run is strong, but... Hazel and Venora.

I let him tug me to the car and guide me into a leather interior. The driver's eyes study mine in the rearview mirror, and he only pulls them away when he pushes the gas and makes a U-turn, bumping over the field so much, I snap my seat belt into place and grip the handle over the window.

The car smells of ash and a familiar but unique spice in a dish I had long ago but can't pinpoint. I don't want to ask him who he is, because I have an idea. The car crashes through a small section of bushes and pops out on an empty road, tires screeching and tail end swaying. The driver chuckles, the sound shriller than it should be. "I enjoy vehicles."

The deity beside me doesn't respond, but his gaze prickles my neck. I keep my eyes out the window, focused on nothing. "You're Moros, aren't you?"

"Yes." A simple word, spoken with no shame or excitement.

The tight knot in my throat refuses to leave when I swallow. I've walked into the God of Doom's trap. "What do you want with me?" He knew my name and said he was the one who routed the plane to me.

We turn onto a street with lights and other cars, and I can see him more clearly. His eyes are shiny black pools with iris and pupil barely a shade apart. "I've been looking for you for a long while...daughter." He squints, pulling his bottom lip between his teeth. Is that the equivalent to how Alex calls Comus and Rath his brothers? Does this stranger think I'm some close ally because that can't...

"That's not possible." I'm a siren. A normal, enthralling, death-dealing siren.

His head tilts again and his studious gaze wanders my face. "You were so young when you were taken from me. Only three. My perfect little songbird with your mother's eyes and my hair." His smile captures another flittery memory. "I knew you'd be lovely."

"Stop the car," I say. "Stop!"

The driver glances at me in the rearview. "No."

I fumble for the handle, but Moros snags my hand and neck, making me face him. "You are my child." His warm fingers are gentler than expected with his aggressive move, but I still lean away from him. He follows.

"You killed my sister," I whisper.

"Did I?" He raises his eyebrows at me. "Do not presume facts by the words of others. What else do you think you know of me?"

"You're the God of Doom. An unkillable divine spirit."

"You've learned much in my absence." With one stroke of his thumb across my cheek, he releases me and leans back into the leather. "So Deimos was correct. The Demigod of Warding off Wars and the God of Revelry got to you before I did." He snarls their titles like a curse, then closes his eyes and breathes out long. "I'm sorry I could not get to you sooner. The world has changed since I've returned, and adapting has been difficult until a couple of my followers escaped Olympus."

I can't deny the similarity, but that's not how our species works. "I'm a siren. Things would be different if I were…" A hybrid? Alex told me how Zeus hunted the powerful deities and banned procreation until the humans' evolution was under control. I didn't think it would be possible to be even more despised by Zeus, but being a hybrid would do it. I wave a hand toward him. "Like Olympians."

"You are not an Olympian." He shifts back and looks out the window as we turn again, this time into a neighborhood of stately houses among tall trees.

His expression is not monstrous as he turns to watch me watching him. He appears thirty in human years, despite his actual age being beyond exact recording. Older than Zeus. Comus told me he's a child of Nyx, a primordial deity, but he was born in a cusp or he's a hybrid so he's not Primordial, Titan, or Olympian, and therefore unkillable by the hand of another divine being—though not for lack of trying.

I don't want to believe that the God of Doom could be my father, but his straight, sharp nose is the male version of my own, and his almond-shaped eyes would be mine if you plucked out his near-black irises and replaced them with light green. They smile as much as his lips.

"You see it, don't you?" he asks.

In the deep recesses of my memories, there's a vague flash of him staring at me, and his silvery voice ringing. I can't grasp it, but it's there. My stomach churns, and I swallow back bile. Moros appears happy to sit, unconcerned that this situation is causing a slew of emotions to run rampant through me. How could this be? My mother is someone no one discusses with me and that rule applies to the deity claiming to be my father as well. Was he there? If he knew my mother... "What happened to Petra?"

His smile slides away into something unreadable. Sadness maybe, or disappointment. Or perhaps he has no idea that Petra was my mother's name.

Anger simmers up my neck with his silence. "Then you didn't know her either." I turn to the window. The houses are scarcer, the trees more abundant. We pull onto a boxwood-edged, paved path next to a red mailbox.

"Your mother was stunning. You have her mouth and chin. Her ears and delicate hands." He fidgets with his fingers. There's a gruesome scar on his right palm. "She was happy, with a laugh far bolder than her voice. There was a time when I'd return home and she'd be waiting for me in her favorite dress." He raises his eyebrows at me. "The blue silk gown with the fifteen tiny pearl buttons. Undoing each one was a treasure." His eyes go half lidded as acid roils in my belly.

He's correct about it being my mother's favorite dress. Amah passed it to me when I moved out at twenty-six, and it has hung in each of my closets since. I bring it out to try on every once in a while, though it's short and baggy on me. "You were in my closet," I whisper. "That means nothing."

"That dress meant much to your mother. Her sister sent it to her. I told you I was looking for you and yes, I saw it in your closet. Where have you been?"

I'm not ready to share with this stranger. We pull up to a stately, white home with columns on either side of the double-door entrance. Red, curved shingles cover the roof, matching the color of the brick walkway and four stairs leading to the porch. The driver steps out and waits in the cold.

"Do you remember us at all?" Moros asks, a quiet hum in the silent vehicle. "Your mother and I?"

There are foggy-paned glimpses of playing in my mother's dark brown hair and singing as she poured water over my head while I sat in a basin and slapped foamy suds. I was held often, then cried for her, but she wasn't there. Amah was.

Brown curls became tight black ones. The scent of honeysuckle shifted to rose. I gained a sister the same age to run around with, skipping rocks in the lake and making willow wreath crowns as we danced and sang until Amah joined us. I miss Lena and I miss the mother stolen from me before I even knew her. There have been times I've wondered if she was real at all. Along with her, two of my sisters have died since I've been alive, and their passing took a piece of my soul with them. There's no way to process the bound link breaking. It's unmanageable agony—a tear inside, a rip, and the heart caving in. It sticks forever, creating an ever-present when-will-it-happen-again anxiety, but maybe I was young enough to block the experience.

Moros leans closer and pops open the seat belt. "It's okay if you don't. You were only three when you were taken from me." With the care he'd give handling explosives, he takes my fingers in his. "They didn't speak of me, did they? Hazel wasn't aware of your lineage."

I lift my head, dislodging the tears that made my vision blurred. "What about Gerty and Venora?"

He gives a nod. "They knew me."

The sick thought that my older sisters always had this information nudges into my brain like an unwanted stranger in my personal space. My father should be human and long gone from this Earth, but he's not. He's sitting beside me, already filling in a mysterious past I've longed to understand. I settle tingling fingers over my tight throat as I beg my lungs to inflate. Why would they keep this from me? Is Moros what Amah needed to talk to me about and what she's warned me of throughout my lifetime, or it was Hera in her mind? Did I misjudge Alex, Rath, and Comus, placing them as the good guys chasing down the dangerous God of Doom to save the world? If I've learned anything from deities, it's not to trust any of them. Sirens wouldn't have killed humans if Moros weren't a monster threatening what they care about most—our other sisters. But Hazel sounded happy. I will figure this out, and being where I am, I'm one step closer to getting Hazel and Venora back. The bushes in the extensive gardens circling the house are gold and red. I bet the dead flowers are beautiful in the spring and summer. "Is Venora here?"

"No." He knocks on the window with a knuckle and the driver opens his door. Moros exits as a king, each movement skilled as if someone has waited on him each day for a century. "Understanding your path in my absence is of great interest to me, and I'd like a few days without interruption to do so." He offers a hand to me. A few days until I get my sisters back. I can do that. I slide over the seat to follow his lead. The chilled air wraps me up, though I was already trembling. Moros doesn't notice and signals to the other deity. "Lula, this is Firthus, Demigod of Standing Water."

Standing water? He's the god of swamps and sludge? If he has something to do with mosquitos, we're not going to get along.

"You're stunned." Firthus licks his lips. "Like what you see?"

"Go inside," Moros says in a way that makes me glad for his presence, which in turn, instills nervousness. "Be sure a room is prepared for my daughter, then keep the house clear for the evening. Inform Deimos."

Firthus sinks into himself like a shamed puppy and backs away. "Yes, sire."

Moros offers an elbow to me, which after a hesitation he waits out with remarkable patience, I take. He leads me up the path. "Firthus escaped Olympus with Deimos when he learned I had returned to the Earth realm. He's used to Olympian ways. Zeus and his minions prevented another from joining me, but others will follow."

"I'm not calling you sire," I say, unsure why when there are a thousand other pressing things to discuss. I am curious though.

His rumbly laugh loosens something in my chest and makes my eyes tingle. "No, I wouldn't ask that of you." We pause at the top step and he turns to me. "Nor do I expect your loyalty yet. I am sorry I could not get to you sooner. We have so much to speak about."

My world feels sideways, churning with unknowns, and Moros holds a manual of information. I hold still in the shadows of an unfamiliar house where he may save or kill me because I have no understanding of the divine.

Chapter Thirteen

LULA

THE HOME SMELLS OF ROT AND STALE AIR. IT'S NOT STRONG BUT makes my nose crinkle. The living room to the right has couches with a pattern more suited to a floral blouse. A dining area with well-designed furniture is directly to the left. A vase of dead roses sits on a half-moon table butted up against the side of a curving staircase, and there are no pictures on the walls but nails poking from bare, sunshine paint. A heavy weight settles in my stomach. On the circular rug next to my foot is a red stain the size of a dinner plate. Wine, I hope. I sidestep to the light oak floor.

"Were Alexiares and his associates keeping you?" he asks. I purse my lips and his dark eyes narrow. "Did they hurt you badly?"

Only my heart. The emotional puncture wound expands with every minute I'm away from the guys and fills up with dread from Moros's words. Alex couldn't hide evil, right? It would have snuck out in stressful moments where we didn't have control. I clutch my shirt. Unless he always had control and I wasn't aware. I've been caught up —whipped around in a tornado I couldn't predict or react to. What if Alex was the wind all along?

Moros touches my chin and I jerk back. "Oh, daughter. They did harm, didn't they? How much?"

"No." *Shit.* I shouldn't tell him anything about the guys but it's too late. No take backs. "You said Deimos told you they got to me. What did he say?"

"Only that Zeus tasked the group with studying humans and otherworldlings and they'd found you and two other sisters."

"Who?" Oh god, if Alex… No. My sisters wouldn't have kept that secret.

"I don't know."

"It's important," I say, hoping that he's withholding information like Amah does.

Moros's shoulders jerk in a small shrug. "They'd listened in on conversations but there were no names."

"Of course, they did," I mumble. Amah was right to cut off my phone.

"The Council is like that. They pry as often as possible in whatever way suits them."

I tilt my head. "Is Alexiares part of the Council?"

"No, though he may as well be." His thin lips dip at the corners. So the Council was prying into the calls the of the guys. My face heats.

"They found me with your sister when I was seeking you." He bows slightly. "This is not a conversation you wish to explore yet, Lula. Come. You have traveled far." He signals to the stairs and moves forward.

"No, I do want to explore it." I stumble after him. "Why wouldn't I?"

"Because you care for him." His words carry a bite and his jaw clenches before he pauses halfway up the steps. "A bad decision on your part, dear, but I will try to understand."

I ball my fists and follow. "Tell me what happened when they found you with my sister. Was it Gerty?" An eerie stiffness slows the air. There's no life in here. "Maybe I'd improve my choices if everyone would stop hiding things from me."

He stops on the upper landing, skin and hair clashing against lavender walls. "I understand what manipulation can do to a being and I need you to listen to my words. For now, I will tell you that filth and his kin locked me in the hell realm." He speaks it as if I should be outraged. "They broke my arms and left me for dead."

"You're immortal," I say. "The unkillable kind. Did you deserve to be in the hell realm?"

"Does anyone? You were a mere babe when they came. They shattered my bones." He encircles his right wrist with his fingers and squeezes. "They tore me from my family and threw me into a realm with beings that only know death. I lost limbs, barely surviving until I dragged myself from there to find you and you ask me if *I'm* the one who deserved that fate?"

He didn't answer the question.

"You have my sisters," I say. "Gerty died with you and—"

"You honestly haven't guessed yet? Your sister's death was a loss to me. You think I would have done such a thing?"

I put a finger in the air and cover my lips with my other hand to keep from speaking or screaming. He can't hint to me that the guys killed Gerty. That's not possible. I can't have slept with someone… went through a heat with someone who ripped my sister from me, then held me as I broke apart from the loss. No. I want to know more though. I shouldn't, but I drop my hands and try to coax the question up my throat.

"Daughter, I am not the enemy. You will learn that in time. Let's get you to your room for some rest. We will meet for dinner, and you will tell me everything I've missed in your upbringing."

I follow him in a chilled fog. The walls surrounding me seem made from an insulating cotton that's barbed and poisonous. Even the air bites at my skin, licking it with sick intention. Each step forward weighs on my bones, but I can't run, and it's far too late to hide. He indicates the room he wants me to stay in with a welcoming palm.

The cream carpet is plush, the purple, damask wallpaper perfectly placed. Between two windows is a frilly bed. The bathroom door is open, showing rainbow-hair mermaids swimming on the shower curtain. This is not Moros's house. It's human, and he stole it. I have a thousand questions, but my vocal cords are as frozen as my tight fists pressing over my heart.

The door clicks closed. A jingle then another click signals a lock. He's wrong.

Everyone is an enemy.

THE LIGHT PEEKING THROUGH THE WINDOW DIMS. MOONLIGHT GLINTS off more nails in the walls. Whoever lived here once didn't move out, but I bet the monsters didn't want the previous owners or their personalities staring at them as they took what wasn't theirs. When someone puts a picture on the wall, it's them displaying themselves, or what they wish they were.

Were my sisters here too? Did they stay in this room with the flower night-light and wonder who lived here before? They probably made the family leave. I hope that's the case. I grab the white, child-sized rocking chair and throw it. It crashes into the corner and drops onto a dead houseplant, spilling dirt over the carpet. The sensation of pinpricks stabs my feet from the movement. I didn't know they had gone numb. I snatch a porcelain unicorn bust painted with flowers from the nightstand and smash it into the door. How much did a little girl love that statue? Did she pick it out with her mom or was it a present from her doting father?

A quick click and Moros busts in with Firthus, who only wears a pair of boxers.

"What happened?" Moros demands.

Firthus hisses as he steps on the shards of a little girl's dreams.

"Where did the family that lived here go?" I yell at both of them.

Moros's stone face slinks into comprehension. "They left."

"Did they?" I laugh, but it's not me. It's a shrill call of someone pushed too far. "Did they leave or are they serving you or are they dead? Did they leave their home as themselves or as shells of what a human should be. You took their lives, but did you leave them alive?"

"Did you rest?" Moros steps forward and offers a hand but I slap it away.

"How would I relax in a child's room with missing pictures? Are my sisters here?"

"No." His hands stay lax at his side, head tilted as if I'm confusing him.

"What else did Deimos say about Alex?"

He exchanges a narrow-eyed glance at Firthus. "Alex? You call him Alex?" He clucks his tongue. "Oh, daughter, I am so happy you are in the right place now."

"This," I yell, swinging my arms around to encompass the room, "is not the right place. Whatever happened here when you decided to make this place yours, was not right."

"Deimos witnessed every wrong your dear Alex and his men made. He was after you, and unfortunately found you first. I hope he did not spoil you too much."

I don't believe Moros understands the spoiling Alex did for me, or what I thought he did for me. He helped around the house as if cleaning dishes and doing laundry was a normal divine task. Fruit and vegetables from all over the world would grace my kitchen counter most mornings. He held me close whenever we were together. He did spoil me and because he lied, he has *spoiled* me as well.

"Tell me, have you had your first heat phase yet?" Moros asks as if he were enquiring if I needed a glass of water or dinner.

My face pinches and I step away from him. "That is none of your business."

"Oh, Lula, it is. Considering the nature of sirens, I assume you have previously communed."

Nature of the—really? "Again, I'm not telling you that."

"Lula, dear. It's important. We do not want such an event sneaking up on us. I must plan who the father of my grandchild will be. The correct union could have splendid results."

My eyes widen and I glance at the door. "You need to stop."

Firthus sidesteps the slightest bit to trail his gaze over me. "Maybe she doesn't understand the terminology, sire. They call it fucking here on Earth. Have you fucked before, Lula?"

I crinkle my nose at him. If a different deity showed up before Alex, would they have captured my heart so completely? I don't think so now. If Firthus had approached me, my body wouldn't have relaxed like it did with Alex. It wouldn't have swooned closer and begged for his touch. Every area Firthus's eyes explore tingles with the need to run. I don't want to speak to him or be in the same realm for that matter. "I'm not speaking about this with you, and no one is planning anything for my body."

Moros's focus pierces through me but not dangerously. He's

accessing. It's too similar to Rath. It's as if they can x-ray emotions and perception instead of bones.

He looks over his shoulder at Firthus. "Leave us. Prepare dinner and then this will need to be cleaned up." He signals to the unicorn fragments.

Firthus backs out the door, keeping his eyes on me. I glare back until Moros steps closer.

"Please forgive me, Lula," he says. "I forget you were not raised as a goddess. Yet it is still important. Have you had a heat?"

Sirens don't have their first heats until around three hundred. If he were so in love with my mother, he'd have known that. She would have told him unless Amah convinced her not to or maybe she didn't share like I do.

I straighten my shoulders. "My mother didn't tell you much about sirens."

"What do you mean?" His face blinks into a sharp stone that drags the breath from my iced-over lungs, but when I take another step back, he tames it into an almost smile. Too late. I saw the monster inside. Not once did Alex look at me with simmering rage.

"Shouldn't you know some basic siren physiology since"—I wave a hand at myself—"I'm around."

"Lula," Moros sighs. "Your mother was an incredible creature, but—"

"Person," I correct. "Being or siren. Darklings are creatures. She wasn't a creature and neither am I."

"Of course you're not a creature." He stands straighter, latching his hands behind his back. "You're my daughter, a hybrid goddess. You, darling, are perfection."

"There is nothing perfect about me." My voice kills. My bravery hides inside my small home with me.

"What did your Alex"—he sneers Alex's name like a curse—"tell you of Olympians?" I hesitate, and he lifts his chin. "How can I show you I'm on your side if you are unwilling to share your mind?"

"How can you expect me to share anything with you when you have my sisters captive?"

"Guests. They're guests. You spoke to your sister and heard the truth, did you not?"

"Do not lie to me. Gerty died, and you're avoiding telling me of Venora. You forced them to kill humans. Do you know how difficult that is on a siren?"

"We needed to gain attention to find you, Lula. I thought you were with Zeus and…" The tight lines on his face ease. "Why they wouldn't take an extraordinary crea—being such as yourself back to Olympus only speaks of their ineptitude, though I'm glad they did not harm you as much as they could have." He takes another step forward, extending a hand, and I bump into the wall. "Zeus has been a fool for a long while. I would have trained you, raised you correctly, but instead Olympians forced my hand. Your sisters and I had to make a statement."

My jaw aches with how tightly my teeth press together. "My sisters would never agree to harm humans. Never. They could have called me on the phone." Moros's lips pout and I point at him. "What lie are you considering telling me next? That Gerty wanted to lay down her life for you? That Venora and Hazel didn't have chargers for their phones so they couldn't call, and instead had to murder to say hi to me? Bullshit."

"You do not know the circumstances."

"No circumstances justify any of this." I rub my forehead. Why me? For all of it. "I'm a siren, not a goddess. The male does nothing more than provide a catalyst for near asexual reproduction. Siren DNA overrides the males, so if you think of me as some weird science experiment, you picked the wrong species."

He's next to me before I can blink, reaching to tug on my curls. I cringe, but he ignores my reaction. "Such words, my daughter. This hair speaks differently. You are unlike any other—the only of your species. A siren, yes, but one that has yet to acknowledge her divine attributes. Once you do, you will become a goddess."

"That doesn't make any sense." I dig myself further into the wall.

"No?" He drops my hair and heads toward the door. "Your sisters tell me you're far more powerful than they are and that you have not adapted to being a siren as the others have." He grins. "And by your expression, they were correct. You are not a siren. That's why it's been difficult for you, Lula. When you acknowledge your attributes, your body and mind will unite, and everything will be as it should. Trust me."

I don't trust him, but I can't argue with the logic that I've never felt comfortable with myself. My sisters understood that? Besides my eyes, I don't look like the other daughters of Aglaope. I'm the only red-headed siren. Grace's line is blonde. Amah's is dark with ebony hair and deep chestnut eyes. I don't belong and yes, I'm more powerful. It's made things difficult. The others can form a relationship for a while. Date even. I can direct actions and words, then break a mind, then kill.

"The death of my sister and thousands of humans was not worth finding me."

"Oh, no? When your divine essence ignites, you will be the most formidable being in the realm. You can do..." His chest rises with a deep inhale. "Anything. Olympus will topple and the world will bow. You will be glorious, child."

"I'm not a child and nothing is worth the lives of others. You took Gerty from us. Give me back my sisters."

"When you have heard my side, when I can trust that you will make the right decisions, Hazel will visit."

I latch my shaking fingers together. "Then tell me your side. Tell me that everything I've heard from other deities is incorrect." Please add to the confusion in my mind, the spun lies tightly wrapped around my insides that prevent my breath and cut into my heart.

"You were in great danger with the company you kept. I do hope you maintained your mind around Alexiares." Moros purses his lips. "I will not let more harm come to you."

Alex made love like he had waited for me each day of his millennia-old life. Rath hugged me when I was upset and talked to me for hours as if we were old friends. Comus kissed my cheek like I was a long-lost sister and tried to gather as much siren lore as he could because I wanted to know more. But they lied. Comus didn't want Alex to tell me, but he did anyway and Rath didn't correct him. A hot tear sears my cheek and I brush it away as fast as possible.

My heart is black and blue with the battering these last few days have given it. Moros steps out of the room. "Tomorrow, we will speak and come to an understanding so that we may trust each other. This is difficult for you to take in, but you will. When you are a goddess and understand your attributes, Olympus will topple." He grips the doorknob. "Olympians should pay for the harm they have caused, then the world will be right again."

The second the door closes and the click of the lock sounds, I drop to my knees and cover my mouth to keep the sobs silent.

Nothing will be right again.

Chapter Fourteen

ALEX

My hands rest, bound and lax over my head until I clench my fists, sending twinges through recently knit bones. It's been five days since I kissed Lula's lips and listened to her tell me she loves me, spearing my heart with the truth illuminating her eyes. Then I wrecked everything. We made love that morning, and if I concentrate, she's under me—soft curves, smelling of rain and raspberries, making me calm and crazy with her sounds. What I'd do for another morning…another minute wrapped around her.

Eight days ago, we caught the sunset together, orange ball blazing as warm as the mere graze of skin. We stood holding hands in a quiet peace that spoke volumes about what we'd found.

Twenty, we drowned in lust under the spell of siren heat and changed everything.

Thirty, I fell completely for her. There was no other choice as she threw a can of olives at me, dragged the deepest laughter from me during a flour fight, and kissed my nose because she refused to kiss my lips, knowing the impossibility of staying apart once we crossed that line again.

A hundred days ago I watched her from shadows at two in the morning while she danced in a downpour. She smiled, heat tilted back as she spun. She reminded me of Rath when he felt rain for the first time and the simple human experience he'd never been privy to overwhelmed him to delighted tears. It took a monumental effort to keep myself from blowing cover. I wanted her to see me, to scoop her into my arms and share the tiny joys she clings to. She made me forget that my primary goal was to observe the power she holds in incredible control.

Now I observe four marble walls, golden bars, and two guards that grow quieter and more sullen each day as they stand as statues, waiting for their owner to release them from their own version of prison. They're not statues though, just demigods like myself, but their grandfather isn't the king of Olympus. He doesn't need them beyond taking orders with no fuss, so that is their role. They each move aside, and Comus strides in with a purpose. The chain binding my wrists clinks as I snap to my feet. It received an upgrade: additional length that's bolted to the floor. It stops me from assaulting the bars and walls, so now I only fight with insults and truth. Comus halts, face caught in a wince of pity. To ease the prospect of war, Zeus allows him to visit twice daily to speak to me, though this time we don't need words. Lula is still missing. He stretches to palm my arm through the cage, and I lean into the touch, gleaning strength from my friend. "I have news," he says in a whisper.

That gets my attention, even if it's not about Lula. We need news on our group, Moros, or progress of any kind. Let it be good progress.

Comus glances over his shoulder at the guards. He crosses to grip the door and slowly close it. Olineus retreats, but Trantus sticks firm to his spot.

"War meeting." Comus shoos him with a fluttering hand. "You know how it is, private counsel and all. Now, move your ass."

With a rise and fall of armored chest plate, the guard abandons his post and the stone swishes closed.

"We have an unexpected ally," he whispers, brows arching into a you-will-not-believe-this expression.

"Who?" Maybe Hera has declared her stand, though I'm not counting on it. She's stood by Zeus through every horrid thing her husband has ever done. She's joined in, but not since the break.

"Hades."

My eyes go wide. That's not necessarily good. "You've got to be shitting me."

"He found me," Comus whispers, gripping the bars. "A couple days ago, I asked the keeper of knowledge about the sirens and the muses, but she ignored me. Then today, he pops up in a sconce to have a chat regarding my questions. Scared the hell out of me." He shrugs one shoulder and grins. "Ha."

Hades is eccentric and far too mysterious for my liking. He's not a fan of his brother Zeus or the Olympian hierarchy—a benefit to us. But he's loyal to no one. If he decides on a whim that trapping us in the underworld or spilling a secret of ours would give him an advantage, he'll do it in a second. "I'm not sure he's a right fit—"

Comas waves me off. "You don't understand. It's Hades. He's in. He acted like he's been in from day one."

My fingers snag in my tangled, singed hair. We're all bedraggled, but I can't imagine what my appearance holds. Nothing Lula would recognize. "Why?"

"Maybe Zeus's ways are affecting the underworld or there's something he wants. He demanded updates and got agitated when I told him we'd meet to discuss when you're free. I'm still surprised."

I stretch my hands as far as the chain allows. My fingertips brush the metal but no more. "We don't like surprises."

"No, we don't." Comus's phone buzzes from his pocket, and when he checks it, he answers with speed. "Please tell me something good." His brows furrow and I jerk against my bindings again.

"Lu?" I whisper.

"Get here." His eyes cut to the wall as he listens, free fist balling. "We need to discuss this now. The guards are outside." Comus hangs up and grabs the lone chair in the corner, wedging the top of the backrest under the doorknob. I smack a bar with my palm. "Not Lu," Comus says. "Grace told Rath to leave Lula alone. The sirens cut all phone lines and are in hiding. He found Deimos, then somehow lost him."

"Shit." Rath doesn't lose people unless the God of Terror attacked him.

"Yep. However, Rath won't stop and I'm worried about him. You need to talk to him."

Rath's shadow forms in the corner. Before he's even solid, Comus steps next to him. "Where?"

"Malaysia and New York. Hey, Alex." He flicks his fingers toward me. "Missed you."

I suck in a breath through my teeth. Rath's eyes are sunken, ringed in dark circles, and his shimmery, pale skin is dull and greenish. I let my gaze run over him, searching for blood or breaks because he looks like he's been fighting. "Brother, are you okay?"

Rath shakes his head in slow, drunken movements. He leans against the wall, closing his eyes.

"When did you sleep last?"

He's silent, then slumps and pops to consciousness with a jerk. "I couldn't say." His words are slurred and he lifts a heavy hand, pointing to me. "I'd let you out, but it's a trap. Sticky stuck."

I give Comus a pained glance. "The bars are adamantine."

"Huh." Rath sighs. "Sucks."

Comus clears his throat. "Deimos was in New York? That's a dangerous spot. Too populated, especially with the rural areas Moros has been hitting with the sirens. Anything like that going on?"

Rath inhales as if he'd forgotten to breathe and starts in a rush. "Manhattan. Scared the hell out of a street of people when I spotted him. Chaos. He did something, threw a thing, and disappeared. Lost him. Signs of him popped up in Malaysia, mass fear, but nothing. London. Nothing. Sorry. No sign of Lu. She's just fucking gone. No Moros. No sirens. Only Grace but...but ssshe'sss n-not..." He closes his eyes again. Gods, he needs to sleep. The door catches my attention —the chair blockade would give an additional five seconds and a plethora of questions to answer.

"This is not safe for him," I whisper to Comus. For any of us.

"Nowhere is safe." Rath jerks, bumping his head in rhythm against the wall.

I blow out a long breath. "What in the hell is Deimos doing in those places? And who's the missing guard?"

"Firthus, Demigod of Standing Water," Comus says. "He's tried to gain the ranks, but his attributes are making swampy areas. He's better with a sword and that's not impressive either. Others swore fealty to Moros and the old ways, but they're not talking." He swishes his hand toward the bars between us. "Because of this shit."

"Is there a defined word on *the old ways* yet?" I ask. Moros is evil incarnate so his beliefs can't be anything but bad news, but are we dealing with literal backstabbings or apocalyptic events?

Rath's head flops from side to side. "Death. Life death. Earth death. No humans. Too complex for him. We did wrong, he says. Start over. Reeeedo." He gives a raspy, squeak of a chuckle and taps invisible buttons in the air. "Boop, beep. Deleted."

Both Comus and I stare hard at Rath.

"Okay." I roll my hands, but then drop them because it looks like I'm doing some odd dance move. Damn bindings. "Let's start with how you know that."

Rath slides to the floor, his head thudding against the marble wall.

"Rath?" I ask.

Eyes closed, he clears his throat. "What?"

"Redo? Boop, um, beep. Spill it, brother."

"Ah." After a long pause he shifts back to life again as if someone put a quarter in his slot. "I visited my father."

My lips part as my jaw drops. "Father" is a loose term when it comes to Erebus. He's technically an Olympian, but could be primordial, a spirit or thing of darkness. He doesn't exactly have a business card for what he is, nor would he be able to use it locked away in the sea realm.

Comus squats and brushes his thumb over Rath's temple "Why didn't you tell us?"

"Cause it sucks." Rath turns his head to show us his bloodshot eyes and a mischievous smile. "And I'm the only one who can get near him." His blink is a slow-motion movement. "Why do you think Zeus wants me dead so...damn...bad. He thinks I'm going to release him, join him, be him." He bares his teeth in a snarl, more vicious with the hollowed darkness encircling his features. "But my father is entitled to Moros's evil plans as a follower of the *true sire*. The God of Doom wishes to end the world and says he has a weapon. Could be the sirens." Rath's face falls to pain. "And I can't find Lu, Grace won't help, and Artie has a problem with our war, and..." His chest rises and he blows out a stressed breath.

Comus glances at me and mouths, "More later." He squeezes Rath's shoulder. "Will she see you?"

"Artemis?" Rath peeks open one eye. "Told me it wasn't safe. Visiting hours closed."

That's not good. Rath and the virgin goddess have maintained a deep yet chaste relationship for decades, all in secret. If she's turning him away now, she's either spooked or chose her side. Rath isn't the kind to keep out though, especially if he believes she's in danger. He's a shadow and uses that attribute to its fullest extent.

"You going to her?" Comus asks.

"I shouldn't." He smirks. "So obviously, yes."

"You need sleep," I say. "There are other places." Other places where there's not a death-on-sight order against him.

"They don't have her there."

I could argue, fight with him to leave Artemis be. It's too dangerous for both of them, but he pushes back if I pry. I give the bars a light kick, sending a warning through my healing ankle. "Thank you, brother."

He opens his eyes and drags himself up the wall as if he's a hundred-year-old human. "I'll find Lula."

"You will, but she is resourceful, and if she wants to stay hidden for a bit, let her. The second I'm out of here though—"

"You're tied up." He points to my wrists. "Is Zeus going to allow you to wear your bracelets to the ceremony? You may start a new trend. The shackled look."

"Olympus's newest way to embellish," Comus adds. His face remains subdued.

I shrug. "All the cool kids are doing it." None of us laugh. "Go rest now, brother. Anice can help if we need it. Take a couple days to eat and sleep. You'll be useless if you're too tired to return from the shadows."

He fades. "I hate it when that happens."

"Anything else?"

Comus removes the chair and sits on it, ankle to knee, and one arm flopped over the back. "No, and they're going to get all growly if we're too long." He smacks the handle to open the door. "Welcome, gentlemen."

Olineus and Trantus glance around, glaring. "There were voices."

I bend my head to scratch at the itch of new beard growth. "That happens when people converse."

With an annoyed sniff, they return to their posts. Comus studies his nails. "So as I was saying, the Northern Coven was glad to see me. They said the guards understand a nymph's body about as well as they understand Earth. Funny as Zeus's lackeys haven't explored that terrain in two thousand years." He grins wide. "It was quite an evening. Besides that, it's the same old shit except for the rioting. Zeus can't hold them back forever. Something has to give, and letting you out would be his best bet for peace."

Both guards scowl over their shoulder at Comus.

I bite my bottom lip to keep my expression under control. I've missed his banter. "He's not going to—"

The door slams shut making both of us jolt. Hades leans against the wall. He cut his dark hair. It's slick and wavy, but shaved on the sides. He wears jeans and a vintage cereal t-shirt and looks so human. He yawns. "Well, hello."

The guards shout and thump, the sounds muffled through the thick stone. Comus and I whisper-yell together, "Are you crazy?"

"You're going to get me murdered," I add.

He smiles, toothy and amused. "Nah. I'm going to save your ass."

"Uh, what?" Comus stumbles. "Right now?"

The grin never fades from Hades. His poker face is legendary. He may pull a mystical weapon from behind his back to stab us both, but appears as though we're out for a chat over tea and cake. "Nope. But soon."

He pushes off the wall and approaches the bars, running a finger down one, then with a flick, makes it clang. "You've gotten yourself into quite a pickle, little war deflector."

I can't help but huff a laugh. He always calls me, Anice, and my father "little." I have at least four inches on him and about eighty pounds of muscle. Though, he's strong in different ways, and in a fight, I wouldn't bet on me.

"You could say that. Who told you?"

"I don't need others to tell me what I've seen with my own eyeballs." He taps the crests of his cheekbones. "She's lovely."

A sharp pang stabs through my chest. "Do you know where she is?"

He shakes his head. "Unfortunately, no. I wasn't watching you all that closely. Just checking in. Waiting and waiting…" He eyes the ceiling and rolls his hand through the air. "And waiting. Heavens, the waiting. Why haven't we hung out through the years, Alexiares? You three, the demons, humans, and I could have had quite a Saturday. And here it took a siren debacle and an overdue mutiny to bring us together. Tsk, tsk."

My face scrunches. Hades is passionate and flighty. Is he really on our side? I witnessed him go toe to toe with Zeus when Rath was born and Zeus demanded the death of both the newborn and Erebus. I'm not sure how either of them came out unscathed with the inferno of their conversation.

The pounding on the door turns into a loud bang.

"And they have a battering ram." Comus rubs his forehead. "What can we expect here, Hades? And why now? You could have taken Zeus out in his sleep."

With a swish of his hand, Hades dismisses the thought. "Where's the challenge in that?"

I raise my eyebrows and my bound hands. "We're sufficiently challenged. There's been a death. We don't need more."

His smile slithers away. "There will be more. Zeus has more safeguards in place to save his ass than even I know about. Moros is out and about, and I can't sense him, but his followers do." He looks between Comus and me. "Can you?"

"Gods no," Comus says, brows furrowed.

"Only when he's starting a war on Earth." I grit my teeth at the loud crack of ram against stone. Thunder rumbles the ground. "Okay, so we're about to get fried."

Hades purses his lips and crams his hands in his pockets. "Mm-hmm. Maybe this will give you a needed push because you're out of time. Work faster. Think faster. If Alex impregnates the goddess, we're all kinds of bad-type fucked."

"Oh yeah?" I ask. "In what way?"

"In ways you have probably touched on a hundred times with the amount of talking you do. You don't want that path."

If he has an Olympian oracle in his hands, we need him. "How do you know lines of fate?"

Hades's serious expression is more terrifying than the underworld he rules. "I know everything," he growls in a demon's timbre.

The air seems to leave the room. Even the thunking outside stops. I jerk when he breaks into cackles.

"You should have seen your faces," he says. "You two should lighten up." He pushes off the bars and shoves his hands into his pockets. "My knowledge is vast, however, I'm not privy to everything. Enough to help…or not. Depends on the motivation."

"What's your motivation," Comus says before I can.

Hades's eyes go half-lidded. "Soon, littles. So soon. I'm so tired of waiting. But hey, I'm in this now. Alex, don't be stingy if you feel Moros. Get your partner here to give me a little ringy ding." He stretches his thumb and pinky against his face.

"Then what will you do?" *Are you on our side or your own?*

Hades shrugs again. "Not sure. Can't wait to find out." He flicks his eyebrows and disappears in a thread of pearlescent smoke.

The door flies open and six guards fall into the room, two splaying over a wooden battering ram.

Zeus steps in over the pile of demigods and golden armor. "Who was here?"

"You're as confused as we are." I stretch my fingers, tucking them one at a time until I'm flicking him off. I examine my two extended digits as if checking how they've healed. "Must be shoddy craftsmanship. You should make some upgrades."

He stares hard, then bares his teeth, pivots, and storms away. *No fight left, old man?* I wish that were the case. The guards test the walls with splayed hands and open and shut the door until satisfied, then station themselves inside and facing me.

Comus's wild eyes portray panic. "I'm going to go, uh, talk to people."

I nod. Inform our taxiarchs that we may have an ally with fists as big as Zeus's.

Comus reaches through the bars to squeeze my shoulder. "Soon." He strides past the guards.

"I'll be here," I yell after him. "Plotting my revenge. Attempting to escape. Definitely scheming like the dirty schemer I am." Waiting for *soon*. Clinging to the thought of freedom, and memories of hugging Lula to me. Dreaming of picking her up to feel her weight safely in my arms and tucking my nose in her hair.

Where in the hell are you, Lu?

Chapter Fifteen

LULA

UNCOMFORTABLE IS SOMETHING I'M FAMILIAR WITH, BUT THE LEVEL OF unease I get around Moros beats the stares, the touches, and the ability to take over a room of humans if I cough. And it's not because he's gross, scum like Firthus, or cruel.

He's…kind, and I'm not sure what to do with that.

This morning he remains silent at the kitchen table, seeming to give me space I desperately need to mill over thoughts and sip coffee. When he's talking to me or trying to get me to work magic I don't have, there's an edge to him—a pompous, commanding attitude overflowing with determination, but I'm missing too many pieces to the whole puzzle so I can't see the full picture of him. He's patient with me, though he's not patient. He wants me to be a goddess like it's his one goal in life, and says it's because I will be stronger and invincible, but there's something else I can't even name to question him. There's a leer in his eyes when I fail or ask a question he doesn't want to talk about. He diverts and dodges. Ducks under the truth or the lie. With his help, I understand more about myself and deities, but not enough. Never enough.

This house is a mess. The dishes stack through the day if I don't do them, then disappear at night. I wake to a cleaner, but not clean, existence and breakfast. Moros still locks my door. For my protection because I'm not ready yet. He needs me. I'm important.

Curiosity gets the better of me and I wander over to take the wooden chair next to him.

He gives me an approving nod, holding out the hand with the black triangle scarred into his skin. "Let's try again." I trace my fingers over the raised lines and press my palm to his. The Olympians attempted to detach his attributes by using witchcraft, though they failed.

They always fail.

Except when Alex, Anice, Hercules, Comus, Zeus, and a bunch of others found him on Earth, broke his arms, and closed him in the hell realm. He said it took him two days to reset his bones because he kept passing out, and weeks to heal, all while fighting off darklings and scrounging for food. They don't have fruit trees in hell.

He gives a compelling story, that's for sure. He's told me about Olympus. Much of what he shared is the same story Alex sold me, but the perspective is from another angle. Lesser deities fill important roles but need leadership. Goddesses aren't even brought up besides mentioning that there are traditions in place. He's explained it as an Olympian culture. Attributes matter most. All are needed, but the more powerful, the more respect a deity gains, helping them climb the hierarchy. Zeus has placed himself as king even though Moros believes he's only there because of the powerful deities he surrounded himself with and still keeps close by use of manipulation and secret keeping. So far, Moros and the guys seem to be on the same page when it comes to Olympus, except I don't know what the guys' endgame is, but my father claims he will rule—we will—if I step into the ultimate unknown.

He squeezes my hand to bring me from the thoughts that live on repeat. "Seek that deep place that's aching to unravel. You can do it, Lula. It's time to embrace your divine nature."

Same words, different day. Same nonsensical meaning. I don't ache. I don't want to unravel, bloom, break through while attempting to reach zenith. He has the wrong person...siren. My eyes hurt. I want my sisters back, but apparently have to prove myself first. Hazel is excited to see me and Venora is glad I'm safe, Moros has told me.

They're carrots poised over my hungry mouth and the line is too short
for me to reach. Amah must be so worried. I should have met with her
a week ago. What did she do when I didn't show? She has to know
I'm with Moros. The Olympians would have killed me by now and
she would have felt that break. Moros often reminds me of the bounty
on my life. Before I was born, he made the mistake of speaking to
Zeus about his relationship with my mother, and the king of Olympus
blew up and sent his army for him. He sent Alex.

He sent *Alex*. My Alex is a liar. A murderer. He's someone who
would chase down another deity for falling for a non-deity. Then the
hypocrite met me. Which means, he may not be a hypocrite at all, but
a psychotic serial killer who needed me for…something. Maybe to
find the rest of my sisters and wipe us all off the planet.

"I can't." I let my hand drop, but Moros holds tight. My lungs
squeeze, making breathing impossible.

Visions flash through my mind in a TV series finale as my heart
crumbles. Our electrifying first kiss. The flutter of every cell in my
body as he tugged me into his arms. Pinning me to the wall after a
fight over pizza and tracing my skin until I swore I'd explode. How he
held me as I bawled for my lost sister whom he murdered. How could
anyone hold another that perfectly after doing such harm? He tried to
stay away during my heat, but *did he really?* He closed the portal and it
was just us. I shattered around him so many times while he whispered
words I never thought I'd hear from a willing, free partner.

You're perfect.

I want you forever.

I love you. You. Everything about you.

How dare he.

I slap my hand over my mouth, but it can't control the wail that
pours from me.

"Lula?" Moros says.

I'm up in a second. Stumbling over a red-stained carpet and up a
staircase that once held family photos. I imagine them happy and
human and alive. Why am I here? As I turn the corner, I bounce off a
hard chest.

"Hey, Lula, darling." Firthus's arms drop around me like
pressurized, burning bands. "Come to see me?"

I've had one run-in with Firthus in the six days I've been here, and I can usually feel the tense presence of his eyes on me, picturing me doing a thousand things I won't ever do with him. He's not a good deity. I'm not sure why my father keeps him here. I shove away from him, but he snags my wrist and drags me back.

"Stop," I growl through gritted teeth.

"You gave it up to the demigod and his crew, why not me? It's a non-deity's responsibility." Hot fingers slip over my hip like fire pokers. "And there are no goddesses here."

"If this is your sick way of trying to get me to reach zenith, I will kick your nuts into your lungs and—" I catch motion behind him. Another person trudges toward us. "Who is that?" I jerk backward, wrenching from his grip on my wrist.

Firthus stiffens and shifts to block my view, but I step around him. A slight man with dead eyes wanders the dark hall, holding a ball of fabrics.

"Daughter?" Moros says behind me.

Firthus drops his hand, but I don't turn. I watch, because the man's motions are familiar, his blank expression not something I expected, and I want to be sure. It's been a long time since I've seen someone this far gone, and my eyes tingle.

He turns to open the laundry closet door, and goes through practiced, slow actions of loading the washer. A garment falls to the floor, but he ignores it—well, doesn't notice, only sticks to muscle-memory actions. Brown hair hangs in tangled waves over a back so thin, his bumpy vertebrae show through his shirt. My stomach lurches so hard I put my hand over it.

"He's enthralled," I whisper. Under a siren's command.

Moros sighs behind me. "We needed help, Lula."

"So you enslaved someone to be your servant?" I keep my voice quiet, but he notices and turns, staring straight through me. Dammit. What else does he do for them? Where are they keeping him during the day? "Did Hazel do this? He's been enthralled too long." I catch a whiff of rot and old urine, and the nothingness in my stomach threatens to come up. I gag when my eyes land on dark red splatter on his filthy shirt.

Moros's hand on my elbow makes me dance backward. "Let's eat.

You need a break."

"Not hungry." How could I be with this poor human wandering around the house in this state? "This is cruelty."

"Make dinner, Harris."

The man comes closer but doesn't reach out. I wish for it in this case. It would mean there was hope for his mind. Instead, we stand still, facing each other. Every weak muscle and tendon shows on his bruise-covered neck. His dirty cheeks sink in and his eyes bug with no fat to put his features at normal proportions. What has my sister done? Moros's hand clasps my arm, and he drags me back. He has a phone at the ready and I should grab it and run, but I'm surrounded. The urge to scream at him is hard to tame, but I'll hurt the man and he's had enough harm. Can he recover or is it too late?

"Now, Harris," Moros says. "The pasta dish you know so well."

The man stumbles past me as if air is too heavy for his bones, and clomps downstairs with slow, methodical steps. Moros's grip is too firm to wriggle away. "Calm yourself, Lula. You do not like that we enlisted someone to help us acclimate to human life?"

I sneer at him. "There is nothing human about this situation. Is this how Olympian servants are treated? That man is not *cared for*. He's starving and unclean. There's…blood." I swallow hard and back another step away from Firthus, glaring at him. "Bruises on his neck. Why are there bruises on his neck, Firthus?"

He raises a shoulder and watches Moros.

This time, when I pull against his hold, Moros lets me go. "I'm sorry this pains you, dear. We will take care of it."

"It's too damn late for that. How is this protecting those who are weaker? Isn't that what you said?"

"Lula, he's human. This is an honorable servitude to deities."

I huff and toss up my hands. "You can't force someone's assistance and call it honor." When I turn to head to my room, sweaty fingers clamp around my wrist. My skin attempts to escape Firthus, shimmying in chills. "Let go." I wish I were a goddess right now so I could strike this asshole down. Bruise him as he has the man downstairs, who's lived too long with a melted mind. My sister did that to an innocent human. Why? I jerk harder, muscles and elbow protesting, but Firthus only releases me when Moros nods at him, allowing his monster to touch me long enough to prove that he has control over me.

I scratch at where he touched me, trying to brush it away. "Why would my sister do this?"

"They wanted to help."

"This isn't helpful. No siren would do this willingly."

Moros crosses his arms and leans against the wall, blocking the path to the stairs. "They did."

I glance down the hall. I've been nearly everywhere in the house, but nowhere near Firthus's room or the locked downstairs. Is there a key in one of those places? A bill with an address or any hint to my sisters' whereabouts, which Moros has kept silent about? "Which sister did this?" My nails pinch into my palms. If I can escape, I'll go door-to-door and ask about Venora and Hazel. Someone must have noticed a red-headed god and two sirens. Then again, people's perceptions are fuzzy when interacting with my species.

"Venora." He smiles. "She's been helpful to everyone."

I tilt my head. "Did she do this because you threatened her or Hazel?" None of my sisters would hold a mortal under permanent thrall.

"Oh, daughter." He turns and steps down the stairs. "Come. Let's not pretend that sirens are innocent creatures. You're made to be powerful and should exercise your skills. Venora did."

"Not like that. The whole world would fall if we did."

He pauses, eyes gleaming as he purses his lips in thought.

"Wait." I hold a hand up. "If that is your plan—"

"Come down here. We need to talk and eat." He continues downstairs, and the creeping heat of Firthus behind me sends me following. I eye the front door and pause.

"I will harm your sister if you leave. Then I would find you. Stop being foolish and listen to him."

I glare back at Firthus. "You were hiding the human because you know how wrong it is."

"It was a necessity, as are many undesirable things to get through this time, daughter of Moros." He points toward the kitchen.

The sound of pots clanking and clattering rise through the silence.

The man pulls a colander from a cabinet with the subtle movements of a sloth.

"Was he the owner of the house?" I whisper, blocked from the hallway by Firthus.

Moros leans against the counter and tilts his head. "No."

"Were those people a necessity like Harris is?"

Moros approaches him and pushes his hair behind his ear. "This truly bothers you, doesn't it?"

"Yes." So much *yes*. I can't believe there's an enthralled servant in the house. I've probably made him worse by talking at full volume. "It's wrong."

"With everything we've spoken about, I'd hoped you would gather that right and wrong does not exist. Things only are." He drags his fingers down Harris's neck with gentleness that makes me cringe. "Damn the Olympians for separating us. I could have taught you so much. Instead, you grew and lived amongst mortals, learning to fear and to judge." Moros scowls. "You've acquired human emotions."

"Good," I whisper.

"Mm." His lips tighten and he wraps the fingers of his scarred right hand around the man's neck. My pulse topples to a breakneck speed, but before I can move, Harris's dead eyes come to life, blank expression morphing into silent-screaming agony as black tendrils slither from Moros's tight hold. "When a deity sees something that needs to change, they change it."

"What are you doing?" I tumble forward and grip his tensed forearm. His skin is ice.

"Our world is simple, Lula. There are the divine, and then everything else. It's a concept you must embrace, daughter."

Harris makes a choking sound then collapses to the ground as Moros's hand drops away. *No.* Wide eyes full of human fear blacken, matching the scorch marks trailing from where Moros touched him. Rath had a similar mark. My father really did burn him, but Rath's a deity. Harris is not.

I cover my mouth and nose with both hands as the man clutches his neck, flopping in the throes of death. He hacks a dry, closed throat sound.

"Help him." I drop to my knees to examine the dark, invisible fire inching across his skin, leaving behind charred flesh from his chin to jutting collarbones. "Moros, please."

"Death is the fate of every mortal life. Focus for me, Lula. Watch him."

I glance up, expecting a demon looming over us, hulking and horned, but his expression is blank. How many deaths would cause this level of desensitization?

"It was too late for the human." The corner of Moros's lips twitch before sinking to a frown. "You said so yourself. He was not healthy. He served us well though. If you wish, you may end his suffering. It will take a while for my gift to end him."

Grasping at his neck, the man chokes out a squeak that sounds like a stretched balloon leaking air.

I flinch. "I cannot kill him."

"You have not taken life before?"

Killing anyone, even the psychotic berserker that murdered my sister Lena, makes my heart hurt. He can't be entirely unsympathetic. Sparks of humanity live in everyone. "I have, but won't describe the torture it does to my mind. No one should go through this type of death. Please, help him."

"There's no shame in ending life when you're a deity. It's ours to control, darling. You of all beings should understand that. Sing a few notes, and he will be out of his misery."

But there is shame. It rolls through my bones, making my palms sweat. This poor man is either my punishment or a test, when he should be enjoying his human existence with his mortal people. The charring has spread, creeping from his eyes and appearing on the tip of his blue-tinged nose. This is too slow.

As if Moros can read my mind, he nods encouragingly. "I'd like to see your abilities in action. You could sing to help him pass, or attempt zenith and then your goddess state can practice new attributes."

Harris's feet tap a beat on the floor as he twitches from lack of oxygen. The scent of his uncleanliness increases, making my stomach lurch. My teeth grind together so hard I may crack them. "You think my goddess state would kill?"

"No, I think your power will make you realize your purpose in the universe. You've lived too long as something you're not. It's not right for my daughter. Reach inside and seek an overwhelming sensation that doesn't belong." He grips the air, making a fist. "Take it and trust how it will aid you."

"Making me a killer won't help me." I focus on Harris, reaching for his wrist, then pulling away at the chill billowing from him. "Can't you reverse this?"

With effort, I pry the man's hand from his neck, and a jolt of energy zaps me as my fingers touch his blackened wound. The sensation was a shock, but within that was a wave that lit me up. My skin continues to tingle.

"Did you feel something, daughter?"

I train my face back into a scowl. "No, his skin is colder than I expected."

His gaze bores into me in a way that has me checking for Firthus. He's there too, leaning against the doorway. I sneer at him, but he ignores me and watches Harris with bored interest. Moros snaps. "Tell me. It may be important."

I doubt the sensation was positive. Harris's eyes are wide with terror. Poor thing. Should I use my thrall to help him move to the veil? Wouldn't a faster passing be a gift?

I snort at the thought. Moros calls his nightmarish ability a gift. If I aid him with murder, I'm no better than he, and I may prove something I don't want to. He's determined to teach me to be a deity, but if deities only care for themselves and use every other being as they see fit, I'll keep my siren life, thanks. Not that there's a choice. I'm a siren, no matter what Moros thinks.

"Look at him, Lula. There is beauty in this. Realize that this man has never felt such agony or basked in the glory of someone so powerful. You can alter his existence."

Moros is revealing a lot about himself in this moment. He wants my reaction. I only want to ease this man's suffering. Glassy, pleading eyes land on me, finally aware of another person.

"You feel no pain from this," I whisper. "Remember the happiest times you've ever experienced. Do you understand? There is no pain."

His face morphs into a calm mask as his rapid gasps slow. I exhale a sigh of relief. I didn't know my ability could turn off pain receptors, but I'd never needed to test it. His eyes close and he smiles, though his breathing is still ragged as his body struggles. I can't stop his passing, but he's at ease.

"Remember those you love," I whisper. "They are safe and happy."

Moros crouches beside me and clasps Harris's throat. More black tendrils appear, along with a pungent smell somewhere between charring meat and decay. "Fascinating."

"Leave him be." I return my focus to the man and stroke his hair. The gray tinge of his skin darkens and his limbs jerk, but the smile never leaves his face.

Moros's fingers tighten around his blackened neck until a sickening crack sounds and Harris's twitching body stills. I give a challenging glare at my father. Now is not the time for celebration, not with a dead human on the floor, but pride surges. I stopped pain that a deity caused. In a terrible way with a horrid loss, I won. It's as renewing as learning how to command before I realized what I sought with interactions was a genuine connection with someone. I'd forgotten the excitement.

The room slides into hazy silence from the placidity of death.

Moros removes his hand and pumps his fingers as he stands. He walks to the sink to wash. "You are far more powerful than the others. You will acknowledge what you are."

When Moros faces me again, I shove at him, though he's as easy to move as Alex was. He's a bolted down marble statue. "Did you put my sisters through this same test?" I ask. "Unleash your *gift* on a helpless human, and challenge a siren to kill?"

He snags my hands, stopping another assault on his chest. "Moments like these are needed. You are more important than this human, the Olympians, or your sisters. How can you not see that?"

"I'm not more important than someone's life."

"Yes, you are," he yells. "They mean nothing compared to you, Lula. Olympians made them too similar—"

Firthus clears his throat, and Moros bares his teeth, but nods.

I wave my hand through the acrid air. "No, no. What were you going to say?"

Moros takes my shoulders in his palms. "When you acknowledge, you will be the most important being in this universe. You're my daughter, and nothing means more to me than you. Can you understand that?"

"You don't need to kill to tell me that." I pull out of his grasp and rub my forehead.

He raises a finger. "You said we were being cruel, and he was too far gone. What else were we to do? This is a lesson. If something is broken, we fix it. We will fix many things together. Now, sit so we may enjoy a meal."

Chapter Sixteen

LULA

In my near consciousness, a warm finger traces out words on my back, making me smile. These are my happiest times. The ones where Alex carefully wakes me, touches me and I'm engulfed in love. I'm home.

The first word he writes is *Beauty*. Then *Sweet*. After that comes *Adore*. Finally, *Mine*. He underlines that one before blazing a tingling trail of fire down my side. His other fingers join, slide toward my thigh and curl in above my knee where they tug. Then lips meet my shoulder, his hard chest slides against my back, hip skims over my ass, and he nudges his way to the place he knows better than anyone else.

He is, without a doubt, correct. *I am his.*

Knocking sounds like gunshots in the distance. I sit up straight with a startled gasp, blinking a few times in a little girl's room that is too cold and smells stale.

"Daughter?" Moros calls through the door.

"Hang on." I drop my head into my hands. "Give me a few minutes." My back still tingles from Alex's phantom touch, and need grips my traitorous body. I miss waking up with him, and I hate myself for that. He's another enemy in a universe of divine assholes, and more dangerous than my father because of the undeniable emotion that connects us. At least Moros is honest about who he is.

He doesn't pretend to be a perfect golden god who radiates warmth and honesty when that's the last thing he's been. Alex is married by now, according to Deimos. The black-haired deity showed up a couple of days ago to take away Harris's body. He had a tall Scottish woman with him—a vampire ally—so I wasn't allowed to speak, which I failed in less than two minutes when I asked about Hazel. She told me my sister was a good girl and her blood was delicious, and then Firthus clamped his hand over my mouth, picked me up, and locked me in my room.

Moros came in hours later with a smile. He praised me for taking control of the situation and acting as a goddess. I will be perfect once I morph. His reactions—the single clap of parental approval, the proud nod, the squeeze to my shoulder when I share my history comfort me. He tells me I'm like him often and that he can't wait until I figure out how to acknowledge and *we* discover my true self. After nearly two centuries, I'm unsure if my true self even exists.

The version of me in the Belize house was me, or so I thought. The guys took that from me. They've soured those memories, and I wish my dreams wouldn't keep reliving the lies during that time.

My father rants daily about the deities who scorned him and his brethren. He's so bitter that those conversations leave the taste of unsweetened cranberries in my mouth. I even defend the guys, only realizing it when Moros presses for information, especially regarding Rath. Being the youngest Olympian and protected by Alex and Comus, Rath is mysterious, but being bred from a key member of Moros's supposed army, my father is interested. What Rath told me about his father checks out. I'm surprised he didn't lie. Moros wonders if I can recruit him, but I always keep quiet. I'm not recruiting anyone to whatever war everyone seems keen on dragging me into. I just want my sisters back and to go home, but I doubt that will ever be possible again. He's grown impatient, yet more gentle with me—coddling me with words and presents as a father would do. He feeds me, clothes me, and provides any amenity he can within the confines of the house. He murdered a man to end his suffering, then pats my cheek with the same deadly hand, and I lean into his touch because although I'm only here biding time until I get my sisters back, I need people. The knock sounds again. "I've brought you coffee."

Deep breath. "Come on in."

"Good morning, daughter."

"Good morning." I yawn and pull closer the comforter of a stranger I've named Holly. She loves fairy tales and magical creatures. I imagine her in an equally darling room out there in the world, unharmed and amused that a siren sleeps in her fluffy bed.

"Rest well?" He sits and offers the hot mug.

A jolt slices through my chest and I huff out a sharp breath, clapping my hand over my heart. Moros goes fuzzy as I fight to stay conscious from the pain. Nausea overflows and I swallow hard. Then I remember this agony I fear so much and wish I could fade back into dreams. Not again.

"Lula?" My father's voice comes from a distant tunnel. I need to return there because it's steadier than the ebb and flow of searing pain and ice shredding my soul.

"My sister," I rasp.

"What's wrong?"

"No, no..." I gasp a series of sobs, and Moros says something that sounds amused, but I shake my head. "One of my sisters is dead. Another one." The ache in my chest is a hot poker that drives fear into my bloodstream. I grasp at his arms, crawling to my knees. "Where are they? I need them. Did you kill her? Hazel? Venora?"

"What?" He looks at my hand clamped around his wrist. "No. I'm here with you." Realization softens his confused expression. "Did you feel a siren pass?" Before I can answer, he yells for Firthus.

The demigod peeks into the room and furrows his brows when he sees me. "What happened?"

"Call Deimos," Moros says. "Do you know who, Lula?"

It doesn't work that way. Did Zeus finally find one of us? How many times will I have to go through this? The others whisper but I can't hear them through my wracking sobs. I lean my forehead against my father's thigh.

He squeezes the back of my neck, easing my ragged breath. It's not a hug, but that's not his way, and I should be happy that he's nothing like Alex, but I'm not. Moros pats my shoulder. "It's time to be strong, my daughter."

I clutch at my searing chest and try to sit up, but the movement hurts. My soul's been severed again. When I finally hand-walk my way upright, Moros's face is red, his lips clamped in a sharp line. Firthus leans on the doorjamb, phone in his palm. He appears as furious as my father.

"What is it?" I ask. "You know who it is." It's not a question. They both wear determined expressions, like they have all the information.

"You have no clue where your other sisters are?" Moros asks with a bite. When I shake my head, he hisses a breath through his teeth. "I'd wager that Alexiares struck again."

His words are borderline playful, sitting so weirdly that they don't land. They should; Alex did lie, but harm my sister? He was so gentle with me. I'm unable to visualize him using his hands as a weapon. I can't even picture an angry scowl directed at me or my sisters. He kissed me out of frustration once, brows angled and jaw set, but I didn't fear him. I melted. He was so good at playing innocent.

Who could it have been? Did Grace escape? Is Amah looking for me? "Zeus has a bounty on my species." Please don't let there be more. Moros looks to Firthus, who starts dialing and walks down the hall, murmuring low.

"Again, you're not a siren, Lula." Moros grabs my chin and lifts my face. "It is time to strike, daughter. I need you strong enough to fight against the Olympians. Do you understand?"

I narrow my eyes at him and lean back so he has to release me. "My siren sister just died. I hurt." All I want to do is find the others and mourn the loss we've had to bear again. I want to be held, but there's no one to do that. Alex ruined me. If he were here, dragging me to him, stripping me down so he could hold me with nothing but lies between us, I'd kill him because I want that again. Replaying how he cherished me that day calms the ache yet hardens my heart further.

"If you're a goddess, you may be able to travel as Alexiares or Hermes does. It would be easy to get to your sisters. You can annihilate Zeus and Alexiares before they do more damage."

"I don't want to annihilate anyone."

"Lula, you must change your mindset. I will help you with that." He stands, all previous anger and concern gone with a paternal smile in place. He taps my chin with a finger. "Get dressed. We shall try something new today. Do you want to see Hazel?"

My hand settles over my heart again. It still throbs hot like an infected wound. "Yes." If I can see one sister, that will settle my mind until we can check on the rest. I'm suspended in a black, unknown chasm, held by loose, frayed threads of fate, but none fall away and none pull tighter. There is nothing to grab. If I can talk to Hazel and check on Venora, then something will settle into place.

I need one string to hold fast.

After a moment, he gives me a knowing smile. "You're nervous about acknowledging."

"That's what you want to try? But—"

"We have covered the basics. Do you remember?"

I wait too long to respond, and he grabs my hand and tugs me to my feet with a hard yank. "Lula, recite the steps. This is our future."

Part of me wants to tell him to walk his stupid basics back to the hell realm, but this will distract me from the hole in my chest. I'll use it as such. I wipe at my eyes and take three long shuttering breaths. "Focus on a repressed emotion. Open my mind and allow it in no matter how overwhelming. There's no shame in accepting everything I am. If I've found my attribute by doing so, I'll become a full goddess."

He nods. "Superb, Lula. Your true state will be glorious." He squeezes my hand and heads toward the door. "Much better than you've had to withstand. We leave as soon as you're ready and fed."

My actual state is siren, and his instructions are vague. He wants me to uncover a stifled emotion? Like what? This pain is overwhelming. I've explored power trips, regret, and guilt a hundred times. I've considered his words and meditated on my faults and difficult situations I've longed to forget. That led to irritation and falling asleep, but no goddess activity when I woke.

"Do not worry, daughter. You need not be nervous. All will be well soon. Now, get dressed and meet me downstairs."

All will never be well again. Another sister is gone. Another hole in my soul that seems more cavernous by the day. The door shuts, and I drop my head back into my hands. My chest burns, as do my eyes. He's not going to let me mourn until I do what he wants. At least I'll see Hazel and maybe together we can get Venora. At the foot of the stairs, Moros offers an elbow and an apple. "Feel better, daughter?"

Not even a little. I bite into the tasteless fruit and take his arm as we head to the car, following Firthus. Through neighborhoods, people walk dogs, work on scrubby gardens, and play with their sweet, innocent children, unknowing of the dangers driving down the street. I could step out and command them to overthrow the world or sing and kill them all. But I'd never do that. The humans have taught me more than Alex and Moros combined.

They teach their offspring to be better than they are, or at least try.

Though Moros says I will be more powerful than him, I'm not sure he thinks in terms of betterment. I picture him raising me and I don't enjoy what that future could have been. If I had become pregnant, would he have shunned her for being Alex's or embraced what she would have been and tried to teach her what I should be learning. The possibility is long gone and I'm glad for it, even when I find my hand over my stomach as if by its own accord. Like now. I ball my fist and rest it on my thigh. Small one-story shops and cafes line the sides of the street we travel, but it's ghost-town quiet. We turn at a gas station with a red sedan parked next to the pump. The door is open but there's no driver in sight. Nausea amplifies my swirling emotions and singed soul. Behind a concrete partition, I get glimpses of people though entrance doorways. I blink, hand gripping the seat in front of me. My sister is here, and she's controlling a big crowd. "What is this?"

"Trust me, Lula." Moros smiles and signals for me to exit the car. The guys told me Moros was killing crowds by the hundreds, but my father said it was required to get the attention of the gods and bring me out of hiding. I'm here though, with him, so why does he need a group? I will not harm these people. The urge to dig in my feet until he tells me what's happening rages through me, but I won't further enthrall the silent crowd with questions.

No one turns to face us as I follow him through an opening in the wall. There has to be a thousand blank-faced humans in lines on the slope of a tiered hill leading to a wood-beamed amphitheater. On the stage is Hazel, one hand entwined with Deimos, the other wrapped around her thinner middle, noticeable even from this distance as she's tucked into a tight outfit. I bite my lip to keep from yelling for her.

She did this to them.

I shift to run, but Moros takes my arm in a firm grasp. "Patience, daughter."

Taking a long breath, I try to calm myself, but my trembling won't cease as we descend a stone staircase centered in the hill.

"Hazel did this for you. She wants to see you rise above your state just as I do." Moros loosens his grip. "Do you want to go to her?"

What kind of question is that? I nod and his fingers drop away.

Careful not to make a verbal sound, I sprint and weave through the crowd taking up a flat, grassy strip in front of the stage. Hazel pulls from Deimos and runs toward the wooden stairs. We crash in a hug. She's so skinny. I pull back to cup her thin cheeks, capturing a silky lock of brown hair that's escaped her high bun. Her green eyes dance with happiness, but I know mine don't. "Are you okay?" I whisper. She's thinner and dressed like a supermodel in a sleeveless jumpsuit. I drag my coat off and wrap it around her, guiding her trembling arms through the sleeves.

"Stop, sister." She makes no attempt to keep her voice low and giggles, but it trails off to a frown. "I'm the best. Why are you looking at me like that?" I try to shush her but she waves me off. "You're here to save us, Lula. You're going to do it. They're coming, but you're going to stop them and I'll help. You just need to do what Moros says. Things are really good when you do what they ask."

"Is Venora here?" I keep my voice so low that I'm more mouthing the words than speaking them.

Her brows crinkle and nostrils flare.

"Come here, Hazel." On the stage, Deimos's hair hangs in damp black waves, leaving dark spots on the shoulders of a gray, wool coat. I glare at him. At least someone gets to prepare for the weather.

"It's fine," Hazel says. "It will be when you're a goddess." She kisses my cheek and pulls away to walk up the stairs and into Deimos's arms. "Did I do good?"

"So good, sweetheart." He keeps his eyes on me.

"Daughter, your attention." Moros coaxes with a crooked finger to where he's standing with a gray-haired man. "I'm sorry, darling, but you need incentive. Too much is riding on your zenith and our time is short."

Before I protest, his hand encircles the man's neck. My father pushes the man toward me and I catch his shoulders. Liver-spotted hands clutch at his blackening throat as he drops to his knees in front of me. "No," I whisper. The other humans stay still, watching me because I spoke to my sister. I should make them run. I will, but not yet. They need direction after an enthrallment like this or they'll draw attention, if they haven't already.

"Don't feel pain," I tell the man and back up, bumping into Firthus. I sidestep, but I'm blocked in a triangle of deities.

Moros gives me a disappointed scowl. "No, daughter. Do not protect them from the fate dealt by a deity."

"If I'm a goddess," I whisper, moving toward the stage. "I can impart fate to them as well." I glance at Hazel and extend my hand to her, but she looks to Deimos, who shakes his head. Hazel bites her lip and stays put.

"You're not a goddess yet." Moros clears his throat and beckons me again. "But you will be. Watch him die. Acknowledge those feelings, whatever they may be. You repress the truth that tells you this is right. It's time to release your true nature. Look into his eyes as my gift overtakes him."

"You said there was no right and wrong." I glare at him, refusing to glance at the human dying at my feet, silent except for ragged breaths.

"But you understand those concepts. I'm adapting to your mindset until you accept the truth."

"If you don't acknowledge"—Deimos stands behind Hazel, toying with a lock of her hair—"I get you until your first heat, and maybe during. Try hard, daughter of Moros." His eyes are brown but glint red, and his smile promises an eternity of nightmares, even when Hazel gives him a hurt-filled glance. If there is a devil, this deity is he.

"You think threatening me will help?" I direct at Moros. "If you believe you'll win my alliance by—"

Moros waves away my words, but Deimos is the one who answers. "It can't hurt, according to your non-divine state. Listen to your father and hurry up. We will draw the attention of the mortals soon and then you will have scores more to deal with."

"I only do this to help, daughter." Moros signals to the man.

"You must look at him. Is the spark there when you see death? Your mind attempts to suppress it, but let it in. Fight to revel in his mortality, because you own this world as a creator. Be happy about this, Lula."

I tremble as much from the cold as from this impossible situation. Whatever he thinks I contain, he's wrong, and I'm not sure what he will do when he learns that. He loves me in a way, or respects and cherishes that I'm his child. I swallow hard and chew my lip. My eyes skim over the man at my feet, face now blue. Nothing inside me revels that he's dying a cruel death or that the God of Terror has possibly brainwashed my sister. She stares at him like he hung the moon and it reminds me of my infatuation with Alex. Alex never made me do terrible things. At least, he hadn't yet.

"It's okay, Lula," Hazel says, her voice tight. "It gets easier. They're just humans."

My blood chills. *Just humans?*

"Another then?" Moros grabs a woman in a business suit and grasps her neck.

I bite back a scream, knowing that reaction will anger or instigate him further.

"Do you feel it?" His twinkling black eyes shift between me, his dying victims, and the huge crowd. "It is beautiful, is it not? Watch my power, daughter. It can be yours."

He grabs a young boy by the shirt and jerks him forward. The kid can't be older than ten.

"Stop," I yell, throwing my hands out. I step close and pull the child to me. He trembles in my arms, though he should be calmly enthralled. Maybe my fear is somehow transferring to them. "Don't be afraid." He settles, little shoulders relaxing. Are his parents in the crowd? The mass of humans seems fearful as well, even under Hazel's command. Their stares are wide, some visibly tremble, and they're panting or baring teeth in a terrified grimace. Moros's focus bores through me, seeking things I can't give him, then he lifts his hand and moves toward another.

"I'm trying, but killing people isn't working for me. All you're doing is stressing me out and making me not like you." I lean and whisper to the child, "Go home, and be careful of traffic."

I may as well have slapped Moros as the boy shifts from my grip and strolls away. He huffs. "Daughter, you need—"

"I know." I wince at the loudness of my voice. "I understand that I need to acknowledge or find zenith or whatever, but killing humans only makes me want to work against you. You have to realize that I've settled among them." I raise a hand when he gets ready to say something that is most likely another rant of why I'm better than mortals. "Let me send them away and I will try to figure it out."

"You don't believe you're a goddess, do you?" His fingers ball at his sides and he simmers with energy, but his voice remains featherlight. He signals to the crowd and to my sister. "You're not afraid as the others are. Did you notice?"

If anything, the humans have grown more fearful. All except the innocent people laid out on the ground, eyes wide and unseeing. Harris died so much slower. Did Moros draw out his death? That wouldn't make his murder a merciful act.

"Lu," Hazel pleads. "Please listen to them." She's trembling, clearly terrified but I can't do what they're asking. I won't.

"Trust me, daughter." Moros scans the crowd and the sky. "You need a push."

A push? This is tossing me off a mountain. My mind flits for an answer to stop this madness but lands on nothing. "I need a minute."

The humans would bolt if they could. Some would at least. If they realized what Moros has done, most might run, but some would fight. They'd engulf him, punching and kicking, outraged that a murderer walked among them. Saving strangers, they'd call for help that would come. Here is a compassionate race. Unfortunately, every one of them would perish.

Moros is right and Alex was also right: Olympus needs to change. Why must deities harm so much?

"I can't instill fear into you." Deimos smiles and grips Hazel's arm to drag her closer. "Do you know my divine calling, daughter of Moros?"

Hazel presses her hands to her ears and wails.

I wince. "Leave her alone, God of Terror."

"Ah, good. Now you're paying attention. I'm exuding my gifts and you're unaffected." He holds Hazel at arm's length as she cowers, face caught in a grimace.

"Because you are a goddess," Moros yells. "Act like one and acknowledge so that Deimos will stop harming the humans and your sister. Non-deities can only take so much."

Chapter Seventeen

ALEX

"No." I pause push-ups to roll my shoulders. *Again, no.* It's my word of the week.

Zeus crosses his arms—a sure sign I'm frustrating him. "Alexiares, your wedding occurs on the day after morrow. I am gifting you one last opportunity to swear fealty and agree to the terms of your release."

When Zeus was born, the universe needed his straightforward views of life, death, and power, but the strategy that once worked for him is faltering in this new age and he refuses to adapt. He no longer understands his people, and I fear more Olympians than we realize think Moros is the answer. Word of the murdered guard and Deimos's treason has circulated, but whispers don't carry an appalled tone. That, matched with Hades's irritation at our long game, has me thinking. Maybe we planned wrong. The God of Doom is patient, but not overly so. Before taking a step out of Olympus, he observed, waiting for his moment, then added to the chaos of plagues while hiding among the wreckage. He sought attention then, and he seeks it now, but why? Unlike Zeus's method of threaten, kill, and then threaten to kill until everyone is bowing before him, Moros skips the threatening part. My brother and I got him off-realm last time by playing to his hubris and feigning loyalty. Moros didn't consider that we could fake obedience and turn against him. He thought we accepted that he was the bigger power, and would trade one asshat for another. When we overthrew him, it shocked him that we disapproved of him killing so many mortals. And here we are again. Except I'm in a cage, scheduled to wed, and when I get out, I have no more cards to play against the God of Doom.

"This is your last chance." Zeus hits the bars, frustration making me smile.

"No." I do five more push-ups, hands overlapping into a triangle so I don't put pressure on the chain. I've improved on most tasks with my arms tied. Clapping is still difficult. I balance on my knees, and try for the hell of it. Only wafty little slaps.

"Alexiares, I will not stand for your resistance to mere conversation."

"Fine. I'm *gifting* you the opportunity to do right by your people and release me before Olympus stumbles into war." Standing, I lean as close to the bars as possible. "By the way, gifts come without payment or expectation."

He raises an eyebrow and one side of his lips. It's an odd facial quirk when he's amused. I'm tempted to try it, but I'd need a mirror and I don't want to see myself in this state. I smell. Unshaven, unbathed, and still wearing a blood-stained shirt from my attack on the barracks—this wedding will have interesting art renditions.

"How can you receive something without payment?" he asks.

"What am I receiving to go through with your nefarious plans?" I ask, standing straighter to show off my unkempt state. A tingle pulses at the base of my skull and my eyes widen. I turn and fiddle with the chain. Zeus drones on, an annoying buzz in the background, because my attribute is waking.

Moros.

He's reaching out with more bodies, more declarations of his intention. The signal is a fuzzy throb scrabbling for purchase, but it's there. This is the worst time to be separated from Comus and Rath. Has anyone caved and spoken to Comus about the connection of Aglaope to Zeus and Moros? In the past, older deities ran from him when he asked; begged him to leave them be or shushed him, commanding that he mind the peace, but these last days have changed

Olympus. Has Rath made any progress or overheard anything of use? I have to get out of here. Stop Moros and find Lula, whether or not she forgives me.

"You owe me out of loyalty to your king," Zeus grumbles.

I laugh and take a deep breath. "There's your issue. You believe we owe you, when you owe it to your people to guide them into the world, yet there are Olympians who have never set their eyes on a mountain from the base or sunk their fingers into snow. They've never spoken to a single creature they influence." I shrug. "Olympus understands the farce you've created and realizes that I'll only commune with Ichnaea if you arrange a rape. Oh, they know you, and when your minions drag me to my *bride*, Olympus will fight for me because they owe you nothing."

"I gave everything for Olympus," he growls.

"You wanted power, and you took it."

"Olympian's needed change. I began a new era."

I grin wide and give my wafty clap in a silent room. "You never fail to prove my point for me. History repeats."

It takes a long moment for Zeus's wrinkled brow to shoot skyward. "Olympus is perfect as it is. This era—"

"Is on its last crumbling leg. Wake the fuck up, Zeus. Even the Council no longer understands your insane notion of leadership. Have you not noticed the shock on their faces with every wrong decision you make? Their silence is not agreement. These fear tactics and lightning-bolt punishments can't keep the world from moving. It's left us in the damn dust because of you."

"Do not spread your lies."

His words fade as the tingle in my mind spreads, wrapping around my head like huge hands, fingers landing over my eyes, thumbs pressing to the top of my skull. Visions splotch into place before dissipating. A wooden structure dwarfs a vast group, but the people are faceless still, the area unrecognizable.

"We must wait," he says. "Until—"

"Until what?"

"I've explained myself enough to you. If you invoke war among my subjects, their blood will be on—"

"Don't push this on me, old man."

"Stop interrupting me, Alexiares."

"It's the only way you listen at all. Anyway, I'm not the one who closed the libraries to prevent younger deities from reading about your horrific deeds and weaknesses. Thousands of years later, the humans still talk about you…" I wrinkle my nose. "And don't look proud about that, you sick fuck. It's a different world now." Realization hits me.

"It may be different, but—" Zeus tilts his head. "What is it?"

I ache to work this concept out with my brother, Rath, and Comus, but I'm alone with my considerations because Zeus banned visiting after the "faulty door," incident, and I'm now guarded by no less than five guards at all times. Breathing life into this thought will spark it to blazing or snuff it out. "Leave and get me Comus and Rath and Anice." I need Eos and Iaso too, but they're too woven into Olympus for me to utter their allegiance. Damn, even Hades could help with this, and my grandmother, though she hasn't returned. I need my taxiarchs, my army, my friends. Lula. Lula would help me work this out over anyone else. *Humans.* It's humans who influence us. It's why deities are born with attributes to serve the modern world. How did I not see this until now? Because a narcissistic king taught me well. Divine rules all.

"The God of Shadows will die for his—"

I throw my palms up. "If you harm the God of Shadows, you will not reach the next exodus."

"Exodus," he bellows, somehow excusing my threat to his life.

I vacantly nod and pull from the thousand rehearsed things I've wanted to tell him over the decades as I wait for my attribute to engage—a gift from the mortals. "My brethren are uprising: petitioning for my release, standing vigil in front of your home, recruiting servants and other deities at an astounding rate. How obstinate will you be when there's no one to feed, dress, fuck, or wipe your royal backside? Get me my people. Now."

A familiar chill runs up my spine, stealing my breath. I glance around the cell as though an ally may hide there, ready to discuss my reemerging attribute and make plans to break me out where I'm needed in the world. It must be my mind playing tricks, making excuses to socialize. *Nope.* Besides the group of guard-dog demis and my grandfather, I have no one. Unless Olineus and Trantus have warmed to me further. What would Lula say about this line of thought? She'd tell me that humans inspire her too. She puts their art in her home, and walks among them, listening in on conversations that she can't join. Zeus is still yammering, pacing in front of the bars, arms clasped behind his back. A scent infuses my mind. I'm imagining things. It's faint, a hint of Lula's skin, enough to make my heart stammer. Maybe it's raining there. I inhale long, hoping to drag more of the imagined smell to me, and for a moment, the invisible presence of her stands beside me.

"Let me through." Anice's voice breaks through my attention. "I need to see my brother. It's important."

The guards at the door shift out of sight. "No one shall pass without—"

A loud crack stops his words, and Anice pops in the doorway before hands grasp, attempting to drag him away. Olineus and Trantus surge forward, but Anice's wild eyes communicate enough. He feels it too.

I nod. *Go, brother.*

As he's shoved out, Comus sneaks past, showing his palms in surrender. His focus remains on me. "One down. Cold weather for me."

"Get them out!" Zeus roars.

Comus backs away, staring at him. "Cool your bolts. It's not our time yet, Your Majesty. You're going to want to free Alex if you want the chance to woo your kingdom back to your side. Arresting him was the worst idea." The cocky grin changes when he shoots a last glance on me. He's scared. Shit.

As guards shove him through the door, I yell, "Humans influence our birth attributes." When he does a quick turn, I add, "Am I right on that, Zeus?"

"Get him out!" He slaps the bars. "What did Comus's words mean? Will there be an attack?"

Comus's boots stomp the hall. *One down and he's going to cold weather?* The chain jingles as I walk three steps and spin. Our Alps house is the place we go most often that is cold. I stumble to a halt, chest seizing. Comus wouldn't reveal himself to Grace unless absolutely necessary. Like if there was a death of one of her sisters. *One down.*

"Fuck!" I grit my teeth to keep from asking Zeus if he killed a siren. He wouldn't act so aloof if he had, and I'll give away that we're in contact with them. What if it's Lula? I flex my fists, pushing the cord into my skin.

"What is it?" Zeus asks. "Are you detecting your attributes?"

"What do you think?" I kick at the bars with everything I have, and Zeus flinches back a step, wide eyes on me. It's good that I can't land a hit. My bones will be intact when I face Moros. "Let me out of here now."

The guards walk in, grumbling and shrugging their shoulders to reseat their armor. Blood cascades from one's broken nose, and the other has a fist-sized dent on his breastplate right over his heart. He breathes with sucking gasps. Zeus will see this as an attack on the royal army—an extension of himself—and punish my brother. We need to move faster than ever.

"Get to Anicetus and detain him," Zeus demands, fists clenched at his sides. He turns his focus on me. "You both feel the pull, do you not?" Stress lines twitch at his mouth. Does he seriously need a reminder of the stakes?

"Let me out of this cage so I can go with him. Otherwise you won't get Moros out of this realm. Each time he does this, we're one step closer to the world falling apart." Guards clatter after Anice. Trantus and Olineus stay, wide eyes focused on me, chained and behind golden bars. I must look insane. Tight muscles tremble with nervous rage under a bloodied, two-week-old shirt. "Anice is there by now, but he wouldn't leave a portal open because that would be irresponsible. Let me go and we'll end Moros's game or die trying."

His worst nightmare is having links to random places for armies of creatures or humans to storm into Olympus.

"Anicetus will perish without help." He lifts his chin as if I hadn't run every scenario through my mind.

I can't get the snarling grin off my face. I've won this round, but I'm not out of this cage. "Then you will lose a portal keeper. If Anice dies and I escape, which I will, I'll open a thousand portals leading to Olympus if my father hasn't done it yet. Mourning people do reckless things."

His golden eyes pierce me. "Do not spout false threats, Alexiares. If I have to imprison your father—"

"There is not a prison in the universe that can hold him. He's done with war though. Do not force his hand." Little by little we're closing in, taking a bite and waiting for more. He will give because he has to. The doom of Moros creeps over my skin. My mind flits between Lula and my attributes. *Let her be okay.* What if he has Venora and Hazel and didn't need both? Did he kill another at the place that flashes into view? An amphitheater. My chest tingles and that invisible drag begins, slowly winding between the location and me. The universe wants me there. The scent of sweat and ash on a chilled winter wind brushes over me with such force, it rustles my hair. A glimpse of auburn sears my mind.

Zeus signals out the door, and a face I didn't expect walks in with a guard. They've also bound Naea's arms, though with iron shackles instead of enchanted gold. She blinks in shock as her blue eyes flit over my appearance, then darts around the room, observing the guards. "Is there anyone you won't put into chains, Zeus?" I ask.

He steps in front of Naea. "You will calm yourself in the presence of your bride, Alexiares."

I tilt my head, studying Naea over Zeus's shoulder. Her eyes are puffy as well as her lips, and tear tracks streak her face. An unruly dark blonde tendril brushes her cheek. *What happened, Naea?*

"Leave us," I tell Zeus. "You want me to marry her? Let us speak in private."

"No." His chuckle rumbles around the small marble room, but there's no one joining now, not even a lip curl from any guard. "There will be no secrets any longer." Zeus gives her a nod. "Maybe your wife can talk sense into your thick head."

Naea shifts on her feet. "The Council shared that Moros returned. Can you find him?"

Well done, Naea. Rumors may fly, but she's so far in, Zeus is sharing information. And yet he has her shackled. I flex my fists. "Moros is in the realm. Yes, I can find him once I'm free."

Zeus steps forward. "If you willingly marry and commune with Naea until you produce a child, you may fight Moros as long as you follow my commands of how the portal is kept open. You will allow

Council members and guards to travel to and from the site. This threat cannot continue."

"As Moros is starting a war at the moment and communing will take a bit, that's not going to work out."

Naea's face is pale and tired. With a glance at Zeus and the guards, she mouths, "Plutus execution tomorrow." I blink at her and she makes the words once more, but unfortunately, I already understood. Zeus is taking out anyone standing in the way of his plans for us. We're in the desperate death throes of an overdue battle.

"Consider your options, Alexiares." His wild eyes widen, and a thrill-seeker's smile lights his face, as if the game's end is in sight. It is, but he doesn't know he's lost yet. "You will agree to my terms."

"No," I say without a pause. "There. They've been considered." While we're both out of time and one must concede, the chanting of discord outside has returned. I have support. The tides have shifted. Even Naea straightens when I answer, her down-set expression hardening. If I give up, I doom us all.

Zeus's smile falls. "Moros will kill your brother."

I step as close as my chains allow. "Then you'll be next. Moros despises you more than me for some reason. He'll find you the second your guard is down and wrap that hand around your throat. Then you won't have to worry about controlling anyone. You'll be a pile of ash, and your overbearing reign will die with you." The scene of war rolls through my mind and I hope I'm not too late. "I'm right. Decide."

He kicks the bars, making Naea jump back and the guards jerk to attention. I laugh because everyone in this room now knows how right I am. Zeus's demeanor boils into fury, releasing rumbling thunder outside.

Naea scrambles backward until she's pressed against the wall. Olineus shifts between her and his king, seeming to have forgotten his purpose is to keep Naea imprisoned. Zeus's own army doesn't trust him. Energetic currents shimmer through the room, flicking white off the ceiling, waiting to snap through the source of Zeus's strife as soon as he wills it to be. He can't kill me though. Not yet. And Lula is out there, I have to believe that. I lift my chin, welcoming his wrath if he decides to be that stupid. "Are you going to let me out of this cage or what?"

Chapter Eighteen

ALEX

THE FRESH SCENT OF AMBROSIA AND BELLFLOWER LACE THE WARM Olympian air. It's a stark contrast to the cell I occupied for a week. Instead of puffy, white clouds in a blue sky, dark gray waves coat the skies. Zeus is pissed, and though still bound, I'm walking away from the barracks with no deal. One task accomplished. Now Moros and then Lula.

My grandfather strides in front of me, Trantus and another walk behind, and Olineus stands at my side, holding the end of my wrist chains, keeping the length slack. Naea walks next to me, head high as if she weren't a king's prisoner. Twelve of Zeus's prized personal army flank us as we make our way along the golden street toward the massive crowd shifting to see over a wall of more guards. Prax is the tall corner of a triangle of Olympians, arms crossed over a black t-shirt. He has made his viewpoint known and several others have followed, wearing garments we've brought in over the years, or donning repurposed himation material to fit modern fashion. The textile deities must be thrilled. Goddesses stand out in greater numbers, unadorned hair loose and flowing over covered shoulders, their faces fuming with determination. Chanting and murmurs drift into pondering silence. Wide eyes watch us approach. Though I washed somewhat in the cell's basin, if Zeus were smart, he would have had me bathed before dragging me in front of this group gathered to support my release. My jeans, also blood-splattered, sit an inch lower on my hips. The onlookers on the sides of the road appear undecided on which faction they should support. They mill about on the grass, concerned eyes latched to the parade slowly marching toward the square. Some are motionless as statues, and several stumble away in haste the moment Zeus or I turn our gaze on them. Athena paces like a second-string reinforcement, swallowing nerves but eager to get in the game. As a Council member and her king's favored daughter, I'm surprised she's not leashed at Zeus's side.

"Alexiares!" My mother rushes forward, but the guards block her.

"Let it be known that I have sanctioned Alexiares's release out of goodwill toward my subjects." Zeus faces Prax and the rows of deities. When there are no cheers for his great line of bullshit, he reaches for my chain, tapping it with the massive ruby ring on his finger. The bindings wither and drip to the ground, writhing into nonexistence. That gets the crowd mumbling.

I stretch my sore arms, wincing at the pull. "All the incredible talent in Olympus and you resort to witchcraft…as usual. Did you at least work on a solution for Moros with your witches?"

Zeus's lips rise in a sneer, but my mother barrels in, taking my scruffy face in her hands. "I won't see you and Anicetus harmed further," she whispers. "Please, do as he asks."

I turn my head to kiss her palm and ready myself to apologize for the stubbornness I still possess, but the crowd gasps. My grandmother appears from between two deities on the grass and steps onto the golden street. "Hebe, none of that. Come here." Where did she pop in from?

Some Olympians drop to a knee, others bow regarding the queen. I nod in thanks, and by the slight tip of her head, she hasn't abandoned me to her husband.

My attribute barrels through me tenfold, blanking my vision to a sea of human faces, spinning to a fuzzy version of my brother's curses. "Anice needs my help," I tell my mother, kissing her cheek. "I'll be as safe as possible."

"And they *both* will return directly after." Zeus snaps his fingers.

The guards move with a swiftness only manageable with planned knowledge. Three block my path, Trantus with a pauldron against my chest, hands on my shoulders. "Settle, Alexiares," he says before I even flinch. Olineus escorts Ichnaea toward the barracks with a gentle hand on her elbow. They talk, heads bowed together as if both understood this outcome. They'd be the only ones. My mother yelps as a guard snatches her wrists and binds them before nudging her to follow the others.

"What are you doing?" I push at Trantus. "You're going to get yourself killed and not by me." I signal to the crowd. Glaring Olympians grumble their dissent, shifting closer. Prax moves forward with four familiar deities, but gets blocked by another line of guards. He glances at me and I shake my head. If we fall into battle now, we lose no matter the outcome.

Hebe struggles in the binding. "Father?"

My grandfather stares at me, stone-faced from behind his soldiers. "I do not trust you to return after completing this task. Your mother and soon-to-be wife will warm your cell. If you do not return the moment Moros is where he belongs, the punishment of your treason starts with your mother. We will go slow to give you time to come to your senses."

"The punishment for treason is death," I yell at him, chest tightening as panic takes hold. "You can't do this. She's your daughter."

"I have many children, Alexiares. Go in haste. I must prepare to meet Moros. Leave the portal open." He walks toward the barracks within the safety of his wall of guards. He is preparing for war because I've had enough. Though it surprises me that he hasn't attacked the group starting to circle me appearing relieved but nervous. One thing at a time. Moros.

Mother gives a sob that claws my lungs, her eyes scanning between the demigods dragging her away and me, but then her gaze sticks on something over my shoulder and she stops struggling.

Behind me, my grandmother stands with balled fists and red cheeks. Thank goodness this wasn't her plan. I shove Trantus off me. Prax steps in beside me, tossing the other two guards toward the barracks. "Follow your master to your doom, little pups."

I didn't expect my guards to join me, but this? "I fear for you, friend," I tell Trantus as he backs away from us. "Don't lose yourself to his lunacy. If my mother or Ichnaea are harmed..." I trail off. He's well versed in my threats.

He gives a faint nod. At least he's not completely lost. The others pull him toward the barracks, coaxing him with commination toward me and the traitors of Olympus.

"Excerebrose cowards," Prax bellows to their backs.

I pat his chest. "They will understand soon enough. Any news on *her*?"

"No. I'm sorry." He turns to face me, squeezing my shoulder. "You look as if you've already been through war. We've missed you, Alex."

I return the gesture, then lean to pat Zephyrus's bowed head. "I've worried for you all and need a full recap, but we have a problem."

"Anice and Rath are already there," Prax says.

"Any idea who could have fallen?" There are too many ears around to be specific.

"No."

"Then it's time to stop Moros." Then find Lula. I've done it before —pinpointed her location because I'm hers. I blow out a long breath. "Okay, here goes."

I pivot to face the crowd edging forward. All of Olympus has turned out and I'm glad to see a hefty portion sending me encouraging nods or aiming outraged glares at the barracks. We weren't wrong to aim for change. My attribute buzzes loud, and visions of a mass of gathered people blank my eyesight for a moment. *One thing, then another.*

"My brothers and sisters." I rub my tingling wrists. "We have many problems on our hands. First, I must open a portal because Moros has returned and is causing trouble on Earth."

The crowd edges forward, and I speak louder over their chatter. "We will stop Moros before he does irreparable damage to Earth and it's beings, so now is not the time to revolt." I raise a palm and focus, allowing my attribute to pinpoint me to the location. "Let's do that when we return."

Several deities laugh, but most still scowl and move closer as the murmuring gets louder. "Do you know where Comus is?" I ask Prax, opening the portal.

He nods, lips tight. "With Grace." Being with Lula during her heat phase was a highlight in my long life, but I'd fallen for her, wanted her. Praxis and Grace were strangers, but no matter how awkward it must have been between them, there's no forgetting something that powerful.

The scent of pine and people hits me along with the chill. East coast America. My stomach drops. That's too close to Lula's house for my liking.

Something makes me turn back. My grandmother remains on the street, hair wound tight and himation perfectly draped. She only watches me, eyes as cunning as a fox.

I jog over to take her hand, pressing it to my forehead. "Will they be okay?" I whisper.

"Do not be careless, Alexiares, and everything will be as it should."

If I return. The remaining undecided deities face us in observation. Even Athena stayed. She grips the hilt of the sword at her side and gives the slightest nod. Taking a deep breath, I turn, nearly toppling a god—oracle. *The* oracle. At least Zeus doesn't have her locked away scrying for Lula. I tilt my head. "Pythia?" Her chestnut eyes are almost angry.

With twitchy motions, she raises a fist, spreads dark fingers, and presses a shaking hand to my chest. "Go in peace and in haste, Demigod of Warding off Wars." She pulls her heated palm away, sending a chill over my shoulders, then pivots, walking alone toward Zeus's home.

I wait for the pain of a curse or a vision she's rumored to be able to project, but there's nothing. Has she ever touched me?

"Alex?" Zeph asks. "You okay?"

When I glance toward the temple, Pythia is gone. Did I imagine her? My attributes sear and I jog to the portal and through it, Prax and Zeph behind me, and Olympians filing in after us. There's drab, winter grass under our feet, a wall of trees to our right, and a vast human crowd tiered on a hill with a staircase. They all stare at a wooden structure to our left. The crunch of a fist against flesh has me running, but I have to dodge a small group of humans running toward an open set of gates.

Deimos stands on the stage of an amphitheater, a brunette woman behind him, clutching his sides. She has to be a siren. Is he protecting her? I sprint up the stairs. His head whips around and he raises a lip to sneer. He kicks out at me, but his timing is off and he misses. I don't, and send him sprawling with a left hook. The siren screams and cowers, clamoring away as if I'm the bad guy, but Rath appears behind her, nods at me, swoops her waist, and they dissipate into the shadows.

"No!" Lula's cry of frustration is heaven to my ears. I whip around but my view is blocked by the Olympians chasing after Deimos and the chaotic scatter of humans. Anice circles the escaped Olympian guard who holds the throat of a little girl and smiles at my brother, though blood seeps from between his teeth over a split lip. Humans scream like they've been harnessed into a torture device and I regret not hanging on to the God of Terror so I could punch him some more. Lula is here though, and her sister is safe. The others clear out of my way and my heart clunks, too big and wild for my chest. She's alive, but standing behind Moros, hand on his shoulder, whispering to him as if I'm not here. Moros keeps his black eyes on mine. "Everyone, calm down," she says, loud, but gentle.

I could melt at the sound of her voice but relief crashes against anxiety. She's still not in my arms, not safe while next to Moros. He found her. The humans sprinting slow to a walk or stop in place and the screaming fades out to silence.

I drop down from the stage. "Get away from him, Lula."

I stumble into a person, accidently knocking them to the ground. "Sorry," I murmur, lifting them up and continuing on. Prax shuffles behind me while others circle around, weaving between the humans, clearly distracted by them. The scent of urine burns my nose like an inhale of astringent. What happened to these people?

Moros holds a woman, his deadly hand clutching her throat but she doesn't fight or even seem to notice. I halt, raising an arm to prevent the others from passing me. He would kill her with no more thought than stepping on a flower.

Moros signals to me. "And see?" he asks, amusement lacing his words. "Our enemies have arrived. More will come. What are you going to do about it, daughter?"

Though I'm not moving forward, it feels like I stumble. The world situates into a bleak, lung-bursting breath-hold. I take in her hard scowl, the shape of her wild green eyes as they track me from head to toe. Her hair is the exact shade of Moros's. "Lula," I whisper.

She looks like she's going to cry or punch me. "It was you."

The hard line of Moros's lips soften and curve upward. There is nothing similar about their smiles.

Chapter Nineteen

LULA

ALEX HALTS SO CLOSE I COULD HIT HIM WITH A WELL-THROWN ROCK. His new beard growth is scraggly and only holds my attention for the splittest of seconds because enough blood coats his clothes to make my stomach do a two-story backflip. He killed my sister in ways I don't want to think possible from any sane being. Tears spring to my eyes and I fight the urge to crumple. I never saw this coming, not from him. I'd hoped the strain in Moros's voice when he suggested that Alex struck again was a tell when he lied. But there's so much blood and Moros has known him longer than me. He warned me so many times.

My father puts his free arm around my waist. "Now is the time to strike, daughter," he whispers against my ear. "You must acknowledge. Sirens are nothing, but as a hybrid goddess you will overtake the Olympians with ease. Send the humans for them so you may concentrate."

"Lula?" Alex asks, brows furrowed as he stares at Moros's hand on my hip, and studies my body like he's checking every inch. Probably making sure his goods aren't damaged. Golden eyes fill with concern and he inches closer, head forward and tilted, reminding me of when Gerty died and he held me, sitting on a hotel room bed pretending my heartbreak was his too. I bet Olympus has never had a better actor.

I pull away from Moros's grip and whisper, "Go home and forget this day," to the nearest humans, who turn and weave through the crowd.

"Lula," my father says through bared teeth.

I shrug, eyeing the woman he grips, hoping he doesn't harm her. "It's too crowded." I turn to Alex, but keep my gaze past him, because looking at him is too difficult. "Where's Hazel?" I rub the soreness still stretching through my chest.

"In a safe place." Keeping a good distance from me, Alex offers a hand as if I'd take it. The days of stepping into his warmth are long gone. "Lula, be careful of them."

"I am," I whisper. "Make Rath bring her back."

"But…" Alex keeps his eyes on Firthus and Moros. "No."

The poor child Firthus is clutching like a shield doesn't deserve this fate. No one does.

Anice takes Alex's side and nods at him, but Firthus keeps his grip until he's beside Moros, then lets me drag her from his grip and send her to what I can only hope is safety. Anice is clean and strong compared to Alex. My heart hurts, caving in and itching, forcing me to clench my teeth to force away the tears. Was Alex tracking Amah through jungles and woods? Did he listen in on our last phone call and track her, or did they catch up with Grace? I didn't think he would do something so cruel to punish me for running from him. I want to question him, but if I open my mouth now, the emotion lodged tight in my throat will escape in uncontainable anguish. I can't hurt the humans.

"Lula?" Alex's head swivels, observing the faces around us, trying to put together the pieces that will sway me to his will. Never again. "What did he tell you?"

"The truth." Moros smiles. "Unlike yourself from what I understand."

I wish I could acknowledge. More deities spill from the blue chasm of Alex's power on top of the hill. We're surrounded and outnumbered. "Ah-ah," Moros says as Alex takes another step. "Don't come closer." He shakes the woman in his other hand until I pat his shoulder. The twinkling joy in his eye dulls when he looks at me and my overblown humanity, but he loosens his hold on her. With a sigh, he turns back to Alexiares. "Bring Hera to me. Tell her I have something I want her to see."

"Lula can't be here," Alex growls. "This stops today and others are coming. Let her and the humans leave. Now, before it's too late." I could laugh. They have us. We're done.

Firthus sidles up next to us, facing the other direction. "Where did Deimos go?"

Moros keeps his eyes on Alex. "To continue my decree. Pull your weapons and be ready if my daughter won't protect herself." How? One by one, the Olympians will kill each of my sisters, and Alex is their death dealer. Odd that his murderous hands are so clean. Why didn't he change his clothes too? The blood is dark brown, layered and splattered far over every inch of cloth, as if the torture he inflicted took hours or even days, and he wears the evidence of his gruesome heart to prove his deeds. A tear escapes, as does a pained squeak from my throat.

Firthus shifts and pulls out two handguns, splaying his arms wide to aim toward Alex and behind us at the others closing in. "Get the queen now. Mortals made superior weapons. You can taste how they die if you come closer."

I put a hand on his shoulder. "Wait. I have to make the humans leave."

Moros claps his hand over my mouth. "No, daughter."

"Stop calling her that." Alex stares hard at me. "That can't be."

"Oh, it is." Moros holds tight, though I struggle, gripping his wrist with both hands. He gasps before going predatorially still. "Greetings, lovely one." His voice is a melted, lax version from normal. "It's a delight to set my sights upon you again, Hera."

The goddess stands between lines of humans, waving a hand in front of faces, then focuses on me. Her wide eyes are a stunning blue, the color of Earth's cobalt oceans from space. I don't want to drag my gaze from their endless pull, but Moros uncovers my mouth and takes a small step to the side.

"I improved your creation," he says. "See what we can do together?"

Her brows knit in perplexity that doesn't fit her physiognomy. She's a stranger, but holds herself like someone who doesn't experience confusion often. I, however, probably have the emotion painted all over my face.

"Creation?" I whisper. He can't mean me.

Alex appears equally shocked and stares at…Hera. The one who told Amah to scatter and stay away from her sisters.

"Flank the area. Enclose them." A booming voice bellows over the growing murmurs of the crowd. "Archers, get in position. Do not let them escape again."

A stream of men with golden armor flood out behind another who has a bushy beard and shoulder-length brunette waves, giving him a ruggedness that doesn't match his full Greek-god warrior costume. His body is as defined and big as Alex's. Zeus? My heart double-times and I shift against Moros. Firthus laughs, a ripped cackle that's the opposite of happy.

Alex snaps out of his confusion and pivots, splaying his arms at the army filing in. "Halt! I need to speak to them."

I'm in a weird time hop back to the days of knights and sword fighting as a bunch of armor-plated archers clank into a surrounding curved line and push forward.

Moros shakes me. "Reach. Now. Firthus, now."

The guns go off and a guard standing next to Zeus cries out, hit in his uncovered thigh. The others halt, helmets turned to watch their fallen comrade.

"Let her go," I whisper to Moros, flitting my eyes to his captor. "The humans need to be out of this."

The imposing armored deity sidles up next to Hera. "Moros," he growls. Hera grasps his wrist to halt him, and my father growls.

"Hera," Moros says. "We must discuss what I made you." To me he whispers, "She won't kill you, but the others will. Find your courage, daught—go no further, Anicetus." Moros drags me closer. "I won't return to the hell realm. The queen and I shall settle this."

"Alexiares," Zeus booms. He jerks free of Hera and storms forward. "Now."

Alex shows his teeth and clasps hands with Anice. They both raise a palm.

Moros growls as they open a portal, spilling amber light through the slip between realms. "I'm not going back. And stay over there,

King." Moros spits the word in a way that proves how little he thinks of the leader of Olympus. "Hera. Come, speak with me."

So that's Zeus. His glaring golden eyes match Alex's.

"This is not the way to gain my attention, Moros." Hera stays where she stands, chin lifted, shoulders back. "Release her. All of them and surrender."

My father snorts. "I will do—"

"Where is Aglaope?" The king stares at me. "You are of her line," he says, as if that would automatically give us a homing device to each other. I wish it would.

I stay silent.

A flinch from Hera pulls my attention. She stares at me then Moros, Zeus then Alex. It's like she can't quite figure out which wire to cut on a ticking bomb and I utterly get that. Clouds roll in as if in a time-lapse movie. "Tell me," Zeus booms.

Alex whips toward him. "Stop. We need to figure out what's going on before you toss bolts at anyone." He points at the surrounding guard. "Stand down."

Moros drags me in front of him. "Aglaope is gone, Zeus."

Under cloudy skies, a silence falls over the huge crowd that is so bated, my own ragged breathing fills the space. The large white feathers attached to some of the soldiers' helmets dance in the gentle breeze. If the archers fire, I won't be the only casualty unless they have impeccable aim.

Moros reaches over my shoulder to turn my face to him. His black eyes are wide and demanding. "Kill them. Reach out with your mind and kill them all."

"What?"

"What if I said you are our only hope?" He grins like a madman, eyes shifting to Hera.

I shake my head. Dammit, what is with the gods and their stupid politics? "I don't want to kill anyone."

"Now, daughter. You must."

"What is this?" Zeus yells. "You created an abomination?"

Alex shifts between me and the group. "Wait. We need to find out more."

What else could he need to know after stalking me—

A deafening crack sounds and green light flashes hot in my vision, blinding me. A hot tingle rolls over my skin, thrumming in my chest. Screams and gasps echo through the rumbling white noise but one bellowed, "no," sounds above the rest. Alex's terrified cry is so raw, that though I'm so angry, a thread of worry for him goes through me. Moros leaves me, and I sink to my knees because whatever is happening surges energy through me until I feel like I'll pop. I clutch at grass that breaks apart in my grip. What happened? Growls and the thwacks of fists to flesh sound around me, but my vision is big spots of red, a negative to the green glow. I flinch and cover my ears as another blast rumbles the ground. Then another. More screams.

I inhale a long choking breath that singes. The smell of charcoal overtakes the air and I slap at a burning sensation on my shoulder. My shirt has a huge hole and dust coats my fingers. My vision clears to fuzzy bubbles of color and zooming shapes that divert when I focus on them. I blink and cough puffs of smoke.

"Alex?" I ask, but I can't hear anything.

The veil of my hair comes into vision first. It's shorter, red curls frizzy with singed ends. To my right, Firthus stares with cloudy eyes. He's on his back on the blackened ground. Smoke billows from his body and the burned grass beneath him. His face is gray, and black blood drips from his nose and ears.

"Oh my god." I scramble backward, bumping into something. My holey, singed pant leg splits, exposing my unmarked flesh up to my thigh, and there's an itch on my left side. My torn shirt flickers with flames. I smack that out and take in the rest of the scene in my overexposed vision. The thing I'm butted up to is the woman my father had kept close, but she's unmoving. Patterns of crimson lightning tattoo her face. All humans within a ten-foot circle around me lie on the ground, smoke curling from their bodies. I cover my broken sob and clutch my chest. Other's stand still, but their wide eyes beam like spotlights of terror. Why didn't I make them leave?

Alex is breathing as if he ran miles, and he reaches for me. I slap his hand and stagger to my feet. He follows me up, sinking both hands in his hair. His eyes are wet. Why? Zeus, Anice, and Prax wrestle Moros to the ground, putting their focus on pinning his arms. Smoke pours from him too. Tattered clothing ripping further as he fights.

Prax cries out and jerks back, gripping his blackening arm. Two men drag him away.

"Lula?" Alex whispers "Lula?" My name is an odd, panicked mantra on his lips. He says it on repeat, always a raspy question that tugs at me.

The fallen bodies smoke. Firthus's clouded eyes stay unblinking at nothing.

The sound of a bone breaking pops through the air, making me wince as someone cries out.

"Stop." Damn this itch in my lungs. So many humans are down. Twenty, maybe? Thirty?

Zeus's shock is brief and he sneers. Bright light flashes again, this time white. Warm tingles travel through me, connecting me to the sky and Earth.

Alex yelps, tossed backward by a stray white streak. Anice tackles him when he pushes himself up and moves toward me.

It's not as jarring now or blinding. Everyone watches me. Hera stands back from the pile of wrestling gods my father is beneath, holding a hand over her heart. "It's true."

"Yes." Moros, face pale, gives off a chuckle I haven't heard before. It raises chill bumps on my neck. "See what we can make together? Unkillable like me. Perfect like you."

Zeus roars and lifts his arms, causing everyone except the mesmerized humans to scream and cower. A barrage of white and green streaks flashes down around me, into me, though I no longer flinch. "Stop," I yell into a void. "You're hurting them." The ground sinks, and another round of ash makes me cough. Is there anything good about Olympians?

When my vision clears, the others stand, slack-jawed and staring, exchanging confused glances. One person stands out, close behind Alex. Dark, decadent…Jordan? He drops his gaze.

My head spins again, taking me to the evening I met Alex. Humans never approached me so aggressively. I was accosted by a gang right after a pediatric nurse confessed his craving for murder. That wannabe serial killer stares at me now, gaze pleading instead of vacant, though I never actually enthralled him, did I? How many other liars did Alex send into my world, and why? The humans remain still and innocent. They lie too, but never to me.

My ability's always been a curse—something I'd do many things to be rid of. I realize now, making anyone honest is my greatest gift. Before I met gods, no one had lied to me. It's all deities do. My pain grows into a living, breathing entity, lighting my chest in flame— though the lightning surrounding me should be what hurts more, but it doesn't. I lift my hand, watching sparks twist like they're tasting my skin or trying to find an entrance to get inside me, but there's none. My father was right. I am a goddess. Have I acknowledged?

No one runs to help, except Anice wrestling Alex to keep him from me. I'm not sure why he's keeping the show up now. The rest watch, silent and complacent as their murderer king attacks, but his weapon only causes an itch over my skin. Lightning still falls in a cascade of flashes, as if enough of it will activate my death sequence. "This is what the Earth has as protectors?" I yell through the sparks, unsure if anyone can hear me. "This is who leads the realm?" A few more humans fall and guilt rises again.

No.

The tingle heats. I drag it in, try to absorb it as if I could grip it and do something, anything to stop Zeus. He should hurt and leave forever.

The lightning slows, and his face contorts to a scrunched-up grimace. He growls, but it slides into a whimper before he falls to his knees, abruptly halting the light show. Alex stares up at me from under Anice. Anice's eye is red and swollen, making him fit Alex's less-than-fresh look a bit more. Moros smiles wide, two deities in the throes of his doom thrashing beside him. They're all evil.

Moros struggles to rise, one arm bent at an awkward angle. "Now, Lula. They cannot kill you. Accept what you are and destroy them. Cleanse the Earth."

I drag a battered piece of fabric up to my shoulder and fight a crashing wave of nausea. The black tips of my hair crumble under my fingertips. I suck in a deep breath and let my intention fill to bursting. "You will remember nothing from today. Go home and live peacefully."

"No, Lula," Moros yells. "Call the humans back and have them attack the gods. Now!" He grabs the throat of the nearest soldier, and before I can yell "stop," it's done. The deity only struggles a moment on his knees before slumping to the blackened ground. The divine onlookers gasp, and some flee around the building. The ones near Moros retreat, taking their places beside Zeus. The mass of humans files away from the site in silence, even those who should be too far to hear me. The shuffle of feet against grass is the only sound, but it stings my ears like buzzing bees. There are too many lying on the ground. Zeus remains panting on his knees as if there's no more energy in him.

Alex struggles out of Anice's grip and stumbles forward, but I shake my head and wave him off, backing away. "Why?" I aim the word at everyone remaining as I take in the death surrounding me. "They were innocent."

Zeus seethes, but he's only pitiful scum on his knees. "Abomination."

"You don't even know me. You tossed my species from Olympus, forced us to walk the Earth alone with a deadly weapon you're immune to, and the first moment you see me, you try to murder me? These people were innocent. They lived their lives here, happy with —" I swallow a sob, bending to close the eyes of an old woman, purse still slung over her shoulder. "With family, friends, and you ended that forever. What is wrong with you?" I ball my fists and look over the crowd. "What is wrong with all of you? You're sick. Psychotic." I pause my glare on Alex. "Manipulating liars."

"Sire?" A thick god lifts Zeus to his feet. The creases of his expression remind me of Comus and I wonder where he is. Probably cleaning up Alex's mess. Hunting my sisters. They have Hazel. I take a deep breath and wipe my eyes with the back of my hand.

Zeus points at me. "Kill her. She must not live."

"Oh, go to hell," I tell him and mean it so much. Damn these terrible beings. I've never appreciated being a siren more. It was good they discarded us for so long. "You've had millennia and you've spent it like"—I signal at him, rucked-up himation now stained with grass and ash—"like this. A closed-minded murderer."

"Get off of me." Alex shrugs free of Anice and puts himself between me and Zeus. "Leave her be."

I rub the ache in my chest, the sore tingling that only warms with my motion. "Too late. Stop pretending to—"

Zeus sneers. "I will do no such—"

"Stop." Hera shushes our argument.

Moros presses close to me. "You've done well, daughter, but it's time to strike out against the gods and end this reign for good. They cannot kill us." He wraps his hand around my throat and squeezes, dragging me in front of him. "Step back, Alexiares," Moros yells next to my ear. There's a tingle against my skin under his choking grip. "I will do what I must."

Why does everyone think that my life is theirs to do whatever they want with?

"Let her go," Alex shouts, and thunder rumbles the ground again as Zeus stands taller. "Her eyes. Moros, let her go." He paces, jaw and fists clenched, face a mask of concern mixed with utter ferocity.

Moros's grasp tightens, and he turns me to look me over. He smiles. "I have been patient, daughter, but time is short and I must help you. Whatever you reject, allow it to surface. You are halfway there. Accept it fully. Focus and release your other side."

"I'm only me," I whine, tapping his arm to tell him to let up.

"Aim," Zeus yells.

"Zeus, wait," Hera says. "Don't—"

"You can't force her into it." Alex gives a harsh growl. "If you care for her at all, you will loosen your grip." He moves forward, and Anice sidles up next to him, hand on his shoulder to hold him back.

Everyone needs to get away from me. I imagine myself in a sea of white emptiness that matches my heart. A place where I don't have to hear the lies of gods. I longed for each one from Alex's lips. For a moment, I believed I was the luckiest otherworldling in the realm.

"Fire!"

The sharp twang of weapons released makes me flinch for the sting, but a wind hits us hard instead, and the arrows slow, then tumble to pierce the ground where humans used to stand. Jordan and another god, similar in appearance and standing beside him, lower their arms.

Stars blink in my vision and ice fills my veins. There's shouting as time slows. Movement that's drunk and wobbly. More words. More wind. Rumbling earth. A woman's voice in my head telling me to be strong. "Keep fighting." It sounds so real. "I told you to stop," the woman says but this time it's outside of my head.

"Too late," Moros says. "You will thank me later."

I shove at Moros's arms as if I'm shoving these deities away from me. Make me alone. Free me from this madness of murderers and control. The chill in my veins heats and tingles. My chest burns, and maybe it's my death this time. My soul breaking from its bonds. I hope I don't hurt my remaining sisters too badly. The hand on my throat flexes, toying with my breath and blood. It's time to leave me untouched. Haven't they all done enough? Can I not die as I lived? Alone.

I grind my nails into Moros's skin, letting my anger boil. Is anyone safe? *Get off of me*, I will into his mind. I grit my teeth and try to growl, but no breath means no sound. *Unhand me.*

The flesh under my fingers gives way until I clench air. I'm falling. Screams are an echo in a distant cave. The grip on my throat loosens then drops away, and I drag in a ragged wheeze, filling my lungs before my chest forces it out again and repeats, trying to catch lost oxygen. Gray fingers part ashen grass, and when I push off the ground, I realize they're mine. My insides swoop as if I'm soaring high on a playground swing and I try to brush off the ash, but it doesn't come off. Charcoal tendrils weave up my hands in a chaotic fishnet. I'd panic, but I'm distracted by the heat in my chest itching to escape. It pushes out to my limbs with a fiery tickle. The world slaps back into place, nearly sending me tumbling, but I remain upright on shaky legs.

"What did you do?" Moros whines.

He lies on the ground behind me, convulsing with trembles, and gripping his arm below a stump where his hand used to be. Where there should be blood and gore, a cloud of black flecks swirl. They also spiral around the dissection point of his severed hand, lying on the grass beside me.

I did this? My fingers go to my throat. It stings and I wince, coughing ash. He tried to kill me too?

"Lula?" Alex's face is pale.

Alex is closer to me than before, and Anice is fully hugging him from behind, arms seat-belted around his chest. The portal rip glimmers behind them.

Alex shrugs off his brother and moves toward me, but I don't want him close. He slows to a stop and presses the air with open palms, but his hands rebound. He leans forward in midair, eyes flicking, searching for something, then glances at the other wide-eyed Olympians before refocusing on me. "Containment field? Let me in, Lu."

"Release me, Lula." Moros trembles, face pallid.

"Attack!" Zeus advances at a jog.

"God, would everyone shut up?" My head is a near-popping balloon, but stuffed with cotton and sharp ice cubes.

Zeus smacks into something a few feet from me and bounces off, crashing to the ground. Three guards do as well. It slices my mind, leaving a spider web of sparks throughout, and I rub my temples, but my fingers are sore too. "Ow."

The gray on my hands darkens—weaving a sparkling pattern on my skin like pixels on a stretched photograph. The flecks glitter and shift as I wiggle my gunmetal digits. Moros's arm jerks, and his freed hand slides toward me across the grass. I ignore his screams and tilt my head. This can't be.

Lifting my fingers gives me the sensation of tugging invisible threads and Moros's arm moves my way, dragging him along. As he travels the ground, he reaches for his detached appendage, but I flick and the hand flies toward Zeus. It smacks him in the chest and drops into his palms. Zeus jerks and releases Moros's appendage to the charred grass.

"Is that what you wanted?" I stretch my arms and take a deep breath that carries a rich, metallic scent like rusted batteries. The world spins and crushes inward like it's trying to squish me out of it. Maybe it is. I don't belong. "How about you, Father? Does this please you?" I raise my hand, and the glitter flecks surrounding his arm tug him to his knees. It stings my chest and sends another sharp slice through my brain. I need to get out of here and figure out what happened to me.

Chapter Twenty

ALEX

Zeus tosses Moros's detached limb to the ground and I can't drag my eyes away from it—the pale skin paler, the place that should gush blood and tendons is a neat line of moving luminous black flecks. Lula disarmed—literally—a deadly, divine weapon. It injured Prax and killed three gods. They lie still on lightning-scarred earth, sending wafts of acrid perfume through the air from their charred necks. One of them is Olineus, and that fact hits me harder than expected, tightening my already tight chest and stinging sore eyes. I'd grown to understand him, and he me, I believe. We didn't agree, but we were working toward middle ground. Oli won't stand again and chastise me for being disruptive and obstinate. There are far more humans scattered around. Zeus holds responsibility for ending most of them, but he will consider the death of deities infinitely worse. But Lula…

A hundred-year plan heads toward fruition, and our key component is a hybrid goddess. Not only a hybrid, but one with Moros's unusual blood, and she's rare-form. Lula's skin is a patterned shimmery ash, her lips and hands a shade from black, and she's still the most beautiful being I've ever seen. It may take her a while to figure out how to turn this phase on and off. Rath is a rare-form. When he acknowledged, it took him a week to shift back from the shadows. His irises were fogged, and gray circled his features for years after. He's not a hybrid, but it makes me wonder about their instant connection. To me, there's never another being like Lula, but I didn't realize she was singular to this degree. Even though her eyes have the color and eerie gleam of hematite, they still contain the same fire and compassion I love about her. I only wish I wasn't the recipient of her abhorrence.

"Lula?" I ask, pressing into the invisible field I can only guess she created. What is she? Protector or fighter? Provider, healer, or element handler? What did the humans need two centuries ago that they created her? "Lula, please."

Her unusual glare slices into me, pouring in shame like a poisoned blade. We've done nothing but hurt her, and with Moros as her father, she will never receive a warm welcome. I tracked her down, followed her, and brought her into this life. The regret is visceral. It rolls over me in crumbling mortar—inflicting sharp smacks of nausea, crushing every cell in my body.

She steps forward, and the invisible wall keeping me from her shifts, but only an inch. I'm not sure where she plans on going. I glance back at Zeus, but he's still staring at the hand. Moros has plagued the king for longer than I've been alive, and Lula disabled his power in seconds as an untried goddess. Zeus should worship her, but he won't.

I should have somehow known this about her. Moros was killing so many during that time; I'm not sure why we didn't think that he could have been forcing himself on otherworldling species as well. Are there others like Lula? Did Zeus's personal oracle miss hunting down some hybrids, or did Zeus and Pythia give up the murder spree when they separated us from the Earth?

The odd, springy force field Lula constructed holds firm under my palms. Words whirl around me, but I miss plucking them from the air. I have no excuses for her. I should comfort her, guide her, tell her it will all be okay, but I keep repeating her name. She's alive after numerous death bolts from Zeus. They may not have killed Moros, but he cried out, giving a few a moment to pin him—though it didn't last—but the bolts didn't hurt her. The worst is over and it can only get better now.

Her mouth firms into a straight line, and she squeezes her eyes shut for a moment before glancing at the hell-plane portal again. Her attention is so steady on it, I wonder if she senses the creatures within. "An oracle needs to read you," I whisper. Zeus won't allow her into Olympus, though he's going to have to. She's ready to inflict pain and is too powerful. "You need training." She could bring down the world. "Let me help."

"Get up," she commands Moros, voice strained.

He gasps, pale and kneeling, gripping his arm as if trying to stop major bleeding, but there's no blood, only the shiny black flecks of Lula's creation.

"Lula?" I ask. "Hey, let me help."

Her jaw sets and she won't look at me.

Rath may get further with her. Blame doesn't fall as heavily on him as me, and he relates to her more being young, unsupported, and born illegally by Zeus's laws. They're two talented peas in a blind, decaying pod. Still, I can't let this riff between Lu and I grow any further. I'm not even sure explaining what she's probably feeling will help until we understand her divine designation and are not surrounded by enemies.

I nudge Anice and whisper, "Get Rath here as soon as he can leave Hazel."

He steps back and pulls his phone from his pocket, gently clicking over buttons.

Moros breathes heavy, tattered breaths as shiny blackness wanders his mangled limb like it's searching for something. "Daughter, give it back, and I promise no harm will come to you or your sisters."

Lula squints down at him, lips parted to say something, though she remains silent. The invisible field she has around her softens against me but still won't give. She erratically moves her fingers. Moros's stub jerks and he cries out. Lula's hand trembles as it moves down, and his forearm lowers, her head tilting as she tests her new power. When someone acknowledges, there's a panel of deities to guide them to their powers and influence. She's alone in her discovery. No one has attributes such as these.

The others murmur curious guesses, but they stay clear while I inch toward her.

"Stand." Lula flicks her hand, and Moros's arm lifts until it forces him to his feet. Besides his moans, there's no sound in the amphitheater, even from Zeus, who now has his eyes up, watching her. Lula controls all the attention and a monster that took us years to get out of the realm. We couldn't handle him, and our only choice was to drop him into hell.

She lifts him until he's on tiptoes and then twitches her fingers, raising him further. "Aren't you so pleased with me...*Father*?" Her voice is shaky but playful until she says "Father." It lights a nervous trail up my spine. Until now, dangerous wasn't a word that would have fit Lula. Even with her previous siren thrall, she was never a threat. With a clench of her fist, Moros drops to the ground with a grunt. She presses both hands to her forehead.

"Lula, tell me what you're feeling." There is so much wrong, but the stress lines on her face and her trembles go beyond stress. "Talk to me."

She jerks up to study her darkened hands. "Fuck you. Good talk."

"Turn him over to the divine guard, siren." My grandfather's voice booms through the silence, though there's a wavering question to it. "You are both summoned to Olympus to stand trial."

Lula turns to give Zeus a chilling look, enhanced by the shade of her eyes. The guards next to him shift back a step.

"I have no intention of going with you anywhere." She holds my gaze. "Going with *any* of you anywhere."

Before I have time to be heartbroken over her statement, Zeus's voice booms again. "You will turn yourself over to us immediately."

Thunder crackles and before I can yell a warning, a bright shot of lightning snakes down and attaches to Lula. When the flashes stop, her eyes are closed and her lips parted in an exhale. She laughs, a dark and honest note of disbelief mixed with disappointment. "You're my father's big challenge?" She tilts her head, her silvery gaze an inextinguishable torch. "You're *the king*? I expected more."

More bolts rain down on her. Current nips at my feet, sending my nerves dancing. I take a few steps back, but Zeus rushes, slamming into the invisible barrier around her. He roars and guards come to his side to fight air. But not all of them. Others stare, shocked and processing. Trantus and another stand over Olineus's body, as does Hera, except her inquisitive gaze is locked on Lula. A guard takes

Moros's hand, placing it on a shield. It could be a Halloween prop at a haunted house, except it's not made of plastic. It raises, and the demigod in charge of it gasps. Zeus dashes to grab at it, lightning ceasing, but Lula twists her wrist, wincing, and it shifts out of reach.

He misses, then tries again, slashing through the air. "Stop. Moros may not have his power back." It becomes a weird game of *try-to-snag-the-hand*. I'd laugh if this situation weren't so dire. Zeus gives up and glares at Lula. "Daughter of Aglaope, I demand that you—"

The hand freezes midair, then flies forward to smack my grandfather on his left cheek. Olympus can probably hear the synchronized gasp of deities. "My name is Lula. You will shut up before I separate your head from your body and toss both parts around the skies. I'm sure I'd succeed if I try hard enough." A furrow creases on her sweat-speckled forehead as if she's concentrating, and for a moment I think she may do it until she clutches at her chest and grimaces.

My fingers tingle with stress. "It can hurt if you don't control it. I can help."

"You've helped enough." A sob tumbles out with her quick words, and I would do a lot of things to erase time or at least clear the area of Zeus and his army. We need a conversation.

My grandfather falls silent, his face apprehensive. Lula has hit a new level. The king is afraid of her. He seems to shake himself and growls. "You will—"

"I'm done with demands and being controlled...manipulated by you horrible people—deities." Lula's attention alternates between the two of us, then the Olympian crowd. Her eyes stick and I glance back to Zephyrus, who appears ready to bow at her feet as he stands next to his brother. *Shit.* She recognizes him. "Don't think I will be a pawn, an Olympian, or a part of your plan. I don't care about your stupid war for power, because I'm not one of you."

"You are, though," I whisper. "Come and speak with me. I swear to do right by you, Lula."

The hand drops on the ground in front of Zeus, and Moros whimpers. The guard picks it up by one finger and places it back on the shield before wiping his hand on his linen exomis.

"You are covered in blood." Lula studies my shirt for a long moment before glancing at her father. "And you are so dangerous. All of you are." She points to the rip between realms. "Is that the hell realm?"

"Can we talk?" I step forward as far as she lets me. "I'll tell you everything."

"You've already done that, Alexiares." She bites my full name as a viper would strike a mouse.

Moros's voice cracks. Sweat drips from his brow, sticking his long hair to his face. His trembles are more like convulsions. "It's hell, Lula. I can smell it. Kill them all before they send us there. You can do it."

"Lu," I whisper. "Please."

Lula doesn't acknowledge me. Her brows are angled in a lost sadness that asks me to wrap her in my arms. She looks at Zeus. "If another one of my sisters dies, I will come for you, though you should be punished for what you did." Her lips purse in the way she does when she's unsure.

Zeus growls. "Attack!"

Chaos unfolds as the crowd shifts, some away, some toward.

Arrows fly with a twang and sink to the ground thanks to Zephyrus and Notus's west and southbound winds. I slide between Lula and the few incoming guards. Anice leaps in front of me. "You're weakened, brother." His tone is firm but apologetic. He kicks a golden chest plate, sending the demigod flying, and nearly taking out Zeus, who slips to the side.

"Traitors," the king yells.

Prax gives a battle cry and though he holds his injured arm close, he takes a guard to the ground with a shoulder in his gut. Two more guards go down, thanks to the younger generation. Athena stands tall next to my grandmother, spear upright in a white-knuckled grip but sitting this one out.

"Stop," Hera yells. "Enough." All activity halts.

"Lula." I would do anything to pull her against me, but she's a new goddess we know nothing about. It's likely she could do things we've never considered possible. "What can I do to help you through this."

"I want nothing from you." She moves around, her gait not correct for her. She's hunched, caving in.

"You need me."

"You are the last thing I need."

Dammit. Where is Rath? We have to get her to Olympus before this standoff draws a human crowd. The damage and death will already hit the news—all we need is a media helicopter overhead.

"No, wait." She halts. "I do need something."

I nod, pushing as close as I can. "Anything."

"Release Hazel immediately. Where is Venora?" She looks to Moros but he juts his chin and turns his head to the side. She grumbles. "Find out where Venora is from Hazel and release them. If anyone harms my sisters, I'll feel it and then I'll return and kill you all. Do not fuck with me. Leave the sirens and humans alone. Go back to"—she winces and holds her head a moment before straightening—"to Olympus and never leave." She crouches to address Moros, who has gone pallid and silent. "The creatures in there that you told me about, are they real?"

He nods. "Yes. They are dangerous. They bring dismemberment and pain."

"Ah, then we will get along fine." She stands. "Come on."

"No." Moros drags himself backward.

She can't mean to go to the hell realm, not when she needs to learn how to control her power and understand what she's become. She won't feel right for a while. No one moves. I look to my grandmother who seems like the only one in control besides Lula. She watches, an odd sadness on her typically stoic features. As if it's a chore, Lula waggles her fingers. Moros cries out as he's dragged to his feet by his injured arm. She turns and glides toward the rip, dragging Moros behind her. I stumble back as her wall pushes against me. She steps over a dead guard, pausing Moros next to him. Moros stands then, staring down at the gaping black hole in the demigod's throat. The bastard gives a quick smile.

"You're sick," Lula whispers to him and continues forward. "I'm horrifically ashamed of you right now."

I trail her, testing the points of her shielding, but while there's give, it's not enough to get closer. "Lula, wait. Please let us help you. You need guidance and Rath can be here soon. He's taking care of Hazel, then he will come back for you."

"I bet. You all do such a great job *taking care* of us otherworldlings. You will never find the others, and if you do, you will die as Gerty did. As…Grace probably has."

"What? No, Grace is fine. She's with Comus."

Her eyes widen, and she glances at Moros, then back at me. "Release her and release Hazel."

"They will be free." I keep as close as I can, hands searching and finding nothing but resistance.

"You do not want to follow me."

"I'll follow you anywhere, Lula."

She steps aside, and with a sharp flick, Moros's body soars through the rip. His scream from the other side makes me wince. "Not today, Alexiares."

I swear her eyes are teary and I push to get closer. "You need me. I can help you figure out what you are."

"I'm only me." She moves to step toward the hell realm. "Close the portal."

"No." I will not do this. "Do not cut yourself off—"

"I have to—never mind, just close us in, Alexiares."

"No, Lula. This is not our end." A chill seeps from my chest to my limbs with the thought of being separated from her. Goddess or siren, dangerous or not, we belong together. "I won't give you up. I'm coming."

Her jaw tightens, and her scowl darkens, though a tear rolls down her cheek. "I don't want you."

"Bullshit. You're angry, but you love me."

"That was a mistake on my part. There is nothing further you can say." She steps into the portal.

I panic, bumbling over words and the space between us. "I will not give up when you love me, and I love—"

A scream ripped from her soul sends out a surge of power. I'm thrown back through the air. The ground catches me, and I knock into others, trying to gain my footing as we tumble like rocks down a mountain. The jumbled world halts when I crash into a tree, taking it down with a pop of broken wood and creaking branches. I lie still, propped against rough bark, attempting to assess the damage. My blood pulses in my ears, numbness circulates through my limbs. This must be what humans feel after a car accident. Moans and curses sound in stereo as I roll to kneel, gingerly setting my weight on my aching right knee and working my sore shoulder.

The ground around the open hell portal is ripped up, shoved back, rolled up in places like fabric over a hard surface. "*Godsdamn.*"

Lula's gone.

Rath appears near the stage, eyes wide as he takes in the scene, then he's sprinting over, offering a hand. "What happened? What did this?"

I wince as he drags me to my feet. My spine aches. I point to the hell portal. "Lula. Go before Zeus realizes you're here."

Chapter Twenty-One

LULA

I FALL THROUGH THE PORTAL AND GRIP SOFT WHEAT-COLORED GRASS, gritting my teeth and wishing the pressure in my chest would explode already. Is the new atmosphere the reason I can't breathe? I clutch my mangled shirt over my equally tattered heart and hope my sisters will be okay. At least they'll be safe from me. My blood sizzles, yet there's dizzying numbness in my head. Sleep is a needed ache, as is running full tilt away from everyone—away from myself. I settle for crossing my arms over my stomach and folding over until my forehead rests on my knees. I hurt them. Alex was spouting off about love and I was being pulled apart, and another lie would have done something, though I'm not sure what. How could he say those things while still covered in my sister's blood? How could he tell me he'd never give me up? No one can use me again. Not if I'm in here. I force myself to drag in a long breath of unfamiliar air and pull myself upright. Hell is lush. Bushy trees with dark orange leaves scatter in clumps on rolling plains of wheat-like grass. With a flick of my fingers, sparkles soar, flitting to the closest thick-trunked specimen. An odd sound between a growl and a sob bursts from me as I slash my hand through the air. Shreds of plant life poof into a colorful cloud until the entire tree is a pile of dust.

"Pull yourself together," Moros says from behind me. "You are my daughter. We go back and take what's ours." He drags himself to his feet, hollowed eyes flitting around the scenery. My stomach clenches as he holds his arm close and starts toward me and the still-open portal chasm.

"I don't even know what I am." My wheezing breaths sting my lungs. I can't believe I gave his hand to Zeus. What was I thinking? How did it happen? Zeus had to be quiet and my throat tingled with deadly threat, and then it was sailing through the air. I rub at the spot.

"Lula?" Rath's voice makes me stumble forward and turn. He stares at me from the entrance, brows furrowed, then sliding high. Gray encircles the blue pools of his eyes. His cheekbones are more prominent and dusted with the same ashy color. I want to ask him what happened, then the ache of everything I've lost over the past two weeks returns tenfold. The world tugs me outward by each of my cells, then crushes me like a soda can, but physically I stand still and unmarred.

"God of Shadows," my father purrs. "Have you come to assist us?"

I open my mouth to question him about Hazel, but my insides shift, smacking together like fighting birds immersed in an aerial battle. "Get out!" I double over and bite back a scream. Am I self-destructing? I can't take out the Earth too. "Leave and make them close the portal."

My sparkles roll through the air, morphing into a sphere as it speeds toward Rath. It connects with a thud, and he sails through the opening. Dispersing, the particles drift to me on a magical breeze. A knot of fear tingles through my chest and I scramble backward, waving my hand through them when they reach me. They attach and absorb into my skin, giving the gray tinge a glittery pattern.

I wipe my wet cheeks with my forearms. "What am I?"

Moros waves his hand toward the portal. "You're my powerful hybrid daughter. Let's invade Olympus and force an oracle to read you. Only then will you know your named attribute. Let's go before we cannot." His gaze flits to the sky and darts around. "Darkness brings trouble."

Can he not see that I'm on the verge of breaking, and my new state may take advantage? I don't have control of myself.

Rath steps back in, paler but in one piece, slightly easing my rampant tension. I clutch at crispy grass stalks and gulp air to settle the flops my heart is experiencing. It's not a pain in my soul like when a sister dies. Or if it is, the spread isn't contained to my soul. No, that's not right either. My body and mind are warring.

"Where's Hazel?" I push myself to my feet, brushing black dirt off my hands before realizing the darkness on my fingers is part of me.

"I'm fine, thanks for asking." Rath studies my face, making me want to hide. "She's safe with Comus and Grace in an undisclosed location so that no one"—he glowers at Moros—"else can harm them."

"Grace is okay?" The fire in my bloodstream cools until I remember how much they've lied. "Then who did Alex kill?"

"What?" Rath tilts his head. "No one? What happened?"

"No more lies, Rath. He was covered in blood. Another sister died." His brows furrow, and he walks closer. I throw my hands up and he pauses. "Was it Amah?"

"I don't know. I'm so sorry about your sister." Rath moves to block Moros's movements toward the portal. "Was it Venora, Moros?"

"He didn't." I grit my teeth as a sensation passes over me that feels like vibrating water over the bones in my arms. "He was with me when it happened. Just tell me and leave."

"Unlike some." He glares at Moros. "We'd never hurt you or your sisters. Stay over there, asshole. The portal is guarded and they will happily shoot you with Firthus's weapons if they don't use all the bullets first." He takes another step toward me, pinches his jeans, and tugs the fabric up as he crouches. "It's not what you think, Lula."

"No? He didn't stalk me? Did you, Rath?"

"Well, yeah. We needed you. Still do, probably even more now, but you mean quite a bit more to us than our original intent." He tilts his head. "You look ill. Zenith is a tough time. Let me walk you through some things."

The ache in my bones shivers out of my skin and the black flecks vibrate together and apart. What in the hell? "No. Alex sent you because he's not getting anywhere with me." The pulse hits my chest and I think my heart stops. My breath falls from my lungs and I collapse to the grass.

"Lu?" Rath stands and steps forward when everything in me pounces alive again. He reaches out a hand, but I don't want him near me. He bounces back a step, then another, like an invisible sumo wrestler is belly bumping him. When he stops, he grins. "Well, that's something. Alex said you had a containment field."

"Leave!" I scream to the ground. It rumbles, but doesn't do anything drastic. I'm glad for that. A tear falls from my nose, catching on a tiny red pod at the end of a beige stalk. "I don't want this."

"Hey, it's going to be okay." He straightens up when I whip my focus to him. "Zeus arrested Alex the day you left. The only reason he's out of Olympus is because he felt the pull to Moros starting a war. We didn't know you were involved. Lu, I've been looking everywhere for you. I'm so glad you're safe." He glances over at Moros. "Safe-ish."

"You call this safe?" A wave of hot nausea floats through me, and I swallow hard to keep the nothingness in my stomach.

"He'd be here now, but he had to go get his mother and… someone else out of the barracks first. It's been a few since you went through. Time is odd between the realms—minutes here to Earth hours sometimes. Other times one day to months. It depends on realm rotations."

"Who's the other person?"

"Doesn't matter."

The flecks pulse harder. There's pressure from the air and it squeezes me. "Who?"

"Ichnaea."

His wife. The grass under my fingers turns to amber dust, then I sink deeper, exposing white roots that get diced as well. Red earth falls away from under my palms, making a crater I have to scramble out of.

"You're upsetting her." Moros stands. "Leave her be and let us speak as gods."

"I'm not here for you. I'm here to take Lula home."

I'd love to go home. I'd curl up on the couch with dinner and a movie, then fall asleep in my lavender-scented sheets. The flecks of glitter pause their chaotic flitting, and warp back into a net. "What are you telling me?" I whisper to them.

"Lula?" Rath asks, ten feet away and holding out a hand. Weeks ago, I'd have taken his offer and had him escort me through his shadow realm within seconds. I trusted him with my life, when he could so easily have taken it.

"I'm not leaving." I choke on watery words. "You don't know what I am." Nor do I.

"You're my daughter," Moros repeats, an old record with a scratchy sound. As if that simple fact provides everything I need. The waves return. The pressure creates a wah-wah buzz in my ears that makes my eyes squint.

"I can't tell you how surprised I am at that," Rath says. "She's nothing like you." Moros glares but remains panting and kneeling on the ground. Rath focuses on me. "Do *you* know what you are?"

I purse my lips. I don't owe him anything and can't trust him.

"Lu, you're a rare-form hybrid-primordial…probably. We need to check with an oracle. I wouldn't believe it if you didn't look—" He signals at me and smiles. "You have serious powers that no one—not even you—understand yet. You have to get a grasp on them though, because they can go haywire if you lose control. You shouldn't have been forced into the change." He glares at Moros. "That was an utter dick move. It's jarring enough when eased into zenith."

Rare-form? What the hell does that mean? Are the flecks of dark glitter along my skin a form? Am I going to stay this way? If my body wasn't struggling for purchase within itself, I'd wonder if I was part of the biggest practical joke the world's ever known, but it's real. I wouldn't be this jumbled up inside if it weren't. I want to fight and cry and be held at the same time I'm screaming until my lungs shred. Whatever's happening is trying to burst out. It's restless.

Rath leans forward, testing the strength of the invisible barrier keeping him from me. "But Lu, we need you and not only for the plan. We love you. You know that. Your place isn't here with this ass, whether or not he's your father."

The pattern on my hands shifts and vibrates. Everyone should leave me alone. "You needed to use me to gain what you want. Alex…" I shove those emotions down where they belong, but heat flows through me and it reminds me of him. Refocus. My new world is interesting and fresh. A smoky scent wafts on the heated breeze. Maybe it will be okay and I won't explode this place into nothingness.

"I'm not like anyone and…it's better this way. Go before I make you go."

"Lu, you're a rare deity. I am too. I'll help you explore what you are. Can you turn back yet?"

The sparkles bristle on my skin as if requesting release. They form tendrils that shift and skim, breathing me in as if in greeting. It's terrifying that they have a mind of their own, but also comforting. They're companions; my only friends now. I run a finger over my hand and they leap, transferring over then returning in a cheerful spiral. "Why would I want to turn back?" I give him a smile that hurts to make, and his brows furrow. "Isn't the new me more interesting? My father thinks so. He needed me in this form. Did you? Did Alex?" Did they know more about me than I did?

I push the sensation off my skin, which doesn't take much prompting, and the flecks settle into a shimmering ball that hovers over my palm.

Moros steps closer, clutching his arm. "If he will not swear fealty to us, help me kill him, daughter. Test your attributes on him, and then we leave this wretched place."

"Kill all the things, Lula," I singsong to keep from screaming. "Destroy, maim, murder with your mighty evilness." I wave my hand, and he tumbles to the ground. Maybe he's just…off-balance. "This attitude is *new*. Where's my calm and rational father?"

His face softens. "I'm sorry. This must be difficult for you. I only push because of your importance in the world."

"Really, Moros?" Rath widens his stance and drags his hands from his pockets, crossing his arms. "What new game are you playing? Alex told me you forced her into zenith—choked her. That was after Zeus threw multiple death bolts at her, which thank Hera, didn't kill her, and for that reason alone, I'm thankful for your blood running through her. Other than that, I wish you were dead." He smiles, displaying bright, shiny teeth. "I've wished that since I saw you drag Lula's sister through a soup of human remains."

"You speak as though innocent." Moros lifts his chin. "Deimos tells me you're long overdue to feel Zeus's lightning as well." He growls and drags himself to his feet, still gripping his wrist. "Sneaking around in the dark, hiding your nature when you could have done so much more with the talents stemming from your father's bloodline. You could worship me as your father does."

"Never." Rath never loses his smile, but his nostrils flair, and his posture stiffens.

Moros stands with more regality than I'm capable of at the moment. "Too petrified of your real power, shadow god? The grandsons of Olympus have you wedged so far under their thumbs that you deny your darkness. You fight what you are and allow those beneath you to direct your actions like a coward. I would show you how to embrace what you are. I would appreciate your attributes."

While Moros isn't nice, he hasn't poked at the festering wounds of others in front of me. Rath's father and mother are the sorest of points for him. I stagger to my feet. He's not my friend anymore, but this is cruel. The flecks—glitterlings—tug on my skin, and threads of irritation amplify until anger hums within me.

"Everything you've done, and you think *I*"—Rath smacks a fist against his chest—"would follow? Does Lula know this is an act or have you painted yourself as the doting father? She's smarter than you. She'll figure you out."

Moros laughs in a way that's a threat but joyful. It's a revelry in pain and has found a source. Rath is his fountain of agony. "Your whore mother begged to leave the universe because she couldn't handle your named intention, and you desire to—" My shiny ball flies at him, expanding to encircle his head. I swipe my hand left, and he staggers sideways, yelling a muffled chant. The sphere shivers, morphing from gray specks to a glassy, solid state. Moros tilts and falls to his knees.

I'm going to kill my father.

Chapter Twenty-Two

LULA

"HOW ARE YOU CONTROLLING IT?" RATH EDGES CLOSER, PALMS displayed as Moros tugs at the sphere adhered to his shoulders. "Mind or emotion?"

"Shut up, Rath."

"Nuh-uh. Explain."

Moros's body flops around it, stuck firm. "Um…" I drag myself to my feet, pulling my battered sleeve back up to my shoulder.

"Lula, how?" He crosses his arms, head tilted as though leaning against a building, watching people on a Friday night. "Tell me."

The heat that touched me before and pressed my insides together switches to a cold chill and slingshots, wrenching me in all directions. The muscles in my jaw strain and I close my eyes against the tilting, fun-house world. "None of your business."

When the whirl halts, I take a deep breath, blink, and flap my hands, willing the fleck back. They remain balled around Moros's head. His flailing becomes more urgent, hand and stub slapping the solid surface, making metallic thuds.

I clamber over, shifting to avoid wild kicks and rolls, and place my palm on the oddity I created. "Come on, glitter friends." My face tingles, sounds tunneling. Moros's flopping turns to convulses. I'm going to commit accidental murder after torturing him, and he's the only one who understands this realm and me.

"Breathe, Lula," Rath's voice cuts through the buzz. "Use both hands and picture yourself dragging them to your heart."

"Where they will probably stab me to death." And my father is dangerous, but I'm the one who can manage him. We're stuck together now for good or deadly attributes.

"Hey, ignore me if you want. Olympus gives its thanks for doing what they couldn't, but if your attributes are based on emotional control, this could get worse because you're stressed. Take a breath and let me help you. It's all connected to your center."

"Help me?" I snort. "Help yourself, you mean. Use me for your plan. Was anything you said to me true?"

"Yes, Lu. Of course it was."

"You make it sound like it's out of the realm of possibility that you'd have fabricated everything you ever told me." I slap the ball and a shock of energy sears my fingers. "Come on," I whisper. "Come back to me."

"Breathe, Lula. You're shifting further. Focus on your breath. Do not lose yourself to this."

"Breathing isn't going to fix me." Moros's movements slow and I chew my lip before abandoning it to hyperventilate. "This is his fault." There's no keeping the trembles from my voice. "Alex and the Olympians. My...father. I shouldn't be in this situation. I wish I'd never met any of you."

"No, you don't." Rath uses the same tone as when he's joking around with me. As if this is another playful banter moment between us. Like we're still friends. "Hey, look at me, not at him. Everything is going to be okay."

"It's not." My eyes sting as they meet his pleading ones, and the breaths that should slow hitch in my throat. "I'd take it back. Every word we shared, each laugh, and every kiss. I want none of it." The memories stick tight in my chest, choking me out.

"You can't. There are no take-backs when it comes to giving your heart to someone, so quit trying to wish away the incredible moments you shared. Hell, *we* shared. I've told you things I don't tell anyone except Alex and Comus because you belong with us, now more than ever. You're hurt. It sucks, but try to see the full picture. It's bigger than you or me or even Alex."

"It wasn't right, and it…hurts to be here." I clutch my chest and growl.

"I know, but you can't erase the past, nor should you. No deity has that attribute."

"Well, they should. You used me when I trusted you. Alex—" I choke on his name. "Alexiares created a false life for us."

"He withheld, but he loves you. I've known him for centuries, Lula. He fucking loves you." The truth in his eyes pleads with me to believe him.

"Withholding something that big is the same thing as lying." Power radiates through me, sending heated rage bubbling in my chest. I clutch my shirt and hiss a breath through my teeth.

"Lu." Rath gives me his, "Really, Lula?" snark face—pressing his smirk into a sarcastic twist.

"Stop looking at me like that!"

Glitterlings smash into him, and he bursts into shadow. Moros gasps so hard the sound is a long, shrill squeak, as though his throat closed in with the force of his inhale. He trembles on the ground, lips blue and chest pulsing with quick, alive breaths.

No patricide for me today.

I retreat from Moros and the cloud of deadly specks follows, swirling around my outstretched hands in two breezy funnels. They reattach little by little, making a pair of long gloves that shift on my skin. The monster inside me seethes, shifting through two centuries of repressed rage, finding each disastrous moment and holding it up like a shiny token to examine in the light. My will to fight myself drains away, leaving raw doom, because that's what I'm composed of. I have a thousand questions, a hundred requests of revenge, and a handful of deities that brought this upon me.

"Ow," Rath states behind me.

I throw a deadly glare over my shoulder. "Leave." I'm going to hurt someone or everything. Why can't they see that?

"No."

"Daughter," Moros croaks, staggering to his feet. "We escape now. Kill him."

"Focus, Lula," Rath whispers. "You can do this. Breathe."

"Hush." My sparkling flecks rise to the sky in a swirl. "Everyone stop telling me what to do. Go. Away."

The need to run catches up with me, and I stomp off along the brown grass toward a thicket of coffee-colored bushes. I wish I had a road map for my life or a time machine so I could undo the last couple of months. I wouldn't have met Alex, and my sisters would still live, and I'd be a plain old otherworldling with the ability to control everyone. Except hiding from everything brought down on me is silly. It would have happened anyway because I am a grain of sand trying to escape a divine undertow. The fury inside tells me to erase them... now. That's how to fix things. My fingers are still gray with black veining that creeps up to my elbow. The crack of fist against flesh has me swinging around. Rath has Moros in a headlock, punching him in the face. The odd sensation that was tugging me in all directions swings to full-body pressure. It's like the atmosphere is trying to squish me into nonexistence. Needles rip through my head again. Everything is so loud.

I cup my hands over my ears. "Can you two knock it off?"

Moros lands a few elbows into Rath's side, seemingly unfazed now by his missing hand. "Release me, you coprophagous child!"

Rath barks a laugh and batters Moros with another hit. "Where's your power now, you archaic, one-attribute shit stain? Huh? Where is it?"

My insides boil, my hands shake, and my glitterlings vibrate with need to join the fray. Alex steps through the portal, glowing through the haze like he brought an Earthly sunbeam with him.

He opens his mouth, and a white noise pulse-blocks all sound. Flecks drag from my skin and snap together with a pop that resonates in my spine. Rath throws Moros and leaps between Alex and the hurtling weapon ball, dissipating with a grunt when it hits him.

He reappears in front of Alex. "Fuck. Would you stop that?" Stretching, he checks over his arms. "Hurts, Lu."

"Get out!"

"Lula," Moros calls again. "Kill—"

"I swear if one more person commands me to do something, I will scream this damn realm from existence. We'll float around space in tiny, silent particles." I hope that's not possible, but blasting the gods on Earth shocked me enough to understand I'm no longer acting. This isn't a nightmare I'll wake up from.

Rath nods over his shoulder at Alex. "Momma Hebe okay?"

Alex tips his head back and forth, eyes on me. "The barracks have fallen, courtesy of my father, though I weakened it."

"Naturally," Rath says. "We at war?"

Alex crinkles his nose. "Olympus is in, um…turmoil."

"Good," I say through gritted teeth. A bunch of deities stood around while the king went psycho on me. What if I wouldn't have been a goddess? My remaining sisters would have another vacant space in their soul. One more break of mind and another reminder of everything these deities have done to us. "And what about the humans. Did you sweep them under the rug? Burn their bodies to hide, or leave them for other *lesser beings* to find?" The pressure slingshots with heat this time. I touch my forehead and check my fingers to make sure my sweat doesn't glow green or something. There's tightness inside that shifts and swoops. Everything needs to be silent. It's too bright. The world is vibrating.

Alex approaches at a cautious, hunched stalk, even as I back away, shaking my head in warning. "I need to speak to you. Please hear me out."

I can't look him in the eyes—seeing him is an uncomfortable pain that my insides grab a hold of with gleeful talons. "I want nothing to do with you. Get the fuck off my lawn. Rath, you too. Leave me in peace before I leave you in pieces." God, that was cliché.

"Lula," Rath says. "That state will drain you and make you careless. Your attributes can go haywire."

"Ha!" I cackle until the stabbing pain makes my jaw clench. "Haywire. That's…accurate."

"We'll help you through this." Alex takes another step forward and I stumble back. He has the audacity to mimic a tail-tucked puppy. "Please, talk to me. I'm worried about you."

Sure he is. I stand straighter. The glitterlings swirling overhead scatter over me, wrapping my arms. My insides wreck together again, vying for control, remaining unsettled and anxious.

Alex peeks back at the portal and Rath. He tugs his phone out of his pocket and looks at that too.

"Waiting for a call?" I ask. "Is it your wife or are you trying to find a good time to update Olympus? Are you going to turn me in now that I'm"—I brush at my hand as if I could swipe away the dark sparkles; they swirl and vibrate—"this?"

"Wife? No, Lula." His pleading eyes only anger me further. "Just Comus and—"

The heat returns and I fight to stay on my feet. "Enough. Calling for backup isn't going to help you here. Did you arrange Gerty's death so I'd be more complacent? Did you kill her right before you came to me at the hotel, or get someone else to do it?"

He blanches and his eyes bug before they glare. "Are you kidding? No—I'd never. That was Moros. It was—"

"No more lies. You're still covered in blood and Moros was with me when…last time. Today." My ears pop, making me wince as I realize whatever happened to me—zenith, I guess—overshadowed the pain of losing another piece of my soul. "What other sister did you take from me?"

The golden color pours back into him, tinting red on his cheeks and nose. If I thought the glare he trained on me was startling, the one he aims at Moros shows a demon I haven't seen. My father grins, sitting in the grass, leaning on an elbow like he's got all day. The expression is seedy and my stomach lurches, adding to the disaster within me. "You made her think I killed Gerty?" Alex growls. "You dragged that poor woman through a dead crowd. She was so scared of you. So thin."

Moros scoffs. "You are undeserving of Hera's blood."

"Stop." A hot wave amplifies sound and I stumble, struggling to stay on my feet. "Stop."

They yell back and forth with clogged, muffled threats. More wah-wah notes assail my ears and chill coats my skin instead of heat. I hate this inside tumble. Everything is so loud.

"Alexiares lied to you, didn't he, daughter?" Moros's voice rises loud through the fog. "That's all Olympians do. He's made you into a weak, poisoned girl and I made you into a goddess."

"Shut up, asshole," Rath yells, spinning toward my father.

Alex turns to me, clutching his shirt. "It's my blood. I was fighting to get back to you. I love you."

The last part is so loud it hurts my ears as much as my heart and I wince, pressing the sides of my head. "Shut up." The empty hole he left behind fills with bees and lava. It's made to hurt and bleed me out as it crashes around to make space or an escape.

"No, listen. I want to help you through this because you're mine and I'm yours. You feel it, I know you do."

"Ah yes, I'm sure those sweet murmurs, the expressions of..." I cannot stop my voice from breaking, "Love was what you had in mind when we met."

Alex moves forward with a slowness that makes no sense in my spinning world. "You don't belong here."

"Get away from him, daughter," Moros yells, moving toward Alex. "He means to murder you. If he touches you, he will curse you or snap your neck—oof." Rath tackles him to the ground, but Moros flips him and connects a punch.

Tension pours in from everywhere, and I take a few more shuffled steps back on wobbly legs. "Go away." My words are a wheeze as my lung crush. Where did the air go?

Alex's chest rises and falls with calmness as if bragging to my uncontrollable breaths. "No. Never again, Lula. I shouldn't have left for Olympus in the first place. I belong wherever you are."

"And then you stole Hazel," Moros yells.

"We had to save her from you." Rath fades into shadow to avoid a punch.

"She was happy," I yell. "Hazel was happy with Deimos. She just wanted to see me. Why do you all have to keep us apart? The divine do nothing but make life miserable. I should kill you all for what you've done to my sisters."

The glitterlings shift and detach from my skin. The sparkling flecks crash into Alex like a wrecking ball, sending him flying. He lands in a pile in the grass and rolls, coming to a stop on his back. Bones crack as his shirt deteriorates into air. His roar of agony vibrates my soul before a jolt pulses the haze. My roiling insides clatter into still silence. The fury or whatever writhes around inside me leaves like it's being vacuumed out.

"Alex?"

He twitches in the grass, because of me. This isn't what I wanted.

I stare at my hands, gray but not shimmery. I've unleashed a weapon and not just on *someone*. On Alex. Stumbling to him, I sink to my knees. His ripped shirt splays open, and the broken chasm of his sternum exposes his pounding heart—a pulsing anatomy diagram in a sloshing crimson pool. He sets one hand over the gap, blocking my view.

"No," I whimper behind my hands. "Alex...I didn't mean it. I didn't—"

His fingers are cold against my arm. "It's okay. Zeniths are..." His words wheeze into a hiss as his face pinches up with the punishment I've inflicted on him. Golden hue drains to a sickening gray pallor. "It will...work out. I love—" His heart stumbles a beat and he gasps. "I love you. Forever."

Rath drops beside us. "Shit. Shit, shit."

Alex's hand drops to the ground, his eyes flutter shut, and I drown at the loss. Breath is impossible, tingles rear in each of my limbs as my mind reels. I cover his wound—the one I'm responsible for. Sparkling power floods from the air to gather over my fingers. The rhythm under my palms slows, speeds, then stops. "Alex?" I whisper into the fuzzy silence.

"Lula, hey..." Rath edges his hands forward then retracts.

The horrid flecks I created slide to Alex's skin. I try to brush them away, but they refuse. "Leave him alone." They swirl, making a tug inside me as they line against each other, but ignore my desperate swats. Covering his chest, they shiver, and another crack of bone sends a wince through me. "Stop!"

"Okay, Lula, I need you to focus for me and breathe." Rath dips his head, meeting my eyes straight on. "I'm not trying to alarm you further, but you're shaking the ground. A lot of things need to happen right now, but not until your attribute detaches from Alex."

I suck in breaths as though gulping water. My nose tingles. The flecks shiver and trail to my fingers, moving in slow synchronicity. The closed gap in Alex's chest is a red line, hot to the touch. The rest of his skin no longer harbors the heat of a sunbeam. It's cold and lifeless marble. No echo of movement. No life remaining. I wanted silence, but not this. I was hurt, but I'd never harm without need. This wretched demon isn't me and now I've… Abandoning him from my touch is merciful, but leaves me a drained, nonexistent mass in a crushing unfamiliar realm.

Rath covers my trembling, lifted hands with his and carefully moves them to my lap like loaded weapons. "Lula, I have to take him." There's an attempt of calmness in his voice but also a telling waver. "I will come back for you, but him first, okay?"

I ball my dangerous fingers and nod. Rath grips Alex's wrist and fades, dragging him into the safety of the shadows.

Gone.

"See?" Moros chuckles, crouching in the grass. A trail of crimson winds into his beard from his nose, and his eye is swollen shut. "Just like me. Well done, daughter."

Chapter Twenty-Three

LULA

Waves of pressure pull, heat, then push and chill me in a frameless cycle, and I weather it without moving or speaking or harming.

Moros paces in front of the realm portal, yelling gibberish in my direction that refuses to absorb into my overloaded mind. He gets close enough to slip through and I drag him back with my will—the only thing in me that listens. He growls and grumbles. After what could be minutes or an hour, the line of blue light coming from home, or what used to be home, fades when surrounding air adheres like an upside-down zipper. Moros runs circles around where the portal stood and rips up grass with his one hand. Thrown fibers and dirt pepper the air in the shotgun blasts of his rage. His stretched-mouthed, bunched-fist screams don't hit my ears, though I understand his mind —his world has shattered too. The humming white noise blocks sound. The sharp, roiling waves of this magical zenith-torture weave through my bones, becoming a pain I bear because I should. If it lasts forever, I'll adjust. The shimmery pattern lays still across my skin, vibrating to the shifts of atmosphere.

It took a moment to want Alex. Hours to love each of the guys in vastly different ways. I spent months in—not paradise, but close. Within seconds, I ruined it all. I proved Moros and the Olympians who believe I'm dangerous right. How dare I read legends of gods and tell myself how foul they were after I lashed out and destroyed the deity I loved. He's gone because of me—another vengeful goddess.

Moros approaches, heavy steps unfocused until he halts a step from me. Green and amber grass stains speckle across his singed jeans, remnants of our old world. I'm expecting a kick, punch, slap, or more yelling, but he drops to his knees in front of me, black eyes locked on mine, cups my neck, and pulls my face to his chest.

There's no stopping the break inside. No holding in the wail that travels from my soul and passes my lips. He holds me against him as I utterly fail to contain my grief. It pours from me in endless, cascading tears and messy, wracking sobs that quake my body, but my father encircles me tighter, resting his chin on the top of my head. He hums something unfamiliar until his quiet song is louder than mine. Even missing a hand, he lifts me with ease and sets me on my feet. He links my fingers in his and walks me through amber grass that becomes sparse, turning to a walkway of red rock, then crude stairs of a purplish-black substance like glass or gems, jagged and sleek. We step into darkness and he grumbles something, releasing me. The atmosphere considers crushing me further, then gives way to the chill of the air, stale with a lingering musk. With heated fingers on my back, he leads me over more black glass, then nudges me to a pile of coarse fur. I curl in a ball, close my eyes, and let the buzz of this realm take me where it will.

I WAKE AT THE SMELL OF FIRE, AND DIM, BLUE LIGHT FILTERING through my achy eyelids. The world bombards my bones, but not as before. It's putting on a weighted coat instead of standing inside a pressure cooker. The fur under my palm is the deepest ebony, each hair sleek and rigid.

Yesterday was real. I'm disconnected from the Earth, shut out along with Moros where we belong. Two monsters living among the darklings. I turn my face into the coarse pelt. No more tears escape, probably from lack of eating or drinking over the last day.

Sound trickles in: pitter-pattering water in a corner and the pops of a fire with logs of crackling, sappy wood. A breeze rustles a dried-up bush at the misshapen cutout entrance of thin purple rock. The beige pods on skeletal branches clack together like a natural wind chime, calming my heartbeat. Maybe this home won't be so terrible. The blue light creeps across the translucent floor, making a sparkling path wherever it moves. It draws me, and when I brush the line between shade and luster on the chilled stone, the glitterlings branch out from each finger in a swirling dance. A pulse thrums in my chest. The taste of metal but with floral notes coats my tongue, then replicates into smell. The flecks adhere and drag me closer. I sit up with a start, ripping apart the attachment. The glassy purple cave gives a slow rotation. When I ball my fingers, the glitterlings return to me, slip into a pattern, and stay still as I twist my hand back and forth to study each inch. *What are you?*

On wobbly legs, I wander the small cavern. Two piles of stacked pelts and rudimentary tools sit scattered in a corner. The rocks fixed inside wood, makeshift knives, and sharpened spears would look fitting in a primitive museum. Most are coated with deep rust of absorbed, dried blood.

The stream of liquid trickling down the wall leaves the same taste in my mouth as the phantom flavors when I touched the odd stone. Is this water? It hits my stomach and sears, but I can't stop bringing cupped handfuls to my lips. *So thirsty.*

Trotting thunks approach from outside and Moros takes up the entrance, blocking the light as he steps inside. "I see you found the hell water."

"It's safe?" *A little late now.*

Moros's head misses the ceiling by an inch in the center. "You're a deity. You could drink acid and it would hurt, but you'd sustain." His lips purse at my expression. "It's true. Accepting that will help you as the sustenance we're forced to live on here is equivalent to such."

"So there's no furniture or diners in the hell realm?"

"It's a primitive planet. There are leaves, wood, rocks, and animals. I trapped beings. Gathered food. Sought escape." He pivots and strides outside.

After a last handful of metallic floral juice, I follow. The rising sun is dark magenta and chases two faint moons to the horizon, one blue, one gray. Instead of the Earth's cerulean, the sky is a purple haze with wispy, unformed, green-tinted clouds. The cave pokes out of an outcrop surrounded by more red rocks and a field full of amber grass, waving on the stuffy, acrid breeze. A few spindly near-black trees make a curtain to our left. Spiky orange balls perch on branches of wide, brown leaves. Are those hell realm coconuts?

Moros had made a fire pit outside the mouth of the cave. He picks up a stick and pokes at the flames, sending sparks into the air. The scent it gives off is high-scale incense, perfumy and rich. It eases the pressure until a sharp pang reminds me I need food.

Moros grabs a floppy white thing from a flat rock beside the fire and hands it to me. I stretch to take it when he wiggles it.

"Think of it as a parsnip." His nose crinkles. "Or pretend."

I bite and grimace as my throat works to gag. A parsnip? Only if the vegetable was pickled, chewy, lukewarm, and smoked. My stomach lurches. If I eat this, it's not going to stay down. I hold it and sit staring out at the field. As the sun rises further, I nibble, swallowing without chewing and try to forget yesterday, but as each moment persists, so does the pressure against my skin and bones.

I need a distraction. "Was that difficult to make?" I ask, lifting my chin at the fire and eyeing his stump. The cut point is lighter. A thread of guilt simmers through me, but also a good deal of anger at what he did with his attribute. Then again, it's not like I'm any better. The world pushes out, stretching me apart.

"Yes, though I've had too much practice." He squats and grips my chin. "The child of shadows was correct. Power of such magnitude is a new creation—dangerous even to whom it belongs. You must wield it as a weapon. Take it before it takes you." His gaze is studious, mind spinning as to how he may use me for his agenda.

"That's what you did?"

The edge of his lips quirk and he releases my chin. "Of course."

"You have one attribute and it's only purpose is to murder?"

He stills to the point where I wonder if the crushing, tugging world around me has stopped.

"I will not be your weapon," I whisper, then swallow my fear of this punishing realm and the broken man before me whose DNA created mine. "My voice is a weapon. I don't need more and nor do you."

"You need much, darling." He tilts his head at me and lifts his stump, holding it out for me to examine, though I stand there in my pressurized bubble, biting my lip, staring at onyx eyes. "You did this as you entered zenith. How can you think you're not meant to destroy so you may survive? And you will. Look at this, what your creation has done." He raises his appendage higher in front of me and then I do see it. The flecks on his skin are pale compared to mine, and when I touch him, a shock zaps my finger. I can't stop my jolt and his eyes fill with purpose, demanding more information and then action. With a shiver of flecks, the gray drains from the outermost edge of his wrist, rolling up to the center of his stump where they return to glittery black and surge to my outstretched finger. Instead of blending into the pattern, the ones living on my skin shift away, circling the returned glitterlings, keeping an inch between them. The pale remainders on Moros release, raining white ash to the ground.

Moros examines his smooth wrist, lips parted and smirking. "Fascinating. Tell me what you felt."

I swallow. Maybe he should know. He existed before calculated time, and I need to figure myself out before the pressure cooker blows. "A jolt. Like an electrical current."

"Interesting." His tone is masked from emotion. He stares at his arm again. "I cannot believe you did such a thing. I'm both angry and proud."

"Proud?" I ask. "How?"

"I would have done the same." His eyes focus on a point over my shoulder and the corner of his mouth raises. "And what you did to—"

"Do not," I growl. A rumble sounds from the rock below.

Moros tilts his head and glances at the ground before standing. "Come." He walks toward the field. "We must test your attributes. Until I have my gift back, you will protect us."

I halt behind him. "It's not a gift. You killed." The moments from before seep in—that heated, agonizing tingle that promised to be the last sensation I'd ever experience. How many people's final experience was my father's dread? "You used it on me."

"I did, and now you are a goddess," he says over his shoulder. "That method has not been used since myself. Some thought it impossible, but they've now seen proof. We will have tomes written of us, daughter, and when we leave this pankataratos land, we will forge the future." He speeds up, glancing up at the skies. "Hurry, we cannot be out in the dark. I lost a leg once to those creatures. It was unpleasant, though at least I had both hands."

"They forced you into zenith?"

"Yes."

"Who?" I ask, scrambling to keep up over unfamiliar terrain. I veer and dodge red rocks.

"Erebus." Moros heads toward a patch of thick trees.

I stumble as the world wallops me again. Rath's father? "Why did he do it?"

He makes a huffy snort. "Like yourself, I was young once. I was told I was not a deity, and I foolishly believed, but Erebus saw my potential, witnessed my naming, and gave me a choice. When I didn't take it, he forced me into zenith, making me my true self. Why do you think Zeus and his brothers locked him up? You're only naive, Lula, because you have yet to experience all sides of the divine."

"Who was he to you?" I ask.

"My teacher until he became my follower." He turns to me. "Naturally, some lead but most look to follow. After you have tested every aspect of your attributes, we will find our way back to Olympus. You will be hated, attacked, and shunned by those who do not understand you and it will make you strong." He steps closer, voice raising and eyes sparkling with excitement. "You won't only force them to hold their tongues, you will cut the insults from their mouths, and they'll bow at your feet. The reign of Olympians concludes upon your arrival." He smiles at the horror that must paint my features. "You will see, daughter. It's why the sire of your children is important. We will cleanse those undeserving and start fresh, create new deities and strong alliances." His words go soft and he turns, renewed in collecting firewood.

"So you think I will accept my life as a murderer—"

"Survivor." He scoops a broken branch from the ground and points it at me. "You will do what you must to persevere until you lead those who want to be led and destroy those who would cut you down." He passes back more sticks that I hug against me. All I've ever done is survive. I built a home wherever I'm hiding, and while I've never felt I was running for my life until deities stormed in, I didn't achieve "normal." Not without harming others. And now, whatever monster is inside me, tugging and pulling and destroying, has made it even harder. I'll never step on the Belize beach again, wake next to Alex, talk with Rath, or call my sisters. The house I molded into my home for over a decade is officially abandoned. The humans will figure it out, go through my collection of trinkets and art, toss them out, and move in. Maybe they already have. Rath said that time was weird here. What did he say? Hours to days or more? What if it's been years while I slept?

"Destroy something." Moros watches me, arms crossed, odd now with the missing hand. "You're panicking and pressurizing the air. Your power needs release. Destroy that tree or the mountain. Do you think your attributes can topple a mountain yet?"

He questions my ability to annihilate miles of life as if asking if I'm able to snap my fingers. I've done enough damage. Does he not remember?

"We can't go back," I say. "So many died. Firthus died." I'd almost forgotten about him. He was an asshole, but now his steamed corneas stick in my brain and won't shift.

Moros blows out a long breath and continues collecting wood. He doesn't think I understand him, but I do. He needs a place in the universe as much as I do, but he's missing the humanity I was raised with. If the Olympians wouldn't have taken him from Earth, and I'd have remained with him and my mother, could I kill as easily? He has to realize that there are other ways—better ways—to be in the world. "If you refuse to listen to me, you will destruct little by little and fall into madness."

My head swims from the pressure. "Is that what you did?"

"I embraced what I was and let myself flourish."

"Then how do you know I'd lose my mind?" With a flick of my fingers, the glitterlings dart off to encompass a broken branch, hanging by a thread of bark. They flit around it like a flock of cautious starlings—coming close, then darting away. "What if I'm not what you think I am?"

"You are. And those who fight their nature begin brittle."

I grit my teeth. "You haven't known me long enough to understand my nature or what I fight." I take a breath and focus on carrying the wood to the cave, but within seconds, the flecks hover like a black cloud raining dust. My heart pounds in my chest, an impossible feat with the crushing world.

"No?" Moros steps closer. "What are you attempting?"

Light leaves, chased by shadows. The moons rise over the horizon. "I'm trying to carry."

Moros drops the branch and backs from me. His features register apprehension mixed with interest and he brings his finger to his lips. A crunch of branches has me swinging around to stare into a shadowy patch of trees, where a purring snort breaks through bated stillness. I retreat too, holding my pile of sticks tight. A dark shadow slips between trunks as the last of the sun dips below the horizon. In the fading light, it straightens upright on bowed legs bent like a dog's. Red silky fur matches the color of the rocks and the face is more familiar than I'd expected.

Moros walks backward faster than I do and whispers, "Darkling."

"No. Berserker." Or close. It has pointed ears and circular eyes but the creature could have been a cousin to Lena's murderer, except without a stitch of animal skins or bones for decoration. The odd chuff it makes is humanlike, but with a raspy bass timbre. It's probably asking if I'm a mate or food. It shifts from side to side in a weird dance, resembling a cat, eager to pounce but indecisive.

"Kill it." Moros's tone tightens my jaw. When a deity sounds afraid, there's something terribly wrong. How does physiology on getting eaten work? "You have to, daughter, or it will rip our throats out. Try. Now."

The creature springs sideways like a spider monkey, showing off talons, but I hold my ground. "Calm down," I say.

It curls into a crouch. Red lips curl up, revealing two sets of fangs. *Shit.* It barrels toward us with a throaty snarl that would make a demon pee their pants.

"Stop," I drag the word from my center, thrall thrumming in my chest and hopefully escaping into the universe through the pressure. "Halt. Stop!" I hold my hands up to protect my face, as if my flesh could shield me against those mouth daggers, but no bite or pummeling happens.

A hot snort shifts my hair, and the scent of burnt popcorn wafts to me. I swallow hard and look way up. Black, horizontal pupils and orange, veiny irises stare down at me. The sound that comes from it is more purr than growl.

"Step back," I say.

It shuffles backward and I blow out all the air in my tight lungs and take in the mass of this huge creature.

I am Lula, siren goddess and commander of darklings.

Chapter Twenty-Four

LULA

Much to the terror of my darkling sidekick I've named Thor, I relearn how to make fire from flint. I braid and bind my singed-shorn hair with twigs, then shimmy up trees to gather the one fruit-like food that doesn't make me throw up. I remember how sore muscles feel. The sensation lasts short hours in my new divine state, but the pressure that tugs on my bones continues on a constant cycle that only changes when I lose control of my emotions. To keep my thoughts off Alex, my sisters, and my still uncontrollable inner deity, I weave grass and chip stone into art until my dark, shimmery fingers bleed. The weeks pass in a hazy blur as I hone skills I've never needed to rely on, and each night when the moons set, I fall onto a spiky fur bed, asleep before my eyes close. I avoid Moros. It's not that I don't want answers to the hundreds of questions I have about the history of gods, the future he's masterminded, what it was like to be near Venora and Hazel, or the one question above all—what happened to my mother, but each time I even consider asking…I'm pressurized. I'm going to explode or implode, I'm sure of it.

The light from the mouth of the cave dims as I guide a strand of long beige grass through diagonal blades. I'll figure out how to make a basket soon. The evening heat wafts in, wet with the stench of sulfur, and my rebelling stomach does a flip. I'd cover my nose with my shirt, but it's just as pungent from sweat and soot, and fragile with holes sewn and patched using hell realm fibers. Tomorrow at first light, I'll wade back into the pool I've made my bathing spot and stay calm if something brushes my foot. Last time, it took me an hour to regather the glitterlings, and they're not as attached as they were, though I'm not feeling attached myself. My thoughts are as hazy as the clouds, my insides have tugged into a tight ball that lives behind my belly button, and sleep is as pressing as my untamed power. Rath's words float through my mind on replay. *It will drain you and make you careless.*

Avoiding my attributes is tiring me, but so does wielding them, not that I understand how to wield them or even what they are. Yesterday, I almost made Thor carry me back to the cave, but his long arms, taloned-thumbs, and hind legs creep me out. Also, his burnt popcorn smell now makes me hungry, and I don't enjoy what that does to my already cracked mind.

"Come." At the cave's mouth, Moros is a silhouette against the evening sky and fire pit. "You must eat."

I follow and sit, taking the charred chunk of meat from the stick Moros holds out. Yesterday's catch is still squishy, and not in a calamari way—in a water balloon way. It may appear to be a piece of blackened chicken, but I know better. I gulp hard and take a bite. It bursts, flooding the flavor of ashy Brussels sprouts on my tongue, but with the texture of thinned pudding. Please stay down. "Foul." I pop the rest in my mouth and swallow it before gagging.

I toss the part of the carcass Moros hasn't prepared behind me to Thor. He claws it with spindly fingers, gives a snorty whine, and rips in with enthusiasm that threatens the contents of my stomach again. Keeping my eyes on the moons, I try to ignore the slurps and spongy snaps of the limbs breaking apart.

Moros chews politely, somehow not heaving or gulping it to escape the texture. He's had more time to adjust. The few bites I took shift and twist in my stomach. Maybe it's because I'm part siren that my body rejects all hell realm food.

He clears his throat and I groan. *Should have known.* He wants to talk again.

Each day he peppers me with questions I don't know the answers to. *How does it feel? Weird. What can you do? Shrug.* He presses me to expand my energy, but there's a disconnect—unknown knowledge that puts the deity living in my siren body into the driver's seat and me scrabbling to stay upright. Moros does not like that analogy. He pitched a fit actually—yelling that I should be connected to my attributes by now, and why wasn't I trying harder? After he returned, limping from the patch of trees on the edge of the field that I accidently tossed him into, I told him my failure in goddesshood is because he forced me into this state. He broke it, he bought it. That was three days ago. Since he's invited me back to the fire pit, he must have gotten over our tiff.

"We need to move on." His jaw is tight under his unruly red beard. "We leave in the morning."

I can't stop from glancing in the direction where the portal used to be. "I'm not ready."

Moros blows a sharp breath out his nose. "They will not return, daughter. Unfortunately, you only removed Alexiares from our path, but because of their attachment"—he rolls his eyes to the side and keeps them on the moons—"now the God of Shadows will have issue joining us when we meet again. Though he does seem to have an affinity for you." He scratches his shoulder and gives me a once-over that reminds me too much of Firthus's gaze.

I drag myself to my feet, trudging to the fur pile. "If they won't reopen the portal, then why leave this cave? It has water and shelter. Are there better locations on the planet? Is there an eggplant parmesan tree you're not telling me about?" I rub my temples, trying to ease the headache that gets worse each day.

He opens his mouth, then closes it. Thor tilts his head at a cawing sound in the distance, then goes back to nibbling at his talons. He's better groomed than my father.

"Great." I take a trudging step toward my fur pile. "This is our home now."

Thor shifts around me and plops next to the trickle inside the cave. Jutting his bottom lip, he sticks it into the stream to get a mouthful of water. He's been the most surprising thing I've found so far in this place. For the first week, I skittered away when I woke to him stretched out beside me. And I've been tempted to make him leave for good when my mind wanders to my sisters, and I remember the berserker that took Lena from me. Their appearance is painfully close, but he's not that kind of monster, or at least I see a different side when we're wandering and he climbs an adjacent tree from me and chirps like a bird, spins circles as we return to the cave, then flops across the rocks with a lengthy end-of-the-day groan. I talk to him more than Moros, and my thrall doesn't seem to hurt him.

"There is a portal in the hell realm," Moros says from the doorway.

Swinging around makes dizziness send me sideways, and I grab the glassy wall—a mistake because the glitterlings adhere again. I jerk my hand away with effort and fidget with my tingling fingers. "A portal? It's open? Where?"

"You will never find it without me."

I tilt my head. "So not one that the Olympian's opened?"

"No."

Interesting. "Don't leave to explore without me or I'll send Thor for you." Even if there was an exit door out there, he can't escape and I won't either. We're too dangerous. "How far is it?"

"A day. Hordes of darklings will attack by evening though, so when we find it, we must go through immediately."

I don't believe that for a second. He should have told me it was in a field of strawberries if he wanted to explore. "Then we won't go."

Moros stalks closer. "You will—"

A deep rumble comes from Thor, stopping Moros's words and his steps. I raise an eyebrow.

My father eyes the darkling puffing up in the dark light and lumbering toward him, talons clicking on the cave floor. "Fine. But once you have a semblance of attribute control, we leave." He pivots and returns to the fire.

"So never," I whisper into the darkness. I drop to the furs and curl up in a ball. There's crackling cinders, a snoring hell beast, and stink; not a rhythmic heartbeat against my ear and the smell of sun-soaked citrus with each inhale. My eyes sting, and I gulp a sniffle. The more I consider the day in the amphitheater, the more memories come to me. Every minute burrowed under layers of my panic and confusion to harbor until I calmed. Now, Alex's phantom bellow echoes in my mind, unveiling the savage terror on his face I didn't recognize until it was too late. Anice had to hold him back from running into Zeus's lightning to get to me. Others kept arrows from touching us. Was that for Moros, Alex, or for me? How many Olympians understood our situation? Whose side were they on?

Why couldn't he have waited a while to follow? He should have feared me, and that would have given me time to let everything that happened sink in. Not that I'm cured or better, but I'm enlightened about that day, Alex, and Moros. I have no doubt now that my father's or his followers' actions harmed my sisters. He has deep-seated beliefs that those who do not have the power of the divine are lesser beings meant to serve the whims of the gods until they're no longer needed. Then, like the human man at the house, he discards them.

The flecks shift on my skin, the deity inside reminding me how much it would enjoy destroying if I only let it. I curl in tighter, hugging myself in the darkness. I'll take my time remembering, and when I can handle it, Moros will tell me about my sisters and my mother. He'll explain the history of sirens, Hera, and the other gods. And I'll teach him about humanity and the culture of humans. But not today or even tomorrow. We have eternity and a hell realm to make home.

Nose in the air, Thor wanders up the rocky pass that leads to the field as I'm knee-deep in reddish murk, scrubbing my skin with a fistful of grass. It smells better than I do, and it's exfoliating off the layers of hell realm covering me, even if the water puts half the dirt back on.

"Stay here, Thor." If a herd of darklings comes to the watering hole while I'm naked with my clothes drying on a rock, the glitterlings will explode something. He chuffs, then crouches to dig. I'm fortunate he's not interested in my nudity or my smell, because I enjoy having him around. I feared mental deterioration, but it's been at least a month, and he listens as much as he did the first day, but maintains independence. He stays close but wanders to chase birdlike creatures and dig for scaled and furry things that live under the amber grass and red rocks. His snacks remain a mystery as there are only tiny remnants by the time I open my mouth to tell him to let me see what he caught.

He makes a whining grunt sound I haven't heard yet. Maybe he smells food. Too bad it's most likely not edible to me. I'd do extraordinary things for pasta. My arms and legs are thin, and my collarbone juts. At least my pants—now fashioned into shorts—still fit, though it's probably because they're denim and shrink-dry in the sun every day. "I'm hurrying," I tell him and dunk my hair, scrubbing my itchy scalp and wishing for a conditioner. I'll end up with dreads before long. As I flick my soaked locks over my shoulder, bubbles pop to the surface of the water a few feet from me.

I scramble backward, then pause and laugh. The flecks didn't scatter this time and the atmosphere didn't crush me. Maybe that's progress. I focus, letting the tension in my chest expand outward and the big, finned something thrashes as it's moved away. "Thor, is that thing edible?" I ask, not that he would answer, but he'd pounce if it were. Instead, his attention is past the rocks.

My stomach rumbles, and I glance at my dark fingers, considering trying to hunt or fish again. I drop my hands to my sides. Maybe one day they can bring home the hell-bacon, but now, I'd leave nothing but creature particles.

Thor stands tall, puffed-up, muscles bulging, and grunts rhythmic calls that force me to cover my ears. He can be louder than a jet engine when he gets the mind to.

I head over to the rock, snatch my damp shirt and shake it out. "Just go."

He takes off in a leap, legs prancing like a running ostrich. I've stepped into an odd fantasyland with crazy creatures. Lifting an arm, I give myself a tentative sniff. It's not Chanel, but it's not offensive either. The grass leaves a scent like ginger root. It's soothing, and the tightness in my jaw and shoulders loosens.

The stone formations around the mini, murky pond are layered into tiers, and provide good hiding spots for naked sunbathing. I lay back on a flat rock, spill my messy hair behind me, and blow out a long breath. The heat in this realm isn't like a sunbeam, or even a sauna. It invades, but that could be the pressure of my annoying divine-ness. Thor doesn't return. Must have been a big meal. I sit up on the rocky outcrop, hanging my legs over and peering at the water below. The hint of reflection shows my dark shape and the unusual glint of my irises, but that's all I can picture out. Who should I talk to today? Amah again?

"I still miss you," I say to the surrounding emptiness. Closing my eyes, I pretend I'm in my kitchen, cutting up root vegetables to roast while Amah's listening in on speakerphone. Everything I've learned over the last few days spills from me. Amah would laugh, reminisce of times she needed to do the same. She'd tell me how to fold the grass to complete my basket and gasp at the antics of my darkling. My voice creaks and sticks like an ancient door when I confess that I'm angry our final conversations weren't full of cheerful gossip from wine-loosened lips. We deserved a better goodbye. I open my eyes and blow out a long breath. The breeze shifts and brings the scent of the stagnant, trapped water in little sections around the pool. It makes me think of Firthus and whether he'd have liked it here or hated it as much as Moros. The rocky edge is oily and covered with a spiny black moss that's not edible. I rap my fingertips over the red stone. The hot wind ripples the pond, and whatever creature lurks in the depths comes up to check out the ruckus. It's scaled and probably tastes like fried mud nuggets. My stomach rumbles and I snort a laugh.

"Thanks for the talk, Amah." My throat tightens. "Please stay safe and away from deities, and when you all get your phones back, tell everyone I love them."

I drag on my almost-dry clothes and follow my makeshift path, a spot between rocks. Harmonized grunting makes me pause, and I peek around to see Thor getting busy with another Thor or... Thorette. *Oh my.*

Behind them, six others mill about in an area I've named Puff Gardens. The reddish grass has pods that poof huge dandelion balls in the air when disturbed...like now. Three circle, wrestling each other to the ground, chuffing back and forth before the white, floating puffs become too tempting and they chase them as kids would play with bubbles. I cover my mouth to keep them from hearing my laughter. My bodyguard is enormous, but another is bigger. He has a dip in his bicep as though something took a bite out of him and it healed badly. Their lightly furred skin ranges from ruddy brown to near-black. The lady-Thors are tiny in comparison and have small, pointed breasts. Two females to six males. Good for them.

I back up behind the rocks, pass the pond, and go a different route to the cave, keeping an eye out for anything that resembles a fruit or vegetable. There has to be something I can eat in this realm. I crawl up on a car-sized rock to get a better look. A map would help…and paper. Jogging up the hill makes my energy sink, and I yawn as the cave entrance comes into sight. Moros sits and struggles with resetting smoking firewood. His stump has changed shape since that day. The center has expanded, a mountain on a hill. I need to ask him about that too, but his shoulders are down and he stares into the fire, ignoring my approach.

"Where's your protector?" he asks, eyes on the flames.

I crouch to move two pit stones back into place. "In the field reuniting with his girlfriend and others of his kind. I hope I didn't steal him from his family."

"What?" Moros's yell nearly sends the glitterlings to the air, but I breathe deep and they settle. He doesn't hide a glare as he stands.

"What's the problem?"

"They don't travel together." He storms away. "Take me to them. I want to see."

I'd like a nap, but I'm game if he'll talk about something besides taking over the world we no longer live in. "Fine." I stretch to the sky with a groan, then shuffle toward the field. It's not far, at least.

When we get to the edge of Puff Gardens, I peek from between some black-bark trees. Two of the males lounge in the grass. Thor and Thorette are nowhere to be seen. They're probably getting a drink after their romp. The big male and little female tussle about in play. The memory of Alex and me, rolling around in Shangri-La, crushing flowers beneath us as we gave into my siren heat pops up uninvited into my mind.

"This isn't possible," Moros whispers. "Not for this species."

"Why not? They seem cozy enough." I smile as one of the males stretches his arm up to bat at a puff in the hazy sunlight, his big chest rising and falling as though this day is defined in joy.

Moros blocks my view, staring at me in the way he does when I accidently move something, but can't replicate it. "I was here for years, Lula. They don't pack. They act as panthers, only meeting to mate or fight for territories." He grabs my chin hard and leans closer. "What did you do?"

"Nothing?" I try to tug from his hold, but he holds tight, and it reminds me of his hand wrapped around my throat. My muscles seize and the already bombarding air presses harder against my bones.

"Lula," he growls. "Did you tell them to get along? You would."

"Let go. I've only spoken to Thor. The others didn't even smell me." Panic and pressure build inside me like a wild, caged bird that doesn't understand barriers. "Seriously. Let go, or bad things will happen."

"Bad things." His dark chuckle sends chills over my neck. "You understand so little, daughter."

I'm not the only one. I shake my head in warning, but he holds fast. Squeezing my eyes shut, I let my force field go. This time feels like a rubber-band snap through my center. Moros's grip slips away and he flies back. I crouch and catch my breath as the pressure flips to tugging me apart, expanding me out as though each molecule of air fights for a piece of me. *I hate this.*

Moros stops rolling about twenty feet from the pack and stays on the ground. The creatures look his way and shift, tilting heads and humming interest. They stalk over.

"Great." Avoiding the red plants is impossible while jogging to catch up, and I leave a path of puffs in my wake. "Back away," I tell the growling darklings as the big one drags Moros by his ankle and tosses him toward the others. They shuffle backward, watching me. "Do not eat him."

Moros scrambles to me, breathing hard. "Command them to hunt for us. Meat." He staggers to his feet and brushes off his already filthy shirt. "You're too thin and you sleep too much when you should explore your attributes. They'll bring you food, you will eat for once, and then regain your strength. We do not have time for laziness." He steps beside me and crosses his arms, waiting.

"Actually…" I stare at the darkling pack. "We have all the time in the hell realm." The littlest female has celery green eyes, the big male, muddy mustard. "Go hunt, and bring what you kill here." They turn and trot off toward the red mountains. I face Moros and signal to the departing hunters. "There. Happy?"

He stomps off, not giving off the irritation he's aiming for with the white puff stuck on the back of his pants like a rabbit tail. "Now, we must return to check for carcasses."

I swish my hand through the air and follow. "It's fine. We'll go for takeout."

"I don't know what that is."

And he never will.

"It's when you order food from a restaurant and go pick it up," Rath's voice sounds behind us.

I swing around, heart hammering. "Rath?"

Hands in his pockets, he raises an eyebrow. "You didn't hit me this time. Progress. Have you been able to drop the morph yet?" The dark circles are gone from his eyes and he seems healthier, though his broody expression is bordering on depressed.

"No." I check behind him, then in the direction where the portal used to be. Just him and a huge bag slung over his shoulder.

"Not good, Lu. We should talk. Go away, Moros."

Chapter Twenty-Five

LULA

"I won't leave." Moros keeps his attention in the direction where the portal used to be. "Unlike you, no secrets lay between us." I scrunch my nose at Rath's raised eyebrow. There may have been a confession venting night because I wasn't expecting anyone to return. Still, Moros and I hide plenty from each other. "Daughter, let's go." He backs away, eyes on Rath.

Rath tut-tuts. "I heard Hercules crushed your arm into a floppy, useless appendage last time they put you in the hell realm. Imagine what he can do when he's not worried about you dooming him to death." He flicks his eyebrows. "He's guarding the portal around the corner, along with others. They will puree you if you even peek through."

Others like Alex? Comus?

"You know nothing about that battle, child," Moros snarls. "You were merely unwanted scat on the sandals of—"

The glitterlings rise, balling into a menacing sphere. With a sharp inhale, my father takes a step backward.

I lift fingers into the center of the ball, and they swirl, absorbing to my skin. "Go to the cave."

Moros bares his teeth and stomps off, sending a few puffs into the air.

Rath snags one to examine and drops the bag from his shoulder. "I brought you stuff. Your house is fine, though it could use a cleaning. Want me to hire a service?"

I stare at him, frozen in place because I'm too scared to ask and it's the only thing on my mind.

Rath sends the puff to the air and shoves his hands in his pockets. "He's not awake yet."

My knees quake and I sink to the ground, covering my mouth. "That means he's not dead, right?"

Rath drags the bag in front of me and sits behind it, cross-legged and facing me. We've had so many deep conversations this way and the ache in my chest escalates. "He's not dead." Rath holds up a finger. "But he's not awake."

"He's in a coma?"

"Open that." He lifts his chin to the bag. "Kinda. We can die like a mortal with enough force or abuse to our system, but we come back unless a deity uses their attributes to take us out. It's not a common occurrence. Turns out deities don't handle forever-death well."

"But I used my attributes." I hesitate, holding the zipper pull on the bag. I have had nothing from Earth in a month. Touching fabric is odd against my fingertips.

His attention drops to my fingers gripping my shirt over my heart. "You didn't hurt him with intent. Your new attributes went haywire, but you didn't want him dead."

My eyes burn. "So is he…" I tilt my head. "Mortal dead?"

"It's more like a divine stasis. There's something that is taking a long time to repair, and when it does, he will come back."

"How long has it been?"

His wince lasts a split second. "It's been six months."

The earth feels like it drops out from under me, and I blow out a breath to regain control. "It's been a month here, I think. The days are not as long as on Earth."

"I'm sorry it was so long. The only ones who can or will open the hell realm portal are Anice, Alex, and their father Hercules. Opening the hell realm, or any realm portal needs two. Anice was arrested until Comus offered to exchange himself if Zeus agreed to release Anice."

"So Comus is a prisoner?"

"No. He invoked old-ass magic with the help of an ancient archivist who finally chose a side. They cursed a particularly spiteful guard to take on Comus's appearance but made him silent. So one of Zeus's own army now sits in a makeshift prison, secured by his comrades. And Anice and Hercules opened the portal."

I soak that in for a long moment. That was a risk for them. As questions line up in my mind, I bite my lip and prepare myself for answers that already send trembles through me. "Is Hazel okay?" I ask.

Rath pushes his lips out and then frowns. "Hazel is…recovering. Moros and I are going to have a talk about her after we catch up." Rath brushes my still fingers from the bag, watching me closely. He nods when I don't combust him and unzips the bag. "I will tell you everything, but it's going to upset you and while you're doing well, you're not quite in control, are you?"

"No." I blow out a long breath. "I-I didn't mean to hurt anyone."

Rath's eyes squint with his grin. It's genuine, unforced and tease-free. It says whatever he's brought isn't a weapon against me, nor is he angry or disappointed in me. He clucks his tongue and tugs a paper bag from the big canvas. "You think we don't know that? Lula, you've proven who you are over and over to us. Even mad—which you have every right to be with the shit you've been through—you were reeling in the first moments of your zenith. It's been over three centuries and I still remember how unsettled everything felt inside, how foreign. We shouldn't have pushed." Inside the crinkly, white bag is a big container. "Baked mac and cheese with broccoli."

"Oh my god!" I snatch the container from him, rip the top open, and take a bite right off the pile, burning my tongue as I blindly search for a fork in the bag. *Worth it.* Gooey cheese and pasta warms a path to my empty stomach, and my desperate fingers wrap around the plastic utensil. Now I can dive in.

Rath doesn't laugh at me. He sits and studies the scenery as I moan over each bite. "We've discussed what happened over and over again with those present—the ones who will make our leaders if"—he gives a slight grin—"when things change for good and Zeus steps down."

"Do you think that will happen? I've replayed those moments too, and he was persistent in ending me. He seems like the unmovable mountain type."

He's quiet for a long moment, observing me with his chin in his hand, elbow propped on his knee. "To take the life of an immortal is seen by deities like how you or I consider the most foul, torturous, invasive action taken against a mortal. The ultimate despicable act. Zeus lost a lot of face that day. His followers who expect him to rule with the hardest fist of all the gods saw him as weak, and those who were intrigued by you pinned him as a brute. Rumors of sirens, you, and Alex have flowed heavier than ambrosia. I've never been more popular, and have had to tell more deities to fuck off over the last months than I have in my lifetime."

I snort around my mouthful and give him an apologetic grimace. "How much of a monster have they painted me?"

"That I have not been quiet about. You're no monster, though your father..." He sets his jaw. "It's unheard of to force someone's zenith through pain and threat. You're actually handling things well."

I shake my head, mouth stuffed with a perfectly cooked crown of broccoli. "I'm not. Inside is in constant motion."

"How?"

I take one more bite and set the box aside. I'm going to finish that once my stomach remembers what food is. Explaining the whirlwind within me isn't easy, but I get through it. Rath listens, as he always does. There are a few stumbling moments that make me mill over doubts—he's lying to me, holding my sisters captive, Alex is dead but they need more information. I squash the thoughts as the atmosphere does to me. Who else can I trust with this? Moros would use my words to stir my tangled mind and aim my destruction at others. Rath...he will listen and help if he can. He's quiet when I pick the box back up and jam in another bite. He tugs a piece of grass and sniffs it, bends it, and rolls it in his long fingers.

"You're holding back," I say, eyes to the mac and cheese.

"I don't want to call you an oddity, but you are. Everything is backward. You flinch and grimace every few minutes. Deities should be more settled after zenith, but you were forced, and I assume with Moros as your hell realm companion, you've lacked guidance."

"He's excellent at helping me practice my force field."

"I bet he is." Slipshod words tumble with amusement before his expression hardens. "We all want you home…"

"But I'm not safe to be around." Doubt stirs the reality I wish was wrong. *And you never will be.*

"Not yet." He reaches over and brushes his finger over the glitterlings on my forearm. They don't rip him to shreds, thankfully, though the pressure cooker increases. "Can we bring someone to you? We have a trusted oracle friend. The visit would be short and highly guarded. We're not sure what the atmosphere will do to a human."

"Or what I would do." The sun starts its setting routine, dragging the moons up into the haze.

"A zenith reading is overwhelming. You said you're spinning inside, but when an oracle reads you, they pry around in there, scooping up your mind and sorting through what you can't see."

My full stomach shifts and I scoot back on the grass and ball my fingers, not that it's ever helped curb my power before. Moros calls it an obvious tell of my learned humanity. I try to hold it and prevent harm. According to him, I shouldn't. The faster I learn to set it free, the better. But I killed Alex when that happened. That will never happen again, and no one can see what's inside me.

"You're shaking your head." Rath chews his lip, eyes squinted at me. "I would be here, as would Comus, and we'd all be near the portal."

"For quick escape?"

Rath shrugs. "Are you going to blow me up if I tell you 'yes?'"

I snort and lean forward to try for one more bite. It's salty and tangy cream bliss in this world of crushing starkness. I had pasta at least twice a week before entering the hell realm. "No. I understand but…" Out of the three guys, Rath has always been the most honest. The connection between us is a relatable kinship I don't have with others. His face is icy stone and astoundingly pretty—stare-at-the-wonder-of-nature pretty—but I'm not attracted to him. I've hugged him, touched him with familiar ease, but there's no burn like with Alex, no need to bask in him, though I want to be near him. If he understood what I was, would he ever sit with me again? Would he listen if my purpose is to be a pressurized weapon?

"But what, Lu?"

I study my fingers, the patterned silvery metallic over gray. "I'm Moros's daughter. He's said it a hundred times since I met him, but it didn't fully sink in until I changed. What if doom is all I'm made of?"

"Do you want to rip me apart, Lula? I withheld information from you too. Actually, I tried to convince Alex not to tell you at all, thinking you'd be safer if you never found out, like I did with your sister Nysa. She doesn't know I watched her before we found you." He goes quiet and stares, tense and ready to dissipate, but I grip the glitterlings to me with difficulty. He exhales, lowering his shoulders. "Olympus isn't Earth. As you have now experienced under Zeus's bolts, truth isn't met with rational conversation. We lie meticulously and often to prevent shit like what happened to you. That being said, you were raised around humans and we should have handled things differently."

"Being honest when we met would have been a good start." I pluck a blade of grass but it falls apart, not to dust, but big flakes.

"You're telling me that when you met Alex, after the night you'd had, you would have been fine if he told you about your new role in a war of deities?" He scrunched his face, lips twisting. "Please. You'd have moved an hour later and never spoken to us again."

He may be right. "Okay, so not then, but soon after."

"Oh, just admit it—there's never a good time to tell someone you were recruiting them to overhaul Olympus." Rath reaches into the bag, pulls out a candy bar, and hands it over. "Especially when you have more than a passing fondness for them. Navigating love is tough, Lu."

He brought me chocolate? I sniffle. "Fine, but Alex should have trusted me earlier. I'd have come around and he shouldn't have left right when he told me." I take a bite and bittersweet heaven melts against my tongue. The tension inside me loosens the slightest bit.

"You have no idea how much he regrets that. I wasn't around before the break to know what he was like, but I haven't seen anything affect him like you." He winces, eyes trailing a tear that slips down my cheek. "But you understand that now?"

I'm not ready to address this. The world flip-flops around me, asking me to rip it apart or disappear from existence. Breathe deep. Another bite of chocolate is a good focal point. I fold the wrapper and put the rest in the bag to save for later, then pop up and pace with crossed arms, sending a flitter of puffs through the air.

"I'll translate." Rath clears his throat and speaks in a pitchy lilt. "I can't talk about it because my attributes are affected by my emotions, but yeah, yes, you're right, as usual." I bare my teeth at him as I pass. He beams back, arranging everything back in the bag, and loops the band over his shoulder as he stands. "Olympus is in turmoil, and getting Anice and Hercules together is a risk. We can't leave a portal open because that puts you in danger, plus Moros could sneak out, and I can't stay." He waves a hand through the air. "The time being off is probably for the better, but I don't like that you're here."

"It's okay," I whisper, pausing my pacing. "Olympus is at war?"

"Not yet."

"And Artemis?"

He groans, tipping his head toward the cave. "Come on. I can't stay much longer. Hercules has probably been standing guard for days." I wince, but he waves me off. "Not your fault. Um, my relationship is even more complicated, plus I'm playing transporter for meetings."

"Is she still on the Council after everything?"

He purses his lips. "How about we stick to you?"

"Oh, that good, huh?" I try not to put pity into my wince, but it can't be helped. Their relationship is as toxic as hell realm water. "Sorry."

Rath tilts his head. "You're fading—or the darkness on your skin is."

I jerk my hands up. The color and shimmer lightens for a moment, then darkens again with another pressure pulse. Blowing out a lengthy breath, I let my arms fall back to my sides.

"What were you thinking about?" He steps in the direction of the cave.

I shrug. "You and Artemis."

His shoulders sink. "Let me guess—it shouldn't be so difficult between two people who love each other? Why do I keep returning when she only pushes me away for literal decades? How come she chooses a king who makes wrong decision after wrong decision over me each and every time?"

"No." A little. I walk beside him and peek at him from the corner of my vision. "I was thinking about how reckless love is. How we bend and break to obtain it, then fight it. How it doesn't diminish." I didn't plan to lay my head on his shoulder. Before confessions, doomed lineage, and an unfamiliar realm, it was a common occurrence between us. I love him as I do my sisters, and if I could rest against them, hold their hand, and loop our arms together to make a physical connection, I would. Nothing fits right now except for hope that Alex will wake, and putting my head on a friend's shoulder.

Rath doesn't pause his slow steps, and drops his head against mine like a cranial hug. "I've missed you, Lu."

I give a small nod as a loud snort brings my attention behind us. Rath startles at Thor, stepping in front of me, arms splayed. Thor bares his teeth and does his hopping, I'm-going-to-pounce-on-you, dance.

"Thor, no. No eating Rath. He's a friend."

Thor snorts again and swipes his talons together, making a threatening *schwing* sound. That's new. He settles though, stepping forward but not too close.

"You can speak to darklings," Rath says, tight and breathless. "Holy Hera, Lula, you can command them?"

"Yes." I step around him and toward Thor. "Did you have fun with your girlfriend?"

He lifts his face to the sky and I cover my ears. He lets loose a cawing roar. The little female peeks out from the rocks and crouches in the grass.

"Comus is going to flip. He may actually leave Grace for a night to see this."

"Grace?" The mention of my sister's name nearly brings me to my knees. "Is she okay? Is Hazel with her? Her and Comus are together?"

Rath nods and backs away, keeping his eyes on Thor. "Grace is fine. Comus is staying with them. Hazel is having a rough time, which is what I need to speak to Moros about, and you need to hear, but it's not…" He blows out a breath. "Lula, you can't trust him."

"I know." I step beside Rath, nudging him to turn around and walk toward the cave. Thor gives a grunt behind us and plops down in the grass, giving the ground a little tremble.

"Do you?" Rath follows, eyes still on the darklings. The female crawls toward Thor, crouching behind him. Maybe she will stay.

I climb over a rock, tiredness re-surging into my limbs. "I have questions about his dealings with my sisters and...my mother, but haven't been able to bring myself to ask without my insides wanting to explode. Maybe it will be fine if I listen, but run if I tell you to, okay?" I wince and give him an apologetic glance.

"I'll slip into shadow if I need to, but feel free to blow up Moros. Though I'm not sure you could kill him. We know you can make him really uncomfortable."

I cringe at the memory of his flailing body and the helplessness of not being able to stop. "What if I hadn't been able to call the glitterlings back? Would he have mortal-died by suffocation?"

He shrugs a shoulder. "This is why we need an oracle. We don't know. It's possible he would have died by your attributes. Or he would restart and die again, until he was released from the ball thingy you made." He grins and I'd elbow him but a thought halts me and I press my palms to my cheek.

"That's not happening to Alex, is it?" I ask. "He's not waking up and re-dying on repeat, is he?" Pressure. So much pressure. I want to let it all go before it crushes me like an aluminum can, but I can't. I'll hurt Rath, Thor, Thorette, and the planet. Possibly everyone at the portal entrance. Earth. Humans.

"Lula, picture the pressure in your chest absorbing into your body."

I laugh a single, cutting note and lean over, hands to my knees. "Not my chest...everywhere. All of me is pressure. It surrounds. Back away." I've mortal-killed Alex and now he's living in a hellish death-loop. "Just tell me."

He tilts his head, brows furrowed. "He hasn't woken. Not once. His heart won't start yet. Things like this take time."

"Like what? This hasn't ever happened before, Rath!" The grass rips apart starting at my red, clay-stained shoes and moving out in a circle, and then he does back away. "How do you know he'll wake? And what if he hurts? What if he never wakes?" And if I saw him again, I'd probably kill him further on accident because he tornadoes my emotions like no other being in any universe. I'd only torture him more. Power vibrates and spirals on my skin. Up close the flecks are organized, keeping exact distance from each other. But all together, they're deadly chaos. "What if your oracle comes and I hurt her, or others? My sisters can't see me. Not like this."

Glitterlings drain in spirals that shoot toward the ground, and the decimated land around me expands, flitting tiny flecks of grass into the air until I cough. Rath's head tilts, a studious expression on his face, but he doesn't coax me down or direct me as he did before. He doesn't run.

I can't take the pressure of this world. "Move, Rath. Get away from me. I'm not…safe."

I don't know where to step, how to move from the damage I'm causing, and my heart somehow still pounds, though it's compressed along with my lungs. Rath straightens and watches the crumbling line of doom roll closer. I yell a garbled nonsensical mix about not wanting him to die, and how I can't do any of this and I'm sorry, he shouldn't have come, all while he calmly resembles a statue as death butts up to his shoe. The destruction makes its way around his feet, but doesn't take him with it. Air finds its way into my lungs and I sink to my knees as the glitterlings slow, then stop.

He swivels, taking in the sheared land around us, then sidesteps to the unscathed grass, leaving an untouched circle—a tiny, safe island in a lake of disintegrated life. Lifting his eyes to mine, he smiles wide. "Your attributes may be a mystery, but you're nothing like your father."

Chapter Twenty-Six

LULA

I'VE LAIN IN SILENCE ON MY FUR PILE AND GLARED AT THE WALL FOR two days. If I see the mask of parental concern Moros wears to hide the cruel demon beneath, he'll wear a new face the glitterlings provide. I understood that his morals were not aligned with a human world, but hoped that once shown humanity beyond Olympus, he could learn. But what he did—what he allowed—his brand of cruelty is too vast to correct. He belongs in this realm, though I fear for the influence he puts on the darklings. There can be no others like him. I won't allow it.

After Rath left, Grace's letter confirmed what Moros had done, as did the barest twinkle in my father's eye while Rath threw disgusted accusations at him. Moros is proud of himself, and while not everything turned out the way he'd hoped, a large portion of his plan has come to fruition. I'm a monster he thinks he controls. He's wrong. Maybe Rath was right to threaten to toss Moros into the shadow realm where he would wander in a fuzzy black-and-white world, seeing food but not being able to eat it. Having bodies walk by, but wispy fingers passing through. It would be torture, but Moros has lived millennia torturing others for what he thinks is his benefit.

He threatened Gerty, pretended to love Venora, and then stole Hazel, taking a vicious approach with her to keep Venora doing what he wanted. My father surreptitiously gleaned information from each, posing as either a lover or an abusive owner, then locked them away to be used when needed. He murdered Gerty when he discovered Venora could control and kill more because she was more powerful. More usable. And then Deimos came along. Moros's dedicated follower, who fled the amphitheater at the sight of Alex, brought in the most manipulative tactics to use on Hazel. Deimos was her savior. He forged such a relationship with her that he convinced her that seeing her mother die in front of her by his hand wasn't real. The glitterlings shiver on my skin when I think of how terrified Venora must have been in her last months. No, my father didn't kill her, but he allowed his men free reign to do as they pleased in the Earth realm with no consequences. It's the divine way of old, and I haven't decided on what justice could ever set right what he's done. I wake with thoughts of Hazel's turmoil. How confused she is, and only now beginning to realize what happened to her, long after Rath took her from Deimos's side. The grief of losing her mother to a deity she loved isn't bearable. It hurts to have felt that to such a small degree compared to her. I thought the worst of Alex, but the worst is being here with the most dangerous deity in existence. Or maybe second most dangerous.

I grieve with my sisters, though from another realm, guilt-ridden that my father caused such pain, and that I harmed the wrong person. But with the truth known, our grief has the focus my lost loved ones deserve. I can say goodbye, remember the light each of them brought to the world and learn so I can protect my remaining sisters. Even if that means keeping Moros here for eternity. If we're very lucky, they'll throw Deimos and Zeus in here with us other monsters.

Validity is present in my world again, settling my insides at least a little. Hazel would not have existed the way she did then shared everything with Comus and Rath if she didn't trust them. I had been wrong to doubt the guys and let my father manipulate me, but that's the past now. I'm moving forward because Rath will return, even if I told him no oracle and no sisters until my attributes behave. They will...eventually. I'll gain control of the inner deity because the letter from Grace made my chest ache with longing to see her and also to have her see me. She doesn't care if I've sprouted horns, scales, wings

—though she noted that would be cool as shit—or even if I fanged-out and bit her, because we're sisters and sometimes biting happens between those we love the most. She said she was coming whether I wanted her to or not, because that's what family does.

Moros stomps into the cave and Thor clicks his talons over the glossy floor in warning. He's a perceptive creature and becoming more protective by the day. He places himself between me and my father now, during sleep and eating and conversations.

"What is wrong with you?" Moros says. "It's been days." He shuffles, dragging something from one side of the cave to the other, no doubt to have something to do other than stand over me and to make Thor more uncomfortable. "Do you miss the God of Shadows?" His tone gives me the notion that his nose is scrunched and lips sneering. It's time to see how deep the destruction goes and how I can either sway or annihilate his sick mindset.

I push myself up and stare at him over my shoulder.

He nods as if we're on the same page. "Let's practice, daughter. You must be ready for your lover to return so we may use him to take us back."

"He's not my lover." I scoot around until I'm facing him. Thor chuffs at me, I believe asking if I'd like him to eat my father, but I ignore him.

Moros stands as tall as he can without bumping his head against the ceiling. "Good. He is beneath you. All Olympians are."

I narrow my eyes. "Tell me about my mother."

"I have." He steps outside and I stand, stretch, and follow.

"No." A wave of heat flows through me, but I need this conversation. "You've told me what she was like but avoid telling me about her end. Were you there?"

Thor gives a snort, shimmies in front of me, and nudges my shoulder with his head. I take five steps backward with quickness. He always keeps a little distance. The ground rumbles and a pop sounds from within the cave. A chunk of the entrance falls and splinters, sending shards flinging across glassy stone. Moros pivots to me and tilts his head, eyes flicking between Thor and me.

I may as well own what I am before he continues to write his own conclusions. What we both do is wrong and I will fix one of us before the other. I stare at the darkling's orange eyes, and smile at the attention he gives me. The bristles under his chin are softer than they appear. He doesn't growl or snarl or even back away. He's a good being. "Go be with your kind. You don't have to come back."

"What are you doing?" Moros yells as Thor ambles off. "We need him to bring food, and when we leave, the other darklings can fight him instead of us."

"I'm tired of using others. It's not the way the world works."

"Yes it—"

The ground rumbles again and I ball my fists. "You will never use another being to gain power you don't deserve. Now, I want to know about my mother."

His throat bobs as he swallows and he sits on a log next to the fire. "Your sisters didn't tell you?"

"No." I take a seat across from him, peeking over the field, but see no sign of Thor.

"Then you should ask them." He smiles as if there's a joke here. There is no humor in the death of Petra, Gerty, and Venora, nor my cutoff state from my remaining sisters.

"Make me understand why you killed her, because I'm positive that's what happened. There will be no more lies. I want to know what led to that." It may be a poor decision, but if I have to live with this deity for eternity, I'll figure out what makes him tick.

He's silent for a long while, but I wait him out, and finally he grabs a stick, poking at the smoking logs until flames rise again. "She ran from me after her phase ended." His jaw clenches. "Decades I waited for that moment, wooing her, letting her love me, and she hid as though I would have harmed you. At the end of her pregnancy, I found her and saw the proof of our union. I obtained a home for us, and she gave birth to you." He raises his eyes to mine, biting his lips together with the first expression of uncertainty I've seen on him. "You were so tiny and frail, but I could see that flicker within. You were *my* child and would serve me well when you came of age. I sought a dark oracle to read your power, but had to travel to find her, and it was unsafe to take you. When I found what I needed, I returned to collect you, but your mother had fled again, stealing you from me. With the oracle's help, I caught her and, assuming you were with her, used my attribute to send her to the veil because I could no longer trust her with your care and raising. However, when I searched her home, you were missing."

I fight to hold tight to the pressure, keeping my balled fists in my lap. I was with Amah already. My mother handed me over to her most trusted sister, understanding that this monster incapable of love would find her again. Amah's disdain for the gods and method of running from them is valid.

Moros's brows furrow. "Do you understand the importance of your existence, daughter? You may weep for Petra, but you will realize her betrayal in time. As I feverishly searched for you, the Olympians caught me with my guard down and sent me here."

My balled hands sparkle with swirling black. "And you found the portal back and abducted my sisters."

"A hundred and eighty-three Earth years apart, daughter. Because of betrayal and lies. Never again. The Olympians will return and attempt to bring us devastation, but your doom will call to the ones who matter, and *you* will lead them."

"You are the doom-bringer, not me."

He stands with fluid grace. "Consider everything I've done for you and all will be well." He ducks into the cave and returns wielding his spear. "I will give you some time and go hunt until you realize that I understand the way things are. The universe is not the lovely field of flowers you murmur about in your sleep, and if Alexiares does live and returns, it will be to tear you apart for what you did to him."

MY DREAMS HAVE BECOME ODD ABSTRACT RENDITIONS OF MY PAST mixed with ethereal floating sensations. I dream of Hera. Her gulping gaze swallows me into a starry funnel before I land in a forest that fast-tracks a thousand years of growth within a few seconds. Amah peeks from around an ancient, twisted tree, her dark eyes twinkling in the double moonlight. Her smile is one I haven't seen since before Lena died—she's lit so bright; it beams from her mouth and ignites joy in every witness. I'm sucked into the mossy ground, falling through hot lava that makes my skin twitch as it disintegrates, before I melt into the liquid center of the Earth and the pressure builds in preparation for my rebirth.

When I slam back into my body with a jolt, I try to decipher what any of these images mean before they wisp away on the sulfur-scented breeze. Why do I always end up in the Earth's core and feel like I belong there? I swallow hard and inhale against a handful of ginger grass to calm the ever-present nausea.

In the deepest sleep, the sisters I've lost invade my abstract world of metal and stars. They stare at me, gray-tinged skin, unmoving, and expressionless before they morph into Alex, but he sleeps. I move close —closer, needing to be near him and then his eyes snap open, gold capturing me until he kisses me, holding me to him with his hand on the back of my head as I swim to consciousness. I expect the half-dreams, half-waking memories to lash out at me like Moros said Alex would, but that never happens. I trace his bare skin with my fingertips until he captures me beneath him. His scent fills my memory to a point where I wake with a gasp and look for him only to find a burnt-popcorn-scented creature who doesn't understand that he's free. Curled up at the mouth of the cave, Thor blinks reflective eyes in the dark, helping stave off the ache, tugs, or crush of my soul, my body, my mind. He returned and won't stay away. Maybe he senses I need him…or he waits for me to crumble and take this world with me. I'm not settling into this form.

The deity inhabiting me is taking over.

Chapter Twenty-Seven

ALEX

WITH ALL THE UNCOMFORTABLE THINGS I'VE HAD TO BEAR IN MY LONG years, waking from death is the most unpleasant.

Thought steps forward before anything else. It's beyond frustrating to live solely in the mind, intangible and working on sludgy blood and used-up oxygen. My first reaction is to scream for my heart to beat and lungs to open, but they stay impossibly still and then I remember what's coming and where I am.

It's happened twice before. Locked in a prepubescent state for over a thousand years didn't do positive things for my mind. Once my body was old enough to explore, Anice and I careened into reckless teenager mode like the universe had never seen. We had the wisdom of scholars, but hadn't felt pain, lust, power, touched others as adults, or had the freedom of privacy. We did a ton of stupid shit trying every new thing we understood but hadn't experienced. Like dying.

But as a deity, dying comes with waking. Thought, then sensation, then life, then agony, then greater agony.

Lula.

Her name whispers, as does the flash of dark silver piercing into me. A surge of pain pummels my chest. The last memory or nerves connecting? I shouldn't have pushed her. I shouldn't have touched, kissed, or made love to her either, but that didn't stop me. She makes me as rash as those long-ago days of discovery, but has certainly slowed me now.

The extended quiet in the solitude of my thoughts settles into dread when another sharp stab assaults my center against my spine. Connection. I shouldn't appreciate the stony silence of death, but the agony will start soon, and then I'll brave the world again.

My mind adheres to Lula—if she's here and okay, but the panic has me retreating. I'm not ready to face her, even here. Even though I love her.

She ripped my chest open, stopped my heart, and killed me.

Each new twitch of a random muscle has me preparing for the worse. The body appreciates either life or death. It's in constant motion, even during the stillest moments, until forced to fight its own end. Reawakening is the reverse of shutting down, and no soma form, not mortal or divine, appreciates waking after it's been allowed a permanent rest. As a bonus, my mind is clear and present for the event. My guess is so immortals never again put themselves back in the position I find myself.

My entire world expands and contracts with a burst of heat and one weak lub-dub of my heart. The itch begins. Fingertips burst into a sensation that—were my body functional—I'd rip my hands off to escape. This is my third waking. My first in this millennium. I haven't forgotten a moment and my mind spins. I can't stop it. If I could, I'd consider it.

Another pulse in my chest gives the sensation of drowning and filling to burst. The tight itch of waking vessels extends, reminding me I have arms and legs, but making me wish I didn't. I give a mental scream of fury at the hellfire the two meager heart pumps created. Searing heat licks my veins as they expand for the first time in long enough.

And this is the beginning.

The following moments are centuries long. It's not every inch that's pissed at restarting, it's each molecule. Each cell singes from the torture of awakening with starved need and reanimating with blood. Breath comes in a brief gasp that is a thousand needles into each alveolus.

End it. Please.

But my body doesn't end. It begins again with gasps and pumps and cells of fire. Muscles contract in tight bunches, remembering their purpose. Organs squirm back to life though it feels like my entrails are being ripped from my abdomen, one by pissed-off one.

Hematite eyes flash in my memories before flashing to green ones sculpted of chrysoprase stone. Only then do I allow my mind to adhere to my siren. She calls to me, and I revel in twisting her soft, red curls around my fingers back in the lifetime when touch was peace. I cling to the smell of rain and raspberries as my lungs heave for life. Phantom echoes of her laugh, her growl, meld into the vision of betrayal in her eyes that I will repair somehow, because she's my anchor, my universe, my firecracker.

"Lula." Raspy vibrations expand my throat.

The senses come in stages. Earthy scents slams into me—an overgrown greenhouse, flooded and warm with stale life and wet dirt. Not unpleasant, but unfamiliar, and not in the hell realm. Where am I? Where's Lula?

Hearing rolls in on an avalanche. I flinch, sending muscles into another round of painful spasms. A jumble of muffled words pans into understanding.

"Hold him still. He shouldn't have woken so quickly." The female's voice is familiar.

"As I recall, he's succumbed to mortal wounds a time or two. It gets easier each occurrence."

Placing the voices is impossible while my body riots. Bands of brimstone clamp over my biceps and my scream is so intense it's silent, moved beyond vocal cords to an undiscovered universe. A jab into my arm may as well be a rusty ax. But then…warmth and sweet numbness flows through the path of fire in my veins, then up to fade my wide-awake mind.

SLEEP IS A SURREAL BLEND OF DREAMS THAT SLIPS AWAY THE MOMENT consciousness returns, then breezes back in colorful mist when the mind falters. I can't stay here though I try. Small sounds shift in the darkness until the curiosity is too much and I force my eyes only to wince at the sting and brightness. Tiny ocular muscles ache and stretch as I take in the room. That's a new sensation. Candle sconces spotlight against dark stone walls, and pale tree roots drape from the ceiling to the floor in one corner.

I squint and groan at each stretched sensation and the headache, then again at the stabbing pain when I move my fingers. My mouth is tight, and I work my tongue, though it's bloated and dry. The earthy scent is unusual, but familiar in a way that only comes with smelling nearly everything. The waft rolls through memory trying to adhere, and halts on one rarely visited location. "Is this…the underworld?"

"Welcome to my humble abode." Hades smiles wide, flopped in a casual open-legged stance from a large wooden chair next to the bed. He snaps twice and a pale creature in the shadows darts for the door. What the hell was that?

I turn my head with a wince. Every muscle strains as if they'll tear. Iaso's smiling face pops into view. "Your brother will be thrilled to find you awake. Then he may pummel you for scaring him."

The skin is too tight on my forehead when I scrunch my eyebrows. Has Iaso ever been to the underworld? "You're…" My throat rasps closed.

"I will call Anicetus."

I inhale long. "Wait." My mind flounders in a sleepy fog. I need a minute to process all of this. Where's Lula? Opening my mouth, I stretch my jaw, moving the thin, rubber channel leading to my nose. I grumble and tug at it until Iaso smacks my hand away and drags it obnoxiously slow until I gag and it's free of my body. A sneeze makes each muscle explode and I wonder if this is a side of death in the underworld I didn't know about. Why would I need a feeding tube?

She squints her dark eyes as I shift from her inspection. "You've been down a while, Alexiares. Though in stasis, some nutrients absorb. Please, let me help you." With a thumb on my chin, she opens my mouth more easily than she should be able to. She shines a tiny flashlight in and frowns, then bombards my vision until I turn my head and blink away blinding circles.

I couldn't have been in stasis. "How long?" I ask.

She gives me an apologetic glance. "It's been eight moon cycles since you returned with the God of Shadows from the hell realm."

Eight months? I'm lucky I woke at all. Breath comes hard and painful. Almost a year away from Lula. A year of neglect toward our cause while my body deteriorated. Needles and tubes spring from my arm, Fluid bags hang from a pole. No wonder every twitch of my muscles feels like the stretch of a chilled rubber band. Is Lula safe? Learning her attributes?

"Where is she?" I croak at Hades.

"Hell realm," he says, thankfully because I'm not sure my tongue works well enough to explain more. I expect details but he nods at Iaso.

Lips pursed, Iaso turns and picks up a phone from a side table. "It shouldn't take Anice—"

"Not yet." I drag my thin, pained body to the edge of the bed, finding tubes everywhere. Iaso disconnects the most uncomfortable ones and I stand on newborn deer legs, wrapping the sheet around my bony waist. She moves to assist but I wave her off. "Hold on the visitors." They can't see me like this. I'd topple with a light breeze.

Hades shrugs and unfolds from the chair. "Let's walk and talk."

Outside the room, four narrow openings are nestled ten-feet apart along the half-moon-shaped chamber. The underworld is the dark brother of Olympus, yet warmer; cozy with the lower ceilings and slate walls.

I wobble, holding the wall and wincing as protesting tendons pop against bone. Hades walks beside me for four steps before he slows, tilting his head. A small smile twitches across his lips. "Prepare for your grandmother."

Hera pops out of a passageway, eyes finding me and softening. "Alexiares."

I nod at her, throat too dry to work. A tremor shakes my spine. We shouldn't be in the underworld. Is this another bigger jail cell? Why? Has Lula been taken or is she after me to finish the job? Unless…has this been Hera's hideout?

"Relax." Hades steps closer to Hera, circling behind her. "I have things in place to keep out those I don't want here. Actually, I don't want most here." Did he just sniff her hair? "Few."

Her eyes narrow, cutting to him before she moves toward me. "I'm glad to see you up, grandson."

Stomping sounds from a corridor to my right and Hades gives off an exasperated groan. "Case and point." He turns to the opening, "You better not have harmed Cerberus, Herc."

My father walks into the cave, crouched and sideways to fit. "That dog loves me. I'd never harm Cerbie. You, on the other hand…" He stands to his full height, imposing as ever, and glares at Hades before he realizes I'm awake. "Son," he says on a quick outtake, rushing to my side to place his hand on my chest over my heart. He cups my jaw, and strokes my cheek with more gentleness than I thought was possible for him. The emotion on his face makes my eyes tingle. He leans, pressing his forehead to mine. "Your mother will rejoice."

"Is she okay?"

Father nods.

"You missed all the fun, Alex." Hades leans against the wall, eyeing Hera as if about to pull her between his wide-legged stance. "Olympus is at an odd peace, but it's the type of silence before the bloodshed begins. Both sides are waiting for a catalyst that will tumble the realm into war."

"Is Ichnaea safe? Plutus?"

"She is," Father says. "Though Zeus's army keeps her and her maids in the temple because Plutus is in hiding." My father winces as he presses my bare chest where muscle used to be. "You need meat, and to throw stones."

My legs wobble. It would hurt to flick a pebble. I hobble back to the room I've been lying dead in for too long and collapse onto the bed, breathless.

Iaso fusses over me until Hera steps in, leaning against roots that seem to shift to support her. "We need to speak."

Hades and my father come closer as Iaso pokes at me, then relents to check a monitor, sighs and steps out.

"Make this quick." Father stands beside me, taking my arm and working muscles that are not interested in any further activity. "Hebe will want to visit."

"She can't," Hades says. "Alex needs a hot second to wake up, and Hebe belongs in Olympus. They'll understand he's awake when she's dancing over golden streets, and if she disappears to come here, Zeus will follow. Predictably, he's waiting for someone to lead him to Alex.

Maybe if you'd have engaged sooner, we wouldn't be in this predicament. It took your wife being locked up to get you off your muscular ass." He lifts his lip in a snarl.

"I would have made things worse. You know that, Hades."

"No, I know you could be king if you weren't such a pus——"

My father takes a quick step forward, shoulders held high, head grazing the ceiling. "You are one to chide about claiming——"

"Gentlemen," Hera interrupts. "Enough. Let us speak."

"I thought we were doing that." Hades leans beside her, twirling a finger around a vine. It bursts with tiny flowers, making my brows ache as they furrow. He should not be able to do that. "Yes, we have much to discuss—like if Herc plays this round or sits on the bench as usual."

My father glowers and grasps my foot, flexing it until the muscles in my calf may snap. I growl. He ignores me and repeats with the other foot. "I brought the barracks down on most of the royal guard and am separated from my wife unless I sneak into my own home, and you question my intent?"

Hades shrugs a shoulder. "Alex weakened it for you."

My snort of laughter turns into a groan with the all-over ache.

"Are you worried for Lula?" Hera asks, fingering the pink, miniature trumpets Hades created. She doesn't look at me, but her words resonate. She's giving me space, but she never answered whether or not she was on my side. That could mean that after the first skirmish Olympus has seen since Moros and my extended unconsciousness, she could still be deciding.

"Of course, I am." I wet my lips. "Is she okay?"

"She's in the hell realm with Moros. What do you think?" Her eyes pierce, seeking something my mind is too raw to explain.

My muscles twitch in my arms, waking back up as my father manipulates my limbs. I'm thin. Undernourished and atrophied. Eight months. How long is that in hell realm time? Is she still there? My legs barely work right now. I can't fight Moros if he's healed. "How long will I be like this?"

"A week," Hades says. "I've seen worse."

"You cannot go to her like that." Grandmother gives a slight tilt of her head, reading me too well. "She hasn't changed back from her goddess state."

"Why not?"

Hades frowns and leans forward. He opens his mouth and closes it.

The silence presses against me, crushing me so hard I nearly yell at him to just tell me the dire news of what can't be.

"I hate to tell you this," he says quietly. "But...I have no idea."

I blow out a long breath and glare at the asshole.

Hera gives Hades a withering glance before giving me her attention. "She is as well as a new goddess can be without readings and guidance. Your men have reported back to us."

Something loosens the fear in my achy chest. She's alive, in a safe location compared to what could be, but unable to find her way to normalcy. I look to Hades. There's something about his flagrant disregard for rules and niceties that resonates with this moment. "What do I do?"

"You sleep off the death hangover, eat meat, throw stones, then catch up with your friends." He pushes from the wall and crosses his arms, face missing its typical mischievous smirk. "Everyone get out, and don't mention his waking to anyone. Any-fucking-one. Iaso will do the same. He's guarded and masked here, giving us time. Not a lot, but some." He flicks his fingers at the door. When Hera and my father step out, Hades tilts his head at me.

"You and Hera?" I ask. She does not take orders, even from kings.

"Have the same goal." He purses his lips, eyes flashing. "And she's married. We came to each other with half information from the ages, and when we combined our knowledge, our path became clear. And don't change the subject, this is about you." He raises a finger. "You get one week, Alexiares. Then you stop hiding."

"I'm not hiding."

His brows both furrow and angle as if even my stupidity is brainless. "If you haven't noticed, I'm the king of the underworld. Death, secrets, escapes, disappearances, and the reactions associated with those things are in my wheelhouse. Do *not* bullshit me. Now, what do you want on your burger?"

Chapter Twenty-Eight

LULA

RATH SHOUTS MY NAME FROM PAST THE ROCKS. THANK GOODNESS, because I'm hungry and antsier than ever. I have to hold the glitterlings now, focusing as though an invisible thread connects us. They shift and dance on my skin, asking to let them destroy. I'm dizzy and grumpy even with bathing in the water hole daily, keeping creatures—except for Thor and Thorette—at bay with my force field. That attribute is becoming second nature. It gives a pop of relief as it falls into place, but the pressure remains. When I wander toward the rocks, Moros follows.

I glare back at him. "Stay here." I've barely spoken a word to him since Rath was here last, not for lack of Moros's efforts. He wants to discuss future plans and I want to toss him across the planet for murdering my sisters and my mother, but then he'd escape and wreck the Earth. It's best if we coexist in silence.

"I will hear the news of the Earth."

"You will stay here." My words clap off stone, but it takes Thor shrugging past him, baring his fangs, to stick Moros in place. When I scramble over the first few boulders, a deep female voice in the distance makes me pause, and I tell Thor to wait as I slip behind a line of red rocks.

"Put the arrows away." Rath's voice is a gentle tease. "Moros is unarmed…well, unhanded." He chuckles, and as I peer between a gap between the rocks, Rath twists in front of someone, blocking my view with himself and another duffle bag. "Get it?"

"Yes." The woman's voice is tight, and she leans to look past Rath's shoulder, doe-eyes darting around the landscape. "You have not told me much. How long have you known her?" The *her* is inflected with a hiss that sends a shiver up my spine, which is probably my power. Sure enough, flecks weave over my skin.

"You're not here for her." Rath sighs and turns to walk beside her. "Correct?"

I've heard a lot about Artemis from Rath, but the irritation Alex had when he talked about them was its own entity—a ghostly tension that sat between them. She's almost as tall as Rath and created the mold for the athletes who break all records. The glare that sits comfortably on her face doesn't hit home because of her innocent eyes. A coiled braid the color of an autumn maple leaf circles her head. Do goddesses have bobby pins or are their perfect braids held with some form of divine magic?

Her fingers squeeze the golden bow and arrow she carries. "I must see Moros *and* his daughter."

Rath halts, dropping the bag from his shoulder, grabbing her elbow, and spinning her to face him, gripping her chin. "What are you not telling me?" His jaw sets as firm as the silent air. "Did Zeus send you?" Another mute moment and he steps back from her, digging his fingers into his hair. "Why?"

She moves in, nuzzling his neck in what must be an uncommon affection since Rath's eyes flutter closed like he's lived a decade for this moment. "You understand what I am," she says, almost too low to catch.

"I do." He blinks, pain twisting at his features. "You won't harm her though. Let go of the Council's demands. They aren't helping you —never have and never will." He wraps long fingers around the back of her neck. "Be with me, Artie." His voice is a whisper carried on the punishing midday breeze. "For real. You know we can protect each other. Don't be on the wrong side through this."

I shouldn't listen, but I can't pull away. Not when he strokes her cheek like he's clearly done a million times, and she grabs his wrist with stiff fingers. I grit my teeth. Her grasp isn't a plea to stay close and touch her forever. It's a tense preparation to fling and escape. Though she's mostly turned to him, I catch the guilt and sorrow of a woman who's made her choice—one that doesn't match her partner's.

Sure enough, she steps back. "I cannot." Her voice is a crumbling rasp. At least she cares. It still doesn't stop my fists from clenching at the situation Rath is in.

"Artie?" Rath asks. "Come here." She slides into his arms and he tilts her chin up. "What did you do?"

Her vulnerable pout twists back into a scowl. "I—you…" Her eyes search the landscape, looking anywhere but on my friend. "My place is with the majors."

"You make your place by your choices."

"My choice is the greater good." She turns away from Rath and faces the cave. "Lula Aglaope, abomination of unkno—"

"She's not an abomination." Rath spins her around. "Do you hear yourself, Artie? You sound like Zeus."

"Leave." There's a tremble to her voice. "No more. I have a job to do."

I stretch my neck, trying to ease the angry pressurized buzz as Rath and Artemis fall into angry conversation. Thor gives a short chuff, but I hold up my finger for him to keep waiting. He doesn't need to get hurt.

I pull myself up on the top rock, standing tall though my knees are wobbly. Artemis, major goddess and long-term girlfriend of one of my best friends glowers at me as she would a sewer rat that's wandered into a pristine throne room. Hope that I could adjust to what I am scurries away like I should, but my legs won't work.

In a blink, her bow is up and twangs. Rath grunts, and when I open my eyes from flinching, he's in front of me, blood-coated gold arrowhead poking out of his shoulder, the tip inches from my eye. A crimson circle grows across his blue shirt. He really does know her.

"Rath?" I lift my fingers, unsure what to do. Past him, Artemis is pale as she gawks up at us, but when her eyes meet mine, she glares and nocks a second glinting arrow.

Rath snaps the metal shaft piercing his chest with both hands. "This is why you're here?" His voice is caught between a sob and a growl. "It wasn't to walk freely beside me for once, or to meet Lula as one would another deity. It wasn't even for Moros."

"Move, Rath."

He tosses the broken piece. "It will never be me, will it? No matter what I do, how I prove myself to you, you'll choose him every time."

"He is my king and father."

"He's sired over half of Olympus," Rath yells. "You are a sacrifice to an unkillable goddess to either test her or start a war."

"He would not do that to me." Petulance oozes in Artemis's tone. "My arrows have power beyond her. He knew that."

They do? I stare at the sharp golden edge, the dribbling blood. It doesn't seem to affect Rath as much as the conversation. He chuckles, dark and burning. "You, my love, need to wake up as the rest of us have. The days of Zeus are numbered for good reason."

Her drawn arrow sinks a few inches. "What do you mean?"

"You tell me. Please, preach to me more about all his amazing decisions in the last two millennia." He winces as he rolls his shoulder and turns his head to glance at me. "Can you pull that out?"

I glare at the arrowhead. I'd have quite a headache right now had it not been for him. I wish this wouldn't have happened. How long does it take for a hole through a god to heal? Hopefully not long. I place my palm on his back to steady us both but jerk it away when the shimmery flecks exit like kids off a school bus.

"Shit." I grip the shaft, right under the tip, giving it a fast yank before they make gold dust inside him or worse. Rath twitches and grumbles curses as the glitterlings pounce on the wound. My gasp is sharp in the quiet. "No, no, no."

"What is—" Rath arches his back and hisses a breath. "Lu?" I tug the neck of his shirt, mopping away the blood, but my power has burrowed through and there's only a small puckered gray dot where the arrow had been. He rolls his shoulder. "That itches. Hey, talk to me. What's happening?"

"I don't know." I move to his front and Artemis's arrow lets loose. Rath leaps to shield me, but on instinct, I release my force field, deflecting not only the incoming missile, but Artemis.

She flies backward in a whirlwind of cream robes and leather, tumbling until she comes to rest facedown in the grass. Rath stays by my side, brows furrowed. I didn't throw him. How did I do that? He jerks down his shirt and a line of gray flecks stream out like smoke over his pectoral, dragging his wound together. "This is what you did to Alex."

I scrunch my face, moving closer to see. "No, I pulled him apart."

"After. It's when you think, isn't it? You consider something and it happens?"

Artemis screams and launches an arrow. It plinks off air. She shoots another, then another.

"I'm sorry," I whisper. I've dragged him into this doomed world with me.

"Take down your field." He stands in front of me, facing Artemis. "Let it go, Lula."

"No. She will kill us."

Artemis pauses, arrow nocked. Her breaths come in heaves, jaw clenched and stance determined. "I am not here for you, Rath. There will not be another warning."

"I knew it'd be you, Artemis." Rath's shoulders sink. "You've been my wicked, impossible love for half a century now. But this? Your father has played you and you've lost." He spreads his arms, welcoming her fury. "We both have." She keeps moving, trying to get a straight line of sight on me, but Rath has her blocked. He glances at me with an expression I never expected to see on him. He's given up. "Take it down, Lu."

He's always had hope for them. A hundred times he's spoken of her as if she was an imprisoned warrior, biding her time until the worlds aligned for them. I held onto that for Alex and I—if there was change in Olympus, we could openly love who we wanted without consequence. Something cracks with that realization, and Artemis tumbles back in the grass before the world vacuums out. I fight to stay upright as my force field rushes into me without my permission.

Artemis fires and I glare at the glinting incoming arrow. It zips wide, but the glitterlings are on it before it hits the wall of stone behind me. Then it's a puff of sparkles.

"Shoot me," Rath yells, shifting between us again. "Right through the heart as usual."

I put my hand on his shoulder. "Stop." Another arrow flies and bursts in the air, raining harmless sparkles over the field.

Thor snorts from behind me, then roars.

Artemis stumbles back, eyes wide as Thor clicks his talons on the rock. Thorette prowls through the long grass from around the corner, lips curtained up to bare her fangs. The hunter goddess lifts her bow once more and pivots, unsure if she should aim at the creature stalking her or me.

"Leave her, Thorette." It's the first time I've commanded her, and she halts, crouching until she's barely seen in the grass. "You do not want to do that," I say when Artemis's nocked arrow pauses on the waiting female, but then it bursts into glitter, shocking me into stillness and making the goddess leap back, staring at her ammunition-less weapon.

Rath leaps the ten feet to the ground and walks forward toward her. "Do you not comprehend that his command set you up for failure?" Lifting his chin to the side, he pulls down the neck of his shirt, I assume to show her the wound—or where it used to be. "You should be ashamed for not speaking to Lula first. You don't even know her. If she is so evil, as I'm sure Zeus has fed you, why would she help me? Why wouldn't she have destroyed you as she did your arrows?"

I descend the rock after him. I may not be willing to blow her up, but she's not going to harm him either. I think he'd let her cut him to bits to make a sad point.

"She means to use you for something." Artemis scrambles for another arrow as her quiver is empty, but I zone in on one in the pressed-down grass as she does, and poof—gold dust is all she has to work with. She balls her fingers.

"Like you did me?" Rath asks in a wispy way that feathers across the back of my neck. He hurts. It drags the marrow from my bones and the breath from my lungs. "Did you tell Zeus I'd do anything for you? I bet you didn't whisper a word about what you feel for me though, did you?"

"You will never understand." Her doe-eyes plead though her stance is rigid as one of her arrows. He steps forward, but she steps back. "No." She tugs a necklace from out of a leather cuff around her wrist and tosses it at Rath's feet.

"Artie." The gruff irritation is gone from his voice, leaving behind raw pain. "Don't do this. Think. Please."

"You are the enemy of the divine. If you show your face in Olympus again, you will be sorry." She turns and strides through the grass, standing tall, but as she rounds a rock formation, she wipes at her cheeks.

Rath glances over his shoulder at me. Tears well in his light eyes, and his shoulders curve forward, shaking. Would she truly kill him? Didn't I do that to Alex? Shame and empathy swirl into a knot in my throat and I wrap my arms around Rath as he once did for me. It feels so long ago when I didn't believe I could be with Alex, even though I was hopelessly in love with him.

Not much has changed.

Chapter Twenty-Nine

ALEX

IN THE MEADOWS OF ASPHODEL, I THROW ANOTHER BOULDER, THEN another. They're not as big as the ones my father bowls toward a grove of trees, but he's Hercules and I've been dead.

The field to my right is a pasture of flowers, reminding me of Shangri-La, where Lula and I came together during her heat, but the mountains beyond are not green. They're fogged, masking the Isles of the Blessed where only the most brave, enlightened remnants of beings are living—well…housed? They live on, preserved in the death realm that only Hades, the dead, and some demons can see. While it's only a silent, peaceful landscape to me, it's full of wandering souls in their afterlife, and I'm intruding.

"More," my father demands, barely winded.

The blood coating my fingers reminds me of Lula's gray, silky morph. The dirt on my clothes and body make me wonder if she's faring okay in the hell realm where there are no bubble baths. Every meal pushed in front of me comes with a side of guilt because Lu's stuck on a primitive planet with no pasta, I assume.

I'm too thin, too weak, and too scared to walk in there and drag her out where she belongs. Not yet. Nor can I make myself call Comus, Rath, or Anice, though I've wanted to. They've been open with Hades, Hera, and my father about our taxiarchs, logistics, the steps we've made through the century, and our plans for peace that go unheard by the Council. Zeus has been calmer if not silently seething during the few meetings there's been between groups. I'd have expected that after everything that happened at the ampitheater, war would have broken out. Comus and the others have made incredible strides to keep chaos from overtaking Olympus. Do they even need me?

"More!" Father yells.

I drop to my knees, shoulders sagging, throbbing arms at my sides. "How many times have you opened the hell realm since I've been gone?"

He tosses a rock the size of a basketball over his shoulder, making the ground shake when it thuds and rolls to a stop. Offering a hand, he drags me to my feet. "Twice."

"That's it? In eight months?" We walk side by side toward the lake, blazing orange with the ripples reflecting the setting sun.

"It has been trying as of late, son. I destroyed Zeus's barracks and your brother has made it known that his place is at your side. If we're together, Zeus knows, because he's moved all oracles. We assume it's to scry consistently for portal usage and divine nexus as they've broken up our intentions to open portals multiple times."

My face pinches. He's looking for me, knowing I use portal travel daily and live on Earth as much as possible. The power we'd conjure opening the hell realm would light up like a beacon, and unless I lived in motion, they could find my location. No wonder the guys brought me here. Zeus probably thinks I'm with Lula and Moros or dead.

"Hades is correct in keeping your awakening secret until you've..." He glances at my still gaunt, weak frame. "Until your body is repaired enough to be seen and feared." He strips from his short workout chiton and steps into the lake.

I snort. Who would fear me? I glance around, noticing a pile of clean linens stacked on a flat rock. Hades has many followers and underworld creatures that serve him. They're as sneaky as Rath. I pull the cording from my waist and drop my chiton to the ground. The water is cool, the sand beneath the surface soft and pliant under my feet. The high minerals soak into my skin and soothe my muscles.

"Rath is the only one who saw her?" I ask.

"Yes. We're afraid to send in Anice as she may think he is you."

That stings right behind my eyes.

My father dunks under the water, then stands and scrubs at his beard. "Though Rath appeared at ease when he returned the first time, but not the second."

Hades mentioned that Rath had been extra sullen after returning from visiting the hell realm last week and not only refused to answer questions, but disappeared. It can't be about Lula though—I don't think. Hades would have heard something, right?

"You love her, and I didn't know." My father scrubs his arms in the water. "Will you speak of your goddess?"

My goddess. There's no hiding after how I acted at the amphitheater. I close my eyes tight as if shutting off one sense may block the visions of death bolts raining on Lula, and when that fails, force my thoughts to the first night I touched her, smelled her, and kissed her in the street tucked among the world of humans. She blushed and trembled. The way she melted against me will always hold a memory in my eternity. My smile breaks free unused muscles.

It feels odd to share anything about Lula with others, but all of Olympus already knows with the way rumors soar. I bet they presume the worst of her because they caught her in a terrible moment and her father is Moros. They haven't accepted Rath after three hundred years and he's not a hybrid, nor has he thrown deities around, so I can't imagine the rumors about my siren are good. It hits me that after everything, I continue to consider her mine. She is, I think. I'm certainly hers. I'll heal and then go to her. We have a long, uncomfortable talk ahead of us, and maybe my father can help. He loves my mother in a way Zeus will never comprehend. My parents fought to be together and won. Hopefully, I'll get that chance with Lula.

I spill everything; what I did, and how I couldn't stay away. How commanding yet kind she is, and how I'm frightened of her reaction when I see her again. I speak until the sky is dark violet and we're re-dressed in clean himations. The final words of my story rasp in my dry throat. "And I've abandoned her in the hell realm with Moros."

"She is as capable as any I've seen," he says, holding a tone of pride that brings my eyes to his. "Living is not always easy. You understand such, especially as of late, but power lays in the lows. Learn from them, son." He squeezes my shoulder and stands, not offering a hand as he has over the last few days. "Tonight, you shall feast and sleep long. Tomorrow, we run Elysium."

———

WHEN I WAKE, HADES IS GLOWERING AT ME. "READY FOR COMPANY yet?"

My heart hesitantly slows its rapid sprint, and I rub my eyes. The motion is easier today, less stiff. "I thought I had a week to get my shit together."

"It's been four days and your men are asking about you. Believe it or not, I'm a terrible liar." He's in ripped jeans and a Lucky Charms shirt.

"You have a thing for cereal."

He glances down, then lifts his grinning face. "You should have seen Hera when I gave her Cocoa Puffs for the first time. I've since invested in certain stocks. Besides, leprechauns are nothing like this. They get a kick out of this lore."

Distant grumbles sound from the hall.

Another day, another workout. More food. More wondering if I'll ever be the same inside or out. But instead of my father's rumbling boulder voice, it's one I recognize as well as I would the scent of Lula's neck. Comus chitters in words I can't catch until he rounds the corner, wide-eyed and sporting a bushier beard. He laughs in pure joy. "We missed the fuck out of you, brother."

Rath pops up from around Comus's shoulder and the angle of his brows—far from brooding—brings a lump to my throat. I lose sight of him as Comus tackles me into the bed. I clap a hand on his back. Mortal death took me from him for months, but I couldn't talk to him for weeks before that while locked away in the barracks. Rath follows and I can't hug him with my arm pinned, but I smile and nuzzle against his head.

"I missed you too," I tell them.

I expect distaste in Hades's gaze but only find twinkling

amusement. He nods. "You all catch up. I'll send for breakfast." He steps from the room and the guys part from me.

Rath looks sallow and his eyes are red-rimmed.

"What happened?" I ask.

He flops into the seat Hades typically occupies and picks up a stone golem from the side table, rolling it in his palm. The leader of the underworld has eclectic taste and has since added dark wood furniture and quirky statues. Lula would love it and bombard him with a thousand excited questions about the origins of each piece. It feels odd to ask without her here, so I haven't.

Comus sits up, but stays seated on the bed. "Rath and Artemis are no longer seeing each other," he whispers. "Courtesy of her death threats. And we missed you. And he's worried about Lula and is pissed he can't enter the hell realm without your Da and Anice."

I wince. Rath glares at the roots in the room's corner.

"Shut the door," I say, and when Comus does, I look to Rath. "I'm sorry. Tell me everything."

When Hades knocks the second time and we ignore him yet again, I've already found out that we have a chunk of Olympus on our side—so does Zeus—but the Olympian's that haven't chosen a side are the biggest slice of pie. There is rubber-band-tight tension where everyone is facing off, waiting for an attack. Our taxiarchs have proven over and over that they're capable of the role. Rath is heartbroken and not handling things well. He dragged a bottle out of his boot and swigged from it throughout our conversation and didn't even banter when I made fun of him for walking out of a classic movie.

He explains what happened with Artemis and Lula, but only gives a summary when I want an encyclopedia. Comus continues when Rath returns to his liquor and sulks.

"The sirens are back online, sorta," Comus says. "Amah is the most skittish of rabbits, but better after Grace tempted her into conversation about Lula. She's always known about Moros but didn't expect Lula to have the opportunity to change, and thought the siren in her would prevail. Amah won't give the other sirens' locations, but will speak of Lula and her lost sisters. She's..." He squints one eye, tipping his head back and forth. "Upset. Nervous."

"She should be." Rath stands. "You need to talk to Anice, and I need to check on Lula. She shouldn't be there. I'll go get him."

Comus shakes his head, "Wait a minute, would you?"

Rath holds his arms out, eyes flitting over himself. "I'd say 'no,' but I can't fade. Why can't I fade?" He puts a hand up, then a leg, then he crouches, and pops back up. "Seriously, what the fuck?"

Comus grabs his wrist. "You're trying now?"

"Yeah. Why else would I be standing here in an angel statue pose?"

I lumber from bed, stretch sore muscles, and lift my hand to open a portal to France, but nothing happens. Grumbling a curse, I grab clothes from the dresser. "It's got to be Hades."

We swing the door open while Rath yells, "Hades!" so loud it echoes.

"Uh, yes?" Hades leans against the corridor wall, next to Hera.

I step out. "Rath can't leave, I can't portal. Why?"

Hades turns to Hera. "We will have to postpone another delicious argument, unless you'd like to discuss openly? I'd be happy to leeway into needed conversation."

Hera's cheeks blaze, though Hades stares back at her, a small smirk playing on his lips. I turn my gaze to the empty hall because even when Hera's stare isn't fixed on me, it's uncomfortable. Zeus would back out of the room now, but clearly Hades hasn't picked up on whatever ability Hera has to instill terror with her fathomless eyes.

"Would you two just fuck it out already," Rath grumbles, struggling with the bottle in his boot. He jerks it free and stumbles down the hallway leading to the meadows. "We're all drowning in your godsdamn tension." His voice echoes off the stone. He tips his head back, swigging as the brightness of the opening door envelops him, then shuts out the light with a slam.

Hera watches after him wide-eyed, but Hades covers a laugh, shoulders twitching to hold it in. He straightens and bites his lips closed when Hera jerks her attention back to him, narrowing her eyes before storming out the door as well. Rath isn't in the best place, but if he's been around them for eight months, he's completely excused.

"Shadow Boy is not handling his breakup well," Hades says with nonchalance. "He's clearly…distressed."

"How do you know that?" Comus asks.

I squeeze the bridge of my nose. "Because he knows everything."

"There we go." Hades grins. "If it helps anything, Artemis has been extra obnoxious to the nymphs. I was hoping those two would make it and she'd find her way, but…can't force these things, can we?"

"Seriously, why do you even question us?" Comus asks.

"To get different perspectives, obviously. Truth lies between sources."

"Then I'm asking the source," I say. "Why are we stuck?"

Hades purses his lips and studies the ceiling so hard I look up at the dark stone too. "You were a flight risk, as is Rath." He points down the hall. "Let's have a late breakfast and talk."

The dining room is a shock of light gray walls and mustard yellow fabrics. The table is dark, but the upholstery is a modern geometric design. I slammed to a halt the first time I walked in because it's the opposite of Olympian style. Even the white marble surrounding the massive fireplace is sleek and human. There are no carvings anywhere of war and pestilence. No golden forks or demigod servants ready to hold out a chair or swipe oily fats from the chins of feasting guests. The dishes are a hodgepodge of charming china patterns, the food plentiful, but not overly abundant. After days here, I can see why Hera has been hiding and why my father seems far more comfortable here than he is in Olympus. The underworld, the place of endings, appears to be more of a middle ground between Olympus and Earth, which my mind can't even wrap around.

Hercules walks in, Hera's hand in the crook of his arm. Rath silently swings in behind her, eyes bloodshot and trained on the floor, and takes his place between Comus and me. I give his shoulder a squeeze.

As we take our seats and my father reaches for the platter of meat, Hades clears his throat. "We have empty chairs around this table. It sure would be nice to have a crazy-powerful hybrid on the team. Where could we acquire one of those?"

"Too dangerous." Hera watches me as if she's asked a question.

My father leans across the table to place a large heap of sausages on my plate and gives a frustrated huff.

"She was scared, angry, and forced into zenith." I wave Father off when he aims another tong-full in my direction. "She won't hurt me again." Still, my stomach tightens and my chest itches. I ball my fist to keep from scratching at the thin scar that proves there was damage.

"How do you know that?" Hera asks.

"Because it's Lu," Rath, Comus, and I say in sync and give each other a curious glance.

Grandmother's eyes crinkle as if smiling, though her lips stay firm. "She was a force. Uncontrollable. Much like her father." She passes a bowl of potatoes to Hades and takes a delicate bite of vegetable quiche, maintaining her goddess manners, though there's more to her now. She's unclenched and calm.

"Absolutely," I say. "And none of it was her fault. Not her birth, her raising, the fall of sirens from Olympus—"

My grandmother's lips twitch and Hades peeks at her out of the side of his eyes.

"What?" I ask.

"No matter." Hera keeps her eyes on her plate. "Continue."

I give it another moment, but neither indicate continuing whatever inside information they have. Okay, then. "I'd say she's handling herself well considering the horrid acts of the divine through the ages. She didn't end me even though she could have." So she's a rare divine siren hybrid…that won't change her personality. I have to believe she repaired the injury, not out of testing or confusion, but because she cared, even though Rath said the fix was an accident. Lula's mad at me, but she didn't kill me. That last look in her eyes…that was regret. Did she talk to Rath about me? He ignores my staring, too busy with ambrosia and scarfing food like he hasn't eaten in a week. Answers will come when he's sober and not recovering from the realm's worst relationship. Maybe he's right to avoid my questions and staring. I need to see for myself that Lula's okay and how her powers work, but even sitting, my knees wobble, and I don't think I could move from the chair if I tried. I'd been out for eight months. She might not harm me again, but what if she shuns me?

"So." Comus takes a long swig from his wine glass. "What's with Rath not being able to shadow?"

"What is with that?" Rath turns on Hades "What changed?"

Hades purses his lips and Comus points at him. "You said we needed to talk."

"But not about that," Hades whines.

Hera makes sure her braid is tucked. "We need to explain."

I've seen Hades create flowers, light, flame, and block attributes. I can't even fake knowing what's going on anymore. "Fine." Hades's eyes darken. "From this moment on, there will be no secrets about the revolution between us. No closed-door conversations, no exchanged glances instead of words. If we proceed, you are in. Am I clear as acrylic?"

I look to Comus and Rath, then wince as I did exactly what he said we shouldn't. The three of us chuckle and nod. "Yes," I say.

"Agreed." Rath and Comus echo the same.

"The same magic I use to keep folks out of the underworld, can keep others in."

"Witchcraft?" I ask.

Hades shakes his head and glances as Hera.

"Hades is the firstborn son of the Titans," Hera says. "They gifted him an attribute that no other being has or will have."

Hades releases a long breath. "A huge mistake, as I cursed my father's abilities right out of him, allowing Zeus to maintain his victorious streak." He flicks his eyebrows at our dropped jaws. "It needed to be done." He waves a hand through the air but his tone isn't as dismissive, nor should it be. "Surprise."

Comus makes an odd squeaking sound that is new to me.

He can't mean…I find words first. "You can take other's abilities?"

Fire flicks in his eyes. "And if any of you talk about it up there, I'll steal yours and murder you with them. Do not test me."

"Must you be so dramatic, Hades?" Hera's calm voice does nothing to settle the chill on the back of my neck.

"For certain things, yes." His eyes trail her, then lock on mine.

Rath snorts. "Why are we having this conversation? Why haven't you gleaned Zeus's attributes and popped his head off?"

Hera releases a tiny huff and glares at him.

"I have to curse him." Hades leans back in his chair. "Touch him, perform the intentions, soul search and find them inside. I need time to wiggle in, and he won't allow me to get close. If I did, he'd fry my ass. No one is strong enough to stop him. Even ol' Herc here. Not that he's tried."

My father throws him a sharp glare, even with a mouthful of food.

The three of us burst into a blabber of questions, but my grandmother waves us off. "This room contains the only beings who know what Hades possesses, and it will stay that way." Her lips twitch as she glances at him. "Until the time is right."

"And that needs to be soon because you all are moving slower than an ice age," Hades says. "You get stuck in your minds. It took my brothers and me a quick decision and eight months of war to oust the Titans. You are hundreds of years into planning, with no action until Alex's little siren got involved."

"We've needed to study humans, access and be cautious with Olympians," Comus says. "You know what happens when someone threatens Zeus's throne. If we would have gone in a century ago spouting about peace and exodus, we would not be sitting here today. Most of us anyway. At least he needs Alex, which has kept us alive and close to the Council, but the more we bring into this, the more dangerous it becomes. He's not killing us yet, because he thinks he has more Olympians on his side then he does, and he knows Alex is alive. The moment he realizes the scales have tipped, or Alex returns to Olympus, he'll snap. We need a solid, forward-moving plan before that occurs."

Hades twists his lips and thumbs to me. "As soon as Alex grows a set and packs on another fifty pounds, it will be showtime."

I snort. "Unless things have drastically changed in eight months, our plan is not to wage war. Tell me that you see the ways of the old are no longer working?"

"And you hiding down here is doing the universe favors?" Hades mocks. "You've been planning for a long-ass time, but understand that you may have to adapt, because if this goes full war, Zeus will strike to win. If you pause to speak of peace, it will only give him a bullseye to aim at."

Comus gives a small growl and I expect him to protest, but he stays quiet then looks to me. "Having you back is going to be a huge relief to everyone."

"Especially Zeus." Rath finishes off his glass. "He'll be glad your nuts are functioning again and will lock you in with Naea."

Hera huffs. "Honestly."

"Yes." Rath nods rapidly.

Comus claps him on the back. "Stop talking, brother."

"I don't know," Hades links his fingers and stretches them out. "Alex's nuts are a decent bargaining chip."

"Leave," Hera states. "Go pick up Anice and Praxis. Eos as well, but not all taxiarchs. If we're not careful, they will be noticed and followed. We need to plan, because as soon as Alex steps into the light, Zeus will strike."

Chapter Thirty

ALEX

Sconces flicker an amber glow, creating shadows that may or may not be entities of the underworld. I should have gone with them. Why didn't I go? With a pivot, I keep on my route, hoping to eventually wear myself out enough to sleep.

A full day of catching up should have slipped me into relaxed exhaustion, because we have a plan, though that plan is one of remaining in the underworld while informing our people little by little of my return. Everyone acts as if I'm some lynchpin when I'm not at all sure of my place, except that it's beside Lula and that's not where I am.

And now my brother and father are taking a risk and opening the hell plane so Comus and Rath can check on Lula, and see how she's doing on her zenith journey with Moros as her guide. I rub the scar that's probably gone by now. It should be me there. I should have spoken up as they made plans around me, but instead, I sat frozen in silence and let them go to her without a word of disagreement or even a message for her.

"I recognize a man in love when I see one." Hera leans against an arched doorway. She fits here. Maybe it's the contrast to Zeus's realm that creates the cozy atmosphere here, or the lack of stringent laws, but her eyes are easier to gaze into. It's as if there's a rigid twin of hers in Olympus.

"Hello, Grandmother."

"You're worried," she says.

I tug my fingers from my trimmed beard, then smooth it down. "They're meeting with her and I'm not."

"Mm, I see. Your dedication to Lula is evident in everything you do, or…it was."

I jerk my head up, straightening my shoulders. "I was dedicated to our plan first and put it above her. Then I didn't and here we are."

"No, dear, she and your plan collided. You could not have known what would happen, but it's now that she needs you most. The poor thing is living in the hell realm, Alexiares."

"She ripped my chest open." I unclench my balled fists and try to calm my breathing. "She was so upset."

"Can you blame her after the impression Olympus has left upon her?"

"I don't blame her. Not after what I did and then what Moros did."

"Good." Hera comes closer and squeezes my tight fist. "And you're correct. She has every right to be aggrieved with you, Zeus, and Moros. I keep thinking back to that day. I was so concerned for you."

"Me? I wasn't getting death bolts. I still can't believe he did that."

"Me neither." Her face scrunches with disgust before she sighs. "But I saw your reaction when he attacked. For a brief moment, I believed she'd perished, but you…she means so much that there was no recovering from losing her. You tried to follow her into death."

"What if I did lose her?" I swipe at my eyes and turn to stare at the wall. "What if nothing will ever be the same between us?"

She grips my chin, turning my face to hers. "Then you start again. The universe is in constant motion, Alexiares. Why should love be any different?"

I swallow, but hold still against her firm grip. "Is that why you've stayed with him? Why you've given him immeasurable chances? You just move around his immobility? You know he won't change, right?"

Her small fingers tighten before releasing. "I know who he is."

"I do too. Dangerous, but historically predictable. Lashing out is his method and we will fall until Olympus is rubble and deities are extinct. We haven't struck out against him because we understand him. He will rule on a crumbling throne in a silent world unless we handle things better than anyone has in the past."

"He's..." Her nostrils flare and her jaw clenches. "He's just..."

I duck my head, a gesture of apology. Hades is right. She's too loyal like Artemis and the other Council members. Blinded by what she wishes he was—a good father and a faithful husband. As if summoned, Hades walks into the corridor smiling, but his expression sours when he sees the tears welling in Hera's eyes. His jaw clenches and he steps forward. "What happened?"

She gives the air another careless swish. "Just...reminiscing."

As she passes him, he blocks her path, getting so close, I'm wondering if he's going to kiss her. She pauses and reaches up to place her palm on his cheek as carefully as if he may bite her. His eyes blaze, and his hand slides over hers. Some unknown conversation passes between them and an ache takes residence in my chest not only for them, but for me.

I miss Lula.

Touching her was my everyday. Once I fell asleep beside her, it was all I wanted to do for the rest of eternity. Sleep, then wake, blinking heavy lids as I stared in awe that she was there, sweet and perfect. Her smile opened a place in me I wasn't aware of until she aimed her attention at me. I miss her presence near me. My heart rolls into an ache of longing because I can't reach out to take her hand and pull her to me. Can't touch her hair and get lost in her green eyes. It was so easy between us, even with my deception. What could it be like now?

Nothing, when I am here and she is there.

Hera pulls away and walks down the hall. Hades stares after her, and I don't believe he's taken a breath since she touched him. No wonder he's on our side.

"Do you need a moment?" I ask, leaning against the stone wall.

He huffs a laugh and drags his palm over his grin, then squints one eye at me. "Infinity moments. What were you two talking about?"

"Lula. And Zeus. We've opened a door against the king we can't close and barricade. He annihilated the Titans, conquered everything he's been up against, and fought until Olympus rained blood. 'Rational' isn't in his vocabulary. His language is more, 'smash it if it doesn't serve my goal.' Is he preparing for another war or does he not take us seriously? Why does he seem calm? Has he found a way to harm Lu? Fuck, I need to get to her and—"

"Chill." Hades beckons me down the hall and into a room with a circular table and four chairs. He flops into a seat, a lazy lion sprawling on a heated rock. "Sit." When I do, he gives a small smile. "My brother had help with the Titans. Sure, he started it, he always does. He had a talented army, much like you do."

"We're not warring, Hades. I can't just kill family or other Olympians even if their beliefs don't match mine. I won't be like him."

"Oh, you're more like your grandfather than you give yourself credit for." He carelessly shrugs. "You're both talented leaders. He's always seen that in you." Before I can consider his words, he moves on. "You say you understand Zeus, what he's made of, so what does that mean? What would change his mind, Alexiares?"

I snort. "The masses. Hera, though I'm not sure about that anymore. She's been…" I raise my eyebrows at him. "Missing."

The corner of his lips twists up. "Aha, the scales would tip with a heavy bandwagon. And his wife." He lifts a finger on each hand, wagging them back and forth. "One does not work with the other, does it? Have you noticed how he treats her? She's a political flag he waves so others know who to follow. He wants her beside him, because the masses follow her. It's always been that way, but trying to get her to believe and choose a different path has been a long road."

My brows furrow. "Deities literally fall to their knees in the streets at her presence. She's strong enough to command the army."

"She's stronger than he is, but she holds crippling guilt that he doesn't. We may be ancient, but we evolve in mindset—or some of us do. Unfortunately, when we realize we're wrong, we have to live with our past decisions, unless we jump universes." He leans forward, tenting his fingers. "The abuse she's endured with him doesn't bother her as much as the torture she's divvied out in his name to gain his attention. It's a plague on her soul, and with immortality there's no escape, only existence and attempts of redemption."

"You think she will leave in the exodus."

His jaw tightens. "I don't know."

An exodus is what we hope for, though the impact of losing most of Olympus if they follow Zeus could tailspin the Earth into another Dark Age. Hera is life and protection. If she goes, the two of them would leave behind an astronomical attribute void. And as much of a hard-ass as she is, I'd miss her.

Hades's mouth is tight. He studies his fingers as if they may offer insight we're missing. "There are things she needs to do before she's comfortable leaving." He taps the table when he catches my quizzical expression. "She will tell you, but it will take prompting and time that we don't have. You know how impatient I am." He smiles as if the weight of it is hard to bear.

"Explain," I say. He's more likely to tell me things than Hera.

Hades rolls his eyes.

Now I do need to speak with Comus and Rath. I shouldn't be stalling; they're trying to help Lula and I should be too, even if I'm not ready. If I stepped in, would she join us or finish me off? Has Moros wound his way deeper into her mind? *No.* She's too skittish and intelligent for that. She would scoff at the appalling things Moros is undoubtedly doing.

Hades snaps his fingers in front of my face. "Again...impatient. You're thinking of your woman again, aren't you?" When I don't respond, he continues. "You're still thin, and need to get yourself in order so that you can go to her and protect yourself. Then you two return and conquer Olympus."

"You sound like that's the easiest thing ever." I glare. "I have to talk to Comus and Rath."

"Alright, but they'll tell you the same, dear nephew, if they haven't already. You will lead us as you've been selected to do."

"We're a group, Hades. We have a following, but it's because the world has moved forward and some Olympians relate to that. We need reconnection with the humans, and allow the otherworldlings to reunite with their worlds if they choose to. Those who follow us, follow our motives, not me."

"Oh, that's adorable. It seems you have much of your grandmother's traits as well." Hades's eyes flick to the entrance a second before the door opens and Hera steps back in, a cell phone in her hand. She keeps her eyes on Hades and I want to shout to gain their attention back to this conversation. Is this what Rath and Comus complained about whenever Lu and I were in the same space? They'd tell me the air was distracting and I can sense that now. I bite my lip tight as Grandmother takes a seat across from me.

"As I was saying," Hades continues. "Gods and man follow strength and purpose. Ideas are dismissed or taken into account only if someone proves to others that their cause is worthwhile. You've sold your motives to more people than you know. The Ichnaea thing? I'm not sure any other god would have walked out of that room given the circumstances. You have given Olympus the idea that they don't have to do what Zeus tells them. Of course, that has sent his royal ass into a rampage, but most understand a snarling animal in the throes of death when they see it. Olympians are quiet and seemingly calm because they are waiting for you to rise and lead them into unknown territory."

That can't be true. "I'm not even a pure-blood god, Hades, and I've been out for months. They've forgotten me by now or consider me dead. Comus has been leading them."

"Comus has been your mouthpiece during your absence," Hera says. "He is loved and respected by both sides, but he's not the leader you are."

"That makes no sense. It's always been the three of us together, equally."

Hades threads his fingers behind his head and leans back, blowing a lengthy breath from his nose. "And you think Comus, Rath, and you will share an equal leadership when the new world arises?"

"No." A weak vein on my thin hand makes a purple roadway for a bony finger that doesn't seem my own. "Or yes. We will take all beings into account and become a panel for them. If we succeed."

"If?" Hades tuts. "Where did that cocky family trait go, Alexiares? Are you not the grandson of Zeus? The son of Hercules? Twin to the unconquerable god, Anicetus?"

I shrug a shoulder.

"I like that you wish to do right by all beings." Hera eyes me in that way that breaks me down. "Lula needs you, Alex, and if we wait much longer, you will not be able to help her."

"Please. She's possibly the strongest deity in the universe." I give a pale smile. "And she doesn't want me."

"She's a powerhouse with no direction," Hades says. "Besides… wants and needs are separate things."

I glare at him. "That's one of our problems, Hades. As deities we assume we understand someone's desires, but we're projecting ourselves upon them to push them toward our agenda. They think differently, act beyond our control, and it's time we accept that there's beauty in letting beings just be." Lula taught me that more than anything, but I didn't listen until it was too late. "I dragged her into this when I should have left her alone to live her peaceful siren life."

"You believe her life has been peaceful?" Hera asks, then quickly averts her gaze. Pink touches her cheeks. I cannot remember her ever blushing.

Hades knocks on the table and stands. "I'll, um…" He points to the door and scrunches his nose. "I can't think of a graceful excuse at the moment, so I'm just going to leave the room. You two talk about the sirens."

"Hades," Hera growls.

He turns and leans close to her. "Yes, Hera?" Cupping her face, he whispers against her ear. Her shoulders droop as he stands. "It's time. Get it off your chest, love. You both need it." He leaves, shutting us into a room of secrets held on bated breath.

I scoot my chair closer to the table and steeple my fingers. "The sirens?"

She keeps her eyes on the door.

"Is this about Lula? What do you know?" The mystery of their origins is something the three of us have sought for centuries. All information is the same the humans have…a myth. "It involves Zeus, doesn't it?" Her jaw tightens. I slap the table at her continuing silence. "Tell me!"

"I made them." Her eyes close tight.

"You did what?"

The tight tendons in her neck shift as she swallows and meets my eyes. "My sisters and I made the sirens."

I slump back in the chair. "You made the original three and kept them secret?"

"Not at first. I know you disapprove of how Olympus treats goddesses and demis, but before your generation was born, it was much worse. You know the stories, Alexiares, all that was taken without care for desires as you stated. It was a handful using their strength to do whatever they pleased. As years passed and more deities were born with attributes meant for creating peace as family and union, some gods listened. Zeus listened."

"Back then, if he acknowledged your presence and called you by name it was considered listening, Grandmother."

Her lips tighten. "He was better than he is now. He fought for us, became our leader without flinching and set things right. It's why I chose him. Then came territorial disputes and aggression. He began trusting his men of war over those of us who spoke of maintaining the hearth and gifting the humans with family structure that didn't revolve around death games. I followed his lead instead of my heart."

I wince. "The legends of jealousy."

She nods. "He wasn't used to having a wife, and my bitterness at a cold bed added to the bite of his increasing dismissal of my ideas. I'd thought once that I'd been his match, but while he wooed, scorned, and feared me, he never loved who I was. I thought I could earn him by showing how much more powerful I was than his countless lovers and comrades-in-arms, but my actions never slowed him, and all the while I became more lost."

"So you created sirens?" I ask.

Her eyes crinkle in sadness and she gives a slight bob to her head. "We each had our reasons, but Aglaope was the essence of who I was before Zeus. I crafted her with sweetness and a loving disposition you'd never recognize." A faint smile crosses her lips and she exhales like a boulder lifted from her chest. "I'd loved my sisters with pure intent, so she did as well. I made her form the tightest bindings to them and any future children so she wouldn't forget herself as I had, though I kept her barren."

"Why?"

She pales and her lip trembles. "Because part of me understood how her and Zeus's meeting would go. I expected indifference or dismissal, and callous, cocky behavior from him toward her. Lust, of course, he lusted for everyone. I did not anticipate infatuation."

I raise my eyebrows. "He wooed her?"

"He *loved* her." The pained disbelief in her words makes breathing difficult. She swipes at her eyes and I reach across the table to offer my hand, which makes her brows crinkle further, though she grasps my fingers and nods. "He respected Aglaope, and that I could not take. I had become a wretch because of him, the furthest thing from my original state, and he cherished a being I'd made to remember myself."

"Hells," I murmur "How can you still be with him?"

"It is complicated. He proved then, that he was capable of change, and of love, and I'd devoted myself to him alone. I'm the Goddess of Marriage." She shrugs as if that explains everything.

She may be my grandmother, but she has much to learn. "New age, new generations. Why stay?" A thought hits, widening my eyes. "Oh, the exodus. You want him to leave peacefully. Is that why you are here, and helping against him?" She looks to the door and bites her bottom lip. Her dedication to Zeus is ridiculous and there's nothing wrong with how she feels about Hades. "Never mind," I say. "It's clear that some do respect you."

Her eyes widen. "It's not like that…not entirely."

I squeeze her fingers and let go. "If you're looking for me to shame you, I will disappoint you. I'm glad Hades is committing to this and to you."

"He has his own motivations."

I raise an eyebrow. "Mm-hmm. What about the other sirens? Lu calls them 'the mothers.'"

"The mothers." She curls her lip. "I like that. Demeter made Peisinoe to prove she could. Birthed her from the earth like a dark flower and gave her love for plant and person. Hestia created Thelxiope to be her daughter, as she'd never have one of her own. When Zeus's attention was dedicated to Aglaope, Hestia gifted Thelxiope with incomparable allure. Because I had linked the sisters' bonds so closely, the three became irresistible to non-deities and similar in temperament. Zeus's attention never wavered. Hestia tried to separate Thelxiope by sharing her immortality and gifts."

"She bound herself to her." I wipe my sweaty palms on my jeans. Hestia was Goddess of the Hearth, inner fire of the home. "She gave her the siren's heat."

Hera frowns and tilts her head. "She did. It burns so brightly within them; it comes out in their voice. You know of their heat?"

The silence in the room is a heavily weighted fog. I stare at my tapping fingers, then slowly bring my eyes to Hera's.

Her lips part. "Oh." That covers it. "It was her first?" When I nod, she lets go of a held breath.

"Where are the original three?" I ask before she diverts me with the questions I practically see swimming in her eyes. Lula's not pregnant. Before I confessed everything, she told me about the signs and seemed sad not to have any of them. I can't say I wasn't feeling the same way.

Hera stands to walk a path beside the table. I'm glad I'm not the only pacer in the family. "The powers of other gods had always unnerved Zeus, but once he discovered Aglaope was irresistible to humans, he locked her and her sisters away. Since there are no secrets between us anymore, this will remain quiet for fear of retribution to others."

"Obviously," I say. "For centuries, only a handful understood our plans before Moros returned. We know how to hold our tongues."

She stops pacing to sit again. "They despised being locked away. Aglaope was becoming afraid of Zeus's aggression toward others, and felt guilty for the situation I was in." She snorts and rolls her eyes. "After everything I did, she was apologizing to me. Hestia took them out of Greece with Hermes's help. She hid them among villages and taught them how to interact with the mortals to maintain their secrecy. But then a heat came. We didn't realize what it would do to humans, though we should have." Her gaze trails off to the wall. "The damage was extensive. Yet another error we cannot atone."

"That was the Punic War shipwreck. You took them to Africa."

"You figured it out." Her voice holds surprise. "One of Demeter's gifts to them was love for water. She was trying to impress Poseidon. It worked, and he hid them for a while, even though they bore a siren daughter each. But with the attention they pulled, and Zeus's endless search, Poseidon asked Demeter to take them from the sea realm to avoid his brother's wrath. I told them to scatter, and stay away from each other to prevent more heats and discovery. Then I convinced Hermes to tell Zeus they had escaped and died by human hands."

"Oh, damn." I rub my tight forehead.

Hera scrunches her nose. "Yes. I did not think he would hate the humans so much after that, but now we are broken from the Earth. I was...wrong."

"And Demeter, Poseidon, and Hestia left in the exodus."

"My sisters decided the best way to forget guilt was to start again in a new universe."

"Okay." I sit, numb as I attempt to absorb everything. Hera remains quiet, eyes on fidgeting fingers. "You didn't leave."

"I wanted to right things and could only do that by protecting the sirens." Her face crumples. "After everything, I found my way here. Hades has been kind, if not mischievous." Her lips quirk at that.

"How did Moros find out about them?" I ask. I'd blame myself for exposing them, but when we started studying the sirens, Zeus wasn't surprised. He wanted more information. Lula is almost two centuries old, so Moros knew they were still around, escaped to Earth, and took Lula's mother. As soon as he returned, he found Gerty, then the others.

"He..." She purses her lips, contemplating. "He has always been patient and observant. Nearly as much as Hades."

Colored light flashes and Hades stands in the room, arms crossed. "You called?"

Hera glares. "I did not."

"Yet here I am." He grins and takes the seat next to her. "What are we talking about?"

"He is jesting," Hera says. "He probably heard every word." Her expression is sulking and firm.

Hades shrugs. "I missed a bit and you pull your punches, so sometimes I need to step in. Like now." He settles his elbows on the table. "Moros is a dick, but he's an infatuated dick. His perfect world is him on the Olympian throne with Hera by his side. It's why he's never left and why he chose the sirens to get Hera's attention, not other, more powerful otherworldlings." He gazes over at her. "Though how can you blame him, and more importantly…" He twists his head back to me. "How can we use that against him?"

Chapter Thirty-One

LULA

I run outside the cave and throw up the tiny amount of meat I forced down this morning. *Dammit.* I'm so hungry. My shirt hangs, and my shorts ride low on my hips.

"What is wrong with you?" Moros says behind me. "Why are you sick?"

It's nothing I'm sharing with Captain Kill-it-All. I spit and wipe my mouth with my hand. "There's not much here besides gross meat. I want oatmeal and pasta. Ice cream." Every flavor of ice cream. Twice. And pineapple. Is it possible to speed-grow that here?

Moros has become even more irritable and quiet, which concerns me. He sits and thinks, and him thinking is never good.

As I settle onto my sleeping mat, I reach for the water. The trickling stream in the cave is now a drippy faucet. "We're running out of water."

"We should leave the realm then." Moros leans against the wall, arms crossed and eyes closed. "Go back to Earth where we belong and…" His lips firm as he goes quiet.

"And what?"

He peeks at me before feigning sleep again.

I tilt my head at him. "You honestly think I'm going to walk into the Earth realm and tell everyone I'm queen now?"

His eyes pop open and he sits up. "Why wouldn't you?" Before I can speak, he holds a finger in front of him. "Before you jabber on about humanity, you won't be accepted anywhere without showing your attributes. I created the most capable being in the universe and she sits…" He signals to me, cradled in the comfort of my fur pile. "Sits or vomits, getting weaker, diminished even. She sleeps when she should train. Remains silent, waiting for another youth to guide her instead of her primordial father." He stands, flexing the two short stumps protruding from his wrist. "She looks the part of a powerful deity that could rule the world, but doesn't recognize herself as one. It's…unfortunate."

It shouldn't, but his words sting. They bring forth the fears I have about the permanent shimmery net on my skin and the lack of control I have over my attributes. I'm not learning, only tolerating myself. I'm still two beings occupying the same space.

"Lula?" Rath calls. There are no other voices and he doesn't sound sad.

I hop up, adjust to the dizziness with a few deep breaths, and make my way around the rocks. Rath smiles and hugs me. There's no bag this time. Maybe he's only here to help me practice.

"How long has it been now?" I ask, afraid of the answer.

"Two months." He sinks into himself.

"Two months? It's only been four days since I saw you." I wince when his numb expression darkens, and while I've adjusted to the shifts that still swirl through me, the turn to pressure cooker throws me off guard and I stumble back, light-headed. "It's speeding up." I've tried to keep up, but the disjointed daytimes make it difficult to measure. "It's been two months here, maybe? Almost nine on Earth?" I press my hand to the slight curve of my stomach.

"Yeah, that sounds right." He turns and I follow his gaze. Comus stands next to a thick patch of trees and the portal opening glimmers blue light behind him. My breath catches and I force my feet to stay still instead of sprinting to the Earth realm where there's food and fresh water. Moros would escape again and hurt more people. I can't leave.

Comus smiles and walks forward, but not too far. He's probably scared of me. I take deep breaths and wait for the dizziness to pass.

"We've missed you, Lula." His eyes flit over me, taking in every detail of my new appearance in quick assessment. At least he doesn't appear shocked or disgusted.

I nod and drop my hand from my stomach. "It's been a long time, Comus."

"Too long. Grace is coming on the next visit too. I brought another letter." He pulls an envelope from his back pocket and hands it over.

I clutch the paper to my chest before tucking it in my back pocket. "Thank you." These letters ground me each time I reread them. It reminds me that while I may be basically alone in this realm, I'm not alone in the universe.

"They're all doing well." Comus's eyes flick by me and glare. "We're sorry you've had to be here with him. Go throw yourself to the hell crows…" He continues a hissed curse in an unfamiliar language. There are clicks and rolls that seem impossible for the tongue.

Moros glares at us from the upper rocks. How long has he been there? He lifts his chin and adds more scathing sounds I've never heard.

"Original divine language." Rath shrugs at my questioning glance, shoulders lax. "You can't understand them?"

"It's just clicks."

"Huh." Rath breaks into a small smile. "I thought I was the only god who couldn't understand it. Most deities can understand and speak all languages because of Hermes, but that one…" He shrugs. "They even tried to teach me, but it ends up translating into stuff like, 'open throb form to your goat's milk.'"

Comus holds up a hand, fingers widely splayed as if he's counting to five, which is apparently insulting by Moros's open-mouthed huff. Walking closer, Comus's attention returns to me. "You still can't change back?"

Ignoring a new thread of furious click-roll words from Moros, I shake my head. "It gets lighter or darker but doesn't go away. Did Rath catch you up?" I don't want to explain everything again.

"He did, but did he catch *you* up?" He smiles but has an expectant expression. I'm missing something.

"Not yet." Guilt floods Rath's features and before I can tell him to spit out what's bothering him, he takes my hand. "Alex is awake."

My breath leaves in a hard whoosh. "Is he…" I can't continue. Is he in a death loop? Disfigured and cursing my name?

Comus swishes his hand. "He's fine. Recovering, getting his strength back and such, but yeah—" He smiles wide. "He's great."

Great? The wave of relief floods into a mini panic and I drop Rath's fingers so I don't hurt him. Will he ever come here? The thought of speaking to him again makes me bite my tongue to distract from the wavering world.

"See?" Rath says. "It's got to be emotional control, but I can't figure out the swing state she's in. It's like a pendulum or a loop that swings faster and shorter or long and wide." He lifts a hand. "Temperature change. Subtle, but it's there."

"Lu?" Comus ducks his head to catch my eyes. "I think you're probably done in this hell zone, yeah? I mean, it does have two lovely moons, but no food and Moros, so…can you let us introduce you to a friend who can read you? She's human."

Taking deep breaths, I swallow hard to curb the ever-present nausea. "I don't want to hurt anyone and…" I glance at Rath, then at Comus. "What if I'm worse than you think? What if my father is right, and I'm a walking apocalypse?"

Comus's amused smile turns cold. "Is that what he told you?"

"Of course, he did, the fuck." Rath crosses his arms.

"It's not like he's wrong," I say. "I can only push away and destroy. No one should be here. Not that they'd want to be." I close my eyes and ball my fingers that were autopiloting to my stomach.

"Hmm." Rath squints, watching my hand. "Show Comus your field and then unleash the glitterlings for us? He needs to see. Moros would make good target practice if you need a focus point."

"Okay, but…" I signal to Comus with my chin. "Get him out if things get wonky." I slowly release, edging Rath away from me.

"Whoa." Comus scratches his beard. He steps next to Rath and pushes against the air. "That's how Alex described it."

The field jumps at my stress at hearing that Alex is talking about it, and Rath has to hop back to avoid falling while Comus bounces, stumbling back but recovering with an agile twist.

"Sorry," I whisper.

"He will come soon." Rath nods. "He's just…recovering." His trudging tone makes me take a step back while the deity inside swells. Was it that bad? Alex needs time. I can't blame him. I'm afraid of me too, but there's something important to discuss, even though the timing couldn't be worse. "Watch this." Rath eyes Comus. Before I can prepare, he throws himself forward, landing punches in midair. It's so odd, I drop the force field, and he falls forward to his hands and knees, laughing. "Lu, you're not supposed to let the bad guys in."

"But you're not bad." I put my hands on my hips, then drop them and fidget. Placing any attention to that area is weird. I clasp my hands in front of me and cock my hip. "I just didn't expect you to do that."

From his knees, Rath stares at me, assessing in a way that sends a chill creeping up my spine. My hands flinch to wrap over my stomach, but I force them back down. He stands and walks forward, eyes piercing into me, then bends, dragging a liquor bottle from his boot.

I raise an eyebrow. "You keep that in your shoe? Really, Rath?"

"No." His tone oozes sarcasm. He unscrews the top, offering it to me. "Clearly not. Here. It's good whiskey. It'll burn the throat like the stench of the hell realm burns the nose. You'll enjoy." He waggles the bottle.

Damn his stupid mind-reading, body-reading abilities.

My stomach clenches. I'm not human, but I've been around them my whole life and they share most traits with gods. I'm not chancing anything more than I'm forced to when it comes to something so important.

Rath takes a sip, spins the cap back on, and drops the bottle back in his boot. He taps the back of my hand, splayed over my stomach with his knuckle. "I would have dragged you right out of here last time, Lu. Why didn't you tell me?"

"I didn't know then," I say, throwing my hands in the air. "The day before yesterday, I swear I woke up and this"—I wave at the tiny bump that feels enormous under my loose shirt—"was like this. I ignored the signs because they weren't normal…for a siren."

"Because you're a goddess." He does an odd wince-smile, confused between pained and happy.

Telling them spurs something in me, as if sharing made the theory solid and true. The evidence is obvious, but, wow…I'm carrying Alex's child.

"Holy Hera." Comus tents his fingers in front of his lips and squats. He could use one of those silly fainting chaises. We all could. "Alex will be so happy." He drops his hands to show off his beaming smile. "I mean, he's going to be a basket case for a bit with everything going on, but yeah. Thrilled."

I bite my lips together. "He will?"

"Absolutely." Rath grips the back of his neck. "I didn't think of him as the family kind until he met you. I can see it now. Lu…" He steps close and pulls me into a careful hug.

Emotion shifts in the universe with Rath's words, and I envision Alex tossing around a green-eyed baby as she cackles rolling giggles of joy. Something loosens in my chest. We could be a family?

Rath grips my shoulders and gently pushes away from me, mouth open to speak, but he closes it and studies my face. "It's fading. How are you feeling right now?"

I jerk my hand up. The fading pattern pulses like a heartbeat. "Relieved, I think." Though it's short-lived and the lines grow stronger. I can't leave here and allow Moros to escape through the mysterious moving portal. The best way I can protect the humans and Earth is to remain here.

Rath backs up and crosses his arms, standing next to Comus.

"We need to go get Alex," Comus says. "And Herc and Anice can't hold the portal much longer."

A wave of nausea rolls through me so quickly, I cover my mouth with my hand.

"And she needs food." Rath crinkles his nose. "I'm an ass for not bringing something. I was just—"

"You've been…distracted, but yeah. Grace is going to flip in so many ways." Comus twists his lips to the side. "We need to get her out."

"I'm standing right here," I grumble and cover my mouth again. I need that ginger grass. If I soak it in water, it's similar to weak tea. "Can't. Moros. K. Have to go now." I point behind me and turn, taking deep breaths.

"Lu, we'll be back sooner than later. I'll bring you whatever you want. Pasta?"

I give him a thumbs up and keep walking. Don't throw up in front of the deities. I say it in my mind like a mantra. Will Grace come too? I need her right now. All my sisters. They'll help, I think. We haven't had a new siren in a century, though I'm not sure what this child will be. A primordial siren demi-hybrid? I'd laugh, but the sickness holds it back. What am I going to do about this place? Moros may be my father, but he's dangerous to the world and to Olympus. His hand is growing and his powers will return soon if they haven't already. He can't be around other people and I can't raise a child in the hell realm, especially with him whispering doom in her little ears.

I duck behind a rock and lose the water that was in my stomach. *Okay, little one. We must come to an agreement. There's not a lot of food here and you're going to need it, so no more making me throw up every half-day or whenever I use my attributes. The dizziness isn't helping us either.* What did Rath mean by sooner than later? Pasta would stay down, I bet. "You'll love pasta," I whisper. "It's the best."

"Whose child is it?" Moros asks from behind me, making me jolt and spin around.

"Stop creeping up on me. You've been doing that lately, and I'm going to send you flying next time."

"The child." His eyes flick to my stomach. "Does it belong to Alexiares, Rathbarth, or humans?"

"She belongs to me."

Rust brown movement catches my eye on my left. Thorette has been following closer lately, and now she's crouched in stalk mode.

Moros presses his forearm to my collarbone and shoves me hard into the rock behind me. A sharp pain digs into my hip. "Stay still. Unless this ends you won't have another heat for centuries."

Thorette's sharp screech joins my scream and a rumble shakes the ground.

Chapter Thirty-Two

ALEX

I'M RAIDING THE FRIDGE, A WHEEL OF GOUDA IN MY HAND, WHEN RATH barges in the door.

"Cheese?" I ask, smiling until I catch the terror on his face. Hades and Hera follow him into the kitchen, grim expressions making my stomach both drop and knot tight. "Lula," I say on an exhale. I grab Rath's wrist. "Go."

The world falls to black and gray slipstreams sailing by at a speed I can't remember reaching while in the shadow realm. With a burst, we fall to sand. I wasn't ready for the stop and fall, rolling back up to my feet directly into a sprint. The portal line shimmers, unmanned in the desert where we found a burning pile of bodies—one of Moros's early calling cards. The sand covers whatever damage was there, though I suppose that was a year ago now.

With a pop of color, Hades and Hera step from flame.

"Where's Anice?" Rath slows to meet them. "He should be guarding."

"What happened?" I ask, stepping into the hell realm. It's eerily quiet and I stretch my jaw to release the pressure in my ears, but it's not me. It's the hot, acrid air. I scratch at my chest.

Rath runs a path through the grass and I follow without question. A rainbow of flame rolls around us in blinks as Hades and Hera flank us. We leap from red rock to red rock, and once we clear a boulder that's broken in two, I see her.

Lula faces away from me, thinner, and hair shorter than last time I saw her. Balling her fists at her sides, she appears to be yelling at Moros, who's in a bloodied heap on the ground with two darklings pacing a line behind him, fangs bared. I can't hear her at all.

Comus and my father stand twenty feet away, whispering to each other.

Each step brings me closer to what feels like home, even in the hell realm. Waiting was asinine. How could I have forgotten that near her is my place?

The ground shakes and a fissure breaks between us. I step over, eyeing the small chasm in case it breaks further.

Comus turns, wide-eyed and pale. "She's not responding to us and is going to break apart the planet." He yells but it sounds like a whisper. "I don't have a clue what she's doing."

My father clasps my shoulder. "Be cautious. The threats we could hear are unsettling."

"Those are my favorite kind." Hades watches Lula with a tilted head. Her skin shimmers dark metallic patterns that shift in chaotic jerks. "What do you mean, *could* hear?" he asks.

Comus taps his ear. "Sound goes in and out along with waves of heat, but finding a rhyme or reason is like listening to bad jazz. Her field shifts and we're blocked from her by the rocks and cave. We can't help her without knowing what we're dealing with." He throws his hands up, then jams them on his hips in total frustration. "I should have brought the oracle and Grace. She could have convinced her."

"Lula?" I step against her force field. With a hand up, I follow it, trying to get closer, but she's tucked into a mini crater surrounded by a tall line of rocks. "Lu." Her shoulders tremble, and her defined leg muscles are tight with tension. As I get closer to seeing her profile, crimson stains her right side and rage infuses my chest. Hades blinks to the top of the rocky cave wall and presses air. He shakes his head.

Rath pops in beside me, but faces my father. "Anice is missing from the portal."

"He shouldn't be." Hercules turns without a word to run toward the opening. That's for the better or Olympus could show up during this and make everything worse.

"Lula?" Rath yells, then looks at me. "We heard her scream as we were stepping out of the portal. Thorette was roaring. Moros did something, and she protected Lula which is just…" He trails off with a huff.

"Thorette?"

"The smaller darkling." He bites his lip as if there's more, but the ground trembles again, so hard it sets both Rath and I on our asses.

Moros drags himself to his feet and takes three limping steps toward Lula before he's flung through the air, hitting the top lip of the cave entrance and landing heavily on the ground. There's no way that didn't break something.

"Lula," I yell. "Lu, look at me." I stand and press the field. It gives the slightest bit.

"And I can't control any of this…" Her voice comes, an echo gaining ground with every word. "Your brand of *help* is the worst. I'm stuck here, babysitting your ass for eternity because you're hell-bent on dooming the Earth. Fuck you, Moros." The last part is so loud, I have to cover my ears and heat surrounds me as if I walked into a dry sauna. "I can't raise a child in the hell realm, and I'll be damned if you get a chance to speak to her. Never, do you understand me? We do not belong to you."

The world around me swirls to an abrupt, hollow stop.

"I…uh, didn't have time to tell you." Rath waves toward Lula. "And I didn't think it would help at this…ah, juncture." He scrunches his nose.

Scrambling forward, I follow the invisible wall she's trapped herself in, frantically seeking an empty or weak spot. If Moros gets up or a rock crumbles…the darkling is too close to her. I climb rocks and slide down dusty gravel. "Let me in, Firecracker." I slam a shoulder against it. "Lula!"

Her matted curls flick as she cocks her head, and then she turns. Blazing silver eyes land on me and her lips part in a gasp.

I exhale and lean into the barrier. "Hey. It's okay." *It will be.* "Can you take down the field?"

"Alex." My name is a mere whimper on her lips.

My chest clenches. "I'm here." I give her a small smile; glad she seems more relieved than angry. "Take down the field?"

The ground beneath her sinks more and another rumble trembles the realm. She steps away from the dip under her feet but keeps her eyes on me. The darklings cower, and though the one is huge, the way he skitters and crouches beside Lula makes him look small. The other leaps to the rocks, blending in with them.

"I don't know how." Lula raises her palms, then balls her dark fingers again, holding them to her chest. "I can't control this. You all have to leave. The portal is open and I don't want to hurt—"

The big darkling presses its snout against her leg and Lula yips and jumps sideways before patting his head as if afraid of him. She may be afraid of hurting him. She points toward the cave and it sulks off, climbing rocks close to the other and perching—a gargoyle overlooking its postapocalyptic city.

"Come closer," I tell her, but she takes a step back. Another pulse of heat hits, making sweat trickle down my back. "Are you injured?"

Her lips tighten and she glances at the pile of Moros, then lifts the hem of her shirt and swipes at a place I can't see through blood. My knees wobble and I have to hold myself back from ramming against the border keeping us apart. The others curse and the old tension of warring gods hits the air. He tried to take our child from her. "Lu." There's too much desperation in my voice, and I take a breath. "Are you injured?"

She drops her shirt. "Not anymore."

Moros isn't walking out of here or anywhere else ever again.

Comus steps in beside me. "What's the plan here? We have a crumbling planet, an open portal, and a field she can't remove that also contains darklings and Moros.

"Moros is the bigger issue." Rath grits his teeth.

"Always has been." I rub my damp neck. "Alright, she's the most powerful deity alive and she's had Moros and a few moments with you two as a guide. Her attributes are still unaligned. Remember your zeniths? What was the first lesson you learned?"

"To accept it," Comus says.

"Go deeper."

Rath pinches between his eyes. "To accept it, you have to allow it to unite with your essence. That's scary as fuck depending on your power level."

Rath's frightened him and the deities that were already distrustful because of his lineage. But he still had guidance, even if he refuses to explore some attributes because of his first round of testing. Lula doesn't have that option. They're bursting out whether or not she wants to unite with them.

Comus runs a hand over his beard and presses against the air. "She wrote to Grace and told her that Moros asked her to kill everyone. Said she could do it easily. She's been holding back, thinking that if she lets go, she'll destroy the universe."

The ground rumbles again and I turn to Hera. "What's your assessment? Is the hell realm in danger of dying?" Hera's mysterious attributes are based around life and protection. She's bound to sense something here.

Hera watches Lula. "No, not at all. Do you feel the shifts under the earth? It's not breaking, it's traveling."

"She's moving plates around?"

"She's most likely pushing them away without realizing it." Rath rolls up his sleeves. "When she gets stressed, her field automatically poofs. I think it siphons energy off her though. Look, she can't kill me. Probably. And her glitterlings can go through the barrier. Sic her on me to ease this pressure? Use her up?"

"She already looks exhausted and—" I bite the inside of my cheek and shake my head. "Nothing can happen to her…" I glance between the guys, warning them to be careful with her. With both of them. They nod and I face Lu, who's clutching her shirt and taking in the damage to the cave. "Come closer," I yell. She needs to be clear from the cave if she takes it apart. Her eyes follow me, but she frowns, hugging herself like she's trying to shrink into nothingness. This uncontrollable wall keeping us apart when we've done too much of that already makes remaining calm a faraway, fluttering dream. I fake nonchalance and wave her toward me. "Closer and then push me further away."

"But I need to contain it." Lula's near tears. "I can't. Alex, I don't know—"

"Which is why you're going to learn. Trust me, baby." The words slip out so easily, but I flinch, unsure of what we are right now with so much past unresolved. "Let's go. Push your field out, see how far and how fast it can go."

She drops balled fists to her sides and takes a deep breath. The invisible wall hits me and Comus like a tennis racket against a ball and we both sail back, hitting the ground and rolling. I climb up to my feet and pop my shoulder back in with a grunt. Lula's covering her mouth with both hands.

"Very good." I smile wide. The ache will settle in a moment. "We're fine. See? Again. Further."

"This is brand new, Alex," Comus whispers, brushing himself off. "What if she can encompass the planet?"

"She's aiming at us." I give a nod toward Hades and Hera, standing off unphased and engrossed in watching us, still testing the air in front of them. "But if it goes beyond? Well, we cross that when we get there." I dust off, taking a few steps back. "Again, Lula."

This time, the push is more gradual.

"Outstanding work," Comus shouts.

Rath pops in ten feet beside me and nods. I lock on Lula's eyes. "Send your power at Rath. Hit him."

She shakes her head.

Rath clucks his tongue. "What? Come on and do it, Lu. If you can get me, I'll bring you mac and—"

A dark ball hurtles at him, and he flicks to shadow when it impacts.

"I did it." Her eyes are wide.

Rath appears on Comus's side. "Again."

She hesitates.

I whistle to get Hera's attention. "Is she and...is she okay?"

"They're both strong. The babe more so." She gives a pained smile.

"Do it, Lula." I shove against the barrier, but it's hard now, ungiving.

"Alex," Comus warns.

"She has to allow it room to exist and it may snap in place."

"I know, but—"

I raise my hand to signal him to stop. "Our attributes surface for a purpose. If hers are to end it all, we might as well find out now."

Rath laughs, inappropriate with the situation, though it feels right for the four of us to work together toward something, even if the mystery goal may be apocalyptic.

"How are you feeling?" I ask Lula, shifting my gaze to her belly.

"Peachy." Lula rubs her face and shakes out her hands. She's calmer and the dry heat slips to a more tolerable hell realm temperature. "Everything is so…tight."

"Good. Push harder, hit Rath."

Moros stirs behind her, twitching as if coming back to life. He may be.

Lula straightens as she takes a deep breath, and the field pushes us away at a snail's pace.

"Hit me, Lu," Rath calls.

The glinting ball surges toward him, but this time stops before his braced body. He peeks open an eye. "Holy Hera. Uh, sorry Hera."

Hera ignores him and instead glares toward Moros, who's rolled to his back, chest rising and falling. I've got to get in there.

Lula's shoulder sag and her eyes are tired. "I didn't want to hurt you. They listened."

"Good job, Lula." I shove at the familiar wall. It now has the slightest bit of give. "Push further. How far can it go? Can you push only me away?"

She rubs her forehead, then flexes her fingers. She eases me back, then I slide faster until I stumble to remain on my feet and white seedling balls float through the air like giant dandelion puffs. Comus and Rath stay put, eyes wide. The ability to manipulate a force field in different locations isn't something that should be possible. She beams at me and I laugh. "Yes, that's it, Firecracker! That's it."

Her face falls, and I lurch forward with the shrink.

"Hold it, Lu," Comus yells. "You can't let emotion change what you want to do. Keep going. Toss him back."

"Brother, I'm looking to make things better," I whisper.

"Yeah, well, you pushing her is working. She needs this and everything is easing. Can you feel it?"

He's right. The temperature is lower, the air more clear and not stealing or amplifying sound. Still, she and I are in an odd spot. But that look from before…she's glad I'm here and I am too.

Moros flips to his stomach and his eyes widen as he takes in the scene.

Every muscle in me tightens. "Let me in."

"What?" She takes a weak side step like her ankle gave out. She doesn't have much energy left.

"Just me. Do it." I slap at the field. *Just fucking let me in.*

"Alex, I—"

"Now, Firecracker."

She closes her eyes, then opens them, determination blazing. Her skin darkens further. Comus and I stumble forward.

"Sorry," she says.

"You're getting it." We walk forward until we hit the wall. "No apologies. Focus."

Moros pushes off the ground.

Lula bends, teeth bared, hands over her heart. "I—"

"Don't you dare give up!" I yell. "Take it down now. Sling shot it out if you need to and let it whip back."

Comus grumbles. He's worried about her. As am I. Rath fades, popping back in and out in a panic to test areas for weakness. The wall in front of me shifts, and I walk forward. The resistance falls away step by step until I'm running. Lula sways, and behind me Comus yells directions. The barrier has fallen.

I catch Lula before she hits the ground. She's too light and her face is pale. Her eyes flutter, the shining hematite of her irises flickering to green. I stroke her cheek. The silver drifts off her skin, and she leans into my fingers. "You're here."

"Of course, I am. I'm sorry it wasn't sooner."

Moros stalks forward with a crotchety growl but Rath tackles him, then dissipates before Moros can touch him. I back away, clutching Lula closer to me. Hera steps in front of us and Hades sidles up beside me. "The hell realm isn't as disastrous as I thought it'd be. I mean, it sucks, but in a Silver Age way." He takes Lula's hand to kiss her palm. "Hello, Lula. It's an absolute pleasure. I'm Hades."

"Oh." Her half-lidded eyes widen the slightest bit. "Hello."

"I like your darklings. Do you have more?"

She almost puts her hand on my chest again, but diverts at the last second, balling her fist and tucking it under her chin. "I'm not sure? They're…I don't know, not mine, but Thor has been very helpful. And Thorette."

"Fabulous." Hades gives her a charming smile. "We are definitely doing brunch soon."

"Hera." Moros coughs. "Still beguiling, even here." His voice is a rasp and I realize it's because the darkling took a good chunk from his throat. He's deathly pale under the dried blood. And I've found a new appreciation of darklings.

"Your conduct has been vile." Hera straightens in front of us. "And you dare to use the sirens to accomplish your wretched deeds."

Lula struggles to get down, and I reluctantly set her on her feet. The space between us is cold and snaps an unease through me. I should snatch her up and out of here; hide away to protect them forever, but it's not my place right now. Not yet.

Moros lowers his eyes and hobbles toward Hera. "I needed to see you."

Lula steps beside my grandmother, turning to face her. "You were the voice. You told me to hang on during the lightning."

Grandmother spoke to her mind?

Hera lifts Lula's chin and gives her the faintest kiss before pressing their foreheads together. "And you did so well." My heart staggers at the familial gesture.

Moros stumbles another step forward. "You may not claim her unless you join with me. She is more mine than yours."

"You killed daughters of my creation." Hera's tone gives me chills and she's on our side. "You harmed my future granddaughter intending to end the life within her and yet you believe I'd consider joining with you? Do you not know who I am, God of Doom?"

I wrap my arm slowly around Lula. She jerks until I splay my fingers against the small curve of her belly, and then she sinks, blinking back tears as her eyes meet mine. My knees weaken when she puts her hand over mine and there's nothing I wouldn't do to start again and make everything right for her and our little one.

"I know you more than anyone, Hera." Moros's words remind me that things are not perfect yet. "Zeus should have given you to me. I deserved you."

"You and Zeus and can go fuck yourselves." Hades studies his nails like he's bored. He probably is. "You know what to do here, Hera."

"I cannot without…" she whispers, then trails off, giving Hades a pointed glance. He shrugs. What is their plan? She touches Lula's shoulder. "What do you choose?"

Lula swallows hard and looks at Rath. "I can't ask you to do this."

He steps forward. "You don't have to."

Lula's fingers tense and tremble against my hand and she presses back against me. Moros bares his teeth as Rath appears behind him and grabs his right wrist. Moros yells, reaching for Hera, then they're gone. Lula sniffles and I wrap my other arm around her as well.

"Where is he taking him?" Hera asks.

Lula wipes at her wet cheeks. "He's abandoning him in the shadow realm."

A whistle comes from Hades. "We're going to get along just fine. Shall we get the hell out of here?"

Rath reappears without Moros and I release Lula so he can hug her. His eyes are distant and as shadowy as his realm. When he turns her around to face me again, we stare in awkward silence. This is a path where I have the destination, but not the map.

I bite my lip and nod toward the portal. "Do you want to go home or to Belize?"

Chapter Thirty-Three

LULA

"I can't leave." I glance back at Thor and Thorette, who dig in the upturned dirt. They don't seem traumatized, but my world is reeling. The pressure has tanked, leaving me empty and dazed, but it could return any second. "I'm not safe to be around."

Alex's brow furrows, and he studies the landscape. "I'm not leaving you." He points to the cave. Rock and shards of broken purple stones fill half the inside. "And that doesn't look habitable." His gaze drops to my midsection and I fight wrapping my arms around myself. "Belize is secluded."

"And it's on Earth," Hades says. "Zeus can scry for both of you." He takes a step closer to me and twists his lips. "And I can't take you to the underworld without knowing what you are. All we need is for your force field to knock a bunch of souls into the next realm or back onto Earth. Anyone up for a zombie apocalypse?"

"Could be fun." Rath keeps his eyes on his boots.

"Maybe tomorrow," Comus adds, looking past us. "We have a different problem though. Shit."

The huge deity covers ground like a freight train and is so big, he blocks out the lowering sun when he gets close. I retreat a step, hoping his ire isn't aimed at me. I can't go through another god wanting to harm us.

"Anice is gone." His voice is gentler than I could imagine coming from a giant. "He would not have left willingly." He spots me and bows his head. I believe he's aware that he's intimidating, or it could be the tight expression I wear, but he pulls his big arms in tighter, and moves close.

"He may have had to transport someone quickly?" Comus asks.

"Did you call him?" Alex's fingers brush my lower back, sending so much heat through me, I have to shift from him before my powers get the best of me. He drops his hand. "Father, meet Lula. Lula…Hercules."

The demigod's blue eyes crinkle at the corners. For a moment, I think he's going to kiss me like Hera did, but he presses his forehead to mine. "I am most honored to meet you, Lula." My throat tightens and I want to return his kind words, but he spins and stalks toward the direction he came. "With me. I must guard the portal and will attempt to call again."

We walk behind Hercules in a small herd. When Thor chuffs behind me, I pause.

"It's okay," I say. "I'm safe." Thor seems to nod and then backs away, before spinning and loping off toward Thorette and the pond. When I turn around to step in line with the others, they're all watching me. "Should I have brought him along?"

Comus huffs amusement and continues on the path. "We need an oracle."

"That's the siren part," I mumble.

Alex steps beside me, hands shoved in the pockets of clean jeans. I can't imagine what I look like. For living in a hell realm, I've mastered primitive chic, but there's red clay under my fingernails and my hair is one step away from mats. My fingers get hung up when I tuck strands behind my ear.

"The siren ability is still incredible," Alex whispers.

I take the slightest step closer and keep my voice low. "The others wouldn't accept me so willingly if I didn't have a goddess side." The glitterlings shift forward again and I rub the back of my hand. Hercules disappears into the rip in the veil.

"It's not a side," Alex says. "It's you, both siren and goddess. And my family accepts you because of how you acted at your zenith and because I love you in a way that Olympus doesn't often witness." His eyes quickly flick to mine, then he steps close to Comus and Rath like they do when they're plotting in their hive mind. My heart races off at a speeding pace. I'm not ready for any of this, yet, I am. In my new normal, I'm at odds with myself. The pressure returns, but lethargic, like I'm staring up at the last hill of a six-mile hike. "Check for Anice," Alex says. "Then update Lula's sisters, please. Then Sing?"

Comus turns to me. "Lula, you need to be read by an oracle. I have one, a human. She lives in Florida and if we know your attributes' named form, we can work further to train you. I could bring Grace too?"

I bite my bottom lip. Hiding here forever isn't an option. If the baby keeps taking what she needs from me, I'll waste away with no one but Thor and Thorette to assist. Guilt riddles me with the thought that I'd rather have them around than my father. I don't have to worry about that anymore; he's gone, lost to shadow. Alex watches me closely, but from a distance. He's leaner with longer hair and a beard which I'm tempted to run my fingers through, except I may destroy it, and it looks good on him. He tilts his head, the corner of his lips twitches up, but there's still a question to his gaze, not pushing, but asking. I'm so tired. If I'm destined for evil, at least I'll know and figure things out from there. "Okay."

"Yeah?" Comus grins.

Alex takes a step closer. "Maybe not Grace. Not yet." His wince is faint. "It's overwhelming and you're already overwhelmed. I know you want to see your sisters but—"

"No, that makes sense." I blow out a long breath. I ache to see them, but when I picture her reaction—the inevitable shock on her face, plus being able to hug her to remember that she's real, healthy, and out there—the world heats and crushes. Even if that pressure is sleepy, it may not be by time they return. I've hurt enough people I love. Alex was dead for months, and Grace wouldn't return from what I did.

Hades clears his throat. "I'm going to check on the big oaf." Flames in a hundred colors blast from the ground, engulfing him, making me gasp and jump sideways, knocking into Alex, who's arm wraps around me with protective familiarity. My muscles ease with comfort, but he drops his hold. We both take a small step apart.

I tuck tangled strands behind my ears. "So Hades can catch on fire and disappear?"

"He can flame travel. It's one of his attributes."

Rath and Comus's tightly knit brows and Hera's scrutiny enhance this awkward moment, but fortunately, Comus offers an elbow to Hera and they step through the portal.

"You need food." Rath disappears.

In silence, Alex stares at me and I stare back. What does someone say to the person they love and also hurt so badly? There are no smiles between us. No jesting or hope of light and airy moments. Those lie in the past and the thought of finding them again doesn't seem possible. Alex, now thankfully in one piece, blows out a long breath with the miraculous movement of his lungs. His heartbeat would be a known rhythm if I rested my head against his chest, but I can't because I've seen it sputter to a stop. I'm both ashamed I hurt him and in awe of how beautiful he still is as he stands, watching me, watch him.

He puts his hands in his pockets. "I want another chance, Lula."

"Alex, I attacked you."

He shrugs like ripping someone apart isn't a horrendous act. "I hurt you first."

"You lied to me. I almost killed you. There's a bit of a difference there."

"I scared you into the hell realm with Moros."

With a jerk, I lift my fingers and Alex flinches, backing up a step. He fusses with his hair, trying and failing to cover his reaction. I lower my hand to fidget with the hem of my shirt. "I scare you now."

"No, I'm—"

"Scared," I repeat. "With good reason."

"No, it's…" He gives a small growl. "Reluctant, yes. Timid, sure. I woke only days ago, I'm adjusting."

"Adjusting to me killing y—"

"No." Alex turns to pace. "I needed a moment to take everything in. It's a lot. And now…" He eyes my midsection. "Lu, you're pregnant."

"Is that what brought you back?"

"No." His eyes angle into a soft awe as he glances at my midsection. "I didn't know until you yelled it. But Moros hurt you and I should have been here. If Rath and Comus wouldn't have heard you, we may not have known. It could have been…" His fists ball at his sides and even under the beard, I can tell his jaw is tight. "Are you okay?"

"Not really." I cross my arms over my sore chest.

He steps closer and takes my hand. The snap of electricity is still every bit as electrifying as before. At least that hasn't changed. I study my small, silvery fingers in Alex's golden ones. So different, but my body remembers the warmth we shared, the drag of need when we're together.

Alex moves in, bringing me closer to the gold I've gotten lost in so many times. His citrus scent isn't the sweet sugar from before. It's more earthy, like he's been living on a mountain of rock and bathing in the purest springs. Wanting to trace my nose against his neck to inhale more of him, I lean in. He's addictive. Always has been.

"Pizza," Rath yells.

My fingers jerk out of Alex's and I step back, brushing my hands on my shorts.

"Oh. Uh…" Rath holds a huge pizza box, and his expression flicks to scrunch-faced chagrin for a second. "Hungry?"

"You know I am." I sprint to him.

He opens the box and I bite my lips together. It's covered in vegetables, including olives. What seems like forever ago, Alex and I fought over what to order on pizza and I may have thrown a can of olives at him. Then he may have pressed me against the wall and came close to breaking Zeus's rules earlier than we did.

Rath tilts his head. "What's wrong?"

"Nothing. Thank you." I snatch a piece, olives be damned, and with difficulty, focus on not cramming the entire thing into my mouth. My stomach grumbles at the inhale of oven-cooked vegetables and melted cheese. Oh my god, this crust. Only New York can make pizza like this. I moan and bounce in place as I take three bites in quick succession.

Alex steps beside me, and I turn to keep him from seeing me

attack my prey to get it into my body as fast as possible. "It has olives." He huffs out a laugh. I glare at him over my shoulder, but the emphasis is probably lost with my mouth being so full. He grins and snags a slice. "You have to admit that's funny." He takes a big bite and hums a happy sound.

That makes me smile and I reach for another piece, taking it toward the trees. I sit and lean against a wide trunk. The guys follow.

"Olives?" Rath asks.

He's not used to not knowing things. I kinda like the cranky face he gives, at least until I remember how shitty Olympus has been to him. He's always been out of the loop, at least when not in shadow. That's how I'll be too, if I'm ever allowed there. Not that I'd go. Assholes.

When I get half of the third piece down, a wave of exhaustion hits me, but Comus walks back into the realm.

"Anice is missing and not answering his phone," he says. "Hades and Hera are searching. They will find something soon. Grace sends her love and wants you to contact her or she won't be happy, and Sing is willing to come here first thing in the morning—Earth time—but needs a ride."

Rath narrows his eyes. "You did not just call me a ride."

Comus pokes at his phone, keeping his eyes down. "Oh, I did. My gallant steed, my trusty pickup, my—"

Rath leaps and drags him to shadow. Alex stares at me and I drop my smile. "You look worried," I say. He gives a small nod while he chews, far more civilized than I'm capable of at the moment. "Do you need to go search for your brother?" I understand missing siblings. Waiting to hear from them is torture.

His brows furrow. "Are you trying to get rid of me?"

I lean back against the tree. I still haven't adjusted to him being here. It doesn't feel like the hell realm with him in it. It's homier, calmer, and more tolerable. "No."

"Good." His voice is soft, and he wears a slight smile as he looks me over. "How are those olives?"

"Don't judge me." I nibble my grinning lip and pull one from what remains of my slice. "Better than anything ever."

Alex watches me closely, then moves his gaze to the hills, the rocks, and to Puff Gardens. "You've been through a lot."

"I have. This is an interesting place. I wasn't able to explore much because I couldn't leave Moros for fear he'd find his way out again." The world does a quick whirl of pressure, then settles again. I peek at his profile. "And I had a tough time leaving where the portal opens." He gazes back at me and nods. I explain the portal Moros claims he left from. Alex doesn't like that one bit, but Rath didn't either. We talk about what I thought I'd see here, but hadn't. I expected trolls or goblins, and I only saw a wendigo pair once, but they steered clear of Thor.

"Moros didn't tell you much, did he?" Alex says. "Some otherworldlings that seem like darklings come from other realms. Like goblins are from the elven realm, and types of berserkers as well."

"In a couple of thousand years will these creatures become civilized?"

"Mm-hmm. I wonder if your influence is helping them now. I've never seen a darkling respond like that one—Thor did. And you have some control over the…glitterlings?"

I run a finger over the pattern on my hand. "They rip everything apart." The image of Alex sprawled with an open chest makes me drop my hands to clutch grass. "As you know."

When I cover my face, he takes my fingers, then keeps them in his. "And put things back together. Don't give me that look. They did."

"Yes, but I don't know why or how. They weren't listening." Or they were, even when I couldn't ask.

Alex releases my hand and moves next to me, crossed legs stretched out, sharing the tree I'm leaning against. "What else can you do?"

I shrug a shoulder and cup my stuffed stomach. "You've seen the force field. I can move items or people further away sometimes, but don't have a clue how any of this works." I trace the veins on the hand that rests on his thigh before balling my fist.

He snatches my fingers back. "Can you pull things closer?"

I sit up and give a gentle push as I focus on a medium sized rock. It's easier this time as it rolls a few feet further away. When I drag the force field toward me, nothing happens. I visualize it wrapping over the stone, and it wavers but otherwise doesn't move. Four more tries and it inches closer in slow jerks. Then it pops and shivers to the ground in a pile of pebbles.

I lift my eyes to Alex's. "That would be no."

I lie back, but he tugs my hand. "Hey, gaining your attributes isn't easy and yours are…dramatic. You're flying blind when you should have instruction."

Comus and Rath reappear with a woman wearing a pink, lip-sticked smile that matches her jumper. She blows a lock of black hair out of her face from a messy bun on top of her head. "My moosh, you weren't kidding!"

Rath steps close to her, arms folded. "You okay? Breathing fine?"

She flares her nostrils with a big inhale and pats her chest. "Burns a little, but I can do it."

Comus eyes my and Alex's entwined fingers, which I unwind. "Sing," he says. "This is Lula. Lu can't talk to you, Sing, because she's part siren. And that's Alex."

The woman's arched brows raise, and she steps forward, reaching to shake Alex's hand. I take a step behind him, not wanting to touch her.

"I've heard so much about you." She pumps his hand with enthusiasm.

"Have you?" Alex gives Comus a glare.

Sing peeks around, giving me a once-over as if I'm a painting in a gallery. "Wow, a hybrid and a hell realm. How long have your attributes been in external form?"

Rath crosses his arms over his chest and stares at me, assessing. "Since she was forced into zenith. A little over two months ago."

She steps closer, smile slowly dropping away. "You have a confused aura. You have another one with you, don't you?" Her gaze drops to my midsection. "Their light is strong. Congratulations."

I swallow hard and Alex backs into me, reaching for my hand. I bite my lip and squeeze his fingers. He clears his throat. "Yes. Thank you."

Her eyes pop and she covers her grinning lips. "Oh my! I should have known from how your auras interact. I've got to hang out with the divine more. This is wildly fun."

It's certainly wild. I force a smile.

Comus steps next to Sing. "Lu, Sing has to touch you and interact with your energy. It's going to be weird, but she won't hurt you. Don't fight it."

"I'll be gentle." Sing smiles and holds out her palm. "Okay, Lula, give me your hands."

Alex lets me go, but settles his hand on the small of my back. I don't flinch this time. "You're both safe with her," he whispers. "Focus on that if it's too much to handle."

Both of us. I nod. Alex's hand drops away.

The moment my palms align with hers, Sing's eyes flash opaque and her lips part in a gasp. Heat trails from her, up my arm like it's following my blood. I should panic—it's invasive and overwhelming, yet peaceful.

"Mother of pearl," Sing whispers and gives a slight smile before frowning.

There's energy that's not mine flowing in my veins, and the only thing keeping me from jerking away is that it's similar to submerging in a warm bath. Sing tilts her head and pressure bombards me. My breath quickens, and I peek over my shoulder at Alex.

He smiles from right behind me, but he's flexing his hands and there's a focused wrinkle between his eyes. "It won't be long."

Sing's eyes are an overcast sky and they focus through me. Rath's arms stretch around her but not touching. In a jolt, the pressure flips to wanting to rip me apart. "Shh," Sing whispers as I try to squirm out of her grip, but my palm is fused to hers.

The glitterlings swirl and leap to Sing's hand. I bite my lip to keep from telling her to stop and run. Would it hurt her if I did?

Sing smiles. "All good. This is…fascinating."

Comus nods at me as if this is everyday stuff, though Rath worries his lip as he watches our hands.

Her coursing energy slows and wraps around my heart, digging into new places that gape wide and air out like opening all the windows in a stuffy house. Vision fades to swirling color and thoughts. Sing sifts through my attributes, sorting them, and somehow I'm with her as she works. My lack of control is embarrassing compared to how she drags energy where she wants it. If pressure spikes, she pulls it back and lets other components rise. It's not on and off, it's a complicated web that stretches from me; my soul and mind and extending out to her, Alex and the guys, and the life on this planet. It tumbles, bounding out to reach for stars and planets…the sun. The tugging heat leaves me in a chilled whoosh. Vision returns from the fog and Sing's head falls forward. Her hand slides from mine and she slumps as I do.

"Wanna do tha' again," she slurs as Rath catches her, laying her on the ground.

I'm up in Alex's arms before I fully sink into a gelatinous mass and absorb into the earth. At least, that's what my body wants to do. He brushes back my hair and strokes my cheek. We're walking… somewhere. Doesn't matter. "Talk to me, Lula."

My energy flooded to the sun. "Sleeping now."

"Go ahead, Firecracker. I'm so proud of you." He shifts me closer and I drift to his heartbeat against my ear.

Chapter Thirty-Four

ALEX

I hope Lula is happy in my arms, because I may never put her down again. She nuzzles against my chest, breaking open a heart that has been hers since I kissed her, maybe earlier. Her breath flutters her slow, steady sleep rhythm, making her unlikely to talk and enthrall Sing. I return to the guys. Their expressions are free from scorn or disbelief, different from the first time they saw me acting foolish around Lula. There's only pure concern for her.

"Has that happened before?" I ask. If I almost lost her again, I'm truly not letting her out of my arms.

"Never like that." Comus checks over Sing again. "She's only read me, Prax, and Rath. She gets tired, more so with Rath, but"—he signals to her unconscious state—"there was a sinking ship moment where I wasn't sure either of them were exiting that trance."

"Wake up time, Sing." Rath grips her shoulder and gives her a gentle shake. "Let's go so I can take you home to rest."

She blinks awake and rubs her eyes under her glasses. "That hybrid power thing isn't a joke." She sits up with Rath's help. We stare, holding our breath, the only sound the hollow taps of dry grass stalks meeting each other. Sing smiles at Lula, passed out in my arms. "Goddess of Magnetism."

"Magnetism?" Comus asks, stroking his beard.

"Yes," Sing says. "It's wild in there. Her energy vibrates and there's so many components to it I don't understand. It's going to take a while for her to grasp them." She puts her fingers close but not touching and moves her hands back and forth. "They polarize, so if one goes off, others retreat or piggyback along, so they spike or drop to get around the fellow…uh, attributes. Wow." She smiles. "I want to do that again, just not yet. She drained me."

"She said there's always a conflict within," Rath says. "Usually to keep the flecks that can escape her skin under control."

Sing staggers to her feet and sidesteps, halted by Rath steadying her. She pats his hand. "Yeah, that makes sense. You probably understand best because she's kinda like you."

"What do you mean?" I ask.

Rath purses his lips.

Sing takes a shaky step from him and shrugs. "You can't tell? There's something different about the two of them. It's like an inner brand or striking the same note." She swishes the air toward Comus. "I'm not entirely helpful because I can only talk it over with Comus and he's not an oracle. I can't bounce ideas off anyone but you all, and Rath's real reading was brief."

It was. Zeus made Pythia do it and she gave a simple, "he's the God of Shadows, pure of blood and will serve Olympus well."

One day I hope Sing can meet another oracle, but she may be elderly or run out of time altogether if we can't change Zeus's mind. She a mini-Pythia with the depth of her reading, though I'm not sure why Rath would be different from Comus or Prax.

"Any insight into her attributes that will help her train?" I clutch Lula closer against me.

Sing takes a deep breath, holding a dainty hand over her heart. Every fingernail is painted a unique color. "She's got a bunch to sort through that I didn't have time to test drive because she was … uh, unsettled, but when she figures everything out, whew! She'll… well, uh, watch her. Compared to Comus and Prax, she has the potential to do"—her eyes get big, and she flings her arms wide— "crazy bad things like dragging us to the sun or something. Oh, not to worry you!" She swipes her hand through the air as if holding the potential to cause the Earth's death is not a massive issue.

"She'll be fine, but needs to meditate a lot and remain calm, okay? Okay."

I'd pinch the bridge of my nose, but my arms are full of Lula. I turn to secret-keeping Comus and stare at him until he winces. "She's a powerful reader, and an empath, and…human? And how old?"

Sing looks between us. "What?"

"Twenty," Comus answers.

I purse my lips. "Did Pythia sneak to Earth and have a kid?"

"Ha!" Rath says. "That's what I asked."

"Okay. That's a later conversation. So Sing…magnetism? Like the world's magnetism?" I stare down at Lula and wish I could wake her up to discuss. "Can she throw the balance off in the world, or move continents?"

Comus tugs his beard. "Sing has abilities but—"

"Uh." Sing scrunches her nose. "I think she could if she wanted to, but she's got a grasp on that part. She's one with the Earth. Two peas in a pod. Oh, except she's here."

"Specifically the Earth?" I ask.

Sing shrugs. "Think so? It was always humans and a field in the visions. Um, green, enormous trees." She closes her eyes. "So tired. Pink—no. Purple flowers. It's like a heart lies in that place, she feels the rhythm of energy, and the people of Earth are blood. Her blood. They matter so much."

My throat tightens, and an ache hits behind my eyes. "Shangri-La." The place Lula and I made another from our love.

"Oh, you know it? Glorious!"

"Anything about destruction?"

"Nah. But she can expand and contract, um…I want to say air, but that's not right."

"Fields," Rath provides. "An energy barrier."

"Yeah, that makes sense. I saw her ability to expand things apart."

I grin. "And bring them back together again."

Comus shares my smile. "We need to research."

"Magnetism had been around since the literal dawn of time. Access to the archives is the only way we will understand more."

"That won't happen with Zeus running Olympus." Rath's hand shoots out to wrap around Sing before she hits the ground.

She startles awake. "What? Yes, please."

Comus offers a hand. "And you're done. Off to rest." He helps her to her feet and hugs her. "Thank you. Let us know if you need anything."

"You take care of me enough." She kisses his cheek, then looks at him, expression dulling to a downtrodden frown.

"Hellish air getting to you?" he asks. "You okay?"

"Um…yeah." She turns to me, eyes staying worried. "It was so nice to meet you, Alex." Placing her palms together, she bows.

"Same. We will see more of you soon."

That brings a smile back, though it's not as giddy as it was before.

As the guys bunch, I step closer. "Comus, can you come with me? Rath…meet us in Belize."

"Can do." Rath disappears.

"Wait," Comus leaps for them, but they're already gone. "Alex, are you sure?"

"There's nowhere for Lula to sleep and she's so thin. She needs food. How long would it take for Pythia to pin us down?"

"A couple of days," he says.

"And if it's earlier, who will they send?"

Comus snorts. "Everyone."

"And we have eyes in Olympus?" I wait for him to nod, then return the gesture. "And what happens if they show up and try to hurt Lula?"

"Okay, I'm with you. The two of you annihilate the army, though that's not our plan…"

"It's not. Call my dad, get him here, and we close this realm."

"On it." Comus jogs out of the portal.

My goddess sleeps with quiet, open-mouthed snores. I'll bring her to visit her creatures when the ash of what's ahead settles, but she can't be here. She belongs on Earth with me and her people. Comus and my father arrive a moment later.

"Are you sure, son?" Hercules asks.

"Yes. She will be fine, but needs rest." I step through and inhale the sweet Earth scent. "Any news on Anice?"

Father shakes his head.

"I called a friend while I waited for your Da," Comus says. "The researcher told me Lu could have wide-open influence. She could balance the axis, increase the magnetosphere, or do a vast array of sciencey things. There are magnetic abilities in nearly every substance, and we still haven't figured out why it behaves the way it does."

"Can you talk to Dionysus about getting into the libraries?"

Comus tics his eyes back and forth as he thinks. "Maybe? Everyone's on edge, and the Council is split. Hermes is missing and Da pleads the Fifth. Athena is antsy enough to bolt if Hera returns or someone gives a better opportunity for leadership." The last part comes out clipped as he stares me down.

I raise an eyebrow. "Do we need a sit-down, brother?"

"I'm trying to keep the peace, Alex, but our people must know you're back."

I'm reluctant, especially with Lula in my arms, and for some crazy reason, I want to talk all this over with Hades.

"Okay. But I'm getting her out of here. Zeus will find out. Alert everyone. Let's go."

I have to pass Lula over to Comus to close the hell realm with my father. I let him hold her while I open a portal to Belize. She doesn't stir, which is also unsettling. Father joins us, muscles tense and head pivoting to take in every inch of the beach. He jogs to the house, grabs the key from under the rock next to the deck, and opens the door.

"You've been here before then?" I ask, following.

"There have been meetings here. It reminds me of Athens's coast, but less rocky."

There are many places deities could explore that would remind them of ancient Greece, though far more would blow their minds with how humans have changed the landscape. Comus gets Lula inside and I signal him to the couch. He settles her down and she gives a soft moan before wrapping herself around a pillow and going still again.

I remove her tattered shoes and cover her with a blanket. Everything is mostly in the same place as it was before, but it's more lived-in and smells a bit like ambrosia, a sign that deities have been here.

"This is headquarters, I take it?"

"Pretty much." Comus taps on his phone. "What's the plan?"

"Rest, regroup, and move forward." I drag my eyes from Lula's relaxed face and move toward the kitchen. Father crosses his arms and stands guard over her.

"Thank you, Father."

He nods, and I get to work checking supplies. There's a good amount of pantry and freezer food and even some fresh vegetables in the fridge.

Rath pops in beside me, then spins, cruising toward the mudroom. "She okay?"

"Tired." I head upstairs. My room is blissfully in order. A quick sheet change and I'm back downstairs. My tight shoulders ease once I'm near Lula. "We're on a clock now. Inform every taxiarch that I've returned with Lula, talk to Iaso and Ceraon about my brother and search for him. You know I'd come but—"

Rath waves me off. "She needs you. The group will want to see both of you though."

I run my hands through my hair. "Give us a day to catch up and rest."

"Let's plan to bring everyone here at midnight tomorrow," Rath says. "That shouldn't set off too many alarms in Olympus. Call Prax when you can. He's been a mess."

"He has?"

Rath tilts his head. "Yeah. We've all been worried and needing you." He brushes a dancing lock of hair out of Lula's face. "Both of you. I didn't know when she'd be able to come back. Every time I left her there with Moros, it felt like giving up on both of you. I thought you'd kill me for leaving her, but there was too much here that needed to be handled."

He's been through a lot and I wasn't here to help with that. I squeeze his shoulder. "Thank you for taking care of her the way you could. All of you. I'm here, and we'll make the best of this as we can."

His shoulders straighten with a lengthy inhale. "The stakes are higher now."

"They've always been high," Comus says. "And now we have Lula. She gets ahold of her attributes and we can't fail. Her mindset, morals, and kindness outrank Zeus's hubris, fear-mongering, and lack of reason. She's more powerful by spades if she's ready, and while she may not yet have a foot in Olympus, she has so many allies."

I feel the blood drain from my face and I sit on the couch.

"Alex?" Comus asks and squats to look at me. "You okay?"

"She's pregnant."

"Yeah." Rath squints in understanding. "I was wondering when that would hit you."

My breath leaves and refuses to return. "Holy hell, I'm going to be a father." We're fighting for more than Rath or Dalia or Lula. We're setting the stage for a new generation. My child's generation.

There's a buzz and Comus pulls his phone from his pocket and chuckles. He types, then tucks it away and pats my cheek. "You're made for fatherhood, Alex. Now…" He stands and stretches. "Grace is going to hike here from Switzerland if I don't give her all the updates immediately."

Everyone is overly affectionate with their goodbyes. It's bittersweet. Each time we part, we wonder what will happen when we see each other again. I should be happy to be in the thick of this progress, but Lula may make me take her back to the hell realm. Or Zeus may find us sooner than later. And where is my brother? Too many things block out the light at the end of this long, inescapable tunnel. But I'm in Belize, with Lula. The radiant orange sun sinks into the deep blue, warming the icy unknowns in my chest. Lula doesn't stir as I talk to Prax, then Zephyrus, and call Anice. There's still no response from Anice.

Carefully shifting myself under Lula, I settle in. I should take her upstairs and let her rest in bed alone like she's been used to, but she's in my arms. It seems like years since we've had this. Did she miss my touch? We'd grown so close that even before her heat phase, there weren't many times we weren't next to, or on, each other. Having her near again, I study each eyelash pressed to the highest point of her cheek. My heart expands in my chest, so much that I'm glad there's no more pain in my wound because it would twinge.

I rest my palm against the tiny rise of her stomach, and my breath catches. Whatever happens when she wakes, we'll work through it together. We can show this world what peace means.

Chapter Thirty-Five

LULA

THE SURFACE I WAKE ON IS BOTH SOFT AND HARD AND IMPOSSIBLY warm. The smell is good—midday sunshine on a rocky outcrop when the heat is considering being too much, which makes it perfect. I shoot up with a gasp and come eye to eye with Alex. He's as surprised as I am, but then tilts his head and smiles. "You still wake up like there's a fire."

When something's different. But *everything* is different. The Belize mudroom is a fuzzy dream that I wouldn't think was real if I didn't know Alex. I'm nestled between him and the back of the cushy, gray couch. He cups the swell of my belly, and his other fingers cover my hip. My leg drapes over his upper thighs, foot pinned under his knee while my pulse pounds so hard, he's bound to hear it. "How?"

"I brought you here."

Swiveling my head to take in reality makes me dizzy, and I prop my forehead next to my hand on Alex's chest and shut my eyes. His scent takes me back to close moments between us, over him, under him, against him.

"Do you remember what happened?" His voice rumbles against my skin and the relief that he's here settles in, soothing my quick pulse and nervous shivering. He didn't leave me in the hell realm. His hand strokes my hip as if I don't scare him.

I lick my dry lips. "Moros. Is Rath okay?" How could he be? I'm certainly not, even if the world already feels safer without my father in it. "Oh, and the oracle—Sing. I didn't hurt her, did I?" I push against him to sit upright.

He balls his fingers as they leave my hip and he lifts as well. "No, she's fine, and wants to read you again as soon as possible. And Rath is more worried about you than anything else." He waits for me to respond, gathering his lip under his teeth. I missed his mouth. I remember what it can do to me. "Are you not interested in your naming?" he asks.

"My what?" I lean forward, mimicking him, until the words line up in my mind. "Oh." Shrinking back, I scrunch my face. He didn't run. That has to be something positive.

"Goddess of Magnetism."

The thoughts trickle in until my brain overloads, snapping twisted lines into place. I can push a force field...no. Repel. The glitterlings... what are they? They've faded, leaving behind a shiny haze.

"You okay?" he asks, reaching to run his knuckles over my tight fist.

"Yes." I stretch out my hands. "Just thinking. I'm—"

Words won't describe what I'm feeling. I need a minute, food, and a bath. My sisters—if I can tame this polarity inside, I'll be able to see them and protect them. *Thirsty.* I pad to the kitchen on bare, dirty feet and grab a glass of water, draining it through moaning gulps.

He stands close, leaning against the counter. "Is this a thinking freakout, or do you need help working through those thoughts?"

I refill and hold the best drink ever to my chest. "Ah, I'm okay, I think. Just...magnets don't hurt people?"

"Depends on how they are used, like all divine attributes."

"Doom can be good? And war?"

Alex's brows furrow. "How can we progress without the stakes of an end and beginning? And sometimes war needs to happen." He lightens, shoulders sinking and face relaxing. "What matters is if it's managed with love and respect or force and revenge."

My father was a force; did I handle him with respect or revenge? And I brought Rath into that as well. How can my most unruly attribute be used with love when it only poofs everything apart?

"Okay…" I back toward the staircase. "I'm going to shower and let this settle."

Alex pushes off the counter. "Lu?"

I hold a palm up. "I'm fine, just need to bathe and think."

Concern and disappointment cling to his frown, but I speed upstairs with my full water glass. A sinking feeling in my stomach has me clutching my shirt. What if Moros was needed for a greater purpose? What am I here for? A thousand other panic-inducing thoughts roll through my mind, but I can't dwell on them if I want to stay in this house with the worried demigod downstairs. I can only accept what's happened and learn. I understand why the guys want peace instead of war. The decision to change the world by taking another from it isn't bearable. I exhale at the pressure swing, but it's not bombarding anymore. It's a nudge, reminding me that there's more to me now. I'll take what Alex said and throw copious amounts of love into what I do until I figure out my purpose.

I step into the bedroom and sigh. Oh my god, I missed those pillows every sunset. But I'm coated in hell realm, so I trod along the dark floors and step into the bathroom that makes me smile because it has clean, warm water. It's been too long, my friend. I laugh in pure joy at the clear streams brought forth from a knob turn. My clothes raise dust when they hit the trash can, and a stranger stares from the mirror. Thin and tan with a silvery hue. And that little bump. I drink more water and grab a new toothbrush from the drawer. Everything is the same except me. I'll eat again soon and sleep and talk to Alex. We can sort through this mess. Thor and Thorette will be better without me, but that fact doesn't stop the regretful twinge of abandoning them. I should have asked Alex about Anice.

It takes a palmful of conditioner to weed through the tangles, and once every grain of hell realm dirt swirls around the drain, I inhale steam and exhale worry. I settle my palms against the stone wall and let my head drop forward. Magnetism. It's odd to think of foreign attributes as part of me. I've treated it as an invading entity because it felt so separate. Whatever Sing did as she was shuffling through my mind aligned something. The oddness isn't gone—there's a buzz in my chest, but it spurs an ache to test it out instead of scaring me.

If there's no separate entity of powers, then I'm the one who needs to control myself to keep everyone safe. I imagine myself as a magnet and the water as an opposite pole. The falling jets waver, then shift. I concentrate and focus on flipping polarity. After several minutes of swiping my hand back and forth, the pressure inside does a jagged exhale and flips. Every stream slaps my palm so fast, I yip and jerk it away.

"What?" I ask, smiling, and try again. Sure enough, when I can drag the pressure and shove past the balance point, water funnels to waterfall into my splayed hand. I want Alex to see.

It gets easier with each pass. Back and forth, ebb and flow. Swing and—

The glass door opens, making water splash in every direction as I gasp and crunch myself into the corner as if I can hide in the steam.

"Are you okay?" he asks, swiping water from his face. His eyes trail over me and fill with heat. "Sorry." He sucks on his lip as he grips the edge of the door hard. "Did you call for me?"

"No. I wanted to show you something, but didn't say anything."

His gaze sticks to my chest, making my nipples tingle. "And what did you"…his eyes make it back up to mine…"want to show me?"

"The water."

"It's great water."

My grin matches his as I bring my hand up to show him my new skills. "See."

"Very nice. Things are easier? Feeling okay?" When I nod, he swallows hard. "Are you done?" His bitten-red lower lip is captivating.

"Yes."

He slaps the water off, grabs my hand, and pulls me against him.

"I'm getting you wet," I say, breathless.

"The exploding water did that well enough before." He tugs a nearby towel, smells it, then works it over my dripping hair, thumbs massaging as he dries me off. I missed his hands. Looping the towel around me, he tugs until we're breathing the same air. "Forgive me, Lula."

Haven't I already? How could he ask for forgiveness after what I did? His words as he was dying ring in my ears, "I love you. Forever." He could have said a thousand other things to me, but with his last breath, he tried to ease my guilt about attacking him. I clutch his shirt, then pull my hand away in case I hurt him again, but my fingers only hold a light dusting of dark silver.

He snatches and brings my fingertips close, dropping the towel. I balk, but he holds firm, brushing them over his lips as he watches my face. "I'll never lie to you again," he whispers, sending my nerves dancing. "Or not tell you everything. Leave you for any reason. Not be there for you when you need me...like when you're alone in the shower." He runs his knuckles over my belly, and my eyes flutter closed. "Or pregnant. I'm sorry I missed so much time."

He seems happy and unafraid of me. I hope so. I'm still adjusting to being here and not with Moros in the hell realm. That thought spirals into the torture I created for my father—no. I'm not dealing with those dark thoughts. Not in Alex's arms and when my powers are lying low.

He taps my chin. "Have I lost you?"

I sink closer against him. "No. I wouldn't listen and lashed out. I was so upset. Still..." I drag a finger down the center of his chest, over his shirt. "I can't believe I did this."

"I can." When I throw a hurt expression his way, he continues. "You were forced into your zenith. You had no training or even knowledge that you were a hybrid goddess. It's incredible that you stopped and repaired me after I handled things so wrong. I can't..." He closes his eyes a moment and takes a deep breath. "I need to know you won't despise me forever. That I didn't ruin what we could have again."

He rubs his fingers against the back of my head, not pushing, but showing his love in one of the many ways he always does. The normalcy of it seizes my chest.

"I forgive you," I whisper. He dips, but I shrink away. "Do you forgive me?"

"Of course, I do," he says as though the decision is thoughtless. He gives me a last, long gaze before soft heat touches my lips, and his eyes flutter closed. Mine do too. When a sob escapes me, he's there to capture it.

I've missed him so much—his taste and familiarity. Warmth swells inside, and I realize I've forgotten the glitterlings for a moment. I startle, unwrapping my arms from around him, but the unruly patterns lie low for once. They don't even register, and for the first time since accepting my attributes, I'm myself again.

Alex pulls me close. The scruffy beard under my palms tickles, and I take a minute to run my cheek and lips over it. It's long enough to be soft. Deft hands explore as though mapping my new shape and I dive back against him, needing him closer and deeper. His fingers get caught in my damp hair and tugs at different angles. He nips me, smiling. "I think you're stuck with me."

My laughter's been missing so long that it feels foreign. "You can't get loose, can you? The hell realm wasn't kind to my curls."

He pulls away enough to see what he's doing as he navigates detaching himself from me. When free, he strokes my face, demeanor dropping to something more serious. "I've missed you." He leans in and kisses to the right of my lips. Then my cheek. My nose.

Fire throbs between my legs. "I missed you too," I whisper, closing my eyes at the tingle he stokes with each touch.

He beams. "I like your eyes both ways." Gripping my ass with both hands, he presses his hips to mine, sending a pang of lust that is uncontrollable.

"What do you mean?" I writhe, unable to help it. I'm going to detonate. "Alex." His name rolls off my tongue like honey-coated sex.

He studies me as though he can see every thought shining in my eyes. The only reason I know that's not possible is because he's not inside me yet.

"You haven't seen?" he asks.

I shrug, mapping his sides and tonguing his Adam's apple. "An odd glimmer in murky water. There are no mirrors in the hell realm."

Alex loosens his grip and turns me toward the big, brightly-lit sink area. "You need to see."

I'd complain, but I get a look in the mirror and gasp. My irises are molten mercury and gunmetal slides up my chest, neck, and darkens my lips. Splaying my fingers on the counter, I will the swaying lines to disperse and leave me be.

Alex tuts, caging me in, dropping a kiss to my shoulder. "No, Lu, let yourself go. Show me."

Even as my eyes flicker between silver and green and patterns swirl over me, I like how we look together—his chin resting on my head and broad shoulders overflowing the shape of my naked body. "Show you?" I ask and arch, pressing my backside against the front of his jeans.

His eyes go half-lidded. "Yes. Your goddess state. Fully. Do you know how?"

"I'm nervous." I entwine our fingers on the countertop. The whip of power expands from my heart. It wants out as if it only needs an invitation. "What if it's too much? I'm not what I used to be."

"No, you're not. But your thoughts are the same, right? Your mind?" He leans to kiss my temple.

"Mostly." Shattered and glued together, but highly turned on. That part of me is working overtime. I'm going to manhandle him to the floor if he doesn't stop asking me questions while pressing his erection against my backside.

He turns me to face him. "You may be scared of who you are, but I'm not. And I want—" He brushes his finger under my lower lip and goes still. He makes another sweep, eyes concentrating on the motion. "Wow."

"What?"

"Your attribute is interacting with my touch."

I turn to look in the mirror and Alex surrounds me again. Sure enough, flecks follow his thumb. They want him too. *No.* I want him. The pattern tightens, and he gives a sharp inhale as I bring him closer to me.

He trails his finger along my chin, neck, and swirls over my heart. "Push out from your center, letting down the walls. You've been fighting yourself."

The sensation is overwhelming—like when Sing was in my mind. Something opens, shifts, and a tight pattern alights across my skin. Certain areas hold the darkest silver—hands and forearms, lips, and nipples. Alex watches as if in his millennia-old lifetime, this may be the most unique thing he's ever witnessed. "So beautiful, Firecracker."

He drags his fingers over my shoulder. A light brush and glitterlings dance around his digit. A heavier press makes more gray follow. He's so calm as he traces my neck and over my chest, darkness following until he taps and they leap back within the net.

I smile. "I'm that kid's toy where you lead magnetic chips over a cartoon face to make hair and a mustache."

Alex tilts his head, raises one brow, and he leads the traveling sparkles in a swoop over my upper lip, but they won't stay in place. They want him or to be back in their lines. He eyes me in the mirror and smiles. "Oh well. Really though, see how beautiful you are?"

The lacing pattern is intricate and dainty. I lean closer. My irises are bright and do a slow lava lamp swirl.

Alex runs his fingers over the fishnet pattern on my cheekbones. "Looks a little like scales. You know what that means?"

I grin. "Mermaid?"

"Yes." He surrounds me with the warmth of his arms. "That will thrill the humans."

Not sure I'll be able to see humans like this, but it would be an interesting test to see if they interact with me the way they used to. The lore of our species has many legends.

I squirm when he gets to my hip, and our exploration takes a different direction. He trails back up, gray chasing his palm as he slides over ribs until he holds my breast. I rest my head against his shoulder. The flame of need sparks in his gaze.

"You don't care that I look this way?" I ask.

He nips my ear. "What? Like power? Strong and gorgeous? There's so much you can do, Lula. Not that you couldn't before, but it's different. You have nothing to fear. Our group will love you as I do." No trace of doubt or deceit shines through his gaze. He means every word as he explores, slow and languid as if our eternity has begun.

Maybe it has.

Moros is gone. As much as it pains me that I'm responsible, my sisters and the entire realm are safe from his broken mind.

Alex's cheek prickles my palm before his lips soothe. The evidence of his want for me pokes my hip. He's close but not pushing.

Turning in his arms to face him, each touch stokes a fire and deep comfort. He thrills but aligns me. He kisses my forehead and breathes me in, far too patient. I grip his shirt in my hands. "Your clothes are still on."

"Mm-hmm," he hums, lips trekking to my ear. "You should take them off."

A wicked idea crosses my mind and my skin shivers. Alex and I used to be playful, even under the pressure of too many terrible things. I'd never laughed with such joy until I met him. Maybe with a taste and time, the rhythm that's always thrummed between us will harmonize better than before. I turn so my lips ghost against his. "Do you trust me?"

"I do," he whispers, heavy-lidded and hoarse, sending a flustered blush to my chest.

Glitterlings spill over him in a gentle wave. I pay close attention to every place they go. I hadn't meant to hurt him before, but in my anger, a part deep in my subconscious had jumped forward and told them to rip his heart out as he'd done mine. They are literal, adhering to my thoughts and emotions, and while it's going to take time to figure them out, I'm learning. I'll never harm Alex or anyone again.

They weave around his torso. He stays still, but his jaw clenches. With a guilty wince, I lean closer, nibbling his lip. He always did love that. The glitterlings attack. I smile at the connection to them, now understanding motives and will. The guys said that I am my attributes, but this part of me is different. It's an extension of my conscious, maybe. Whatever they are, they're as delighted to uncover Alex as I am. We need him.

Tiny puffs of cotton float to the floor. I raise a palm. Dragging the glitterlings back is no longer a fight as they leap back to my skin.

Alex raises an eyebrow at me. His chest is still defined—even with lost weight—and flawless.

I release the breath I was holding. "Sorry about your shirt." I nibble my grinning lip.

His hand tucks into my hair, and my back bumps against the linen cabinet. "Show-off," he purrs against my lips. "You forgot my pants."

I lick his smile. "I thought that'd be a sensitive point."

"Good call."

We stare, fighting grins, energy surging between us. The bare skin right above his waistband is soft. I nuzzle his pectorals and inhale. "Your scent is different."

"So is yours. But are your moans?" He tugs my hair to pull my lips to his and crashes against me. *Finally.*

I melt into a squirming mass Alex holds together with strong arms and lips that I'll never leave if I don't have to. He bombards my senses —my hot, sweet summer breeze. How he wasn't named God of the Sun makes no sense to me. He embodies it.

We move, connected in a sloppy dance through the bedroom. I tug at his pants, needing nothing more than him closer; within me, as he nips at my neck, then hums in approval at the whimpering sound of desperation I make. Why has such a simple thing—physical love— caused such anxiety and joy for us. Jeans and boxer briefs hit the floor and Alex stands tall and bare. I wrap my fingers around him and stroke as he sends my ear into tingles of bliss. "Lula," he says in a raspy whisper. "I missed your touch."

He pulls me close against him and guides me back onto the bed, then drags me to the center of the soft mattress. Eager lips ignite my skin as Alex works his way from my lips to my chest. Each brush of his fingers against my thighs ignites my need as he opens me and glances over my body like he's unsure what he wants to explore first. This moment etches another memory into a chapter of our existence. I'm a siren who fell for a god, but hooked him along the way, then joined the divine. He loves me—has always loved me. He wouldn't be able to fake that now. Not after the path we've stumbled through.

I shiver at the confused sensation of his soft lips mixed with coarse beard.

Alex chuckles. "Are you okay, Firecracker?"

"The beard tickles." I grin up at him as he leans to kiss me.

"I'll get rid of it tomorrow." He wiggles his lips against my neck until I'm squirming.

"No." Three shades of gold make up the coarse hair I rake my nails through. "It tickles in a good way. And it's sexy. Distinguished even." I swipe my thumb over his peeking bottom lip. "Thank you for coming to get me."

"I will always follow you. But how about wherever we go from now on, we go together?" He slides the underside of his hard length against my throbbing center, sending a spike of energy to my chest. "Agreed?"

I lick my bottom lip and roll my hips against him. "Agreed."

Chapter Thirty-Six

ALEX

Lula's "need you" expression is the same, no matter what eye color she shows.

I need her too—to work myself into her until the overwhelming pleasure we create together becomes our only thoughts. Her hands tremble as much as mine as she touches my chest, sliding a finger where the mark used to be.

"Look at me, Lula." There won't be regrets between us in this monumental life point—a time that will forever ingrain and repeat in memories we'll relive in two years or two hundred. Silver shimmers in her eyes, and she wraps one leg over my hip, reminding me of how incredible it is to be needed by her. I thought she was gone. First from my stupidity, and then from trauma. I tease us both between her legs and fill my palm with her breast, exploring new curves with the attention of every sense. Dropping my head, I breathe her in; taste her skin with an exploring tongue. Each nuzzle and grope between us grows more impatient, and she gives a strangled moan, arching up to get closer.

"You want me," I grumble around her nipple. Testing it with my teeth, I peek up at her.

"Yes, and you're teasing me. How long are you going—"

Shushing her with my lips, our tongues dance, then I flip her, lifting hips to grip her firm backside and watch, pressing my cock the slightest bit between the slick apex of her thighs, then back out, savoring her sounds, muffled against the bed. The way she arches and glares over her shoulder when I retreat instead of giving her what she wants makes a sweet pang hit my chest. A dark flush flutters over her skin in a mesmerizing rhythm. Her body has changed, curves leaner and harder, smell and taste slightly different, but she's still my firecracker. I work myself up with almost-thrusts until every muscle is as tense as my cock. She responds with hums that turn to growls when I travel away from where she wants me. I grin. "This okay?"

She rolls to her back and writhes. When I line up again, she jerks me forward by her now-familiar invisible force. "Yes," she hisses into a moan. My jaw drops at the shock of pleasure and I fall to encircle her, fists to the mattress. She lifts to kiss my slack bottom lip—a soft contrast to the forceful pull to her. We take a minute to breathe each other's air and adjust to joining. She can do more than she thinks. But that thought is for later.

I lose my hesitation and gather Lula under me, caging her in, keeping her warmth engulfed in mine. She grips my sides with piercing nails and gasps sounds that I've woken to in memory, craved like sunlight in a pitch-black world. I savor each sensation with every slow and deep thrust, staring at her studying me back. Merciful kisses free the emotion in my chest and I drag my teeth over the curve of her jaw, remembering the pull, the universe of what we shared. Our lips meet endlessly, overwhelmingly, until they become salt-tinged. We both smile over that. Then Lula grips my hair and whispers my name like she used to. Her signal surges my desperation, replacing the play between bodies, the calm romance between us. She drags her leg back over my hip, bringing me deeper and I brush fingers everywhere I can reach. I'll relearn every inch repeatedly.

Falling back together erases time, and eases the painful expanse we've had with flawless rhythm. I burn with an ache that borders on torture, if bliss didn't also blaze wild in my blood. The build is so high there's only one escape.

Lula cries out, arching in a welcome for me to nip her neck as she digs her nails into my back and shudders with blissful jerks of grinding hips. I bury my nose under her ear, grit my teeth, and give in as her body pulls me under with her. Vision blinks to stars and soft darkness with every pulse of passion between us. Instincts engage and I roll, though refuse to relinquish our closeness and take her with me. There's a deep ache behind my eyes from the hard curve of her midsection against me. It's the most welcome foreign feeling I've ever had. So slight, yet monumental. We stay in the echoes of fast breathing, me gently stroking skin, and her fingers twirling in my beard until she shivers, and her stomach rumbles against mine.

Lula stares up at me, head on my chest and cheeks burning pink even through the silvery tint, reminding me of my first visit to her house. We'd peeled bits of information off each other in fragile layers, both hiding enormous pieces of our lives as we gravitated in each other's orbit. She'd been magnetic then too. From her blush to her sexy awkwardness around me, she teased me to a frenzy with her mere presence. My want was a visceral, needy beast who didn't care if Olympus stood in the way. How ironic that we're back to that, free from lies, but still facing divine hurdles.

I tip her chin up to kiss her. "Come on. Let's get you some food."

LULA WRIGGLES AROUND BESIDE ME. SNAKING AN ARM UNDER HER, I drag her against me and dammit if I'm already hard for her again. The night was more a series of naps between testing if our bodies still synchronize. We're a seasoned orchestra. "Are you sore?" I ask, floating my fingers down her thigh until I'm clutching behind her knee.

"Not sore enough." Her voice rolls an electric purr over my skin.

"Gods." I tug her leg and slip in with a rasped grunt as my hips press against her backside and fuzz all thoughts but pleasure and closeness.

"Goddess, you mean." Lula gives a throaty moan that licks my spine with heat each and every time she makes it.

"Yes," I whisper in her ear. "My goddess."

My thrusts turn her giggles to more perfect sounds, shuddering breaths while the scent of us lingers in the warm air. I find her clit with wandering fingers and her sharp keen as she comes makes me grin against her neck, press in deep, and let her pulsing pleasure pull me into mine. Lula flops against me, a pile of boneless hybrid. I trace her jaw with my nose. "Morning, beautiful. Are you awake?"

"Kinda. FYI, that whole horny-when-pregnant thing is no myth. Humans and deities have that in common?"

Her shoulder is bony under my lips. "I guess so, unless it's a siren trait?"

"No. Amah said she didn't want anyone close to her." She blindly searches over my body until she finds my arm, then follows that to my hand and drags it over her, tucking it between her breasts. "I want to be near you."

"I want to be near you too." Twirling a curl around my finger, I give it a slight tug. "I'll pay close attention to the moments you need me. Like when you glance my direction or stand at the fridge or are sleeping next to me."

The pillow muffles her voice. "That works."

The power that lies on her skin has faded to a shimmer in the full-day sun beaming through the window. Our time for indulging is short. The guys will arrive soon with others to discuss the latest plan and I need to check for Anice. Hades must have found something by now. I hold Lula tighter. One back and one missing. If Zeus has my brother, he'll use him as a bartering chip but won't hurt him. Not as he would have done—tried to do to Lula. Keeping peaceful is becoming an extensive test.

"We have to get up, don't we?" Lula asks, squeezing my tight fingers before turning and curling against my chest.

"Eventually. Our group will be here this afternoon for a meeting."

She halts kissing my collarbone to peek up at me. "I understand that I won't be accepted, but what should I expect? No one is going to try to curse me, are they?"

"No. Our most trusted friends and allies have grown. And if Hera treats you as she did before, most of Olympus will bow to you."

Lula shifts, dragging her leg out from under mine and dropping it over my knee. "I didn't imagine that then. It seemed..." Her pretty lips press out. "Important."

That's an understatement. My grandmother treated Lula as she would a beloved daughter. "She welcomed you as family." Her eyes angle to a shape that makes me pull her closer and stroke her cheek. "It's true though, yeah?"

Her gaze dives headfirst into mine. "I'd like that."

A blue glow lights the corner of the room and I snarl, snatching the sheet and dragging it over Lula. "Privacy, Hades."

The flame blasts up in swirls, then fizzles, leaving behind the king of the underworld. Concern burns cold in my stomach at him in a himation. He showed himself in Olympus?

"Good afternoon," Lula says dryly.

"Hello, Goddess of Magnetism." He grins, but it's tired and not laced with mischief. "We're going to need you two together for this conversation. Get cleaned up and come downstairs."

"What time is it?"

"It's time." Flames burst then suck him down.

Lula untangles herself from me, springing out of the bed and toward the bathroom. "If I don't throw up from morning sickness, I will from nervousness. He has news on Anice, doesn't he?"

It takes me three steps to catch up to her. "I'd wager he does."

"Hades seems like he'd tell you if it's an emergency, right?"

Leaning over her, I flip on the water. "He would." Maybe.

"So not too much to worry about?" she asks, knotting her curls on top of her head, then testing the temperature. When she gives a contented sigh at the warmth, I nudge her in, keeping close. "Alex?" she asks.

I give up distracting myself with kissing the back of her neck. "He wouldn't be here if there wasn't something. And Anice would have shown up instead. He's been worried for you...and me. And us."

Zeus has him—he has to—but how? More attribute-deadening chains probably, but how would he have made it to the portal to capture him? Hermes is the only answer unless Zeus traveled on the lightning, and he hasn't done that for millennia as far as I know.

"Okay." Lula looks at me over her shoulder, then kisses me with a carefulness that cages the air in my lungs. "Let's hurry then."

The shower is an odd blend of rushed movements and Earth-halting moments. Her glance tells me that this is the exact place she wants to be for eternity and everything staggers into gracious slow motion. She nuzzles my beard as she reaches for soap. I steady her, splaying fingers over her stomach. She settles her hand over mine in a pause that means everything. I'd do anything for her. For them.

We dress in stale clothes. She worries over a gray t-shirt and a flowy, sheer thing until I tug at a cream-colored, silk blouse. "This one."

She abuses her lip another second before slipping on the blouse. It slides off her shoulder, and she retreats to the bathroom. When I can't take the silence any longer, I follow. Silver flickers in a quick lava swirl as she stares at herself in the mirror, fingers clamped to the counter. I always see when she's nervous, but now everyone else will too. I wrap around her and kiss her cheek. "There's nothing to fear with this group, and anything we face, we do it together."

She blinks at me. "It's heavy. The weight of it. I don't understand what my role is or how to help. I don't know enough true history, only myths that don't paint any of you in a rosy light. What if they curse me or rip me apart and scatter pieces around the Earth? That's possible, right?"

"Shh, no. No one will touch you with ill-intent. And if they do—"

"You'll destroy them?" The corner of her lips raises, prompting mine to do the same.

"No, Firecracker, you will." I pinch her ass, making her jump. "Then, I will." I spin her, getting lost in her eyes, then the lines of concern on her face. It makes her structure statuesque, and I can see her in marble. "You are so beautiful. Ripe with power and carrying the first deity since Rath. Well, and you." I kiss her, taking time to breathe her in and absorb her energy. "Humanity prevails every time."

Lula blows out a long breath and sets her forehead against my chest. "You turn all…Olympian when you're about to go to Olympus. That's where we're headed, isn't it?"

"Let's find out." I link our fingers and tug her with me.

Before we arrive in the kitchen, Rath pops around the corner and scoops Lula up in a hug. Zephyrus follows, as does Prax, who nearly tackles me. When I'm more stable on my feet, we give each other hearty slaps on the back. His arm is covered with a black, metal vambrace from elbow to wrist. I knock on the hard surface. "That covering the wound from Moros?"

He nods. "It's healing. Just slowly. You are smaller."

"Everyone is smaller, compared to you." I give him a smile and he nods, shoulders sinking with his long exhale. Lula and Rath's whispered chatter relaxes her tight stance as they stand close, heads bowed together. Zeph hesitates, then steps next to Rath and bows in front of Lula on one knee.

Lula peers back at me. "This is Jordan, right?"

I scrunch my face. "Yes. Well, his name is Zephyrus, God of the West Wind. I'm sorry for that first meeting too." Add it to the list.

She stares down at him, head tilted. "What are you doing? I'm not... Rath, what is happening here?"

"It's an apology," Rath answers. "He's asking you to forgive him."

Lula kneels in front of him and touches his shoulder. "You protected me from the arrows, didn't you? When Zeus and the army attacked." I grin at the way she handles what could be an uncomfortable start to our group's introduction.

Zeph lifts his head. "It was not a difficult task."

"It meant something to me. I remembered...later. Thank you. All is forgiven."

He presses the back of her hand to his forehead, shocking the hell out of me. Rath's eyes blink to mine and we both give a *huh* expression. I haven't seen that gesture in a long time. *Respect. Follow. Protect.* Zeph turns to the kitchen as if he didn't just enact an ancient oath.

Rath snaps as we pass through the doorway. "Oh, I forgot."

Hades sits at the table with Hera and..."Ares?" I step in front of Lula.

The God of War stands, red eyes blazing. "Alexiares." His expression is anything but welcoming.

Lula peeks around me. "Oh good, I'm not the only one with wacky eyes. Hi." She waves from under the arm I'm using to hold her behind me.

"Why is he here?" I ask, keeping a sharp gaze on him, waiting for a sword or spear to appear.

"I am preparing for war," he says, as if I should know this already.

"Then why are you *here*?" I signal around the room to the people hell-bent on keeping the damn peace.

Hades drops his head back, groaning loudly at the ceiling. "Get in here so we can explain." Pulling himself up, he looks at me in irritation. I've never seen him look aged, but he does today. "Uncage your goddess before she tosses you across the room. Come on in, Lula."

Lula ducks under my barricade. Hera crosses to her, taking her hand and touching her cheek. "How are you feeling?"

Ares crosses his arms, seemingly fine that my grandmother is treating an enemy of Zeus as family. I glance at Hades. Hades rolls his hand through the air as if telling me to catch up. It's Ares. I can't catch up with this. The door outside opens and Comus grins until he sees Ares. As always, Comus and I are on the same page.

"It's so gorgeous," Grace says from behind him. "I haven't been to the beach in—Lula!" She bounds in, nearly tripping over Hera to leap on Lula.

Lula's face eases some tension as she holds tight to her sister, who babbles in fast, quiet talk I can only catch half of. The sisters have been wrecked over Lula, Hazel is slowly recovering, though still watched closely, Amah is still secretive, and the others are hiding. Grace holds Lula's shoulders, bouncing as she talks, face bright with happiness even in a room of amused onlooking deities. I don't even think she realizes that Prax is here, leaning against the counter with his hands shoved in his pockets. I give Grace a quick kiss on the cheek as I make my way to the table. "Where's Anice?" I ask. "And seriously, why is Ares here?"

Rath and Comus step in beside me.

"Your brother is being held captive by Zeus." Hera sits, prim and proper, as if she's on a throne in an Olympian great room instead of a kitchen table. "Who has had him possessed by shades. That is why Ares is here."

The world stumbles and I jerk my head to Rath. Color slips from his face like someone's dragging translucent beige cloth down his skin. He wouldn't have done this, nor has he even attempted the attributes he's ashamed of possessing since his zenith.

"How?" I ask.

"Zeus has invoked the powers of a necromantic demon witch with a mate who can talk to shades," Ares says. "Much to the disdain of the Council who did not realize the king had kept them close after the break."

Rath may bite his lip off. I elbow him, but he keeps his gaze on the floor. I'm going to need his insight on this.

"Is Anice okay?" I ask. Every person at the table averts their eyes, making an uncomfortable spike of tension tighten my shoulders. I roll them. "Someone talk to me. Tell me he's not being killed by a shade and a necromancer is raising him."

Ares growls. "I cannot tell you that is untrue, unfortunately. Zeus has done the same to Hermes."

I press between my eyes to alleviate the utter devastation ripping through my skull. Will either of them be the same if we get them out of this? "Where's Ceraon and Iaso?"

"Underworld," Hades says. "Zeus called for their capture. We will have to search for Ceraon. He was not happy with me for locking him in my territory, but he was aiming to invade Zeus's temple which would have made him dead, and Anice will have a hard enough time if…" He winces. "We'll get him back."

"It's possible to do that, right?" Lula sits on the kitchen counter beside Grace.

"In theory." I put my attention back on the table of original Olympians "And what does Zeus want with them?"

"You, obviously." Ares gestures with a palm. "He wants you to publicly swear your allegiance and do as he says. And…" he trails off and glances at Hera.

Hades leans forward, elbows on the table. "No."

"Hades." Hera puts a hand on his arm. A golden bracelet on her wrist slips along her forearm exposing a bruise.

"No," he repeats, strapping his hand over hers as she retracts. "Fuck no, never, nope, numquam."

Hera scrunches her nose and eyes the ceiling. "He wants us, me and him to…"

Hades huffs. "Remarry to show their solidarity to Olympus. Have more children. Not after everything and not after yesterday. No more, Hera." He taps her wrist and she bares her teeth and jerks from him. A bristle of rage trails up my spine. Zeus did that?

"That was too much," Ares says, as if he cares. His eyes stay on the invisible pattern he traces on the table.

"Everything Zeus has done is too much. I'm with Hades on the 'no,' but you, Ares?" I cross my arms. "How odd for you, of all gods, to show up with this information. Smart move for Zeus to send his warmonger to convince us to head into a trap."

The chair crashes to the floor and red eyes are inches from mine. "The king has forgone his Council's insight and works alone. He's kept Pythia locked away for too long, having her scry in secret—every hour from what I understand. The only reason the king isn't here yet is because the oracles must be protecting you. Or her—" Without looking, he waves toward Lula. "That means something."

I bare my teeth at him. "*Her* name is Lula, Hybrid Goddess of Magnetism."

"That sounds awesome, sis." Grace sips from a cat-shaped mug. "It's very official."

Ares straightens, tilting his head to the side until his neck pops. "You understand how the king can inflict great punishment, but if he finds I was here, I will die. War calls to me, Alexiares, and unlike yourself, I understand the stakes and must react to what fate requires."

"I'm familiar with how Zeus works, and you've proven who you are. You and Deimos watched my *punishment* with grins on your faces. No one should have brought you here."

Hades clears his throat loudly in obvious warning, but we ignore him.

"You disobeyed." Ares narrows his red eyes.

"Your son is a psychotic piece of shit who lives to inflict pain and I will *disobey* at every opportunity to protect others from him. And he's just like you."

I was expecting the punch.

What surprises me is Ares's fist hovers so close to my cheek that the heat of his knuckles tingles my skin, and the fabric of his himation drapes over my hands, though I'm not making contact with his ribs as I intended. We bounce apart in three smacks from Lula's invisible wall, both landing on our asses on opposite sides of the room.

"Oop," Grace squeaks. "You didn't tell me there's nothing under himations."

"We'll have to introduce Ares to boxer briefs." Comus covers her eyes with his palm.

"Or not." A squeal follows Grace's words, and she jerks from Comus's pinch, then slaps at him. I haul myself off the floor.

Lula gives me a disapproving scowl with hematite eyes. "Can we talk about how to get Anice back, please? Is it a spell or something?"

"Thank you, Lula." Hades tells her what Olympians know about shades which is vague and not the whole story while Comus, Rath, and I exchange subtle glances.

We need to talk, but Rath looks ready to fade out of here. We've categorized the shadowy creatures as darklings, but that's never quite fit. They are a mystery, and if they infected Anice and Hermes, our only hope may be Rath. He wouldn't have the ability to manipulate them without a fated purpose. Though last time, they took him over. After his zenith, we'd traveled and tested. Just outside of Greece, one came in the night and attacked him. He said it siphoned his sanity from him, and worse—he liked it. There was nothing Comus or I could do but talk him through it. Rath remembered himself, sending it to shadow. Sometimes he feels it, like it's following him in his realm. He's sent two more to shadow since then and can feel when they're close.

"So that's that." Hades raises an eyebrow at Rath, but Rath puts his attention on the wall. Hades rolls his eyes and looks between Lula and me. "What do you say?"

Lula slides from the counter. "We leave in ten. I need to eat something or I'm going to throw up." She fans her face and roots around in the fridge.

Chapter Thirty-Seven

LULA

ALEX WAS RIGHT ABOUT OLYMPUS. MILES OF SMOOTH, WHITE MARBLE buildings are more suited for a fairy tale movie than a mystical city of unrest. Golden glimmers twinkle in the sun from cobblestones that snake through thick flowery ground cover made of the brightest colors strutting against fat jade leaves and sprays of celadon. If we weren't walking into what must be some kind of trap, I'd pause to lie in the wispy, soft grass beyond that. A warm breeze brings the sweet smell I pick up only when I inhale right against Alex's skin.

"Well?" Alex asks, squeezing my hand.

"Oh, it's just dreadful." I bite my lips together to keep from gasping as a flock of rainbow butterflies ballet past us. "Give me the hell realm any day." That may be true depending on how this impromptu meeting goes. Alex gives an exasperated huff and I catch his arm, pressing against him. "It certainly appears heavenly."

"It's broken though. A shiny fruit, rotten through."

I nod. "It certainly has a few worms."

"We will meet those soon enough," Hades growls. "Hera?"

"Not yet." Hera stares toward the biggest building, then behind me.

Grace steps beside me, setting her head on my shoulder and I squeeze her trembling fingers. Comus stands close behind, ready to bite someone. The argument they had right before we left was promptly ended by Hera telling him that Grace would be with us and if he didn't like it, he could stay home from the revolution he's been planning for over a century. I'm glad for Hera. I'd be worried if Grace wasn't here, and I'm more dangerous than any Olympian. I can protect us while Hades does what he needs to. Turning, I check for Rath. Hera spoke to him in a hush-hush conversation, and he disappeared from the kitchen right before we left. Comus seems as salty about that as I am. Paired with not wanting Grace here, and the boiling point of a war we're trying to win without a fight... I squeeze his fingers too.

Hera catches her eyes on something behind us and nods. I follow her sight line and my knees buckle, breath halting in my lungs. Amah holds on to Rath's arm, her dark eyes on me. Then I'm sprinting toward them, the world soundless as I grab other's shoulders and arms, passing them on the way to my eldest sister. She's just as beautiful as I remember, but no longer in an Edwardian dress. Her black hair is free to curl where it pleases instead of being trapped in braids. Grace stays beside me as we crash in a tearful pile that Rath steadies so we don't topple. I hold them tight as words tumble from us in a flurry of "missed you" and "love you" and "I'm sorry."

Amah presses her forehead to mine. We wipe our faces with a laugh, and Amah bends to kiss the tiny lump of my belly. "We will protect you as we can, wee one."

As long as it's not running. No more of that. I feel stronger with my sisters here and grin at Rath over Grace's shoulder, reaching to touch his cheek in thanks. He pats my hand and makes his way toward the men and Hera who's whispering to Hades. "Oh, Lula, dear?" Hades lifts his head from Hera's ear. "Big reunion later, okay? We've been spotted. Rath, it's super-spy time." Rath fades into the shadows where he will stay until needed.

Between two marble buildings comes a trail of golden-armored gods, giving me a flashback of them firing arrows at me when I was having the worst day of my immortal life. I move next to Alex as they march in lines, sandals drumming the ground loud enough to be a parade band, but not enough to be an army. Fanning out, they create a line between our group and Olympus.

"No women?" Grace asks, stepping beside me. "I thought goddesses fought."

"They did," Hades answers. "Except they are on the Council, locked away, or told to sit out because they follow Hera, even if they also follow Zeus. Same with some male deities like Zephyrus and Praxis."

Zephyrus shrugs. "I never followed Zeus. Team Hera since 19 BCE."

The troops halt with a synchronized stomp. The line of armored deities part and a god steps forward. Or at least I think that's what he may have been, before he stopped eating, sleeping, or walking fully upright. He's a reanimated corpse with patchy, slovenly hair and gray skin. He's followed by a tiny figure in a beige, hooded cape. Alex and the others around gasp. A few shrink back from our line. The caped person walks to the left, snaps their fingers, and the creature limps to their side.

Hades gives a grumbly sigh. "We know what we're up against, people." He puts his attention on me and raises his eyebrows, asking if I'm ready for this. I'm not. Harming goes against everything I've learned, everything I am. But if this is what I'm up against? I try to swallow down the nervous lump in my throat. The newest plan is to convince Zeus to have a conversation, and when that inevitably fails, separate him from his people with Rath's help, then protect Hades so he can get close. Fly by the seat of my cutoff shorts if all else fails.

"Knowing and seeing are two different things," Alex says. "Is Hermes too far gone to save?"

My grip tightens on Alex's rigid arm. That monstrosity is Hermes? I've seen humans come back from wicked things, but this?

"I'd like to say no," Hades says.

"Because my brother is in the same state?"

"Because Hermes is a peaceful ally. But your brother isn't at this state—not yet—from what I understand. Even I cannot get where I need to in this forsaken place."

From the irritation in his voice, that doesn't happen often. A few deities in plain himations peek from small structures and wander close to the path, whispering to each other. More approach from behind the line of guards, women holding baskets and men with crossed arms.

Hades, Hera, and Alexiares's names are mentioned loud enough to catch, and several women turn and dash away.

"What? No town crier?" I ask, fidgeting with the hem of my shirt.

"Too modern for Olympus," Alex says.

Hades chuckles in amused rumbles. "Even my demons have cell phones."

I snap my attention to Hades. "You have demons?"

The corner of his lips raises. "Let's live through this and then you can visit my neck of the universe. Incoming." He lifts his chin at the lines of guards parting again.

Anice's eyes are so dark and sunken, they mimic black holes as he hobbles beside Zeus. The king is decorated in golden greaves, chest armor, and shin plates. He carries a sword, and it's a slight relief that the gods haven't yet entered this era and discovered its weaponry.

"Where is your spear, brother?" Zeus yells, halting in the chasm between his men. If he's noticed me, he doesn't care.

"We were thinking we could have a conversation before the stabbing commenced," Hades returns.

A goddess in golden armor steps beside Zeus, bow in hand. I glare at Artemis, but her eyes flit from face to face on our side. She has to be looking for Rath, and I worry for him watching from the shadows. Zeus would target him first, though I wonder if he's aware of Rath's relationship with Artemis. She'd probably be in trouble if he did. Zeus may hate Rath more than me because he's had more time reminding Zeus that he was born under the ban—as if that was his fault. I stroke my stomach. They will not treat this little one the way they did him. Zeus points his sword at us and his soldiers lift shields and take one step forward. The thing that is Hermes groans a sound more animal than human, and the being beside him begins a quiet incantation. With a deep breath, I ready myself to throw my barrier at them. I'll need to pull Zeus forward, and Rath will shove him and slip back into shadow, then Hades…we can do this. It will be quick.

"It's time Olympus saw peace," Alex says. "We've come to discuss the future, not to war with you."

Zeus trails his gaze from my flats to my messy bun. "Yet you bring an enemy here."

"The Goddess of Magnetism is no enemy of Olympus. She and Rathbarth have conquered Moros."

That gets the crowd chittering, but Zeus only chuckles and stabs his sword between golden cobblestones, less than a foot from Anice. "Are you ready to agree to my terms, Alexiares?"

"To pledge myself to you?"

Zeus begins to nod but Alex continues, "You, who have used a necromantic witch and *shades* to hold my brother and Hermes hostage? You, who pledged to murder my love and a goddess who has done nothing but attempt peace with Olympus—"

"Peace?" he roars.

"Yes." I allow my full tone and inflection to rain down because it's time to flex my power. "Peace. Do you know the meaning?"

I get a deeper scowl from Zeus as a reply.

Alex grins and stands straighter. "My path is my own to choose just like every deity, otherworldling, and human."

The surrounding crowd has grown and they're listening. Some hold wooden or metal shields, though they are unlikely to use them due to their lack of armor or weapons.

Zeus scoffs, head swiveling at his men who don't laugh as I believe he wants them to. "That was not an apology, Alexiares. One last chance to embrace your king and your betrothed Ichnaea."

I thread my fingers with his and he squeezes them before straightening with an inhale. "I've always had fondness for Ichnaea, but I won't marry her. That would be agreeing to enslave us both, and you have enough slaves. Release Anicetus and Hermes."

"No." Zeus stretches, pulling his sword from its scabbard. The blue of the sky disappears with a fast roll-in of clouds and a warm breeze that dances in my curls. "Pledge your loyalty and I may find a suitable punishment without annihilation."

"We need a conversation," Comus says. "Not bloodshed."

Zeus glares past us. "Hera and Ares. Come here." He calls them with the confidence of a master calling in his hounds. The two step forward and my stomach sinks. Zeus's grin spreads until Ares stops beside Comus and Hera takes the space between Hades and me, raising her chin with enough defiance that the crowd behind Zeus visibly shrinks with concern. *We are not yours.* Warmth calms my nervous trembling, and I mimic Hera's proud stance. Thunder rumbles as sourness slams over Zeus's face. Alex cups my cheek and kisses me, murmuring, "I love you," against my lips, reminding me there's nothing I won't do to protect those who are mine. When he takes a step forward, I do as well.

"We come in peace," Alex yells. "But you are no longer our king."

Zeus whispers something toward Anice, or most likely to the hooded figure behind him. Anice lurches forward, baring his teeth in a joker's smile. A few of those standing to watch gasp, backing away or raising shields. I blow a long, slow breath through pursed lips. We talked about this at the house. I know what to do.

"Don't do this, Zeus," Alex says. "Think of your people."

As soon as Anice is within pouncing distance of Alex, I fling him to the left, trying to brace his fall into the field where Hercules puts him in a headlock and drags him backward and away from this danger. Anice twists, hands flailing for purchase and snarling like an animal, but there's no getting out of the grip of his father. I don't notice the warning hum until Rath appears in front of me, an arrow through his shoulder again, but this one thicker than the last time he was shot. Another slams into my bicep a second later, the punch so fast, I yip, but don't feel it.

"What the fuck, Artie?" Rath yells.

Alex runs forward, hands out to stop any more from firing. Zeus raises his sword, and the army marches forward. I throw my force field out except the soldiers keep coming.

Rath mumbles a curse. "I can't fade. Lu?"

I send the glitterlings to take care of the massive arrow in my arm, but there is no movement. My hands are clear from their silver tinge. My heart pounds against my sternum. "Nothing. My attributes are gone."

Alex leaps next to me, cupping my hip and my cheek, then growls at the arrow in my arm. "You okay?" His eyes shift to my waistline. Protective looks even better on him when it's aimed at keeping our child safe.

"I have no power. Not okay. Pull it out."

"Attribute-blocking adamantine." Hades checks my arm, then Rath's. "We need to—"

"Alexiares," Zeus yells. "Surrender the enemies. Hades, return to your realm." Lightning crackles around us, hitting Hades and spinning him from us. Another shoots Alex ten feet to the left. He rolls to stand, but limps backward to avoid the barrage of strikes surrounding me and Rath, separating us from the others like an electrified birdcage. I try to drag the bolts to me, except I can't because my attributes aren't working. Utter panic trembles my blood and I wish for the pulls and pushes of the atmosphere. I long for the deadly patterns across my skin that would stretch to the sky like tiny, unruly puppies ready for destruction. I could end this now. Protect everyone. "Get my sisters out of here," I yell toward Prax and Ares through the bright flashes.

The red-eyed god looks past me with bared teeth, then pulls a curvy dagger from a thigh sheath and gets in a protective, arms-extended position in front of Amah and Grace. Unexpected and appreciated. When Prax moves behind them, completing a circle of divine protection, I breathe a bit easier.

"Push the front line," Alex yells.

Hades's fire bursts ten feet in the air like a wild pyrotechnic show in front of the quickly encroaching army. The lightning halts as the soldiers jerk back, and strong gusts pick up and push them further away. A twang of arrows makes me cringe and cover my midsection, but the incoming shafts burst into a spray of water, dropping harmless mist on us. Looks like Artemis is out of her adamantine ammo. Comus runs toward us, yelling something, then thick, green-tinted lightning cracks from the sky, smashing into Rath, then me, brightness blinking the world into an overbearing glow. I scream as the tendrils tingle my skin, remembering the smell last time—ozone; old, rusted metal; and sickening, seared meat. I remember Firthus's dead eyes. *Rath.*

The fire around me stops, but my vision is a spotlight that blanks anything I try to focus on. Someone grabs my arm and I scream, this time from the sharp jerk of the arrow being pulled all the way through, feathers and all. My knees hit the stones and I block the hot gush of blood from the hole in my arm with trembling fingers as the atmosphere slips over me like the gentlest wave before swelling to a roar. *Control yourself, Lula.* I grit my teeth at the tug of skin and muscle drawing together from the glitterlings. With rapid blinking, sight returns, and Hera stands in front of me, expression caught in fury. She drops the arrow from blood-coated fingers and moves my hand to check my wound. Past her, I take in the scene, and my nose and fingers tingle, blood pulsing in measured, age-long beats behind my eardrums.

Rath stands tall, staring at his hands, clothing smoking and dotted with charred holes. He jerks his eyes to me, then past, where they stick, infused with horror. Comus is on the ground not far from me. Alex kneels beside him, patting out the fire on his clothes with panicked, splayed fingers.

Comus lies still. Not even a twitch.

Chapter Thirty-Eight

LULA

Alex gives a choked sound and holds Comus's face, then roars an agonized, rusted bellow before crumbling. Rath's open-throat anguish ricochets against Alex's as he scrambles to his friends, hand holding the arrow still lodged in his shoulder.

No. No, this can't be.

The anger lining Zeus's features has melted away, as though that damn bolt squelched his fire. Now, he's left an indifferent shell, staring at Rath. "How?" he asks.

"My son!" I remember Dionysus from the amphitheater, but his stoicness has disappeared as he sprints for us. A group of soldiers follows like Dionysus's pained scream was a war cry.

"Comus. No, no, no...my boy." He pulls Comus's limp body into a hug, rocking him as he wails.

The army moves faster.

"Lula," Hades growls. "Stop them or I will."

The pressure in my chest amplifies, and I shove out my barrier—hard. "Repel," Alex had said. The line of golden-armored deities flies away from us, landing on others, crashing into marble structures, rolling over perfect golden cobblestones, or tipping onto flowered yards.

I drop next to Alex. Blisters pepper Comus's skin, and the tip of his nose and ears are black charcoal. His brown eyes stare straight up to the gray clouds. Rath gasps in choking sobs, feeling Comus's forehead, then cheek, then shoulder as if searching for a piece of him that may still have life in it. Grace drops beside him, tears streaming as she slowly reaches for Comus—Comus's body. Prax stands behind her, eyes bloodshot and wild as he looks to the other side.

Alex takes my wrists and pulls my palms to his chest. His eyes are lost and wet and tell me that hope left on our friend's final exhale. I want to melt into him. Crawl into his lap and press my wet cheek to his as we settle into this new existence, but the peace Comus tried so hard to obtain left with him. We are at war and must see it through.

Hera storms forward. "Zeus! You promised me."

Hades follows, snatching her around the waist to pull her against him. He whispers to her while she shoves out of his grip, but he keeps up, murmuring against her ear again. She turns in his arms and punches his chest, but he holds her like newly-forged glass—burning, but at its most fragile state, until she buries her face against him.

Alex squeezes my hands. "Force field," he says through gritted teeth.

The few soldiers still pursuing a fight bounce off my barrier. Hera, cheeks flushed and chest rising and falling in fast pulses, moves close to put a hand on Dionysus's shoulder as she looks down at them, brows drawn as if thinking hard.

"Lu." Alex swallows hard. "Please get the arrow out of Rath. It's time to end this."

His voice is a hollow monotone that sends a fresh clench to my chest, but I nod and touch the shaft still lodged through Rath's shoulder, but my attributes won't come near it. "I can't get this out."

"Hades," Alex says so softly I'm not sure many could hear, but Hades steps behind Rath, eyes filled with the flames he controls.

"Fucking witchcrafted adamantine arrows," Hades growls. "All my godsforsaken days—this is going to hurt." I squeeze Rath's fingers as Hades sets a palm on Rath's back and yanks the arrow. It takes three hard jerks to send a spray of blood in the air with the arrow's exit. Rath folds forward as he cries out, and when I touch near the wound this time, the glitterlings do leap and work on pulling his gaping wound back together. Hades throws the arrow toward the other side.

It pings and rolls off the pathway, then flames rise high, purple, blue and white. Encompassing heat billows, pulling all attention. There's a shift in the air, and I feel the lightning before it strikes. Leaping up into a jog toward the enemies, I drag the stray bolts to me and slow to a walk toward the other side, letting the electricity sink deep into the ground. It's a drain on my border, but not enough to break it.

Hades lets the fire die as I get close and stop, glaring past the melted area at Zeus. I glare at his furious gaze, his hatred. I see everything he is now. He is a plague, a darkling, a danger to everything that needs to be. He...*took* from us. So much. I stifle a sob. Later.

His sword and Artemis's arrows ping off my field. Some guards stab the unmoving air, but some stand back, weapons lowered—at a loss. More deities arrive from around buildings, flooding in, faces drawn, some cheeks wet as they take in the army fighting my barriers, then beyond to one honorable, fallen god as if they didn't know this is what Zeus, and therefore Olympus, was all about. Do they finally see? Is that what it took? The price was too high.

A half-moon of silent emotion chills my back. Before me lies a line of weapons and yells of frustration because one death isn't good enough for some of them. Wide eyes of the bystanders ask what's next, but I only know what will never happen again. Alex slips his fingers into mine, gold against silver. His red-rimmed eyes hold determination and I know he sees that in mine too. We nod at the same time. Today is Zeus's last day in control of Olympus.

"Zeus," Alex says, pain of loss still tight in his voice. "We demand you step down."

An arrow twang sounds and I check the sky for the attack, but Zeus is the one who jerks, then seizes again as a guard sinks his sword into the king's side, right into an open nook in his armor. Zeus slashes and the guard cries out, his arm dropping to the ground.

"Trantus!" Alex yells, stepping forward.

The other side breaks out in battle. Goddesses on the sidelines pull daggers from baskets they were carrying and leap between soldiers. Ares sprints past us, through my barrier, and leaps into the fray. Zephyrus and Prax follow, but Alex yells, "Stop. Do not add to this madness. Use your gifts from a distance. Zeph—" His commands and names fall to fuzzy mumbles as I take in the pops of light, a sonic boom, and black feathers poofing to the clouds creating an odd chaos. Zeus's mouth opens in a roar as a woman slaps her palms on his temples. Fuchsia shines from her fingers and then Artemis is there, dragging her off by her braids.

"Lula?" Alex tugs my hand. "See what you can block."

I absently nod and shield a thrown dagger, sending it to an empty grassy spot. A gust of wind tumbles two armored soldiers to the spot as well. A dark swarm of buzzing bugs funnels in, increasing the frantic arm movements from the crowd. A falling ax bursts into a rainbow of flame, making the wielder yelp and toss it aside. "Moros will end you," a guard yells over the cacophony before Zeus's sword falls.

I avert my eyes and wince at the crunch of bone under the blade, then turn back and try to separate the fighters, but there are too many. I fling one away and another takes the spot. They're too jumbled to shift apart.

"Lula," Hera yells, grasping at those of our group trying to get to the battle. "Sing."

"What?"

Amah starts the siren's song of death as she holds Grace next to Comus's body. My heart drops, but Amah beckons me, and the notes fall from my throat without thought. Grace's voice comes in as well, a wet, quiet sob at first. She pauses to kiss the back of Comus's hand, then stands, holding on to Amah, and reaches for me. I make my way to my sisters, connecting our circle. The glitterlings lie still, shifting to a mere glimmer.

The same horrid notes I sang to kill darklings and when I met Alex and thought the worst of him fall from my lips. My sister's songs are different, except they match mine. We harmonize in places, land on the same long note, then veer out as we enter the chorus. Fear spins my mind and I glance around to make sure we aren't killing gods like we do everything else, but we're not. The fighting slows, the attention dragging to our fascinating, unrehearsed singing. Do each of us have a piece to a master song? I glance at Amah's black hair, skin, and dark russet eyes, then Grace, blinking sea-glass blue, wheat hair flipped by the breeze. My green irises are my only physical link to my siren mother. Three lines—Peisinoe, Thelxiope, and Aglaope. Note after note drags out, still matching my sisters. Amah tugs my fingers and nods as if she's done this before. For all I know, she has. If this is what we could do, why haven't we kept close from the start? We could have stood against the gods. I glare at Amah, who winces as we trail off, leaving Olympus silent. Weapons lie on the ground, along with several bodies and more blood than any of us wanted. Smoke plumes and confused, fat beetles are the only movement. All eyes watch us, except Rath, who aims his furrowed brow at the other side as he stands guard over Dionysus, still holding Comus's body, and Hera, who strides across the empty gap.

I blow out a long breath. "We could have stayed together."

"It didn't work on your father," Amah whispers. She pulls my palm to her wet cheek. "I only wanted you and your sisters safe." Her eyes flit to the other side of the courtyard. "And you are."

Zeus is on the ground, a line of crimson drifting over the golden cobblestones. Hera kneels beside him, setting a hand on his armored chest.

With a keening wail, Grace drops next to Comus's still body. Amah and I hold her, one on each side. We've all had far too much heartache this past year. Knowing what it's like to lose your love is too familiar, but I was fortunate enough to not say a permanent goodbye, even though this is hard to take. It doesn't sink in that Comus is really gone, but his skin is ashy gray, fingers singed. Someone closed his eyes.

Rath stands, breathing hard into his tented hands, puffy eyes lost in this oddly quiet moment that isn't peaceful with Alex too far from me, and my other sisters scattered on Earth while we're here, competing over humanity in this unfamiliar, deceptively beautiful war zone. Olympus is less of a rotten apple and more of a damaged fine art painting. It needs restoration.

"They're coming around, Lu," Rath says.

The other deities watch me and my sisters, silent but shifting on their feet, bobbing as if regaining their sight after walking out of a fog. They're not picking up their weapons to maim each other yet, so that's a win.

"Go," Amah says, and I do, but I'm stretched between Alex, my sisters, and Rath. Even Hera and these Olympians I've met. Prax and

Zephyrus flank our group, statuesque protectors. My chest tightens. I take a deep breath and stride toward the other side to keep my mind focused so I don't lose control and drag Olympus into a tense cuddle. I cross to Alex and kiss his slack lower lip before remembering that, while enthralled, Olympus is watching. He blinks at me, seeming to want to say something, but not able to form the words. His fingers slip over my hip then move to my stomach and he swallows hard, nodding. "You?"

I put my hand over his. "We're fine, I think." I lead him toward Zeus. They've been through much, but no matter how they've disagreed and the horrid things that have transpired, there was a time they were family. We pass a few deities pinning others to the ground, but they aren't struggling. Hermes puts up the biggest fight. Thrashing under two guards and a goddess, he hisses. The cloaked figure is nowhere to be seen. I glance to the empty field where Hercules grabbed Anice. They better be okay.

"Decide," Hera whispers, running her fingers through Zeus's hair as his breathing staggers. Red tinges the whites of his eyes, and black veins creep under the ruddiness of his cheeks. Beyond that pop of color, he's pale—no more golden sheen to the skin Alex inherited.

"No more," he gurgles, blood spilling from his lips. "Use me." His gaze flicks toward Comus's body and Dionysus, who glares back. Amah holds Grace beside him. "Send me to my Agie." Hera retracts her hand, balling her fingers, but Zeus snatches them. "Do it. I didn't mean…" His eyebrows furrow. "There have been mistakes. Please, Hera. I want to see my love."

Hera caves inward, and Hades steps beside her from nowhere. "One moment," he whispers, hand on her back. He waves to bring our side closer. "We need privacy." Though confusion paints his features, Alex helps herd people into a tight wall around Zeus, with a goddess giving a firm shove to move Artemis, who holds her ground until Rath appears between them.

"Don't," Rath growls. I prepare to use my force field if she decides to be even more of an idiot, but she diverts her eyes and backs away.

Hades presses a hand to Zeus's forehead. "You shock me, brother, and there won't be room for you in the underworld." His eyes flick to me. "Be ready, little hybrid."

Ready for what?

A flash of crystalline light pops under Hades's palm, and Zeus takes a sharp, bubbling inhale and arches. A few members of our standing curtain gasp too. All but Rath and Alex are as confused as I am. Hades grits his teeth and I swear his eyes snap white, but the moment I see it, it's gone.

"Now you may go," he rasps. He staggers to his feet, sweating, face red and scrunched. He ambles toward me. "Hold still, this shouldn't hurt."

"Hades," Alex warns, moving close behind me.

"Have to." Hades holds up a palm, singed and crackling with lightning. The skin around his eyes darkens like embers in a smoldering campfire. "Stay back, Alex." He cups my face, tingling my cheeks with his heated palms, and sets his forehead to mine. An archaic language I don't understand brushes past his lips, but it translates in my mind. *Take what's yours and wield it true.*

An electrifying tingle surges into me, warming my chest and straightening my spine as I grip his wrists. The glitterlings spring forth, shifting on my skin, scratching the itch of electricity dancing over me. There's no pain, only a pleasant warmth as whatever I am—no, as *I* —grasp the magic with my mind and tuck it among the attributes that meet the company of lightning with open arms.

"Lula?" Alex asks with an edge of desperation.

Hades leans back and Alex takes his place, first brushing my hair aside, then touching my neck. My skin tingles at the contact. He glares at Hades. The God of the Underworld pumps his fingers, puffs of smoke falling from his lips as he pants. "Whoa," he rasps. "Glad I didn't have to hold on to that for long." He studies my eyes. "How do you feel?"

Loopy. The fishnet pattern is gone from my skin, now weaving lines of lightning. It's warm and comfortable. "Fine, I think. What did you do?"

"Gave you a gift. I'm sure you're the only one at the moment who can handle Zeus's voltage, so thank you. It's an inopportune day to self-destruct."

"May Olympus remember the good I did," Zeus moans, gasping. "And the sacrifices I made to better the realm. I did *good* here."

Alex tenses, glancing at Comus's prone body. My emotions sink from the odd giddiness of new power to crushing defeat again. Zeus is dethroned, but we've lost. We need to tend to Comus. After that, we stick together and heal. I move, but Alex keeps me locked to his side and shares a glance with Zeus. They both nod.

"Do right." Zeus's eyes flick to mine.

"Go in peace," Hera says. "Husband." She inhales a long breath and color drains from Zeus's face. His lips part in a final exhale, eyes dulling as they focus on the sky.

There's no way. Did she just…kill him? As our people shift and move toward guards or back to Comus, Artemis drops beside Zeus and drapes herself over his chest. She jerks with quiet sounds. I snag Rath's hand and pull him with us. I have no clue what tomorrow will hold, but Rath and my sisters are safe.

Hera rises, straightens, and lifts her chin, displaying the streaks of tears cascading her cheeks. "Back away from the God of Revelry."

We follow one step behind her and Hades. Dionysus carefully shifts, bowing on the ground, trembling fingers clasped together as his pained sobs tremble across my skin. Grace wipes at her face and releases Comus's hand when Amah tugs at her.

Hera kneels, pressing her palm to Comus's chest. The world stills as we wait. I lean into Alex for his warmth and peer up at the sky, wanting the blue back.

The clouds disperse, rolling away as if by a strong wind, except there's no breeze.

Chapter Thirty-Nine

ALEX

Processing everything that just happened isn't possible, but my mind adheres to the shred of hope that flickered back to life because of my grandmother. Holding Lula's hand like the anchor she is, I stand, still and mute, watching Hera with her palm over Comus's unmoving chest. Speech would be difficult anyway, with my body numb from the sirens' singing. In the middle of chaos and heartbreak, their song was the warmest bath, smoothest whiskey, and sweetest orgasm rolled into verse.

Comus jerks, and my knees nearly buckle. "Stay back," I mumble as Grace shrieks and jumps to get to him, but Amah holds her tight with the help of Prax. Whatever Hera is doing needs concentration and space. Dionysus sobs a wheezed breath and grasps at his himation, white-knuckled fists stretching the fabric so taut, he may rip it apart.

Please, I chant in my head. Waking from a mortal death isn't just difficult on the one who died. My heart pounds so hard, I wonder if it's trying to be an example to his. I want him up, moving. I need his voice and to have him drink coffee from his ridiculous mugs because I can't imagine ever seeing one of them without it being in his hand. My world wouldn't be my world without him in it. Hera sags and Hades leans her against his chest. "Good work, Hellfire," he whispers with a wobbly rasp. She turns and curls into him, shielding her face against his neck and then…

Then Comus's eyes flutter open.

Rath drops to his knees, Amah lets go of Grace, and they both sprawl over him, asking questions that make little sense through the hopeful tears. I can't think to move until he sucks in a long breath and coughs ash. His wild gaze finds mine, and I move from Lula's side to intervene.

"Give him space." I tug at Rath. "We need healers over here."

I understood my grandmother's name had to do with life, but I wasn't aware she could take from one to give to another. She's always been excellent at her secrets. I glance back, but she and Hades are missing. He must want her as far from this place as possible, but we're not done yet.

Lula reaches to touch Comus's shoulder, and I lean to kiss his cool forehead. "Brother." I choke on relief. "Never again."

"Ditto." His voice is a wheeze that rolls into another round of coughing. "We win?"

"Still working on it."

"Go." He nods as two healers lean in, placing hands on his temples and chest. "Party later."

Wiping my eyes, I take a deep breath and stand, waiting for Lula as she hugs her sisters, drags Rath up, and gives Comus a devastating smile of appreciation. I kiss her knuckles as she takes my hand. There's a lot to sort out and my mind does a fast spin through the tasks, options, and immediate fires to be squelched then managed to make this vision we've worked so hard for become the future. I turn to the crowd, some of them shifting around the bodies of the fallen, others hunched in whispering bunches, and some staring at Lula, Rath, and my approach. Zeph falls in behind me, and I squeeze his shoulder, pulling him even with our steps. Zeus taught me that time is critical under this type of turmoil and now is the moment to strike hardest to prove the victory. Olympians crowd around his body, blocking my view. His death wasn't what I wanted, but after what he did to Comus, I can't say I'm regretful.

I step among the withering chaos, hand proudly tangled with Lula's. "Everyone, listen please. We have so much to do, but we'll manage together. For those loyal to Moros, he's gone from the realm for eternity." A few gasp and exchange wide-eyed glances. There are seven I have to worry about first and I share a glance with Rath who nods in agreement. I tug Lula closer. "But his daughter understands his mind and will guide you." If that freaks out Lula, she doesn't show it and raises her chin. I squeeze her fingers and return my attention to the crowd. "If you followed Zeus, we mourn with you and continue the traditions to put him to rest as an honored Olympian. We harbor no ill intention toward any deity, but will accept no more violence. This is our chance for peace and change. Tell me, Olympus, will you work together to walk into a new, better age?"

There are many head bows and "ayes" of agreement. And several silent scowls.

Dionysus steps beside us, still tear-streaked and shaky. "Pythia predicted an exodus and Zeus imprisoned her because of it," he yells to the crowd. "Upon her release, fate will continue without interruption. If you cannot agree to peace, then may you be blessed in the next universe." He steps in front of me, drops to his knees, and presses the back of my hand to his forehead.

––––––––

THE MILKY WAY SPILLS BRIGHT ACROSS THE SKY'S BLACK BACKGROUND by the time Lula, Rath, and I walk into the makeshift barracks of Zeus's temple. Since my father toppled the original building, Zeus installed locks on doors or jammed metal bars into the meeting room door frames, imprisoning Olympians who supported our rebellion.

The servants have already caught word of Zeus's passing, but they need to stop dropping to the ground and bowing in front of us. Olympus has stayed stagnant for a thousand years. Through the evening, Lula and Rath have gone where I've needed them, but haven't spoken much.

I tug Lula closer. "Are you okay," I whisper.

She nibbles her lip. "Um. Yes."

When Rath purses his lips, fighting his words, I shove his shoulder toward a room, herding them both in. "What's wrong? You're both quiet."

Rath runs a hand down his tired face. "He hit me with a death bolt. It killed Comus."

"Yes," Lula adds. "And our siren song didn't affect Rath or Hera." They exchange a nervous glance, then Lula takes his hand, and only then do I see the shake of his fingers. His eyes seek answers I don't have. It makes little sense.

"Hera created the sirens with Hestia and Demeter. But you?" I shrug at Rath. "Do you think Moros is your father?" I already know the answer. Even when young, no one could deny his father's icy coloring and sharp jaw, or his mother's brooding eyes and left dimple when she smiled, which was rare.

"No."

"Do you have a theory?"

"Maybe I'm linked to the shadow realm and not of here." Before I can tell him of course he is "of here," he continues. "Or my father is something in-between like Moros. Or...when I took on the shades. There could be a remnant." He looks at the marble ceiling. "That makes no sense. I'm just grasping at illogical ideas cause I don't fit within the facts, or in Olympus."

I grip his shoulder, giving him a shake. "You're exactly where you belong, brother. Your father's background is fuzzy, so that's the most likely possibility, but I don't believe for a second that a shade still inhabits you." If that were true, what I'm going to ask of him will be far more difficult. "Whether they are darkling or witchcraft, they cannot withstand lightning. Which is why I think Hades did what he did." I thumb Lula's cheek and give them both a smile. "You were the only one who could handle it, and our best shot at success for what needs to be done."

Lula snags my hand as I turn to the door. "Are you okay?"

They both still appear concerned. "Yeah," I answer. "We have a lot of work ahead of us, but I have far more hope than I've had in a long while." They both furrow their brows, and Lula blows out a breath and steps in to hug my arm. I wrap her up. "What?" She's probably exhausted.

"Zeus is dead," Rath says. "He was your grandfather."

That he was. "I'll mourn him once Olympus is under control. Maybe I always understood there wouldn't be the perfect exit we'd hoped for. He'd become so lost, and...he killed Comus. He aimed to kill you both. You don't understand what I wanted to do to him." My eyes sting again and I ball my fists tight, trying to ease the simmering rage of what I could have lost. "Though it makes me callous, Olympus needs Comus and you two far more than Zeus. It will take months to figure out everything that led to this and learn from it, and because he's gone, we now have that opportunity. We are safe. Comus is alive. Grace and Amah are with him and your other sisters can join us soon." I kiss Lula's worried pout and brush my fingers over her stomach. "This is a good day."

We now have the opportunity to raise our child without waiting for retribution. I can't be sad about that.

A rainbow flickers in my side vision and Hades pops in. He's in jeans and a Zeppelin shirt. "Zeus had Athena and Pythia locked away. They need to see you. All of you." There's no humor to his clenching jaw and furrowed brow, nor the way he sweeps from the room expecting us to follow.

I kiss Lula's knuckles and she drags Rath along as we work through the maze of rooms that have become colder and emptier through the years. I didn't realize it when it happened, but Hera had started pulling away even before the break. Little at a time, old tapestries fell and weren't replaced. Sculptures and painters left in the last exodus or stopped working because Zeus didn't approve of art inspired by humans unless it was war and sex. Paint chipped, flaked colors cleaned from bare floors until all that was left was white, pristine marble.

Murmurs get louder as we approach the corner, and when we turn in the echoing corridor next to the old Council rooms, Hera peeks at us over her shoulder. Red rims her puffy eyes. Hades breaks from us, capturing her and tugging her to the side of the hallway to reveal Athena, appearing just as wrecked, but she bows her head as I introduce Lula. Pythia stands behind her. Her curves have diminished and she looks older from the time she pressed her hand to my chest in the square. Realization makes me stumble. She had to have seen the future of what would happen to me.

Her eyes angle to relief when she spots us. "Finally," she says with a teary laugh. "Took you long enough." There's no anger to her words and I'm glad Zeus didn't break her sarcasm.

I bow my head to her, and Lula and Rath do the same.

"Tell them," Hades says. "Please." It may be a nicety, but it sounds like a command.

I glare up at him then put my focus back on Pythia. "I'm glad to see you…" I can't find the right word. "Well-ish."

Her bosom rises and falls with a sigh. "It's been a long road and these next few actions will set the path of this universe." That could mean we have an important day ahead of us, or an important century. It's hard to tell when talking to one so ancient.

I turn my palms to her in a show of peace. "Can you please help us on this path?"

She arches an eyebrow. "Just like that? Do you not wonder about the missteps, the treason? Do you not wish to cut me down for tying you to Ichnaea?" She lifts her chin as if taunting me to slice her neck.

Rath raises two fingers in the air. "Uh, I'd like those answers."

"Of course, you would." Pythia seems pleased by his outspokenness when all Zeus has tried to do is shut him up. "As you should understand by now, an exodus is upon us. The universe has called for two millennium but he wouldn't hear of it."

"I didn't realize it was that long." That's why Zeus separated the realms and banned birth. He didn't want a new age encroaching on his reign.

"And what will you do, Alexiares? Will you keep us here, in this state?"

I lift a shoulder, confused. "It's not my decision, but in my opinion, the split should not have happened." I glance to Rath and also wish Comus was here. "And preventing the universe from its will was asinine."

She watches me for a long moment then blink at Hades.

He shrugs. "I told you he wasn't keen on ruling."

She straightens further, looking over Lula. "May I have a moment with you?"

Athena straightens and limps down the hall. "I'm at your service when needed."

Hades and Hera don't move. "There will be transparency in the new age," Hades says. "Right, Lula?"

"Yes, please." She steps closer to Pythia. "We'd like to know as much as possible without getting lines crossed by rumors. From what I understand, what Olympus needs now is to be on the same page."

Pythia studies Lula's face as one would stand in front of art at the Louvre—gaze touching every angle in appreciation. "I knew of your birth two centuries before you were born. You are a wonder, second champion of the new age." She blinks under her lashes at Rath. "I'm sorry I could not make things better for you, Rathbarth. Fate prevented intervention, though many put themselves on the line for your existence."

My lips part as I try to work through what she's telling us. "We moved into a new age?" An exodus has occurred around the time of each rising generation; the Primordials, the Titans, then the Olympians, though we thought it was coincidental or the order was opposite.

"So…" Rath squeezes one eye shut, tipping his head. "The turn of the millennia marked a new age and—"

"No," Pythia interrupts. "*You* marked the turn of a new age and brought forth a realm. You are the first."

Rath goes paler. "I'm not an Olympian?"

"No."

I run my hand through my hair and huff a laugh of relief. "That makes so much sense. Gods, I wish we would have known."

"Zeus would have killed him before he acknowledged." Pythia balls her hands before stretching her fingers at her sides. "I was so relieved to make it to that moment, but even after that, if anyone would have attacked Rathbarth and discovered his immunity to Zeus's bolts, none of us would be here."

"Like what happened today?" Lula asks. "That certainly stood out. That would have made an…apocalypse?" She places her hand over her stomach and I want to do the same, as if our combined touch could stave off the fall of a planet to keep our little one safe.

"Yes."

"Okay. Um. But that won't happen now?" Lula blows out a long breath when Pythia shakes her head. "Good things from now on, right?"

Pythia winces.

"There's something else, isn't there?" I ask.

She wets her lips. "I lied to Zeus about your child and told him your heir would be born of Ichnaea so he wouldn't alter the path. I didn't expect you to balk in the way you did. You two were close and made a suitable match." Her eyes widen and she stares as if waiting for Lula to strike her down. "I did not mean to cause harm but couldn't find another way."

Lula swishes her hand through the air. "It's weird, but fine. That was then." Her face scrunches until she glances at me and it melts to something that reminds me I'm ready to be home in bed with her after this long day. She slides her fingers into mine. "And this is now."

I smile. "When I met Lula, I'd thought the worst because I'm not sure you've ever been wrong, Pythia."

"I haven't," she says, factual and unfeeling. She glances at Lula's stomach, tilting her head. Finally, she gives a grin that lights her face. "So strong. Your child will be a leader on Earth. Zeus understood it as control, and I couldn't convince him otherwise."

My eyes widen.

Pythia nods. "When the child is born, I will read her abilities, but I've seen fate's pleasure surrounding her birth."

"She?" I ask, a warm heat tingling my temples and making my ears go fuzzy.

Lula shrugs. "Sirens only have girls."

"You are a hybrid goddess," Pythia says. "You will have championesses and champions."

A wave of dizziness takes over. How could everything come around in such a manner so quickly?

While Lula gives me a smile that sends a shock wave through me, Pythia's demeanor sinks. "What will you do with me?"

Even though I know she's nervous about cursing and the touch of gods, Lula wraps her fingers over Pythia's fidgeting ones. "What do *you* want to do?" She is perfect for Olympus.

When Pythia gapes and struggles to find words, I chime in. "We'd appreciate your abilities if you share them as intended, with truth only. While we'd miss your counsel if you left us for the next universe, we will respect your decision and wish you well."

"You don't want me to go?" she asks, head tilting.

"Of course not," Rath says. "I need help to figure out what the hell all this means and how to do what Alex is avoiding asking me. Can you clear that up?"

I crinkle my nose at him in apology. Hermes and my brother can't stay in that state, and I'd ask for a lot to heal them. Even have Rath control the one thing that terrifies him most.

"The shades." Pythia's voice turns deep, and she scowls.

"Oh, you sneaky little—" Hades points at him. "I knew you were hiding something big."

Pythia settles her hand on Rath's crossed arms. "As we all have needed to do. Yes. To clear them from Olympus will require you and the queen."

Lula looks to Hera, who smiles at her. "You, dear."

"But—"

"Ugh." Hades sends a long groan to the ceiling. "You two are in control of Olympus. It's decided. I've decided. Any protests? No. Now shush and accept your fate already." He marches down the hall, dragging Hera with him. "Never in all my days did I expect to find people who didn't want to rule the realm. Can you believe this shit? What are we going to do with them?"

She hugs his arm, leaning against him. "Let them lead."

I CARRY LULA INTO THE BEDROOM AT HER HOUSE. HER SLOW, SLEEPY breathing fans against my neck, making me smile. It's still dark here, though the sun was up and blazing through Olympus by time Rath and Lula burned the last shade from Anice. My brother and Hermes will live, but need a lot of care for a long while. Rath will too, after touching the deepest shadows in his mind, calling the beings out of the bodies they inhabited.

We've learned so much through the night from Pythia and the archivists who had feared death if they spoke of the past. The mysterious shades are ghosts of old gods, though Pythia couldn't explain how they came to be. Hades has a solid theory that Rath's father can create them, which explains why they answer to the God—Champion—of Shadows. When Rath is ready, we'll go together to the pits in the sea kingdom to question him.

My Championess of Magnetism doesn't stir as I settle her on her side of the bed and strip her of her clothes. After I do the same, I crawl in and pull her to me, sighing in utter ease at the heat of her skin against mine. Later, I'll watch her wake. We will touch each other thoroughly and freely, because that's what we are now. *Free.* We won our place. We will exude peace for eternity.

Epilogue

LULA

I find Alex and Alessa in the Hall of Lost Majors, my little girl's chubby hand gripping Alex's finger. Today, he tells her the story of Poseidon and Medusa, the love they had for each other, and how they were likely ruling another universe together without scorn. I'm surprised Comus isn't in here as well, telling her all the details he's learned over the last year from hours in the reopened library. Alex wanders to the statue of Zeus. He moved it from Zeus's temple to here. "This is your great-grandfather, baby girl. You can learn much from his story."

She will grow, learning from the successes and faults of the past as we press forward into this new age. I've been studying long hours as well: the history of the gods, the diaries of those who left in previous exoduses. Zeus wasn't all bad, but he wasn't good, and then he got lost along the way, oddly because he fell in love. I hope to meet the mothers one day when we figure out the world and how to reconnect. Hera hid them in the fae realm. If Zeus hadn't cut off Olympus from everything, he may have seen Aglaope again. Alessa gurgles and drags Alex's digit to her mouth so she can gnaw on him with her gums. He lifts our tiny treasure to kiss her forehead. Her green eyes half-close and she yawns. When he shifts rhythmically from foot to foot, I cross the room, passing all the marble faces of past heroes, heroines, royalty, and the biggest influencers of positive change in the universe. The newest statues standing guard outside the doors aren't done yet. Artists have found new life with visits to Earth and working with Amah and my other sisters. My mother's face has been carefully carved, but not detailed. Only the shape of her eyes, a generalization of her sharp nose, and my chin give me a hint of her appearance.

"Don't you dare put her to sleep yet." I peek around Alex's shoulder to smile at Alessa.

"That's right!" Grace barrels through, snatching and lifting Alessa. "Aunty Grace needs her girl time." Our baby forgets about her father's magic sleep-inducing abilities and kicks her feet, shoving her fist in her mouth. Grace contorts her face, looking like a deranged, grinning loon. "Yes, she does. And we're going to have so much fun together. Yippee!"

I take Alex's hand, keeping him from snatching Alessa back, though he sneaks in a kiss on her head as she drools around her fist. He loves putting her to sleep, rocking as she drifts off, her rosebud lips pursed and twitchy as he stares at her with an overflowing love that makes me teary to witness. Comus trails in, wrapping Grace in his arms, and grazing Alessa's little amber curls as she babbles up to a melodic, though high-pitched, squeal. He whispers to Grace and she turns to kiss him. They can't wait for another siren heat to take hold and give them an opportunity to expand our happy family.

There's been no lack of babysitters with my sisters pitching a fit if Alex closes the portal from our house to Olympus. He shut it for one day two months after Alessa arrived, and after Anice, Hercules, Rath, and Hermes refused, my sisters convinced Apollo to find us and make sure the baby "wasn't bored." Even with the intrusive nature we've never been able to experience, I love having my sisters visit when they want after being apart forever. Alex and I compromised, and we leave the portal open during waking hours. He placed it in a closet with a bell on the doorknob, so we know when someone arrives.

While the sirens take up the biggest chunk of baby time, Olympus has fallen for our championess. In her eight months, she's received enough gifts to fill the Colosseum, and we pull a crowd wherever we go. Alex's mother is always at the lead, taking her granddaughter and giggling back at her, face warm and beaming. Hebe has flourished with being able to visit the Earth realm, but not everyone has been so open about change. Many of the older deities left at the exodus, causing a diminution in the inspiration in the human realm. It's not the Dark Ages, but there needs to be recovery for all beings. They struggle with the drop in powerful emotions from Ares, Zeus, and Artemis. It's left many humans confused and lacking purpose—even if their motives were hatred. I thought we may lose Rath too when Artemis ran to him, threw herself in his arms and kissed him, then settled her hand on Pythia's swirling ball before disappearing through that wild, purple, glowing portal. He flinched, fists clenched at his sides, but he stayed. When the last Olympian departed, and the gateway closed, he shadowed away. We didn't see him for a week. But things will smooth out. We've sought ways to reconnect, and the guys think once that happens, all realms will flourish.

Alex wraps me up and kisses my hair. "Are you ready?"

Alessa giggles in rolling peals as Grace snuffles against her neck.

"I suppose." I steal Alessa back, loving her tiny, squishy weight in my arms. She kicks her feet and smiles up to her wide eyes. I kiss her pudgy cheek. "Be good for your aunties, and if your uncle tries to teach you how to shadow travel again, tell him Mommy says he needs to cool it for ten years."

"Fifteen." Alex kisses Alessa's forehead.

"Five tops. Right, nugget?" Rath approaches and tickles Alessa's chin. "Better shadow than flame."

She waves her arms and shrieks until he takes her from me.

He makes a big show of grimacing as she bites his finger. "Ah, monster. When you're tired of girl time, give a screech, and I'll take you to visit the underworld. You like it there, don't you? Cerberus is fun."

"Ugh." I crinkle my nose. "She always comes back with her hair full of drool when you do that."

Rath's eyes don't leave Alessa. "That's because Cerberus is a big baby dog who loves kids. Besides, Hercules is down there. She loves getting tossed about by her granddad."

"Are they searching today?" Alex asks.

When Hades learned shades were the ghosts of gods, he started combing the underworld for the spirits he knew—a near impossible task as they don't stay still. Olympus lost seventeen the year I became a goddess. None have been spotted, nor has Deimos. The moment a fear event or shade activity appears, all of Olympus will work to end it. We've proven there's a future on Earth for us, and everyone is invested.

Rath nods. "Also, you have a crowd outside that wants to check out the city. Enjoy yourselves."

We do?

Alex and I fawn over Alessa for one more second, inhaling her baby smell and kissing her pudgy cheeks as we say our goodbyes, then clasp hands and head to the door.

A group of twenty deities wait in dresses, or jeans and t-shirts. Some faces are beaming, some biting their lips and tugging at the human garments. Change isn't easy for immortals, especially ones who were closed off from the progress for so long. It's a new, fantastical world out there—so different from what they're used to, that we've recruited some humans and otherworldlings as guides.

"Does everyone remember the rules?" I ask the crowd.

Ichnaea steps forward, beaming, arm locked with Plutus. Her little baby bump is majestic in that yellow shift. "No announcing we're deities, no stealing, no cursing or murdering, even if someone appears to deserve it. Don't walk in front of cars, trains, or mobile vehicles of any kind. Do not scream or harm the things we see, and stay with our assigned Earth guide. Can we go to New York? I want to shop and visit Broadway. Let's say six hours at the meet point?"

Naea is one of our most enthusiastic travelers. She's been to all major cities, mapping with vigor to detail everything she hasn't been able to do in two millennia. I'm waiting for her request to stay permanently, and even with another little champion on the way, it'd be good for them and the Earth.

"I'll take you." Hermes steps forward in an outfit that looks Rath-approved. He props his caduceus against his shoulder. The wings at the top of the golden staff are folded in rest. Alex's hand tightens and I squeeze his fingers. *Give him a chance.*

The elders from the old Council have been difficult. It's a struggle for them to learn to listen, collaborate, or accept they must undo the laws they put into action thousands of years ago. And with what

Hermes has been through, he's only recently used his attributes again. Olympus has new methods now—we've installed technology throughout, introduced human and otherworldling culture, and have tossed aside many traditions that needed to go. The more modern gods embrace the change with enthusiasm, but it's a lot to take in, and a few retreated to the hell realm to work in a simpler world. It's nice to visit there and check on Thor and Thorette. But Hermes, the one Alex wasn't sure would adapt with what he'd gone through, holds his chin up, appearing comfortable in human garb, offering to escort a group to New York. They're coming around.

I squeeze Alex's hand again, sending him a tiny flick of electricity that makes him jump.

"Yes, of course," he says. "Thank you."

Hermes bows—Alex still hasn't been able to curb that gesture—and signals the travelers to surround him. "Hope I remember how to do this." Shaking his staff, he turns it upside down.

Alex puts a fist up to his lips, hiding his laugh with a cough. Hermes doesn't need the caduceus to travel or his infamous sandals. He wills himself and anyone else to where he wants to be. It's incredibly powerful. But the staff is calming for those around it, especially him. Alex said he hasn't seen him without it since the revolution.

Ichnaea turns to me with wide eyes. "Maybe we should—"

Hermes rights the caduceus and smiles. "I jest, Goddess of Tracking. Just breathe." The circled group disappears.

Anice approaches, holding hands with Ceraon. "Are we having family dinner tomorrow?"

Alex claps Ceraon on the shoulder and bumps his forehead against his brother's. "I wouldn't miss it." I kiss them both on the cheek and they head toward the dining hall, probably for Ceraon to direct the kitchens and see what creative meals he can conjure for the week. With the visits around the world, he's been getting requests.

Six remain, and a few of those are new travelers. Eos herds them forward. "It's okay. We'll follow the queen to her little city and have lunch. It's a great introductory place."

"Stop calling me that, E," I say.

Eos grins. "Not a chance, Queenie."

"Fine. Come along then, Sunshine."

I grin and sure enough, Eos drops her jaw in a huff as two demigoddesses beside her giggle into their palms. Eos straightens up to banter back, but Alex holds up a palm.

"Nope," he says. "Date night. You two can smack talk each other later at movie night or whatever you call it."

"Goddess Get-together," Eos and I say together.

"Though anyone is welcome," Eos adds.

"Great. Save it for then." Alex opens a portal and waves the group through. "This way, please." Eos and I share a grin and I follow Alex into an alley.

"We will meet back here at ten. Have fun, you two." She explains cars and sidewalks to the murmuring gaggle of deities as they head toward the main street.

Eos and I have grown close, and she spends a ton of time with Grace as well. Getting to know everyone in Olympus has been a joy, whether we've been accepted or not. Amah still doesn't trust any deity completely, though Hera walks the forest with her often, discussing the past and how the world has changed around them. Their chats have been equally good for the emeritus queen, who harbors more guilt than anyone should. I think Hades asks her to marry him daily, but she's not ready. "How are Hera and Hades doing?" I whisper to Alex as we wait for the group to turn the corner.

"Hades is a bear, so I assume not as well as he'd like." He closes the portal, then turns to me and lifts my chin to give me a gentle kiss. "Hi."

I smile and wrap my arms around his neck, going on tiptoes for a less than chaste follow-up. "Hi." Alone time is fleeting, though there are few moments that we're apart.

"You sure about this? I'd like to have a conversation with you."

Me too. I drag him toward our destination. "We'll be quick, and then I want to take a city tour." The farmer's market calls, as does the city garden that has grown and expanded to other neighborhoods.

Little candles flicker in the front window of the Italian restaurant where I ate the night I met Alex. "I can't believe you chose this place," Alex says.

"Hey," I whisper. "There's nothing that will keep me away from their pasta primavera. Besides, all is forgiven."

Alex kisses me again before we step through the door and get smacked with the scent of garlic and baked bread. "Okay, this was a superb choice."

I squeeze his hand.

We press together in a booth, watching humans interact and converse, though as usual, their attention travels to us. When I almost moan from the first bite of pasta and the waitress returns yet again to stand close and stare, I decide it's time to test what I've been working on without telling Alex.

I imagine the opposite of the magnetic pull, and push a barrier that's easy to conjure, but dropping the physical element. The glitterlings brush the tops of my hands but I ignore them to focus on the tingle in the back of my skull.

The woman blinks a few times and smiles, pouring more wine into each of our glasses. "Need anything else?"

"No." I place my hand on Alex's, keeping him from answering. "Thank you."

She nods and walks away as if I were a normal human at her table. My eyes sting.

Alex whips his head to me, cupping my face. "What? How?"

I beam at him. "I've been practicing and studying more about magnets, and now I can repel humans without moving them. We can talk, I think."

The other patrons aren't staring. They don't stand, waiting for my command. Instead, they eat, smile, and enjoy their own conversations. I've put us in a bubble of normal.

Alex swipes at an errant tear on my cheek. "I'm so proud of you, Firecracker." The way he looks at me sometimes stills my breath. He makes me feel as if I'm capable of every grand design. "It's only going to get better and better."

I put my palm on his warm chest. "I can't imagine it getting better than this." We have eternity to explore the Earth and realms, but there's no doubt that I'm his world and he's mine.

***

Thank you for reading! Did you enjoy? Please add your review because nothing helps an author more and encourages readers to take a chance on a book than a review.

And don't miss more from Poppy Minnix with **HOLIDAY HOTEL**. Turn the page for a sneak peek!

Also be sure to sign up for the City Owl Press newsletter to receive notice of all book releases!

Sneak Peek of Holiday Hotel

Whoever invented corset boning is definitely on the naughty list.

This red velvet monstrosity makes breathing problematic, and there's marabou stuck in my lip gloss. But it will all be worth it when James walks down the hall and finds me stretched out on the living room rug.

It's been one month, three weeks, and five days since he's touched me or kissed me or even tried to catch a glimpse of me in the shower. I can't remember the last time we laughed ourselves into a vigorous ab workout or the last time I earned one of his you're-a-goof-but-you're-my-goof grins.

That changes now.

Blowing aside the poofy ball that keeps bombarding my cheek from my Santa hat, I shift in my corset to see which angle is best. On my stomach in a pin-up pose with my ankles in the air and crossed, I think. Good cleavage angle with that one.

The clock I put on the wall yesterday says seven fifty-three, and James will be heading for the front door at eight to run. In this sexy Mrs. Claus getup, with a playful pose with my candy cane rod, I'm going to get us out of this stagnant stage in our relationship. He will love it. I wince and reconsider my hopes. He will pay attention and hopefully remember that he likes my company for more than movies on the couch.

The tight ball in my stomach could be from the steel boning tucked in crimson velvet, but my sweaty palms tell me it's beyond that. I need more fun times and I'm going for it. Besides, Christmas is the ultimate time for antics. It's also a time for decorations, but I'm missing those. With our recent move, that would be too much stress, according to James. That's valid, as I take holiday decor to a ridiculous degree, but I still have antics—my wheelhouse—and it's been a while since I allowed myself to fly free.

We need a push. We've been working nonstop—him at his new location and me on a particularly demanding client—all while unboxing. And we were drifting before the move, existing side by side yet alone. Maybe while making the best of this untypical holiday, I'll start a new tradition. The Mrs. Claus surprise—pre-coffee Cozette laid out on a fuzzy white rug to set the alluring scene, ready for a fun-filled day of sexiness.

Footsteps. He's awake and moving from the bedroom. My heart smashes against the corset's marabou trim. I'm shocked he didn't notice how excited I've been over the last few days. Was this the best idea? I shake that thought away. I think I'm sexy, and so will he. It will be fine. One deep breath and I prop the end of the thick candy cane stick in my mouth, mindful of my bright red lipstick, and throw my shoulders back, displaying my heaving bosom, which I don't need to fake because I'm panic-panting.

"Cozette?" James asks from the hallway. "Why do you have Christmas music playing so loud?" He steps into the living room and keeps going toward the door, eyes on his phone, probably routing his morning run.

"Ahem," I mumble around peppermint.

When he drags his eyes up, they pop in surprise for a split second, then sink into an expression he aims at me when I've done something out-of-bounds—a blank hazel-eyed stare, plus the slightest nose scrunch.

But no heat.

No interest.

No sexy.

"What are you wearing?" he asks.

My eyes widen. Heat burns my cheeks at this asinine idea. I'm onstage and the one person in the audience, the man who is supposed to love and support me, just discarded his complimentary tickets to this performance.

"You know what? Fa la la you and your little dog too!" I leap up and bite back a hundred angry, hurt words that would only give him more ammunition to judge me. Sorry for trying to have a sexy Saturday before the holidays.

"I-I don't have a dog." He tugs at his winter running shirt and eyes the door to freedom.

I chirp a crazed note of sarcasm. "Well, get one to keep you company, because I'm gone."

Hey, now that follow-up turned out better than expected. One micro-win for me. With a pivot on my shiny red stilettos, I catwalk down the hall. My fast strides send a chill over my bare backside, as the sexy Mrs. Claus skirt I'm wearing isn't exactly full coverage. At least the Santa hat is keeping my head warm.

James used to have fun, used to smile at my shenanigans. He's never been the kind to tackle me, though I'd appreciate that treatment when my lady parts are busting out of a scrap of red velvet and I'm sucking on a candy cane as if it's the best lover I've ever had. Hell, it's the best lover I've had in months.

I'm getting nothin' for Christmas except a Cozette-is-weird face and a *What are you wearing?*

I tug my teal suitcase from the closet shelf and pitch in my clothes from the oak dresser. Everything in our bedroom is beige or wood except for two bright, patterned throw pillows I bought while James was at work. He shoves them in the closet each night, and I toss them on the bed each morning.

"What are you doing?" he asks from the doorway.

"I told you, I'm out, done, finito. It's the motherfrolicking end scene, James."

"Cozette." His tone as he groans my name is an exasperated complaint about my overwhelming nature. Or that's what it sounds like to me. "You need to tone it down. You're upset."

My cheeks heat again. Yes, I am *upset*. I've let this man "tone me down." My style, my language. I've altered everything about me because feelings and bright things make James squirmy.

"How could I let this happen?" I whisper to myself.

"What?"

I move to the closet, jerking everything that's not black or gray off hangers and cramming it all in the suitcase. "We've been together for two years, and I've pushed myself aside to be what you want because I love you."

I'm not feeling the love at the moment, and my heart is racing for freedom instead of embracing my this-relationship-is-over panic. That can't be good.

"Cozette," James grumbles, rubbing his forehead. I wait for him to continue into a reprimand as he always does. Three...two... "That's not—"

There it is.

"No." I slam my suitcase shut, but it won't close all the way. I jab the cascades of unruly fabric inside with my finger. "It is the truth. Somewhere along the line, I forgot about me in this relationship. Today I let myself out, and you don't want me. You want tame and easy and boring. I'm not that person, James. I'm sexy Mrs. Claus, and you're not my Santa."

"This is about sex?" He displays his palms at me, lanky fingers splayed. They haven't been in my vicinity for too long. So long, I'm not sure I want them on me anymore. "I guess it has been a couple of weeks," he says. "Sorry. I'll try to—"

"Hold it right there, Jack Frost." I jerk my bag off the bed, tuck an accent pillow under my arm, and brush by him to head toward the bathroom. "That's the problem. You shouldn't have to try. When it's been over a month, and you walk in the living room to me fellatioing a candy cane while wearing this getup, the obvious path is to replace the peppermint stick with your dick. Your mind didn't even go there."

If our sex life had been a passionate romp long ago, I'd worry about stress from his job or the move, but that's not it. We don't match. Never have, and I'm not sure why I thought a relocation would somehow make things better between us.

"It's fellating. And it's not always about sex, Cozette."

I shove toiletries and makeup into a shoulder bag. "No, it's not. It's about talking, laughing, going out, and making up words like 'fellatioing' because it's more fun to say. We act like we're settled down with kids, but we don't even have pets tethering us to this tiny prison. Is it too difficult to leave the house on a Friday night? Maybe go to a brunch and meet other people our age? You don't want me to explore without you, but you won't leave the apartment. There's a massive city out there, and I've gotten only as far as the coffee shop."

"We've gone farther than that." James tugs at the waistband of his running shorts. "I'd rather stay in. I enjoy our quiet time." His monotone voice grates on the one nerve I have left.

"It's all quiet time!" Except for now, because I'm yelling. "Not to mention, you haven't even attempted to stop me from packing. We're done."

I zip the bag closed, exit the bathroom, and drag the suitcase, my laptop bag, purse, and throw pillow down the hallway, bumping into the wall twice. The stilettos aren't helping my graceful exit.

"What do you want me to do, unpack your stuff?"

"I want you to care," I toss over my shoulder.

At the front door, I eye my corset and gratuitous cleavage. "Ugh." I drop everything to the floor and shuck my shoes.

James steps aside as I pass him on my way back to the bedroom. How can he not get this? Did the hundred times I've asked to go out not give him a clue to my state of mind? I should have gone alone, met some friends or taken on some smaller local projects, but he'd pout if I went exploring without him, and when he went in search of running routes, I had no hope of keeping up with his speedy strides.

I pause in the bedroom and take a cleansing breath. "I want you to show an ounce of emotion that the woman you claim to love is leaving you."

The black sweatpants I left in the drawer are good enough for now. While I think it'd be poetic to walk away dressed as a holiday temptress, it's December in New York. I've had frostbite-free legs for twenty-five years, and I'd like to continue that streak.

"Hey, don't go. We can work this out. The Christmas party is tomorrow."

I stop dead in my tracks. "Oh, is my presence requested at your holiday party? Your boss will not like this breakup one bit, and you know why? Because I'm the only one who talks. I'm entertaining." Regathering my pile of stuff, I head to the door. "At least someone appreciates that."

Stomping my bare feet into my boots, I shove my stilettos into my winter coat pockets, loop my laptop bag and purse over my head, and walk out the door. "I'll pick up the rest of my stuff later."

"Cozette," he says from our apartment door.

The elevator dings. He's not even going to follow? Fully dressed, with no obligations but his self-imposed running time, he stands in the hallway, one foot from the safety of home, watching me walk away.

The stupid part of me that thought he'd simply *try* when our relationship boiled down to this inevitable moment withers away as the elevator doors shut. Sure, he takes longer to vocalize. Unlike me, he thinks everything through before he speaks, but still. He won't even attempt to convince me to stay?

Leaning against the wall, I wipe away a dumb, hot tear.

Two years of sweet moments had dissolved into bitter boringness.

It's over.

James further dashes my teeny hope of a passionate reunion when I get to the empty lobby. He and I have watched enough romance movies to know that when one person leaves, the other sprints the stairs, or races through the airport, or borrows a flippin' bicycle to cut off their true love's escape.

They do anything to win them back.

But James doesn't burst through the stairwell door, chest heaving and stammering about what a fool he's been. I'm absolutely certain he's already gone back into our apartment.

Oh, he'll consider coming after me, pace the hallway while biting his thumbnail, antsy because he's missing his typical running time. Then, he'll call his twin and they'll chat about how irrational and reckless I am. How my exit is one of my tantrums and I'll return home forthwith. Except they'd never use "forthwith." Too uncommon.

My luggage wheels rattle across beige tile as I roll my suitcase to the door. Outside the glass doors, people pass, bundled up in scarves and hats. The city is a wall of gray stone that blocks out the sky.

I have nowhere to go. We moved three months ago for James's programming career. Since then, I've been working my virtual event planner job from the couch or coffee shop. The closest friends I have are the three baristas on rotation, and only one of them remembers my name. But I do exemplary work when caffeinated and free from beige everything, so that will be my think-this-through spot.

The ding of the elevator makes me jerk to attention. Maybe? Possibly? Could it be?

The doors slide open and a couple hobbles out, bundled up in near-matching gray wool coats. Snowflake-white hair peeks out from under her beret and from his fedora. He leans on a cane, and she leans on him like they're posing for a greeting card geared toward couple goals.

How many times have they broken apart and patched themselves back together? He mumbles something laced with the rasp of decades, and her lips quirk, revealing aged beauty carved from a million laughs.

Past them, the elevator clanks shut. The glowing yellow floor number stays halted on *L*.

James will expect me to come back. It's my M.O. Freak out, cool down, slink home. I'm reliable like that.

Not today.

I swing open the door and slam into an arctic wall of cold. A squeak crosses my lips, promptly freezes, plummets, and shatters on the concrete. Why did I ever agree to move to this popsicle hell?

The hundreds of holiday-decorated windows a few blocks away help thaw me out a little. And it's rumored that I can find any obscure material item in city stores. Oh, the pizza and bagels are so delicious that nowhere else in the world could hope to replicate the taste and texture, but whatever—it's cold.

As I shiver my way to the coffee shop, cars travel the potholed grid like Pac-Man chasing dots while ghosts follow, weaving between each other and popping out of adjoining streets. All I can smell is frozen concrete and exhaust. The dancing neon mug in the window just beyond a wall of steam billowing from a sidewalk grate is a beacon in this gray, frantic world. I take the seat closest to the back to keep away from the frigid whoosh each time someone enters, but it's still freezing. The woman next to me scowls at my haul of bags, and I refrain from flipping her off as I place my throw pillow on the seat to mark it as mine. At the counter, I'm greeted by one of the baristas who doesn't know my name.

Marco is an aspiring actor from Venezuela. He lives in a flat with four other theater friends—one of whom steals all his rice pudding and he is *not* pleased. He spells my name C-O-S-E-T.

The cup of chocolate ganache peppermint espresso with cream and whip warms my hands. After one sweet sip that heats a path to my soul, I declare it the ultimate beverage for a 9:00 a.m. breakup. I fish my phone out of my overstuffed purse. No calls. Fine, then. It looks like I'm headed home for Christmas after all.

I'd told my parents we were staying in New York because of James's new job and the holiday party, but that's not an issue anymore. North Carolina, here I come.

Dad answers on the second ring. "I was about to call you. Hello, daughter of mine from the great big city of New York!" He sings "New York" so loud I have to pull the phone away from my ear and the scowling woman levels up her bitch-face.

When his long note tapers to silence, I tuck the phone back against my ear. "Hello, father of mine, who now gets to spend the holidays with his loving daughter."

"What? Did James get off work for Christmas Eve?"

"No, but we broke up, and now I get to come home for Christmas." I take a deep breath to calm the tightness in my throat. "Yay."

The woman stops scowling and stares into her coffee cup.

"Oh, Cozette. Sorry, sweet pea. Can you work it out? You two have been together a while, and you just moved. It's probably stress."

It's boredom, actually. A nonstop need to bolt to the door and be loud, reckless, and alive has been biting at my toes for a while, and that doesn't match James's need for the safety of dead quiet.

"Coming here with him wasn't smart," I say. "I thought since New York has so much to do, we'd explore and reconnect, but nothing has changed." Except me, as I've tried to make myself what James needs. "I can get a ticket and fly out this afternoon."

"I'm sorry it didn't work out. Maybe you need time apart. And about Christmas…we're in Quebec, remember?"

What are my parents doing in Canada? It's colder there than in New York.

"Nope, I don't recall Quebec."

"Mom didn't mention it? Huh." There's shuffling and mumbling. "Oh. Mom says she didn't want to bug you with details during your busy season. We figured since you and James couldn't make Christmas, we'd head up north. She's always wanted to see the nativity tour, so we're staying in Old Quebec, and they've decorated everything—I mean everything. We've walked into a Dickens Christmas village."

"That sounds nice. Chilly, but nice." I don't want to go to Canada. It doesn't have my carousel or smell like cinnamon pinecones.

"It is. I'd tell you to come here, but we could only book because someone canceled two minutes before we called. Hang on, and I'll go see if there's another room available."

"I don't want to interrupt. Can I go to the house?"

Dad hisses through his teeth. Ooh, that's going to be a no.

"Oh, well, you know that Airbnb thing?" he asks, and I visualize him scrunching his face and biting his lips until his mouth disappears into his dark, gray-speckled beard. "A family rented the house for the week."

"You let someone rent the house?" I take a long gulp from my cup, washing down the last vestiges of hope for a normal holiday.

"Yeah. They're pleasant folks. Just a family wanting to visit the lake during the winter vacation."

"What if they steal everything?" Someone is sleeping in my bed right now or staring at the old photos on my pin-board. I don't live there anymore, but it's the house I grew up in, and my parents didn't change my space.

"We locked up the important stuff."

"What if they have six dogs that eat all the furniture? Oh! Or they make a porno on the couch?"

"Cozette," he chides. "Like that couch hasn't seen its fair share of—"

"Dad!"

He laughs in rolling melodic waves. "Sweet pea, it's fine. I'll check on an additional room and call you right back."

We hang up and I pull out my laptop, opening emails. There's one request for location research on the East Coast. Easy peasy. Another requests a forty-person full workshop design in Portland. Fun.

Too bad I didn't have any clients over Christmas; otherwise, I could pop into one of the events I plan. Some of my clients beg me to show up in person to the conferences I set up while sitting on the couch in my yoga pants. Not having to wear a suit and heels is a massive bonus after years of doing so.

I accept the two and get to work creating new client spreadsheets. I may not know where I'll sleep tonight, but these electronic folders are perfect: ordered, to the point, and exactly like the others—on the path to success with little fuss.

I've planned gatherings my entire life, starting with my fourth birthday party. When Dad told me that taking my ten best preschool buds to Disney World's princess castle wasn't within the budget, I sat on his lap and instructed him to look for something similar. We found a princess and unicorn duo that would come to the house for pony rides and pictures. The decorations and details were easy once the entertainment fell into place.

After that, it was friends' parties and school functions, then city festivals. By the time I graduated high school, I'd built a résumé that some people twice my age with full college degrees didn't have yet. A huge, international conference company hired me two weeks out of high school, and each year I received a higher title and more demands of my time.

I just get it, and I love it—the budgets, the people, coordinating a hundred things at once and having parts go wrong. There's a thrill in having to turn on a dime and work a secret miracle to keep things appearing like they're not falling to pieces. Everything about it is what I want in a career, except for the hours. There was no life outside of conferences. I faced hundred-hour workweeks and so many flights, I'll have frequent flyer miles for a decade.

I made so much money in exchange for my early twenties.

My phone beeps.

It's James. *Hey, where did you go? Come back home so we can talk.*

Nope.

The phone chimes again, and this time it's Dad calling.

"Hi," I answer and brace myself for a very wintery holiday.

"Bad news, there's nothing available. The nearest vacancy is miles away, and the innkeeper said she wouldn't put anyone she loved there."

I'm sad but relieved. Alone for the holidays, but not destined for the arctic. "That's okay. I'll think of something."

"Need us to come back? We could go to a B&B."

I love my parents so much. "No. You two kids have fun. I'll let you know what I'm doing in a few."

That puts me on the clock. If I don't have a solid location in the next hour, the dad timer will detonate, and my parents will be on a plane and not living out their Dickens fantasy Christmas.

We hang up, and I jump feetfirst into an internet search. The potential Christmas getaways are endless. Disney? Booked. Christmas spa excursion at Hershey? Booked. A wine country Christmas in Cali? Not this holiday.

Tropical locations keep popping up in my search. Hanging out with Santa by a palm tree while I drink yuletide cheer out of a coconut? *Yes, please.*

The options are daunting. Hundreds of self-proclaimed paradises vying for my attention with deals that may or may not be a dream come true, and in locations I've never heard of.

Helena. I need Helena.

I scroll through my emails to find the best travel agent ever's contact info. She's assisted with many of my out-of-country event bookings and cuts the best deals.

However, booking three days before Christmas? Maybe she can work a miracle.

"Cozette," she says, in a tone that wraps me in a winter hug. "Happy holiday season."

"You, too. I have a request, and it needs to be speedy quick."

I explain my predicament in less than a minute without taking a breath.

"Oh my. Give me your budget, what you're looking for, and I'll see what I can do. You have to leave today?"

I'd get a hotel room, but that's not plan A. As pissed as I am, if James starts his super sad lament highlighting the good times we've had and poses a convincing argument about how we'll work it out, I'll cave. It's best if I surrender thousands of miles away so I have time to come to my senses and realize this has gone on too long.

"I'd prefer it, yes."

"Woman, that's a tough order. Most flights for the tropics leave JFK in the morning, but...maybe today we'll get lucky." Her sweet voice whips to schoolteacher-fierce. "Give me your needs."

She's in business mode, and I love that about her. Someone is on my team.

"Five grand, max," I say. "But I'd prefer under three, a week stay, tropical weather, alcohol, all-inclusive because bikinis don't have pockets, Christmassy, and fun. Oh, but not a family resort. That's entertainment I'm not ready for. Peaceful ocean sounds, sans screaming."

Clicking and scribbling sound through the line. "Mmkay, I have four places in mind and your credit card on file. Do you trust me?"

"I do," I say with a nod.

"Gonna burn up this card. I'll call you with details."

She hangs up without another word, and I smile into my now-chilled beverage. Still chocolaty.

The scowling woman stands and taps her fingers on my table. "Good for you, hon."

"Thank you." It *is* good for me. I'm bailing out of this coldbox and away from Mr. Boringpants. I'll sing drunken carols with surfer Saint Nick and stick my toes in the sand on Christmas morning instead of snow.

I roll up my puffy sleeves and get cracking on venue research to keep busy. The temptation to browse the net for the tropical places Helena could send me is strong, but then I'll fall in love with an unavailable resort, and anywhere else she finds won't hold a candle to my long-lost paradise.

A half hour later I'm tapping my empty cup, boots propped on my luggage. The phone rings, nearly sending me into the air. I fumble it, then answer.

"Get thee to JFK," Helena announces. "Your flight leaves in one hour and twenty-three minutes for Simona Island."

Don't stop now. Keep reading with your copy of <u>HOLIDAY HOTEL</u> available now.

Don't miss more from Poppy Minnix with HOLIDAY HOTEL and check out all her books at www.poppyminnix.com

---

Sometimes, it takes a corset and an island getaway to bounce back from a disastrous breakup.

In the winter chill of New York City, Cozette Fay attempts to turn up the heat with a fun and sexy Ms. Claus roleplay. Unfortunately, her aloof boyfriend is more confused than aroused.

She says fa-la-la to her fizzled relationship and escapes to the tropics for Christmas where she meets Nico, a van-driving beach-hunk who secretly owns the hotel on private Simona Island. He upgrades her room, takes her on adventures, and can't seem to keep his eyes or his hands off of her despite claiming there's a non-fraternization policy.

It shouldn't matter that Nico won't share anything about himself outside of their tropical snow globe—she's there to reunite with herself, after all—but the closer they get, the more it seems he may be the Santa to her Mrs. Claus all year round.

Acknowledgments

Family, you've persisted through my obsessive writing at all hours every day for all of eternity, and I love you.

Tee! You took a chance on a newbie writer who had a story but not so much the skills to make it what it should be. Thanks for teaching me how to make it glorious. You've made an author out of me and I am grateful.

To my critique and beta partners who helped hone this story over the years: Cass, Immy, Lori, Rebecca, Davis, Raisa, Jackie, Owen, Jaycee, Lourdes, Barbara, Rex, Violet, and I've probably forgotten a few over the years, so those lovely people too. So many thanks!

Khalia! You were the first to read this book in its almost-done state. Thank you for assuring me it didn't suck.

To NaNoWriMo for giving me an excuse to drop everything and make this short story a full novel—or two novels.

To my book-blogger friends Alexa and Jen; thanks for your amazing reviews and for answering questions and giving insight about reader wants. You are shiny gilded gems in the bookish world.

To the countless people who told stories of the gods through the ages. Lore is meant to be shared, learned, then maybe tweaked and extended and enjoyed and loved for ever and ever.

About the Author

POPPY MINNIX is an award-winning paranormal romance and urban fantasy novelist living in Maryland. When she's not writing, she's chasing after two young kids, reading, playing board games with her hubs, or plotting her next writing project. She has a love for powerful men and women who are already exceptional but find that together they can conquer their inner demons—or actual demons.

www.poppyminnix.com

 twitter.com/PoppyMinnix

instagram.com/poppyminnix

facebook.com/poppymwrites

goodreads.com/poppyminnix

About the Publisher

City Owl Press is a cutting edge indie publishing company, bringing the world of romance and speculative fiction to discerning readers.

Escape Your World. Get Lost in Ours!

www.cityowlpress.com

 facebook.com/CityOwlPress

twitter.com/cityowlpress

instagram.com/cityowlbooks

pinterest.com/cityowlpress

tiktok.com/@cityowlpress